JOSEP[H]

Youth: A Narrative
Heart of Darkness
The End of the Tether

With a Prefatory Note by the Author

Introduction by C. B. Cox
Professor of English, University of Manchester

Notes by Norman Sherry
*Mitchell Distinguished Professor of Literature
at Trinity University, San Antonio, Texas*

J.M. Dent & Sons Ltd: London
EVERYMAN'S LIBRARY

© Introduction and notes, J.M. Dent & Sons Ltd, 1974
All rights reserved
Photoset by Deltatype Ltd, Ellesmere Port
Made in Great Britain by
Guernsey Press Co. Ltd, Guernsey, C.I. for
J.M. Dent & Sons Ltd
91 Clapham High Street, London SW4 7TA
First included in Everyman's Library 1967
New edition 1974
Last reprinted 1990

ISBN 0 460 87046 7

JOSEPH CONRAD was born on 3 December 1857 at Berdiczew in Poland, and christened Jósef Teodor Konrad Nalecz Korzeniowski. At the age of three, Conrad went with his parents into exile in northern Russia. Orphaned by the age of eleven, he was cared for by his uncle in Cracow. In adolescence he began training as a seaman, first in Marseilles and then with the British merchant navy. He sailed to the West Indies, India, the Far East and Australia and was briefly master of a river steamer in the Belgian Congo. On publication of his first novel, *Almayer's Folly*, in 1895, he gave up the sea for full-time writing and in 1896 married Jessie George, by whom he had two sons. His experiences at sea inspired some of his greatest novels, such as *The Nigger of the 'Narcissus'* (1897), *Lord Jim* (1900), *The Shadow-Line* (1917) and *The Rescue* (1920), but he wrote other novels with different settings, such as *Nostromo* (1904), *The Secret Agent* (1907) and *Under Western Eyes* (1911), as well as some fine short stories. Recognition of his genius came slowly, but when he died on 3 August 1924 his reputation was firmly established.

C. B. COX is John Edward Taylor Professor of English at Manchester University. His books include *The Free Spirit* (1963) and *Joseph Conrad: The Modern Imagination* (1974). He has also published two books of verse, *Every Common Sight* (1981) and *Two-Headed Monster* (1986).

NORMAN SHERRY, FRSL is the Mitchell Distinguished Professor of Literature at Trinity University, San Antonio, Texas. His books include *Conrad's Eastern World* (1966), *Conrad's Western World* (1971), *Conrad: The Critical Heritage* (1973), *Conrad and His World* (1972), *Jane Austen* (1966) and *Charlotte and Emily Brontë* (1969). He is now writing the official biography of Graham Greene.

CONTENTS

Introduction by C. B. Cox   vii
Select Bibliography   xix
Author's Note to the 1917 edition   xxiii

YOUTH: A NARRATIVE   3
HEART OF DARKNESS   35
THE END OF THE TETHER   125

Notes by Norman Sherry   254

INTRODUCTION

I

Conrad was possessed of two quite different personalities. To many acquaintances he seemed energetic and steadfast, a lover of the sea, who had proved his mettle by qualifying as a British master mariner. In his own words he was a Polish gentleman cased in British tar. But his wife and close friends knew a different side to his temperament. He was often moody, eccentric, neurotic, and frequently gave way to feelings of suicidal despair.

The first and last stories in this collection illustrate the two parts of his nature. 'Youth' is an autobiographical account of his own first exhilarating journey to the East. It exudes confidence and *joie de vivre*. The atmosphere of 'The End of the Tether' is quite the opposite. As the old captain compromises his integrity for the sake of his daughter, we feel weighed down by the indefatigable power of evil. Both these narratives illustrate Conrad's great virtues as a story-teller, but with 'Heart of Darkness' we enter another dimension of aesthetic achievement. This masterpiece has become one of those amazing modern fictions, such as Thomas Mann's *Death in Venice* or Kafka's *The Trial*, which throw light on the whole nature of twentieth-century art, its problems and achievements. In 'Heart of Darkness' the two sides of Conrad's temperament are both fully expressed. The seaman's code of discipline and work comes into conflict with the dark secret areas of the imagination. The result is a great parable concerning, among other things, the role of the artist in modern times.

II

In September, 1881, Conrad started out from London as second mate on the *Palestine*, a barque of 425 tons scheduled to collect a cargo of coal at Newcastle to be transported to Bangkok. In 'Youth' the name *Palestine* is changed to *Judea*, but the names of the captain, Beard, and the mate, Mahon, are left unaltered. The events at Newcastle and Falmouth, and the eventual disaster near Java Head, are presumed to be accurate records of Conrad's own experiences. But in the concluding sections he deliberately increased the drama by giving his young hero the chance to steer his little cockle-shell for many days, whereas in fact the journey took only a few hours. Conrad objected when the name was revealed of the real port, Muntok, where his voyage ended. 'Muntok is a damned hole without any beach and without any glamour', he commented, not at all a suitable place to symbolize the potent spell of the East.

Conrad had every right, of course, to alter real events for fictional purposes. He is trying to grasp the essence of his youthful response to the test of life and to the exotic attraction of the East. How far the story is literally true does not matter when we are considering its aesthetic effect.

'Youth' was first published in *Blackwood's Magazine* in September, 1898. Conrad had been bogged down by his frustrating inability to make progress with his ambitious novel, *The Rescue* and the writing of 'Youth' must have seemed an easier and more pleasant task. In this story Marlow appears for the first time as narrator. He is supposed to be recounting his memories to a group of companions, all ex-merchant seamen, on a convivial occasion. We are reminded of this by Marlow's requests to his friends to pass the bottle. The device appealed to Conrad, and he immediately used Marlow again, in a much more complex role, in 'Heart of Darkness' (1899), and in several subsequent novels. In his first works, *Almayer's Folly* (1895), *An Outcast of the Islands* (1896) and *The Nigger of the 'Narcissus'* (1897), Conrad narrates the story in the conventional manner, as if he were the omniscient author who is in charge of the plot. For temperamental and ideological reasons this method did not satisfy him. He wanted to suggest his own uncertainties about the meaning of events, his own deep-rooted scepticism, his belief that illusion and reality are inextricably intertwined. In 'Youth', Marlow looks back nostalgically at the passionate enthusiasm of his youth, recognizing both its naïveté and its honesty. It is significant that this indirect method of narration liberated Conrad from the impotent state into which he had been thrown by *The Rescue*, which was to be presented in the orthodox straightforward manner.

In 'Youth', as in 'Heart of Darkness', the hero is engaged in a voyage of self-discovery. As the *Judea* pitches and wallows in the storm west of the Lizards, Marlow recalls: 'To me she was not an old rattle-trap carting about the world a lot of coal for a freight – to me she was the endeavour, the test, the trial of life.' The youth asserts his manhood by his strength of will, his fortitude in calamity, his unending vitality. The older Marlow feels he has somehow become smaller and diminished, compared with the dynamic exuberance of his lost self. His memory wanders across time, grieving for the departed energy, stoically conscious of the gains in common sense and wisdom.

As often in Conrad, the ship represents a microcosm of the ideal society. Captain Beard retains a boyish innocence, 'a rare internal gift of simplicity of heart and rectitude of soul'. His solicitude for his wife, and her motherly affection for Marlow himself, are depicted as slightly comic, but full value is given to the couple's integrity. Marlow's trust in human nature is further illustrated by his comments on the crew's bravery after the explosion. Even the Liverpool hard cases have in them the right stuff, he tells us, a capacity for endurance given to them by the vastness of the sea, that 'loneliness surrounding their dark stolid souls'. Marlow believes this instinctive courage is peculiarly English, and his words reflect Conrad's own loyalty to his adopted country.

The *Judea*'s voyage is made to seem no ordinary adventure. It is as if the youthful Marlow on his way to the East passes through a strange underworld, where he discovers his true self:

> There was for us no sky, there were for us no stars, no sun, no universe – nothing but angry clouds and an infuriated sea. We pumped watch and watch, for dear life; and it seemed to last for months, for years, for all eternity, as though we had been dead and gone to a hell for sailors.

He feels 'bewitched', responds to 'magic light', and, on one occasion, describes the sky as black as Erebus. In this delicate, poetic manner Conrad draws attention to the archetypal quality of the voyage.

The ideal society is opposed by the alien sea, which attacks them with 'malice'. It is as though Nature acted in conscious 'spite' to frustrate their purposes. In the storm west of the Lizards the deck-house is shattered as if a shell had exploded inside, and the steward is driven out of his mind. Eventually when the ship itself explodes, a plank is left like a gangway protruding over the deep sea, leading to death, inviting the crew to walk the plank and be done with their ridiculous troubles. The youthful Marlow is unperturbed by this violence of Nature. His exhilaration makes him impervious to these suggestions that the universe is absurd and intent on his destruction. For the mature Marlow, youth is a deceptive illusion, whose self-confidence lures us on 'to joys, to perils, to love, to vain effort – to death'.

And so the conclusion is ambiguous. As Marlow at last arrives in port, the East itself gleams like an illusion: 'The mysterious East faced me, perfumed like a flower, silent like death, dark like a grave.' He responds to its romance, its danger, its beauty, and so assumes an heroic stature that the older Marlow has lost. Yet the language hints that the self-confidence of youth depends on ignorance, and the journey inevitably ends in death.

III

Like 'Youth', 'Heart of Darkness' draws heavily on Conrad's personal experiences. These two stories are romantic like Wordsworth's *Prelude*, Proust's *À la Recherche du Temps Perdu*, or D. H. Lawrence's *Sons and Lovers*. The artist explores his own memories in search of self-understanding and perhaps to exorcize psychological conflicts by which he is still possessed.

In 1890, when he was 32 years old, Conrad was engaged by the Belgian Société Anonyme pour le Commerce du Haut-Congo to take command of one of the Company's steamers on the Congo. In 'Heart of Darkness', Marlow's visit to the Company's office, his medical inspection by the doctor with the bizarre sense of humour, and many details of his journey to Matadi and beyond are taken directly from fact. For Conrad the journey was an unmitigated disaster. He was disgusted by the ill-treatment of the natives, by the vile scramble for loot. In his notebook he records a series of unsavoury details – the horrid smell from a dead body lying by the track, rows with carriers, the lack of water, the heat, mosquitoes, the shouts and drumming, a skeleton tied up to a post. The steamer, *Florida*, which he was supposed to take over had been badly damaged, and instead he journeyed as super-numerary on the *Roi des Belges* to Stanley Falls, picking up a dangerously ill Company Agent named Georges Antoine Klein. Klein, like Kurtz, died on the return journey. In the manuscript of 'Heart of Darkness' Conrad starts by writing Klein, and then changes the name to Kurtz. At the conclusion of this trip Conrad suffered further frustrations in his hopes of obtaining a command, and he fell ill with fever and dysentery. Disgusted, he returned to England in December, 1890.

It is difficult to assess the influence of the journey on Conrad's character, but there is no doubt that for many years afterwards he was haunted by the Congo. He never forgot what he had witnessed of the horror of human corruption. His imagination remained obsessed by images of native wildness, of huge forests and indescribable evil. Other great works by Conrad, such as *Lord Jim* or *Nostromo*, include sections that most readers agree are unsatisfactory. 'Heart of Darkness' suffers from no such deficiencies. It is a short, brilliant parable in which Conrad dramatizes his own conflicting attitudes to passion and reason, savagery and civilization.

'Heart of Darkness' has been interpreted in many different ways. Anti-Imperialists emphasize the suffering and torture of the natives in the scenes at Matadi, and so the story is used as a tract against the Colonial Powers. From the Marxist point of view, Kurtz is seen as an embodiment of all the evils which are produced by free enterprise in a capitalist system. In complete contrast, some readers find in Kurtz a devil whose fascinations, like those of Milton's Satan, it may be difficult to resist. The Jungians discover in the story a night journey into the unconscious, a trafficking with the secret criminal energies which civilization represses. The adventure down the Congo has also been analysed as a Freudian voyage into the wilderness of sex, a discovery of the Id. Marlow penetrates down a narrow channel to find in the darkness an orgiastic experience. Other readers stress the fascination with the primitive, typical of later artists such as Picasso or D. H. Lawrence. Lionel Trilling, the American critic, believes Kurtz is a type of the modern artist, who courageously explores the hell which is the historical beginning of the human soul. The artist can only escape what he feels are the bland lies of civilization by self-degradation. In contrast to the conventional inhabitants of Western Europe, lost in a grey sleep of security, the artist-outlaw dares to transgress the taboos of his society, and so participates in a terrible rebirth. Kurtz foreshadows modern writers such as Ernest Hemingway or Norman Mailer, who cultivate extreme experiences as a means of escape from the depressing super-ficialities of contempory life.

The wealth of interpretation indicates the kind of fiction with which we are dealing. There is no one key which will unlock the secret meaning of 'Heart of Darkness'. In this way it is very different from the comparatively straightforward 'Youth' and 'The End of the Tether'. It is an example of the kind of art Henry James described in his short story, 'The Figure in the Carpet'. The pattern is involved in every detail of the narrative, and cannot be reduced to a simple paraphrase. Conrad declared that his purpose in writing fiction was to present the truth. He tries to draw out all the possibilities suggested to him by the image of Kurtz; his own philosophical scepticism makes him unwilling to commit himself to one kind of interpretation. Marlow and Kurtz, the natives and the wilderness, remain enigmas on which the narrative may throw some light, but the darkness will never reveal the ultimate source of its mystery.

'Heart of Darkness' includes a famous description of the method of narration adopted by Conrad in his greatest works. Before Marlow begins to recount his adventures, he is introduced by an anonymous narrator, who comments on the peculiarity of Marlow's stories:

The yarns of seamen have a direct simplicity, the whole meaning of which lies within the shell of a cracked nut. But Marlow was not typical (if his propensity to spin yarns be excepted), and to him the meaning of an episode was not inside like a kernel but outside, enveloping the tale which brought it out only as a glow brings out a haze, in the likeness of one of these misty halos that sometimes are made visible by the spectral illumination of moonshine.

This explanation is itself an image which cannot be translated into rational analysis. There is no kernel of meaning that we can take away from 'Heart of Darkness'. Instead, the whole narrative gives off uncertain lights, a spectral illumination which is all that is possible when we consider how inadequately words portray reality.

The title of the story is therefore evocative but ambiguous. The wilderness may possess a heart, a source of life, which the reader, guided by Marlow, may discover. The quest may end in a place where we shall recognize the secret vitality covered over by the conventions of Western Europe. But, in direct opposition to this interpretation, heart of darkness may imply that our journey will end in complete darkness, in the incomprehensible unknown. Perhaps we are on our way to an ultimate blackness in which human nature is transformed back again into its brute origins. Marlow's narrative circles round these possibilities, and never reaches a final solution. The anonymous narrator tells us we are about to hear 'one of Marlow's inconclusive experiences'.

The narrative begins with a fine evocation of the lower reaches of the Thames, with to the west the dark shadow of London. The sun is setting, and on the *Nellie*, a cruising yawl, the anonymous narrator responds to the sense of history, to the 'venerable stream' with all its immemorial associations: men such as Sir Francis Drake or Sir John Franklin set out from here on their great voyages of exploration, carrying a torch into strange lands unknown to civilization. In these opening paragraphs, as throughout the story, there is a subtle interplay between light and darkness. The language hints at symbolic meanings, as if the lurid glare of the red sun and the brooding gloom of London reflect the great conflicts of the centuries. As darkness thickens, Marlow's voice floats across to the listeners, like an emanation of night itself, or an echo of a dream. He sits cross-legged, in 'the pose of a Buddha preaching in European clothes and without a lotus-flower', and his words seem to whisper secrets from the very depths of consciousness. As he starts his story of Kurtz, he admits his adventure proved 'the culminating point of my experience'. He recalls that in Roman times England itself was a place of darkness, the very end of the world, where the Roman legionaries confronted the savage origins of their own being. At first it might seem that light and civilization are benevolent forces tackling an inferior primitive state of human development. But the darkness retains its own potency; the civilized man may succumb to 'the fascination of the abomination'. In contrast to the knights of old, Marlow's quest may end in a new awareness of the inadequacies of civilization.

Like Conrad himself, Marlow travels to Brussels to sign on as skipper for the Company. It is made clear that it is specifically the evils of colonial policy under King Leopold II which are being attacked. Marlow is pleased to notice on the map a vast amount of red, the areas controlled by Britain, where 'one knows that some real work is done'. Brussels reminds him of 'a whited sepulchre'. In the Company office he is received by two women, one fat and the other slim, knitting black wool. They guard the entry to darkness, and recall the Fates, spinning and breaking the thread of man's life. Marlow passes from one kind of death to another, from the dead civilized conventions of Belgium to the dangerous sub-human cults in Africa.

There are many references which compare Marlow's journey down the Congo to the classic expedition to the underworld, passing down through the circles of Hell, the Company Station, the Central Station, and the Inner Station, to the final confrontation with the devil incarnate, Kurtz himself. Such mythic journeys into the underworld fascinated Conrad's imagination. He felt that at crises in their moral lives men enter an area of reality which normally they prefer to ignore. In later stories such as 'The Secret Sharer' or *The Shadow-Line* the heroes make a similar voyage into the subterranean regions of Erebus, and we have already seen a hint or two of this idea in 'Youth'. On such occasions the active life of the seamen may seem an illusion, an evasion of the truth. The Conradian hero must confront the ultimate meaninglessness of the forms and conventions of society. Exposure to this dark side of reality may drive him to suicide, like Decoud in *Nostromo*.

It may persuade him to indulge in the sexual orgies and killings so attractive to Kurtz. Yet perhaps only by this confrontation with absolute darkness can we release the potential sources of energy repressed by the illusions of society. Conrad's response to the underworld voyage is ambiguous, a mixture of fascination and repulsion.

This double attitude is demonstrated by the contradictory use of the word 'reality'. Marlow is disgusted by the squabbling and self-interest of the Europeans, the hollow men, the pilgrims as he ironically calls them. He turns with relief to the task of repairing the battered, tin-pot steamboat. 'I don't like work', he admits, but he believes that through his labours he can achieve self-discovery: 'your own reality — for yourself, not for others — what no other man can ever know'. This is the reality which the young second mate in 'Youth' discovers as he bravely refuses to be defeated by the tribulations of the *Judea*. This is one kind of test, one way in which a man may find an acceptable identity.

But in 'Heart of Darkness' Marlow is not satisfied with this work ethic. He admits that his absorption in keeping the steamboat afloat prevented him from responding fully to another kind of truth, to 'the overwhelming realities of this strange world of plants, and water, and silences':

> When you have to attend to things of that sort, to the mere incidents of the surface, the reality — the reality, I tell you — fades. The inner truth is hidden — luckily, luckily. But I felt it all the same . . .

He too is tempted to go ashore for a howl or a dance, so Marlow must not be accepted as an absolutely authoritative reporter. He acts as a kind of mirror to events, but what he reflects does not emerge as a rationally consistent view of reality. Coleridge's Ancient Mariner speaks saving truths about love and Nature; in contrast, Marlow needs to tell his story because its conflicts still remain unresolved, because Kurtz and the wilderness still tantalize and disturb his imagination.

The story is built around these oppositions and tensions between the values of work and the fascination of the wilderness. The natives enjoy degraded rites, and they foolishly worship Kurtz as a god; yet the cannibals are respected by Marlow as 'men one could work with'. The book *An Inquiry into some Points of Seamanship* strikes Marlow as 'unmistakably real', as a symbol of honesty in its faith in the seaman's code; yet the tattered manuscript seems ironically inappropriate and absurd in the context of the wilderness. The young Russian, Kurtz's disciple, dressed in patchwork clothes like a harlequin, retains an innocence lost by the hollow Europeans. Yet in his naïve enthusiasm for Kurtz he appears simple-minded. He is transported by Kurtz's eloquence, its breathtaking charm, yet the conclusion to Kurtz's seventeen-page report to the International Society for the Suppression of Savage Customs blows away his false rhetoric: 'Exterminate all the brutes!' Kurtz's savage woman, with her animal vitality, contrasts with his European fiancée, who dedicates herself to his memory, to a lie, in her home that resembles a cemetery. And finally, how are we to interpret Kurtz's last words: 'The horror! The horror!' Is he at last realizing the evil of his past ways, and so proving that the attraction of the wilderness is indeed an abomination? Or is he looking at the horror of death, which will remove him from the scenes of his lusts and triumphs? Marlow returns to Brussels, the sepulchral city, broken down in physical and mental health by the heart of a conquering darkness.

IV

Conrad began writing 'The End of the Tether' in 1902. He had just finished *Romance*, in collaboration with the novelist Ford Madox Hueffer, and it is likely that Hueffer also assisted with the new story. Conrad had promised it for *Blackwood's Magazine*, where it eventually appeared in instalments from July to December, 1902. He had difficulty in keeping up with his deadlines. One night in June his lamp exploded, and the whole manuscript of the second instalment was burnt. Until the end, it was a race against time, and this probably explains a certain flatness in some parts of the writing. The account of the voyages of the *Sofala* corresponds closely to the actual journeys of the *Vidar*, on which Conrad served as mate from August 1887 to January 1888. But the element of autobiography is slight, and this may be a second reason why the style lacks the vitality and symbolic potency of his greatest fictions.

Yet 'The End of the Tether' is a forceful narrative, whose main character, Captain Whalley, has a tragic dignity. Dare-devil Whalley has been a most successful seaman, who never lost a ship or consented to a shady transaction. Like Captain Beard in 'Youth', his glance has the innocence of a boy's. Now he is old, yet his sturdy frame still reflects an unquenchable vitality and vigour. Like Redcross in Spenser's *Faerie Queene*, he is an ideal Christian knight; on two occasions the long white beard covering his heart is compared to a silver breastplate. He is punctilious and methodical, and confidently trusts the Creator who endowed him with such a healthy body and made him so at home in life. He explains to his friend, the Dutchman Van Wyk, his simple faith in divine mercy. He believes that men are naturally good, and that the world is progressing in decency, justice, order and honesty.

But his ship, the *Sofala*, is a microcosm of a very different kind of society from that exemplified by the *Judea* in 'Youth'. Massy, the owner, is a despicable specimen of humanity, with his fawning loquacity, bursts of resentfulness, plaintive whining and gambling mania. Sterne, the mate, is sly, impudent, instinctively disloyal. The second engineer is so taciturn he seems to have lost the use of speech; only two or three times a year when he is drunk he spits out venomous scandals about his associates, as if all of them had offended him. Among this group, Whalley's serenity and manly gentleness seem to Van Wyk 'an amazing survival from the prehistoric times of the world'. Conrad repeatedly suggests that the old world of heroic endeavour has been replaced by a debased, corrupt materialism. Even his old comrade, Captain Eliott, now wheezy and waddling, dare not invite him home for fear of offending his wife. As he walks through the Eastern port after selling his ship, *The Fair Maid*, to provide money for his daughter, Whalley seems a revenant from a lost paradise.

The background of land and sea reflects this changed world, and appears as a product of the morbid side of Conrad's temperament. In the opening paragraphs the *Sofala* approaches a low, swampy coast, a mere 'smudge' of darkness. The coast is 'without a single feature to arrest attention'. The three palm-trees by which they steer have 'dishevelled heads'. The ship passes down a river of brown liquid, three parts black earth and one part brackish water. The darkness of the primeval forest flows into the cabins with an odour of rotting leaves, of sodden soil. These effects are completely different from the violent energies of the storms in 'Youth' or the mysterious abundance of the forests in 'Heart of Darkness'. The atmosphere here is one of decay, of stagnation, of a *tedium vitae*.

This is reality, at least in the terms of this story, and Whalley himself discovers that even he can be corrupted. To help his daughter with money he makes his bargain with Massy. He had never allowed anybody before to remain under any sort of false impression as to himself, but now he allows Massy to think he is a rich man. As he walks from the quay, the bargain concluded, he shivers in the darkness. He feels he is corrupt to the marrow of his bones. The Christian knight is finding his ideals unsuited to the demands of the new world.

And so he is tempted to commit his great crime, by which he endangers his ship. His passion of paternity makes him sacrifice his own past of honour, of truth, of just pride. As the ship crosses the bar, it grazes the sand, and voluminous, yellowish convolutions roll up from the mud to stain the surface of the blue water. His honour too is stained, and he wishes only to die. He proves defenceless before the work of adversity, 'like a cliff that stands unmoved the open battering of the sea, with a lofty ignorance of the treacherous backwash undermining its base'. This is the truth about Nature which he has never understood.

Plot, character and description in 'The End of the Tether' all witness to the corruption of man and the hostility of Nature. Fortunately this was not Conrad's last word. In subsequent great novels such as *Nostromo*, *Under Western Eyes* or *The Shadow-Line*, he continued his search for viable forms of moral heroism. But a man like Captain Whalley must go down to inevitable defeat because he has remained blind to the powers of evil.

1974   C. B. Cox

SELECT BIBLIOGRAPHY

JOSEPH CONRAD'S WORKS

1895 *Almayer's Folly – A Story of an Eastern River.*
1896 *An Outcast of the Islands.*
1897 *The Nigger of the 'Narcissus' – A Tale of the Sea.* (First edition to
     include Preface, 1914.)
1898 *Tales of Unrest.* (Contents: 'Karain: A Memory', 'The Idiots', 'An
     Outpost of Progress', 'The Return', 'The Lagoon'.)
1900 *Lord Jim – A Tale.*
1902 *Youth: A Narrative; and Two Other Stories.* (Contents: 'Youth',
     'Heart of Darkness', 'The End of the Tether'.)
1903 *Typhoon, and Other Stories* (Contents: 'Typhoon', 'Amy Foster',
     'Falk', 'To-Morrow'.)
1903 *Romance – A Novel.* (In collaboration with Ford Madox Hueffer.)
1904 *Nostromo – A Tale of the Seaboard.*
1906 *The Mirror of the Sea – Memories and Impressions.*
1907 *The Secret Agent – A Simple Tale.*
1908 *A Set of Six.* (Contents: 'Gaspar Ruiz', 'The Informer', 'The Brute',
     'An Anarchist', 'The Duel', 'Il Conde'.)
1911 *Under Western Eyes.*
1912 *A Personal Record.* (First published as *Some Reminiscences.*)
1912 *'Twixt Land and Sea – Tales.* (Contents: 'A Smile of Fortune', 'The
     Secret Sharer', 'Freya of the Seven Isles'.)
1913 *Chance – A Tale in Two Parts.*
1915 *Victory – An Island Tale.*
1915 *Within the Tides – Tales.* (Contents: 'The Planter of Malata', 'The
     Partner', 'The Inn of the Two Witches', 'Because of the Dollars'.)
1917 *The Shadow-Line – A Confession.*
1919 *The Arrow of Gold – A Story between Two Notes.*
1920 *The Rescue – A Romance of the Shallows.*
1921 *Notes On Life and Letters.* (Essays, mainly from periodicals; 13 in
     Part I on Letters, 13 in Part II on Life.)
1923 *The Rover.*

1925 *Suspense – A Napoleonic Novel.*
1925 *Tales of Hearsay.* (Contents: 'The Warrior's Soul', 'Prince Roman', 'The Tale', 'The Black Mate'.)
1926 *Last Essays.* (19 essays, uncollected in book form at the time of his death.)
1923–8 Uniform Edition of the Works of Joseph Conrad. Re-issued as Collected Edition, 1946–54, 21 volumes, containing all the works listed above. All published by J. M. Dent & Sons.

CONRAD'S LETTERS

The Life and Letters of Joseph Conrad (2 vols.), edited by G. Jean-Aubry, 1927. *Letters from Conrad, 1895–1924*, edited, with an introduction, by Edward Garnett, 1928, *Letters from Joseph Conrad to Richard Curle*, 1928. *Letters of Joseph Conrad to Marguerite Poradowska*, New York, 1940. *Joseph Conrad: Letters to William Blackwood and David S. Meldrum*, edited by W. Blackburn, 1959. *Conrad's Polish Background: Letters to and from his Polish Friends*, ed. by Zdzisław Najder, 1964. *Joseph Conrad's Letters to R. B. Cunninghame Graham*, ed. by C. T. Watts, 1969. *The Collected Letters of Joseph Conrad*, ed. by F. R. Karl and L. Davies, 1983.

BIOGRAPHICAL AND CRITICAL WRITINGS ON CONRAD

Joseph Conrad, A Study, by Richard Curle, 1914. Essay in *Notes on Novelists*, by Henry James, 1914. *Joseph Conrad*, by Hugh Walpole, 1916. Essay on Conrad in *A Book of Prefaces*, by H. L. Mencken, 1917. *Joseph Conrad, a Personal Remembrance*, by Ford Madox Ford, 1924. Essays on Conrad in *The Common Reader*, by Virginia Woolf, 1925. *Joseph Conrad as I knew Him*, by Jessie Conrad, 1926. 'Reminiscences of Conrad' and 'Preface to Conrad's Plays', in *Castles in Spain*, by John Galsworthy, 1972. *The Last Twelve Years of Joseph Conrad*, by Richard Curle, 1928. *The Polish Heritage of Joseph Conrad*, by Gustav Morf, 1930. *Joseph Conrad's Mind and Method*, by R. L. Mégroz, 1931. *Joseph Conrad and his Circle*, by Jessie Conrad, 1936. *Joseph Conrad, Some Aspects of the Art of the Novel*, by Edward Crankshaw, 1936. Introductory Essay by Edward Garnett to *Conrad's Prefaces to his Works*, 1937. *Joseph Conrad, the Making of a Novelist*, by John D. Gordan, 1940. *Joseph Conrad, England's Polish Genius*, by M. C. Bradbrook, 1941. Introduction by A. J. Hoppé to *The Conrad Companion*, 1946. *The Great Tradition* (George Eliot, Henry James, and Joseph Conrad), by F. R. Leavis,

1948. *Joseph Conrad*, by Oliver Warner, 1951. *Conrad, a Re-assessment*, by D. Hewitt, 1952. *Six Great Novelists*, by Walter Allen, 1955 (Conrad is the sixth subject). *The Mirror of Conrad*, by E. H. Visiak, 1955. *The Sea Dreamer: Life of Conrad*, by G. Jean-Aubry, 1957. *Joseph Conrad*, by Thomas Moser, 1957. *Joseph Conrad, A Study in Non-Conformity*, by Osborn Andreas, 1959. *A Reader's Guide to Joseph Conrad*, by Frederick R. Karl, 1960. *The Art of Joseph Conrad: A Critical Symposium*, ed. by R. W. Stallman, 1960. *Joseph Conrad, A Critical Biography*, by Jocelyn Baines, 1960. *Conrad's Heart of Darkness and The Critics*, ed. by Bruce Harkness, 1960. *Joseph Conrad, Giant in Exile*, by Leo Gurko, 1962. *The Political Novels of Joseph Conrad*, by E. K. Hay, 1963. *Joseph Conrad and the Fiction of Autobiography*, by E. W. Said, 1966. *Conrad's Eastern World*, by Norman Sherry, 1966. *The Sea Years of Joseph Conrad*, by Jerry Allen, 1967. *Conrad: A Psycho-Analytic Biography*, by B. C. Meyer, 1967. *Conrad's Politics: Community and Anarchy in the Fiction of Joseph Conrad* by A. Fleishman, 1968. *Conrad the Psychologist as Artist*, by P. Kirschner, 1968. *Joseph Conrad*, by J. I. M. Stewart, 1968. *Joseph Conrad's Fiction: A Study in Literary Growth*, by J. A. Palmer, 1968. *Conrad's Short Fiction*, by L. Graver, 1969. *My Father: Joseph Conrad*, by Borys Conrad, 1970. *Conrad's Western World*, by Norman Sherry, 1971. *Conrad: The Critical Heritage*, ed. Norman Sherry, 1973. *Conrad and his World*, by Norman Sherry, 1972. *Joseph Conrad: The Modern Imagination*, by C. B. Cox, 1974. *Conrad's Romanticism*, by David Thorburn, 1974. *Joseph Conrad and the Literature of Personality*, by Peter J. Glassman, 1976. *Joseph Conrad: A Commemoration*, ed. Norman Sherry, 1976. *Joseph Conrad: The Way of Dispossession*, by H. M. Daleski, 1977. *Joseph Conrad: Language and Fictional Self-Consciousness*, by Jeremy Hawthorn, 1979. *Joseph Conrad: The Three Lives*, by Frederick Karl, 1979. *Conrad in the Nineteenth Century*, by Ian Watt, 1979. *Joseph Conrad and the Ethics of Darwinism: The Challenges of Science*, by Allan Hunter, 1983. *Joseph Conrad: A Chronicle*, by Zdzislaw Najder, 1983. *Coercion to Speak: Conrad's Poetics of Dialogue*, by Aaron Fogel, 1985. *Conrad and Imperialism*, by Benita Parry, 1983. *The Deceptive Text*, by Cedric T. Watts, 1984. *Conrad and the Paradox of Plot*, by Stephen K. Land, 1984. *Coercion to Speak: Conrad's Poetics of Dialogue*, by Aaron Fogel, 1985. *A Conrad Companion*, by Norman Page, 1986. *Conrad and Religion*, by John Lester, 1988.

BIBLIOGRAPHIES

A Bibliography of the Writings of Joseph Conrad 1895–1921, by T. J. Wise, 1921. *A Conrad Library*, collected by T. J. Wise, London, 1928. *A Conrad Memorial Library*, collected by G. T. Keating, New York, 1929, with 'Check List of Additions', 1938. *Joseph Conrad at Mid-Century, Editions and Studies, 1895–1955*, by K. A. Lohf and E. P. Sheehy, 1959. *A Bibliography of Joseph Conrad*, by Theodore G. Ehrsam, 1969. *Joseph Conrad: An Annotated Bibliography of Writings About Him*, compiled and ed. by Bruce T. Teets and Helmut E. Gerber, 1971.

AUTHOR'S NOTE

THE three stories in this volume lay no claim to unity of artistic purpose. The only bond between them is that of the time in which they were written. They belong to the period immediately following the publication of the 'Nigger of the 'Narcissus', and preceding the first conception of 'Nostromo', two books which, it seems to me, stand apart and by themselves in the body of my work. It is also the period during which I contributed to *Maga*; a period dominated by 'Lord Jim' and associated in my grateful memory with the late Mr William Blackwood's encouraging and helpful kindness.

'Youth' was not my first contribution to *Maga*. It was the second. But that story marks the first appearance in the world of the man Marlow, with whom my relations have grown very intimate in the course of years. The origins of that gentleman (nobody as far as I know had ever hinted that he was anything but that) – his origins have been the subject of some literary speculation of, I am glad to say, a friendly nature.

One would think that I am the proper person to throw a light on the matter; but in truth I find that it isn't so easy. It is pleasant to remember that nobody had charged him with fraudulent purposes or looked down on him as a charlatan; but apart from that he was supposed to be all sorts of things: a clever screen, a mere device, a 'personator', a familiar spirit, a whispering 'dæmon'. I myself have been suspected of a meditated plan for his capture.

That is not so. I made no plans. The man Marlow and I came together in the casual manner of those health-resort acquaintances which sometimes ripen into friendships. This one has ripened. For all his assertiveness in matters of opinion he is not an intrusive person. He haunts my hours of solitude, when, in silence, we lay our heads together in great comfort and harmony; but as we part at the end of a tale I am never sure that it may not be for the last time. Yet I don't think that either of us would care much to survive the other. In his case, at any rate, his occupation would be gone and he would suffer from that extinction, because I suspect him of some vanity. I don't mean vanity in the Solomonian sense. Of all my people he's the one that has never been a vexation to my spirit. A most discreet, understanding man. . . .

Even before appearing in book-form 'Youth' was very well received. It lies on me to confess at last, and this is as good a place for it as another, that I have been all my life – all my two lives – the spoiled adopted child of Great Britain and even of the Empire; for it was Australia that gave me my first command. I break out into this declaration not because of a lurking tendency to megalo-mania, but, on the contrary, as a man who has no very notable illusions about himself. I follow the instincts of vain-glory and humility natural to all mankind. For it can hardly be denied that it is not their own deserts that men are most proud of, but rather of their prodigious luck, of their marvellous fortune: of that in their lives for which thanks and sacrifices must be offered on the altars of the inscrutable gods.

'Heart of Darkness' also received a certain amount of notice from the first; and of its origins this much may be said: it is well known that curious men go prying into all sorts of places (where they have no business) and come out of them with all kinds of spoil. This story, and one other, not in this volume, are all the spoil I brought out from the centre of Africa, where, really, I had no sort of business. More ambitious in its scope and longer in the telling, 'Heart of Darkness' is quite as authentic in fundamentals as 'Youth'. It is, obviously, written in another mood. I won't characterize the mood precisely, but anybody can see that it is anything but the mood of wistful regret, of reminiscent tender-ness.

One more remark may be added. 'Youth' is a feat of memory. It is a record of experience; but that experience, in its facts, in its inwardness and in its outward colouring, begins and ends in myself. 'Heart of Darkness' is experience, too; but it is experience pushed a little (and only very little) beyond the actual facts of the case for the perfectly legitimate, I believe, purpose of bringing it home to the minds and bosoms of the readers. There it was no longer a matter of sincere colouring. It was like another art altogether. That sombre theme had to be given a sinister resonance, a tonality of its own, a continued vibration that, I hoped, would hang in the air and dwell on the ear after the last note had been struck.

After saying so much there remains the last tale of the book, still untouched. 'The End of the Tether' is a story of sea-life in a rather special way; and the most intimate thing I can say of it is this; that having lived that life fully, amongst its men, its thoughts and sensations, I have found it possible, without the slightest misgiving, in all sincerity of heart and peace of conscience, to conceive the existence of Captain Whalley's personality and to relate the manner of his end. This statement acquires some force from the circumstance that the pages of that story – a fair half of the book – are also the product of experience. That experience belongs (like 'Youth's') to the time before I ever thought of putting pen to paper. As to its 'reality', that is for the readers to determine. One had to pick up one's facts here and there. More skill would have made them more real and the whole composition more interesting. But here we are approaching the veiled region of artistic values which it would be improper and indeed dangerous for me to enter. I have looked over the proofs, have corrected a misprint or two, have changed a word or two – and that's all. It is not very likely that I shall ever read 'The End of the Tether' again. No more need be said. It accords best with my feelings to part from Captain Whalley in affectionate silence

1917   J. C.

'. . . but the Dwarf answered:
"No, something human is dearer
to me than the wealth of the world." '
GRIMM'S TALES

YOUTH: A NARRATIVE

THIS could have occurred nowhere but in England, where men and sea interpenetrate, so to speak – the sea entering into the life of most men, and the men knowing something or everything about the sea, in the way of amusement, of travel, or of bread-winning.

We were sitting round a mahogany table that reflected the bottle, the claret-glasses, and our faces as we leaned on our elbows. There was a director of companies, an accountant, a lawyer, Marlow, and myself. The director had been a *Conway* boy, the accountant had served four years at sea, the lawyer – a fine crusted Tory, High Churchman, the best of old fellows, the soul of honour – had been chief officer in the P. & O. service in the good old days when mail-boats were square-rigged at least on two masts, and used to come down the China Sea before a fair monsoon with stun'-sails set alow and aloft. We all began life in the merchant service. Between the five of us there was the strong bond of the sea, and also the fellowship of the craft, which no amount of enthusiasm for yachting, cruising, and so on can give, since one is only the amusement of life and the other is life itself.

Marlow (at least I think that is how he spelt his name) told the story, or rather the chronicle, of a voyage:-

'Yes, I have seen a little of the Eastern seas; but what I remember best is my first voyage there. You fellows know there are those voyages that seem ordered for the illustration of life, that might stand for a symbol of existence. You fight, work, sweat, nearly kill yourself, sometimes do kill yourself, trying to accomplish something – and you can't. Not from any fault of yours. You simply can do nothing, neither great nor little – not a thing in the world – not even marry an old maid, or get a wretched 600-ton cargo of coal to its port of destination.

'It was altogether a memorable affair. It was my first voyage to the East, and my first voyage as second mate; it was also my skipper's first command. You'll admit it was time. He was sixty if a day; a little man, with a broad, not very straight back, with bowed shoulders and one leg more bandy than the other, he had that queer twisted-about appearance you see so often in men who work in the fields. He had a nut-cracker face – chin and nose trying to come together over a sunken mouth – and it was framed in iron-grey fluffy hair, that looked like a chin-strap of cotton-wool sprinkled with coal-dust. And he had blue eyes in that old face of his, which were amazingly like a boy's, with that candid expression some quite common men preserve to the end of their days by a rare internal gift of simplicity of heart and rectitude of soul. What induced him to accept me was a wonder. I had come out of a crack Australian clipper, where I had been third officer, and he seemed to have a prejudice against crack clippers as aristocratic and high-toned. He said to me, "You know, in this ship you will have to work." I said I had to work in every ship I had ever been in. "Ah, but this is different, and you gentlemen out of them big ships; . . . but there! I dare say you will do. Join to-morrow."

'I joined tomorrow. It was twenty-two years ago; and I was just twenty. How time passes! It was one of the happiest days of my life. Fancy! Second mate for the first time – a really responsible officer! I wouldn't have thrown up my new billet for a fortune. The mate looked me over carefully. He was also an old chap, but of another stamp. He had a Roman nose, a snow-white, long beard, and his name was Mahon, but he insisted that it should be pronounced Mann. He was well connected; yet there was something wrong with his luck, and he had never got on.

'As to the captain, he had been for years in coasters, then in the Mediterranean, and last in the West Indian trade. He had never been round the Capes. He could just write a kind of sketchy hand, and didn't care for writing at all. Both were thorough good seamen of course, and between those two old chaps I felt like a small boy between two grandfathers.

'The ship also was old. Her name was the *Judea*. Queer name, isn't it? She belonged to a man Wilmer, Wilcox – some name like that; but he has been bankrupt and dead these twenty years or more, and his name don't matter. She had been laid up in Shadwell basin for ever so long. You may imagine her state. She was all rust, dust, grime – soot aloft, dirt on deck. To me it was like coming out of a palace into a ruined cottage. She was about 400 tons, had a primitive windlass, wooden latches to the doors, not a bit of brass about her, and a big square stern. There was on it, below her name in big letters, a lot of scrollwork, with the gilt off, and some sort of a coat of arms, with the motto "Do or Die" underneath. I remember it took my fancy immensely. There was a touch of romance in it, something that made me love the old thing – something that appealed to my youth!

'We left London in ballast – sand ballast – to load a cargo of coal in a northern port for Bankok. Bankok! I thrilled. I had been six years at sea, but had only seen Melbourne and Sydney, very good places, charming places in their way – but Bankok!

'We worked out of the Thames under canvas, with a North Sea pilot on board. His name was Jermyn, and he dodged all day long about the galley drying his handkerchief before the stove. Apparently he never slept. He was a dismal man, with a perpetual tear sparkling at the end of his nose, who either had been in trouble, or was in trouble, or expected to be in trouble – couldn't be happy unless something went wrong. He mistrusted my youth, my common-sense, and my seamanship, and made a point of showing it in a hundred little ways. I dare say he was right. It seems to me I knew very little then, and I know not much more now; but I cherish a hate for that Jermyn to this day.

'We were a week working up as far as Yarmouth Roads, and then we got into a gale – the famous October gale of twenty-two years ago. It was wind, lightning, sleet, snow, and a terrific sea. We were flying light, and you may imagine how bad it was when I tell you we had smashed bulwarks and a flooded deck. On the second night she shifted her ballast into the lee bow, and by that time we had been blown off somewhere on the Dogger Bank. There was nothing for it but go below with shovels and try to right her, and there we were in that vast hold, gloomy like a cavern, the tallow dips stuck and flickering on the beams, the gale howling above, the ship tossing about like mad on her side; there we all were, Jermyn, the captain, everyone, hardly able to keep our feet, engaged on that gravedigger's work, and trying to toss shovelfuls of wet sand up to windward. At every tumble of the ship you could see vaguely in the dim light men falling down with a great flourish of shovels. One of the ship's boys (we had two), impressed by the weirdness of the scene, wept as if his heart would break. We could hear him blubbering somewhere in the shadows.

'On the third day the gale died out, and by-and-by a north-country tug picked us up. We took sixteen days in all to get from London to the Tyne! When we got into dock we had lost our turn for loading, and they hauled us off to a tier where we remained for a month. Mrs Beard (the captain's name was Beard) came from Colchester to see the old man. She lived on board. The crew of runners had left, and there remained only the officers, one boy and the steward, a mulatto who answered to the name of Abraham. Mrs Beard was an old woman, with a face all wrinkled and ruddy like a winter apple, and the figure of a young girl. She caught sight of me once, sewing on a button, and insisted on having my shirts to repair. This was something different from the captains' wives I had known on board crack clippers. When I brought her the shirts, she said: 'And the socks? They want mending, I am sure, and John's – Captain Beard's – things are all in order now. I would be glad of something to do.' Bless the old woman. She overhauled my outfit for me, and meantime I read for the first time *Sartor Resartus* and Burnaby's *Ride to Khiva*. I didn't understand much of the first then; but I remember I preferred the soldier to the philosopher at the time; a preference which life has only confirmed. One was a man, and the other was either more – or less. However, they are both dead and Mrs Beard is dead, and youth, strength, genius, thoughts, achievements, simple hearts – all dies. . . . No matter.

'They loaded us at last. We shipped a crew. Eight able seamen and two boys. We hauled off one evening to the buoys at the dock-gates, ready to go out, and with a fair prospect of beginning the voyage next day. Mrs Beard was to start for home by a late train. When the ship was fast we went to tea. We sat rather silent through the meal – Mahon, the old couple, and I. I finished first, and slipped away for a smoke, my cabin being in a deck-house just against the poop. It was high water, blowing fresh with a drizzle;

the double dock-gates were opened, and the steam-colliers were
going in and out in the darkness with their lights burning bright, a
great plashing of propellers, rattling of winches, and a lot of
hailing on the pier-heads. I watched the procession of head-lights
gliding high and of green lights gliding low in the night, when
suddenly a red gleam flashed at me, vanished, came into view
again, and remained. The fore-end of a steamer loomed up close. I
shouted down the cabin, "Come up, quick!" and then heard a
startled voice saying afar in the dark, "Stop her, sir." A bell
jingled. Another voice cried warningly, "We are going right into
that barque, sir." The answer to this was a gruff "All right," and
the next thing was a heavy crash as the steamer struck a glancing
blow with the bluff of her bow about our fore-rigging. There was
a moment of confusion, yelling, and running about. Steam roared.
Then somebody was heard saying, "All clear, sir." . . . "Are you
all right?" asked the gruff voice. I had jumped forward to see the
damage, and hailed back, "I think so." "Easy astern," said the
gruff voice. A bell jingled. "What steamer is that?" screamed
Mahon. By that time she was no more to us than a bulky shadow
manoeuvring a little way off. They shouted at us some name – a
woman's name, Miranda or Melissa – or some such thing. "This
means another month in this beastly hole," said Mahon to me, as
we peered with lamps about the splintered bulwarks and broken
braces. "But where's the captain?"

'We had not heard or seen anything of him all that time. We
went aft to look. A doleful voice arose hailing somewhere in the
middle of the dock, "*Judea* ahoy!" . . . How the devil did he get
there? . . . "Hallo" we shouted. "I am adrift in our boat without
oars," he cried. A belated water-man offered his services, and
Mahon struck a bargain with him for half-a-crown to tow our
skipper alongside; but it was Mrs Beard that came up the ladder
first. They had been floating about the dock in that mizzly cold
rain for nearly an hour. I was never so surprised in my life.

'It appears that when he heard my shout "Come up" he
understood at once what was the matter, caught up his wife, ran
on deck, and across, and down into our boat, which was fast to
the ladder. Not bad for a sixty-year-old. Just imagine that old
fellow saving heroically in his arms that old woman – the woman
of his life. He set her down on a thwart, and was ready to climb

back on board when the painter came adrift somehow, and away they went together. Of course in the confusion we did not hear him shouting. He looked abashed. She said cheerfully, "I suppose it does not matter my losing the train now?" "No, Jenny – you go below and get warm," he growled. Then to us: "A sailor has no business with a wife – I say. There I was, out of the ship. Well, no harm done this time. Let's go and look at what that fool of a steamer smashed."

'It wasn't much, but it delayed us three weeks. At the end of that time, the captain being engaged with his agents, I carried Mrs Beard's bag to the railway-station and put her all comfy into a third-class carriage. She lowered the window to say, "You are a good young man. If you see John – Captain Beard – without his muffler at night, just remind him from me to keep his throat well wrapped up." "Certainly, Mrs Beard," I said. "You are a good young man; I noticed how attentive you are to John – to Captain—" The train pulled out suddenly; I took my cap off to the old woman: I never saw her again. . . . Pass the bottle.

'We went to sea next day. When we made that start for Bankok we had been already three months out of London. We had expected to be a fortnight or so – at the outside.

'It was January, and the weather was beautiful – the beautiful sunny winter weather that has more charm than in the summer-time, because it is unexpected, and crisp, and you know it won't, it can't, last long. It's like a windfall, like a godsend, like an unexpected piece of luck.

'It lasted all down the North Sea, all down Channel; and it lasted till we were three hundred miles or so to the westward of the Lizards: then the wind went round to the sou'west and began to pipe up. In two days it blew a gale. The *Judea*, hove to, wallowed on the Atlantic like an old candle-box. It blew day after day: it blew with spite, without interval, without mercy, without rest. The world was nothing but an immensity of great foaming waves rushing at us, under a sky low enough to touch with the hand and dirty like a smoked ceiling. In the stormy space surrounding us there was as much flying spray as air. Day after day and night after night there was nothing round the ship but the howl of the wind, the tumult of the sea, the noise of water pouring over her deck. There was no rest for her and no rest for us. She

tossed, she pitched, she stood on her head, she sat on her tail, she
rolled, she groaned, and we had to hold on while on deck and
cling to our bunks when below, in a constant effort of body and
worry of mind.

'One night Mahon spoke through the small window of my
berth. It opened right into my very bed, and I was lying there
sleepless, in my boots, feeling as though I had not slept for years,
and could not if I tried. He said excitedly—

' "You got the sounding-rod in here, Marlow? I can't get the
pumps to suck. By God! it's no child's play."

'I gave him the sounding-rod and lay down again, trying to
think of various things – but I thought only of the pumps. When I
came on deck they were still at it, and my watch relieved at the
pumps. By the light of the lantern brought on deck to examine the
sounding-rod I caught a glimpse of their weary, serious faces. We
pumped all the four hours. We pumped all night, all day, all the
week – watch and watch. She was working herself loose, and
leaked badly – not enough to drown us at once, but enough to kill
us with the work at the pumps. And while we pumped the ship
was going from us piecemeal: the bulwarks went, the stanchions
were torn out, the ventilators smashed, the cabin-door burst in.
There was not a dry spot in the ship. She was being gutted bit by
bit. The long-boat changed, as if by magic, into matchwood
where she stood in her gripes. I had lashed her myself, and was
rather proud of my handiwork, which had withstood so long the
malice of the sea. And we pumped. And there was no break in the
weather. The sea was white like a sheet of foam, like a caldron of
boiling milk; there was not a break in the clouds, no – not the size
of a man's hand – no, not for so much as ten seconds. There was
for us no sky, there were for us no stars, no sun, no universe –
nothing but angry clouds and an infuriated sea. We pumped
watch and watch, for dear life; and it seemed to last for months,
for years, for all eternity, as though we had been dead and gone to
a hell for sailors. We forgot the day of the week, the name of the
month, what year it was, and whether we had ever been ashore.
The sails blew away, she lay broadside on under a weather-cloth,
the ocean poured over her, and we did not care. We turned those
handles, and had the eyes of idiots. As soon as we had crawled on
deck I used to take a round turn with a rope about the men, the

pumps, and the mainmast, and we turned, we turned incessantly, with the water to our waists, to our necks, over our heads. It was all one. We had forgotten how it felt to be dry.

'And there was somewhere in me the thought: By Jove! this is the deuce of an adventure — something you read about; and it is my first voyage as second mate — and I am only twenty — and here I am lasting it out as well as any of these men, and keeping my chaps up to the mark. I was pleased. I would not have given up the experience for worlds. I had moments of exultation. Whenever the old dismantled craft pitched heavily with her counter high in the air, she seemed to me to throw up, like an appeal, like a defiance, like a cry to the clouds without mercy, the words written on her stern: "*Judea*, London. Do or Die."

'O youth! The strength of it, the faith of it, the imagination of it! To me she was not an old rattle-trap carting about the world a lot of coal for a freight — to me she was the endeavour, the test, the trial of life. I think of her with pleasure, with affection, with regret — as you would think of someone dead you have loved. I shall never forget her. . . . Pass the bottle.

'One night when tied to the mast, as I explained, we were pumping on, deafened with the wind, and without spirit enough in us to wish ourselves dead, a heavy sea crashed aboard and swept clean over us. As soon as I got my breath I shouted, as in duty bound, "Keep on, boys!" when suddenly I felt something hard floating on deck strike the calf of my leg. I made a grab at it and missed. It was so dark we could not see each other's faces within a foot — you understand.

'After that thump the ship kept quiet for a while, and the thing, whatever it was, struck my leg again. This time I caught it — and it was a saucepan. At first, being stupid with fatigue and thinking of nothing but the pumps, I did not understand what I had in my hand. Suddenly it dawned upon me, and I shouted, "Boys, the house on deck is gone. Leave this, and let's look for the cook."

'There was a deck-house forward, which contained the galley, the cook's berth, and the quarters of the crew. As we had expected for days to see it swept away, the hands had been ordered to sleep in the cabin — the only safe place in the ship. The steward, Abraham, however, persisted in clinging to his berth, stupidly, like a mule —from sheer fright I believe, like an animal that won't leave a stable falling in an earthquake. So we went to look for him. It was chancing death, since once out of our lashings we were as exposed as if on a raft. But we went. The house was shattered as if a shell had exploded inside. Most of it had gone overboard – stove, men's quarters, and their property, all was gone: but two posts, holding a portion of the bulkhead to which Abraham's bunk was attached, remained as if by a miracle. We groped in the ruins and came upon this, and there he was, sitting in his bunk, surrounded by foam and wreckage, jabbering cheerfully to himself. He was out of his mind; completely and for ever mad, with this sudden shock coming upon the fag-end of his endurance. We snatched him up, lugged him aft, and pitched him head-first down the cabin companion. You understand there was no time to carry him down with infinite precautions and wait to see how he got on. Those below would pick him up at the bottom of the stairs all right. We were in a hurry to go back to the pumps. That business could not wait. A bad leak is an inhuman thing.

'One would think that the sole purpose of that fiendish gale had been to make a lunatic of that poor devil of a mulatto. It eased before morning, and next day the sky cleared, and as the sea went down the leak took up. When it came to bending a fresh set of sails the crew demanded to put back – and really there was nothing else to do. Boats gone, decks swept clean, cabin gutted, men without a stitch but what they stood in, stores spoiled, ship strained. We put her head for home, and – would you believe it? The wind came east right in our teeth. It blew fresh, it blew continuously. We had to beat up every inch of the way, but she did not leak so badly, the water keeping comparatively smooth. Two hours' pumping in every four is no joke – but it kept her afloat as far as Falmouth.

'The good people there live on casualties of the sea, and no doubt were glad to see us. A hungry crowd of shipwrights sharpened their chisels at the sight of that carcass of a ship. And, by Jove! they had pretty pickings off us before they were done. I fancy the owner was already in a tight place. There were delays. Then it was decided to take part of the cargo out and caulk her topsides. This was done, the repairs finished, cargo reshipped; a new crew came on board, and we went out – for Bankok. At the end of a week we were back again. The crew said they weren't going to Bankok – a hundred and fifty days' passage – in a something hooker that wanted pumping eight hours out of the twenty-four; and the nautical papers inserted again the little paragraph: "*Judea*. Barque. Tyne to Bankok; coals; put back to Falmouth leaky and with crew refusing duty."

'There were more delays – more tinkering. The owner came down for a day, and said she was as right as a little fiddle. Poor old Captain Beard looked like the ghost of a Geordie skipper – through the worry and humiliation of it. Remember he was sixty, and it was his first command. Mahon said it was a foolish business, and would end badly. I loved the ship more than ever, and wanted awfully to get to Bankok. To Bankok! Magic name, blessed name. Mesopotamia wasn't a patch on it. Remember I was twenty, and it was my first second-mate's billet, and the East was waiting for me.

'We went out and anchored in the outer roads with a fresh crew – the third. She leaked worse than ever. It was as if those confounded shipwrights had actually made a hole in her. This time we did not even go outside. The crew simply refused to man the windlass.

'They towed us back to the inner harbour, and we became a fixture, a feature, an institution of the place. People pointed us out to visitors as "That 'ere barque that's going to Bankok – has been here six months – put back three times." On holidays the small boys pulling about in boats would hail, "*Judea*, ahoy!" and if a head showed above the rail shouted, "Where you bound to? – Bankok?" and jeered. We were only three on board. The poor old skipper mooned in the cabin. Mahon undertook the cooking, and unexpectedly developed all a Frenchman's genius for preparing nice little messes. I looked languidly after the rigging. We became citizens of Falmouth. Every shopkeeper knew us. At the barber's or tobacconist's they asked familiarly, "Do you think you will ever get to Bankok?" Meantime the owner, the underwriters, and the charterers squabbled amongst themselves in London, and our pay went on. . . . Pass the bottle.

'It was horrid. Morally it was worse than pumping for life. It seemed as though we had been forgotten by the world, belonged to nobody, would get nowhere; it seemed that, as if bewitched, we would have to live for ever and ever in that inner harbour, a derision and a by-word to generations of long-shore loafers and dishonest boatmen. I obtained three months' pay and a five days' leave, and made a rush for London. It took me a day to get there and pretty well another to come back – but three months' pay went all the same. I don't know what I did with it. I went to a music-hall, I believe, lunched, dined, and supped in a swell place in Regent Street, and was back to time, with nothing but a complete set of Byron's works and a new railway rug to show for three months' work. The boat-man who pulled me off to the ship said: "Hallo! I thought you had left the old thing. *She* will never get to Bankok." "That's all *you* know about it," I said, scornfully – but I didn't like that prophecy at all.

'Suddenly a man, some kind of agent to somebody, appeared with full powers. He had grog-blossoms all over his face, an indomitable energy, and was a jolly soul. We leaped into life again. A hulk came alongside, took our cargo, and then we went into dry dock to get our copper stripped. No wonder she leaked. The poor thing, strained beyond endurance by the gale, had, as if in disgust, spat out all the oakum of her lower seams. She was recaulked, new coppered, and made as tight as a bottle. We went back to the hulk and reshipped our cargo.

'Then, on a fine moonlight night, all the rats left the ship.

'We had been infested with them. They had destroyed our sails, consumed more stores than the crew, affably shared our beds and our dangers, and now, when the ship was made seaworthy, concluded to clear out. I called Mahon to enjoy the spectacle. Rat after rat appeared on our rail, took a last look over his shoulder, and leaped with a hollow thud into the empty hulk. We tried to count them, but soon lost the tale. Mahon said: "Well, well! don't talk to me about the intelligence of rats. They ought to have left before, when we had that narrow squeak from foundering. There you have the proof how silly is the superstition about them. They leave a good ship for an old rotten hulk, where there is nothing to eat, too, the fools! . . . I don't believe they know what is safe or what is good for them, any more than you or I."

'And after some more talk we agreed that the wisdom of rats had been grossly overrated, being in fact no greater than that of men.

'The story of the ship was known, by this, all up the Channel from Land's End to the Forelands, and we could get no crew on the south coast. They sent us one all complete from Liverpool, and we left once more – for Bankok.

'We had fair breezes, smooth water right into the tropics, and the old *Judea* lumbered along in the sunshine. When she went eight knots everything cracked aloft, and we tied our caps to our heads; but mostly she strolled on at the rate of three miles an hour. What could you expect? She was tired – that old ship. Her youth was where mine is – where yours is – you fellows who listen to this yarn; and what friend would throw your years and your weariness in your face? We didn't grumble at her. To us aft, at least, it seemed as though we had been born in her, reared in her, had lived in her for ages, had never known any other ship. I would just as soon have abused the old village church at home for not being a cathedral.

'And for me there was also my youth to make me patient. There was all the East before me, and all life, and the thought that I had been tried in that ship and had come out pretty well. And I thought of men of old who, centuries ago, went that road in ships that sailed no better, to the land of palms, and spices, and yellow sands, and of brown nations ruled by kings more cruel than Nero the Roman, and more splendid than Solomon the Jew. The old bark lumbered on, heavy with her age and the burden of her cargo, while I lived the life of youth in ignorance and hope. She lumbered on through an interminable procession of days; and the fresh gilding flashed back at the setting sun, seemed to cry out over the darkening sea the words painted on her stern, "*Judea*, London. Do or Die."

'Then we entered the Indian Ocean and steered northerly for Java Head. The winds were light. Weeks slipped by. She crawled on, do or die, and people at home began to think of posting us as overdue.

'One Saturday evening, I being off duty, the men asked me to give them an extra bucket of water or so – for washing clothes. As I did not wish to screw on the fresh-water pump so late, I went forward whistling, and with a key in my hand to unlock the forepeak scuttle, intending to serve the water out of a spare tank we kept there.

'The smell down below was as unexpected as it was frightful. One would have thought hundreds of paraffin-lamps had been flaring and smoking in that hole for days. I was glad to get out. The man with me coughed and said, "Funny smell, sir." I answered negligently, "It's good for the health they say," and walked aft.

'The first thing I did was to put my head down the square of the midship ventilator. As I lifted the lid a visible breath, something like a thin fog, a puff of faint haze, rose from the opening. The ascending air was hot, and had a heavy, sooty, paraffiny smell. I gave one sniff, and put down the lid gently. It was no use choking myself. The cargo was on fire.

'Next day she began to smoke in earnest. You see it was to be expected, for though the coal was of a safe kind, that cargo had been so handled, so broken up with handling, that it looked more like smithy coal than anything else. Then it had been wetted — more than once. It rained all the time we were taking it back from the hulk, and now with this long passage it got heated, and there was another case of spontaneous combustion.

'The captain called us into the cabin. He had a chart spread on the table, and looked unhappy. He said, "The coast of West Australia is near, but I mean to proceed to our destination. It is the hurricane month, too; but we will just keep her head for Bankok, and fight the fire. No more putting back anywhere, if we all get roasted. We will try first to stifle this 'ere damned combustion by want of air."

'We tried. We battened down everything, and still she smoked. The smoke kept coming out through imperceptible crevices; it forced itself through bulk-heads and covers; it oozed here and there and everywhere in slender threads, in an invisible film, in an incomprehensible manner. It made its way into the cabin, into the forecastle; it poisoned the sheltered places on the deck, it could be sniffed as high as the mainyard. It was clear that if the smoke came out the air came in. This was disheartening. This combustion refused to be stifled.

'We resolved to try water, and took the hatches off. Enormous volumes of smoke, whitish, yellowish, thick, greasy, misty, choking, ascended as high as the trucks. All hands cleared out aft. Then the poisonous cloud blew away, and we went back to work in a smoke that was no thicker now than that of an ordinary factory chimney.

'We rigged the force-pump, got the hose along, and by-and-by it burst. Well, it was as old as the ship – a prehistoric hose, and past repair. Then we pumped with the feeble head-pump, drew water with buckets, and in this way managed in time to pour lots of Indian Ocean into the main hatch. The bright stream flashed in sunshine, fell into a layer of white crawling smoke, and vanished on the black surface of coal. Steam ascended mingling with the smoke. We poured salt water as into a barrel without a bottom. It was our fate to pump in that ship, to pump out of her, to pump into her; and after keeping water out of her to save ourselves from being drowned, we frantically poured water into her to save ourselves from being burnt.

'And she crawled on, do or die, in the serene weather. The sky was a miracle of purity, a miracle of azure. The sea was polished, was blue, was pellucid, was sparkling like a precious stone, extending on all sides, all round to the horizon – as if the whole terrestrial globe had been one jewel, one colossal sapphire, a single gem fashioned into a planet. And on the lustre of the great calm waters, the *Judea* glided imperceptibly, enveloped in languid and unclean vapours, in a lazy cloud that drifted to leeward, light and slow; a pestiferous cloud defiling the splendour of sea and sky.

'All this time of course we saw no fire. The cargo smouldered at the bottom somewhere. Once Mahon, as we were working side by side, said to me with a queer smile: "Now, if she only would spring a tidy leak – like that time when we first left the Channel – it would put a stopper on this fire. Wouldn't it?" I remarked irrelevantly, "Do you remember the rats?"

'We fought the fire and sailed the ship too as carefully as though nothing had been the matter. The steward cooked and attended on us. Of the other twelve men, eight worked while four rested. Everyone took his turn, captain included. There was equality, and if not exactly fraternity, then a deal of good feeling. Sometimes a man, as he dashed a bucketful of water down the hatchway, would yell out, "Hurrah for Bankok!" and the rest laughed. But generally we were taciturn and serious – and thirsty. Oh! how thirsty! And we had to be careful with the water. Strict allowance. The ship smoked, the sun blazed . . . Pass the bottle.

'We tried everything. We even made an attempt to dig down to the fire. No good, of course. No man could remain more than a minute below. Mahon, who went first, fainted there, and the man who went to fetch him out did likewise. We lugged them out on deck. Then I leaped down to show how easily it could be done. They had learned wisdom by that time, and contented themselves by fishing for me with a chainhook tied to a broom-handle, I believe. I did not offer to go and fetch up my shovel, which was left down below.

'Things began to look bad. We put the long-boat into the water. The second boat was ready to swing out. We had also another, a 14-foot thing, on davits aft, where it was quite safe.

'Then, behold, the smoke suddenly decreased. We redoubled our efforts to flood the bottom of the ship. In two days there was no smoke at all. Everybody was on the broad grin. This was on a Friday. On Saturday no work, but sailing the ship of course, was done. The men washed their clothes and their faces for the first time in a fortnight, and had a special dinner given them. They spoke of spontaneous combustion with contempt, and implied *they* were the boys to put out combustions. Somehow we all felt as though we each had inherited a large fortune. But a beastly smell of burning hung about the ship. Captain Beard had hollow eyes and sunken cheeks. I had never noticed so much before how twisted and bowed he was. He and Mahon prowled soberly about hatches and ventilators, sniffing. It struck me suddenly poor Mahon was a very, very old chap. As to me, I was as pleased and proud as though I had helped to win a great naval battle. O! Youth!

'The night was fine. In the morning a homeward-bound ship passed us hull down – the first we had seen for months; but we were nearing the land at last, Java Head being about 190 miles off, and nearly due north.

'Next day it was my watch on deck from eight to twelve. At breakfast the captain observed, 'It's wonderful how that smell hangs about the cabin.' About ten, the mate being on the poop, I stepped down on the main-deck for a moment. The carpenter's bench stood abaft the mainmast: I leaned against it sucking at my pipe, and the carpenter, a young chap, came to talk to me. He remarked, 'I think we have done very well, haven't we?' and then I perceived with annoyance the fool was trying to tilt the bench. I said curtly, "Don't, Chips," and immediately became aware of a queer sensation, of an absurd delusion, – I seemed somehow to be in the air. I heard all round me like a pent-up breath released – as if a thousand giants simultaneously had said Phoo! – and felt a dull concussion which made my ribs ache suddenly. No doubt about it – I was in the air, and my body was describing a short parabola. But short as it was, I had the time to think several thoughts in, as far as I can remember, the following order: "This can't be the carpenter – What is it? – Some accident – Submarine volcano? – Coals, gas! – By Jove! we are being blown up – Everybody's dead – I am falling into the after-hatch – I see fire in it."

'The coal-dust suspended in the air of the hold had glowed dull-red at the moment of the explosion. In the twinkling of an eye, in an infinitesimal fraction of a second since the first tilt of the bench, I was sprawling full length on the cargo. I picked myself up and scrambled out. It was quick like a rebound. The deck was a wilderness of smashed timber, lying crosswise like trees in a wood after a hurricane; an immense curtain of soiled rags waved gently before me – it was the mainsail blown to strips. I thought, The masts will be toppling over directly; and to get out of the way bolted on all-fours towards the poop-ladder. The first person I saw was Mahon, with eyes like saucers, his mouth open, and the long white hair standing straight on end round his head like a silver halo. He was just about to go down when the sight of the main-deck stirring, heaving up, and changing into splinters before his eyes, petrified him on the top step. I stared at him in unbelief, and he stared at me with a queer kind of shocked curiosity. I did not know that I had no hair, no eyebrows, no eyelashes, that my young moustache was burnt off, that my face was black, one cheek laid open, my nose cut, and my chin bleeding. I had lost my cap, one of my slippers, and my shirt was torn to rags. Of all this I was not aware. I was amazed to see the ship still afloat, the poop-deck whole – and, most of all, to see anybody alive. Also the peace of the sky and the serenity of the sea were distinctly surprising. I suppose I expected to see them convulsed with horror . . . Pass the bottle.

'There was a voice hailing the ship from somewhere – in the air, in the sky – I couldn't tell. Presently I saw the captain – and he was mad. He asked me eagerly, "Where's the cabin-table?" and to hear such a question was a frightful shock. I had just been blown up, you understand, and vibrated with that experience, – I wasn't quite sure whether I was alive. Mahon began to stamp with both feet and yelled at him, "Good God! don't you see the deck's blown out of her?" I found my voice, and stammered out as if conscious of some gross neglect of duty, "I don't know where the cabin-table is." It was like an absurd dream.

'Do you know what he wanted next? Well, he wanted to trim the yards. Very placidly, and as if lost in thought, he insisted on having the foreyard squared. "I don't know if there's anybody alive," said Mahon, almost tearfully. "Surely," he said, gently, "there will be enough left to square the foreyard."

'The old chap, it seems, was in his own berth winding up the chronometers, when the shock sent him spinning. Immediately it occurred to him – as he said afterwards – that the ship had struck something, and ran out into the cabin. There, he saw, the cabin-table had vanished somewhere. The deck being blown up, it had fallen down into the lazarette of course. Where we had our breakfast that morning he saw only a great hole in the floor. This appeared to him so awfully mysterious, and impressed him so immensely, that what he saw and heard after he got on deck were mere trifles in comparison. And, mark, he noticed directly the wheel deserted and his barque off her course – and his only thought was to get that miserable, stripped, undecked, smoulder-ing shell of a ship back again with her head pointing at her port of destination. Bankok! That's what he was after. I tell you this quiet, bowed, bandy-legged, almost deformed little man was immense in the singleness of his idea and in his placid ignorance of our agitation. He motioned us forward with a commanding gesture, and went to take the wheel himself.

'Yes; that was the first thing we did – trim the yards of that wreck! No one was killed, or even disabled, but everyone was more or less hurt. You should have seen them! Some were in rags, with black faces, like coal-heavers, like sweeps, and had bullet heads that seemed closely cropped, but were in fact singed to the skin. Others, of the watch below, awakened by being shot out from their collapsing bunks, shivered incessantly, and kept on groaning even as we went about our work. But they all worked. That crew of Liverpool hard cases had in them the right stuff. It's my experience they always have. It is the sea that gives it – the vastness, the loneliness surrounding their dark stolid souls. Ah! Well! we stumbled, we crept, we fell, we barked our shins on the wreckage, we hauled. The masts stood, but we did not know how much they might be charred down below. It was nearly calm, but a long swell ran from the west and made her roll. They might go at any moment. We looked at them with apprehension. One could not foresee which way they would fall.

'Then we retreated aft and looked about us. The deck was a tangle of planks on edge, of planks on end, of splinters, of ruined woodwork. The masts rose from that chaos like big trees above a matted undergrowth. The interstices of that mass of wreckage were full of something whitish, sluggish, stirring – of something that was like a greasy fog. The smoke of the invisible fire was coming up again, was trailing, like a poisonous thick mist in some valley choked with dead wood. Already lazy wisps were beginning to curl upwards amongst the mass of splinters. Here and there a piece of timber, stuck upright, resembled a post. Half of a fife-rail had been shot through the foresail, and the sky made a patch of glorious blue in the ignobly soiled canvas. A portion of several boards holding together had fallen across the rail, and one end protruded overboard, like a gangway leading upon nothing, like a gangway leading over the deep sea, leading to death – as if inviting us to walk the plank at once and be done with our ridiculous troubles. And still the air, the sky – a ghost, something invisible was hailing the ship.

'Someone had the sense to look over, and there was the helmsman, who had impulsively jumped overboard, anxious to come back. He yelled and swam lustily like a merman, keeping up with the ship. We threw him a rope, and presently he stood amongst us streaming with water and very crestfallen The captain had surrendered the wheel, and apart, elbow on rail and chin in hand, gazed at the sea wistfully. We asked ourselves, What next? I thought, Now, this is something like. This is great. I wonder what will happen. O youth!

'Suddenly Mahon sighted a steamer far astern. Captain Beard said, "We may do something with her yet." We hoisted two flags, which said in the international language of the sea, "On fire. Want immediate assistance." The steamer grew bigger rapidly, and by-

and-by spoke with two flags on her foremast, "I am coming to your assistance."

'In half an hour she was abreast, to windward, within hail, and rolling slightly, with her engines stopped. We lost our composure, and yelled all together with excitement, "We've been blown up." A man in a white helmet, on the bridge, cried, "Yes! All right! all right!" and he nodded his head, and smiled, and made soothing motions with his hand as though at a lot of frightened children. One of the boats dropped in the water, and walked towards us upon the sea with her long oars. Four Calashes pulled a swinging stroke. This was my first sight of Malay seamen. I've known them since, but what struck me then was their unconcern: they came alongside, and even the bowman standing up and holding to our main-chains with the boat-hook did not deign to lift his head for a glance. I thought people who had been blown up deserved more attention.

'A little man, dry like a chip and agile like a monkey, clambered up. It was the mate of the steamer. He gave one look, and cried, "O boys – you had better quit."

'We were silent. He talked apart with the captain for a time, – seemed to argue with him. Then they went away together to the steamer.

'When our skipper came back we learned that the steamer was the *Somerville*, Captain Nash, from West Australia to Singapore *via* Batavia with mails, and that the agreement was she should tow us to Anjer or Batavia, if possible, where we could extinguish the fire by scuttling, and then proceed on our voyage – to Bankok! The old man seemed excited. "We will do it yet," he said to Mahon, fiercely. He shook his fist at the sky. Nobody else said a word.

'At noon the steamer began to tow. She went ahead slim and high, and what was left of the *Judea* followed at the end of seventy fathom of tow-rope, – followed her swiftly like a cloud of smoke with mast-heads protruding above. We went aloft to furl the sails. We coughed on the yards, and were careful about the bunts. Do you see the lot of us there, putting a neat furl on the sails of that ship doomed to arrive nowhere? There was not a man who didn't think that at any moment the masts would topple over. From aloft we could not see the ship for smoke, and they worked carefully,

passing the gaskets with even turns. "Harbour furl – aloft there!"
cried Mahon from below.

'You understand this? I don't think one of those chaps expected
to get down in the usual way. When we did I heard them saying to
each other, "Well, I thought we would come down overboard, in
a lump – sticks and all – blame me if I didn't." "That's what I was
thinking to myself," would answer wearily another battered and
bandaged scarecrow. And, mind, these were men without the
drilled-in habit of obedience. To an onlooker they would be a lot
of profane scallywags without a redeeming point. What made
them do it – what made them obey me when I, thinking
consciously how fine it was, made them drop the bunt of the
foresail twice to try and do it better? What? They had no
professional reputation – no examples, no praise. It wasn't a sense
of duty; they all knew well enough how to shirk, and laze, and
dodge – when they had a mind to it – and mostly they had. Was it
the two pounds ten a-month that sent them there? They didn't
think their pay half good enough. No; it was something in them,
something inborn and subtle and everlasting. I don't say
positively that the crew of a French or German merchantman
wouldn't have done it, but I doubt whether it would have been
done in the same way. There was a completeness in it, something
solid like a principle, and masterful like an instinct – a disclosure
of something secret – of that hidden something, that gift of good
or evil that makes racial difference, that shapes the fate of nations.

'It was that night at ten that, for the first time since we had been
fighting it, we saw the fire. The speed of the towing had fanned the
smouldering destruction. A blue gleam appeared forward, shining
below the wreck of the deck. It wavered in patches, it seemed to
stir and creep like the light of a glowworm. I saw it first, and told
Mahon. "Then the game's up," he said. "We had better stop this
towing, or she will burst out suddenly fore and aft before we can
clear out." We set up a yell; rang bells to attract their attention;
they towed on. At last Mahon and I had to crawl forward and cut
the rope with an axe. There was no time to cast off the lashings.
Red tongues could be seen licking the wilderness of splinters
under our feet as we made our way back to the poop.

'Of course they very soon found out in the steamer that the rope
was gone. She gave a loud blast of her whistle, her lights were seen

sweeping in a wide circle, she came up ranging close alongside, and stopped. We were all in a tight group on the poop looking at her. Every man had saved a little bundle or a bag. Suddenly a conical flame with a twisted top shot up forward and threw upon the black sea a circle of light, with the two vessels side by side and heaving gently in its centre. Captain Beard had been sitting on the gratings still and mute for hours, but now he rose slowly and advanced in front of us, to the mizzen-shrouds. Captain Nash hailed: "Come along! Look sharp. I have mail-bags on board. I will take you and your boat to Singapore."

' "Thank you! No!" said our skipper. "We must see the last of the ship."

' "I can't stand by any longer," shouted the other. "Mails – you know."

' "Ay! ay! We are all right."

' "Very well! I'll report you in Singapore. . . . Good-bye!"

'He waved his hand. Our men dropped their bundles quietly. The steamer moved ahead, and passing out of the circle of light, vanished at once from our sight, dazzled by the fire which burned fiercely. And then I knew that I would see the East first as commander of a small boat. I thought it fine; and the fidelity to the old ship was fine. We should see the last of her. Oh, the glamour of youth! Oh, the fire of it, more dazzling than the flames of the burning ship, throwing a magic light on the wide earth, leaping audaciously to the sky, presently to be quenched by time, more cruel, more pitiless, more bitter than the sea – and like the flames of the burning ship surrounded by an impenetrable night.

'The old man warned us in his gentle and inflexible way that it was part of our duty to save for the underwriters as much as we could of the ship's gear. Accordingly we went to work aft, while she blazed forward to give us plenty of light. We lugged out a lot of rubbish. What didn't we save? An old barometer fixed with an absurd quantity of screws nearly cost me my life: a sudden rush of smoke came upon me, and I just got away in time. There were various stores, bolts of canvas, coils of rope; the poop looked like a marine bazaar, and the boats were lumbered to the gunwales. One would have thought the old man wanted to take as much as he could of his first command with him. He was very, very quiet, but off his balance evidently. Would you believe it? He wanted to take a length of old stream-cable and a kedge-anchor with him in the long-boat. We said, "Ay, ay, sir," deferentially, and on the quiet let the things slip overboard. The heavy medicine-chest went that way, two bags of green coffee, tins of paint — fancy, paint! — a whole lot of things. Then I was ordered with two hands into the boats to make a stowage and get them ready against the time it would be proper for us to leave the ship.

'We put everything straight, stepped the long-boat's mast for our skipper, who was to take charge of her, and I was not sorry to sit down for a moment. My face felt raw, every limb ached as if broken, I was aware of all my ribs, and would have sworn to a twist in the backbone. The boats, fast astern, lay in a deep shadow, and all around I could see the circle of the sea lighted by the fire. A gigantic flame arose forward straight and clear. It flared fierce, with noises like the whirr of wings, with rumbles as of thunder. There were cracks, detonations, and from the cone of flame the sparks flew upwards, as man is born to trouble, to leaky ships, and to ships that burn

'What bothered me was that the ship, lying broadside to the swell and to such wind as there was — a mere breath — the boats would not keep astern where they were safe, but persisted, in a pig-headed way boats have, in getting under the counter and then swinging alongside. They were knocking about dangerously and coming near the flame, while the ship rolled on them, and, of course, there was always the danger of the masts going over the side at any moment. I and my two boat-keepers kept them off as best we could, with oars and boat-hooks; but to be constantly at it became exasperating, since there was no reason why we should not leave at once. We could not see those on board, nor could we imagine what caused the delay. The boat-keepers were swearing feebly, and I had not only my share of the work but also had to keep at it two men who showed a constant inclination to lay themselves down and let things slide.

'At last I hailed, "On deck there," and someone looked over. "We're ready here," I said. The head disappeared, and very soon popped up again. "The captain says, All right, sir, and to keep the boats well clear of the ship."

'Half an hour passed. Suddenly there was a frightful racket, rattle, clanking of chain, hiss of water, and millions of sparks flew up into the shivering column of smoke that stood leaning slightly above the ship. The cat-heads had burned away, and the two red-hot anchors had gone to the bottom, tearing out after them two hundred fathom of red-hot chain. The ship trembled, the mass of flame swayed as if ready to collapse, and the fore top-gallant-mast fell. It darted down like an arrow of fire, shot under, and instantly leaping up within an oar's-length of the boats, floated quietly, very black on the luminous sea. I hailed the deck again. After some time a man in an unexpectedly cheerful but also muffled tone, as though he had been trying to speak with his mouth shut, informed me, "Coming directly, sir," and vanished. For a long time I heard nothing but the whirr and roar of the fire. There were also whistling sounds. The boats jumped, tugged at the painters, ran at each other playfully, knocked their sides together, or, do what we would, swung in a bunch against the ship's side. I couldn't stand it any longer, and swarming up a rope, clambered aboard over the stern.

'It was as bright as day. Coming up like this, the sheet of fire facing me was a terrifying sight, and the heat seemed hardly bearable at first. On a settee cushion dragged out of the cabin Captain Beard, his legs drawn up and one arm under his head, slept with the light playing on him. Do you know what the rest were busy about? They were sitting on deck right aft, round an open case, eating bread and cheese and drinking bottled stout.

'On the background of flames twisting in fierce tongues above their heads they seemed at home like salamanders, and looked like a band of desperate pirates. The fire sparkled in the whites of their eyes, gleamed on patches of white skin seen through the torn shirts. Each had the marks as of a battle about him – bandaged heads, tied-up arms, a strip of dirty rag round a knee – and each man had a bottle between his legs and a chunk of cheese in his hand. Mahon got up. With his handsome and disreputable head, his hooked profile, his long white beard, and with an uncorked bottle in his hand, he resembled one of those reckless sea-robbers of old making merry amidst violence and disaster. "The last meal on board," he explained solemnly. "We had nothing to eat all day, and it was no use leaving all this." He flourished the bottle and indicated the sleeping skipper. "He said he couldn't swallow anything, so I got him to lie down," he went on; and as I stared, "I don't know whether you are aware, young fellow, the man had no sleep to speak of for days – and there will be dam' little sleep in the boats." "There will be no boats by-and-by if you fool about much longer," I said, indignantly. I walked up to the skipper and shook him by the shoulder. At last he opened his eyes, but did not move. "Time to leave her, sir," I said quietly.

'He got up painfully, looked at the flames, at the sea sparkling round the ship, and black, black as ink farther away; he looked at the stars shining dim through a thin veil of smoke in a sky black, black as Erebus.

' "Youngest first," he said.

'And the ordinary seaman, wiping his mouth with the back of his hand, got up, clambered over the taffrail, and vanished. Others followed. One, on the point of going over, stopped short to drain his bottle, and with a great swing of his arm flung it at the fire. "Take this!" he cried.

'The skipper lingered disconsolately, and we left him to commune alone for a while with his first command. Then I went up again and brought him away at last. It was time. The ironwork on the poop was hot to the touch.

'Then the painter of the long-boat was cut, and the three boats, tied together, drifted clear of the ship. It was just sixteen hours after the explosion when we abandoned her. Mahon had charge of the second boat, and I had the smallest – the 14-foot thing. The long-boat would have taken the lot of us; but the skipper said we must save as much property as we could – for the underwriters – and so I got my first command. I had two men with me, a bag of biscuits, a few tins of meat, and a breaker of water. I was ordered to keep close to the long-boat, that in case of bad weather we might be taken into her.

'And do you know what I thought? I thought I would part company as soon as I could. I wanted to have my first command all to myself. I wasn't going to sail in a squadron if there were a chance for independent cruising. I would make land by myself. I would beat the other boats. Youth! All youth! The silly, charming, beautiful youth.

'But we did not make a start at once. We must see the last of the

ship. And so the boats drifted about that night, heaving and
setting on the swell. The men dozed, waked, sighed, groaned. I
looked at the burning ship.

'Between the darkness of earth and heaven she was burning
fiercely upon a disc of purple sea shot by the blood-red play of
gleams; upon a disc of water glittering and sinister. A high, clear
flame, an immense and lonely flame, ascended from the ocean,
and from its summit the black smoke poured continuously at the
sky. She burned furiously; mournful and imposing like a funeral
pile kindled in the night, surrounded by the sea, watched over by
the stars. A magnificent death had come like a grace, like a gift,
like a reward to that old ship at the end of her laborious days. The
surrender of her weary ghost to the keeping of stars and sea was
stirring like the sight of a glorious triumph. The masts fell just
before daybreak, and for a moment there was a burst and turmoil
of sparks that seemed to fill with flying fire the night patient and
watchful, the vast night lying silent upon the sea. At daylight she
was only a charred shell, floating still under a cloud of smoke and
bearing a glowing mass of coal within.

'Then the oars were got out, and the boats forming in a line
moved round her remains as if in procession – the long-boat
leading. As we pulled across her stern a slim dart of fire shot out
viciously at us, and suddenly she went down, head first, in a great
hiss of steam. The unconsumed stern was the last to sink; but the
paint had gone, had cracked, had peeled off, and there were no
letters, there was no word, no stubborn device that was like her
soul, to flash at the rising sun her creed and her name.

'We made our way north. A breeze sprang up, and about noon
all the boats came together for the last time. I had no mast or sail
in mine, but I made a mast out of a spare oar and hoisted a boat-
awning for a sail, with a boat-hook for a yard. She was certainly
over-masted, but I had the satisfaction of knowing that with the
wind aft I could beat the other two. I had to wait for them. Then
we all had a look at the captain's chart, and, after a sociable meal
of hard bread and water, got our last instructions. These were
simple: steer north, and keep together as much as possible. "Be
careful with that jury-rig, Marlow," said the captain; and Mahon,
as I sailed proudly past his boat, wrinkled his curved nose and
hailed, "You will sail that ship of yours under water, if you don't

look out, young fellow." He was a malicious old man – and may
the deep sea where he sleeps now rock him gently, rock him
tenderly to the end of time!

'Before sunset a thick rain-squall passed over the two boats,
which were far astern, and that was the last I saw of them for a
time. Next day I sat steering my cockle-shell – my first command
–with nothing but water and sky around me. I did sight in the
afternoon the upper sails of a ship far away, but said nothing, and
my men did not notice her. You see I was afraid she might he
homeward bound, and I had no mind to turn back from the
portals of the East. I was steering for Java – another blessed name
– like Bankok, you know. I steered many days.

'I need not tell you what it is to be knocking about in an open
boat. I remember nights and days of calm, when we pulled, we
pulled, and the boat seemed to stand still, as if bewitched within
the circle of the sea horizon. I remember the heat, the deluge of
rain-squalls that kept us baling for dear life (but filled our water-
cask), and I remember sixteen hours on end with a mouth dry as a
cinder and a steering-oar over the stern to keep my first command
head on to a breaking sea. I did not know how good a man I was
till then. I remember the drawn faces, the dejected figures of my
two men, and I remember my youth and the feeling that will never
come back any more – the feeling that I could last for ever, outlast
the sea, the earth, and all men; the deceitful feeling that lures us on
to joys, to perils, to love, to vain effort – to death; the triumphant
conviction of strength, the heat of life in the handful of dust, the
glow in the heart that with every year grows dim, grows cold,
grows small, and expires – and expires, too soon, too soon –
before life itself.

'And this is how I see the East. I have seen its secret places and
have looked into its very soul; but now I see it always from a small
boat, a high outline of mountains, blue and afar in the morning;
like faint mist at noon: a jagged wall of purple at sunset. I have the
feel of the oar in my hand, the vision of a scorching blue sea in my
eyes. And I see a bay, a wide bay, smooth as glass and polished like
ice, shimmering in the dark. A red light burns far off upon the
gloom of the land, and the night is soft and warm. We drag at the
oars with aching arms, and suddenly a puff of wind, a puff faint
and tepid and laden with strange odours of blossoms, of aromatic

wood, comes out of the still night – the first sigh of the East on my
face. That I can never forget. It was impalpable and enslaving, like
a charm, like a whispered promise of mysterious delight.

'We had been pulling this finishing spell for eleven hours. Two
pulled, and he whose turn it was to rest sat at the tiller. We had made
out the red light in that bay and steered for it, guessing it must mark
some small coasting port. We passed two vessels, outlandish and
high-sterned, sleeping at anchor, and, approaching the light, now
very dim, ran the boat's nose against the end of a jutting wharf. We
were blind with fatigue. My men dropped the oars and fell off the
thwarts as if dead. I made fast to a pile. A current rippled softly. The
scented obscurity of the shore was grouped into vast masses, a
density of colossal clumps of vegetation, probably – mute and
fantastic shapes. And at their foot the semicircle of a beach gleamed
faintly, like an illusion. There was not a light, not a stir, not a sound.
The mysterious East faced me, perfumed like a flower, silent like
death, dark like a grave.

'And I sat weary beyond expression, exulting like a conqueror,
sleepless and entranced as if before a profound, a fateful enigma.

'A splashing of oars, a measured dip reverberating on the level
of water, intensified by the silence of the shore into loud claps,
made me jump up. A boat, a European boat, was coming in. I
invoked the name of the dead; I hailed: *Judea* ahoy! A thin shout
answered.

'It was the captain. I had beaten the flagship by three hours, and
I was glad to hear the old man's voice again, tremulous and tired.
"Is it you, Marlow?" "Mind the end of that jetty, sir," I cried.

'He approached cautiously, and brought up with the deep-sea
lead-line which we had saved – for the underwriters. I eased my
painter and fell alongside. He sat, a broken figure at the stern, wet
with dew, his hands clasped in his lap. His men were asleep
already. "I had a terrible time of it," he murmured. "Mahon is
behind – not very far." We conversed in whispers, in low
whispers, as if afraid to wake up the land. Guns, thunder,
earthquakes would not have awakened the men just then.

'Looking round as we talked, I saw away at sea a bright light
travelling in the night. "There's a steamer passing the bay," I said.
She was not passing, she was entering, and she even came close
and anchored. "I wish," said the old man, "you would find out

whether she is English. Perhaps they could give us a passage somewhere." He seemed nervously anxious. So by dint of punching and kicking I started one of my men into a state of somnambulism, and giving him an oar, took another and pulled towards the lights of the steamer.

"There was a murmur of voices in her, metallic hollow clangs of the engine-room, footsteps on the deck. Her ports shone, round like dilated eyes. Shapes moved about, and there was a shadowy man high up on the bridge. He heard my oars.

'And then, before I could open my lips, the East spoke to me, but it was in a Western voice. A torrent of words was poured into the enigmatical, the fateful silence; outlandish, angry words, mixed with words and even whole sentences of good English, less strange but even more surprising. The voice swore and cursed violently; it riddled the solemn peace of the bay by a volley of abuse. It began by calling me Pig, and from that went crescendo into unmentionable adjectives – in English. The man up there raged aloud in two languages, and with a sincerity in his fury that almost convinced me I had, in some way, sinned against the harmony of the universe. I could hardly see him, but began to think he would work himself into a fit.

'Suddenly he ceased, and I could hear him snorting and blowing like a porpoise. I said—

' "What steamer is this, pray?"

' "Eh? What's this? And who are you?"

' "Castaway crew of an English barque burnt at sea. We came here tonight. I am the second mate. The captain is in the long-boat, and wishes to know if you would give us a passage somewhere."

' "Oh, my goodness! I say. . . . This is the *Celestial* from Singapore on her return trip. I'll arrange with your captain in the morning, . . . and, . . . I say, . . . did you hear me just now?"

' "I should think the whole bay heard you."

' "I thought you were a shore-boat. Now, look here – this infernal lazy scoundrel of a caretaker has gone to sleep again – curse him. The light is out, and I nearly ran foul of the end of this damned jetty. This the third time he plays me this trick. Now, I ask you, can anybody stand this kind of thing? It's enough to drive a man out of his mind. I'll report him. . . . I'll get the Assistant

Resident to give him the sack, by. . . ! See – there's no light. It's out, isn't it? I take you to witness the light's out. There should be a light, you know. A red light on the–"

'"There was a light," I said, mildly.

'"But it's out, man! What's the use of talking like this? You can see for yourself it's out – don't you? If you had to take a valuable steamer along this God-forsaken coast you would want a light, too. I'll kick him from end to end of his miserable wharf. You'll see if I don't. I will–"

'"So I may tell my captain you'll take us?" I broke in.

'"Yes, I'll take you. Goodnight," he said, brusquely.

'I pulled back, made fast again to the jetty, and then went to sleep at last. I had faced the silence of the East. I had heard some of its language. But when I opened my eyes again the silence was as complete as though it had never been broken. I was lying in a flood of light, and the sky had never looked so far, so high, before. I opened my eyes and lay without moving.

'And then I saw the men of the East – they were looking at me. The whole length of the jetty was full of people. I saw brown, bronze, yellow faces, the black eyes, the glitter, the colour of an Eastern crowd. And all these beings stared without a murmur, without a sigh, without a movement. They stared down at the boats, at the sleeping men who at night had come to them from the sea. Nothing moved. The fronds of palms stood still against the sky. Not a branch stirred along the shore, and the brown roofs of hidden houses peeped through the green foliage, through the big leaves that hung shining and still like leaves forged of heavy metal. This was the East of the ancient navigators, so old, so mysterious, resplendent and sombre, living and unchanged, full of danger and promise. And these were the men. I sat up suddenly. A wave of movement passed through the crowd from end to end, passed along the heads, swayed the bodies, ran along the jetty like a ripple on the water, like a breath of wind on a field – and all was still again. I see it now – the wide sweep of the bay, the glittering sands, the wealth of green infinite and varied, the sea blue like the sea of a dream, the crowd of attentive faces, the blaze of vivid colour – the water reflecting it all, the curve of the shore, the jetty, the high-sterned outlandish craft floating still, and the three boats with the tired men from the West sleeping, unconscious of the land and the people and of the violence of sunshine. They slept thrown across the thwarts, curled on bottom-boards, in the careless attitudes of death. The head of the old skipper, leaning back in the stern of the long-boat, had fallen on his breast, and he looked as though he would never wake. Farther out old Mahon's face was upturned to the sky, with the long white beard spread out on his breast, as though he had been shot where he sat at the tiller; and a man, all in a heap in the bows of the boat, slept with both arms embracing the stem-head and with his cheek laid on the gunwale. The East looked at them without a sound.

'I have known its fascination since; I have seen the mysterious shores, the still water, the lands of brown nations, where a stealthy Nemesis lies in wait, pursues, overtakes so many of the conquering race, who are proud of their wisdom, of their knowledge, of their strength. But for me all the East is contained in that vision of my youth. It is all in that moment when I opened my young eyes on it. I came upon it from a tussle with the sea —and I was young — and I saw it looking at me. And this is all that is left of it! Only a moment; a moment of strength, of romance, of glamour — of youth! . . . A flick of sunshine upon a strange shore, the time to remember, the time for a sigh, and — goodbye! — Night — Goodbye. . . !'

He drank.

'Ah! The good old time — the good old time. Youth and the sea. Glamour and the sea! The good, strong sea, the salt, bitter sea, that could whisper to you and roar at you and knock your breath out of you.'

He drank again.

'By all that's wonderful it is the sea, I believe, the sea itself — or is it youth alone? Who can tell? But you here — you all had something out of life: money, love — whatever one gets on shore — and, tell me, wasn't that the best time, that time when we were young at sea; young and had nothing, on the sea that gives nothing, except hard knocks — and sometimes a chance to feel your strength — that only — what you all regret?'

And we all nodded at him: the man of finance, the man of accounts, the man of law, we all nodded at him over the polished table that like a still sheet of brown water reflected our faces, lined, wrinkled; our faces marked by toil, by deceptions, by success, by love; our weary eyes looking still, looking always, looking anxiously for something out of life, that while it is expected is already gone — has passed unseen, in a sigh, in a flash — together with the youth, with the strength, with the romance of illusions.

Heart of Darkness

HEART OF DARKNESS

I

THE *Nellie*, a cruising yawl, swung to her anchor without a flutter of the sails, and was at rest. The flood had made, the wind was nearly calm, and being bound down the river, the only thing for it was to come to and wait for the turn of the tide.

The sea-reach of the Thames stretched before us like the beginning of an interminable waterway. In the offing the sea and the sky were welded together without a joint, and in the luminous space the tanned sails of the barges drifting up with the tide seemed to stand still in red clusters of canvas sharply peaked, with gleams of varnished spirits. A haze rested on the low shores that ran out to sea in vanishing flatness. The air was dark above Gravesend, and farther back still seemed condensed into a mournful gloom, brooding motionless over the biggest, and the greatest, town on earth.

The Director of Companies was our captain and our host. We four affectionately watched his back as he stood in the bows looking to seaward. On the whole river there was nothing that looked half so nautical. He resembled a pilot, which to a seaman is trustworthiness personified. It was difficult to realize his work was not out there in the luminous estuary, but behind him, within the brooding gloom.

Between us there was, as I have already said somewhere, the bond of the sea. Besides holding our hearts together through long periods of separation, it had the effect of making us tolerant of each other's yarns – and even convictions. The Lawyer – the best of old fellows – had, because of his many years and many virtues, the only cushion on deck, and was lying on the only rug. The Accountant had brought out already a box of dominoes, and was toying architecturally with the bones. Marlow sat cross-legged right aft, leaning against the mizzen-mast. He had sunken cheeks, a yellow complexion, a straight back, an ascetic aspect, and, with his arms dropped, the palms of hands outwards, resembled an idol. The director, satisfied the anchor had good hold, made his way aft and sat down amongst us. We exchanged a few words lazily. Afterwards there was silence on board the yacht. For some reason or other we did not begin that game of dominoes. We felt meditative, and fit for nothing but placid staring. The day was ending in a serenity of still and exquisite brilliance. The water shone pacifically; the sky, without a speck, was a benign immensity of unstained light; the very mist on the Essex marshes was like a gauzy and radiant fabric, hung from the wooded rises inland, and draping the low shores in diaphanous folds. Only the gloom to the west, brooding over the upper reaches, became more sombre every minute, as if angered by the approach of the sun.

And at last, in its curved and imperceptible fall, the sun sank low, and from glowing white changed to a dull red without rays and without heat, as if about to go out suddenly, stricken to death by the touch of that gloom brooding over a crowd of men.

Forthwith a change came over the waters, and the serenity became less brilliant but more profound. The old river in its broad reach rested unruffled at the decline of day, after ages of good service done to the race that peopled its banks, spread out in the tranquil dignity of a waterway leading to the uttermost ends of the earth. We looked at the venerable stream not in the vivid flush of a short day that comes and departs for ever, but in the august light of abiding memories. And indeed nothing is easier for a man who has, as the phrase goes, 'followed the sea' with reverence and affection, than to evoke the great spirit of the past upon the lower reaches of the Thames. The tidal current runs to and fro in its unceasing service, crowded with memories of men and ships it had borne to the rest of home or to the battles of the sea. It had known and served all the men of whom the nation is proud, from Sir Francis Drake to Sir John Franklin, knights all, titled and untitled – the great knights-errant of the sea. It had borne all the ships whose names are like jewels flashing in the night of time, from the *Golden Hind* returning with her round flanks full of treasure, to be visited by the Queen's Highness and thus pass out of the gigantic tale, to the *Erebus* and *Terror*, bound on other conquests – and that never returned. It had known the ships and the men. They had sailed from Deptford, from Greenwich, from Erith – the adventurers and the settlers; kings' ships and the ships of men on 'Change; captains, admirals, the dark 'interlopers' of the Eastern trade, and the commissioned 'generals' of East India fleets. Hunters for gold or pursuers of fame, they all had gone out on that stream, bearing the sword, and often the torch, messengers of the might within the land, bearers of a spark from the sacred fire. What greatness had not floated on the ebb of that river into the mystery of an unknown earth! . . . The dreams of men, the seed of commonwealths, the germs of empires.

The sun set; the dusk fell on the stream, and lights began to appear along the shore. The Chapman lighthouse, a three-legged thing erect on a mud-flat, shone strongly. Lights of ships moved in the fairway – a great stir of lights going up and going down. And farther west on the upper reaches the place of the monstrous town was still marked ominously on the sky, a brooding gloom in sunshine, a lurid glare under the stars.

'And this also,' said Marlow suddenly, 'has been one of the dark places of the earth.'

He was the only man of us who still 'followed the sea'. The worst that could be said of him was that he did not represent his class. He was a seaman, but he was a wanderer, too, while most seamen lead, if one may so express it, a sedentary life. Their minds are of the stay-at-home order, and their home is always with them – the ship; and so is their country – the sea. One ship is very much like another, and the sea is always the same. In the immutability of their surroundings the foreign shores, the foreign faces, the changing immensity of life, glide past, veiled not by a sense of mystery but by a slightly disdainful ignorance; for there is nothing mysterious to a seaman unless it be the sea itself, which is the mistress of his existence and as inscrutable as Destiny. For the rest, after his hours of work, a casual stroll or a casual spree on shore suffices to unfold for him the secret of a whole continent, and generally he finds the secret not worth knowing. The yarns of seamen have a direct simplicity, the whole meaning of which lies within the shell of a cracked nut. But Marlow was not typical (if his propensity to spin yarns be excepted), and to him the meaning of an episode was not inside like a kernel but outside, enveloping the tale which brought it out only as a glow brings out a haze, in the likeness of one of these misty halos that sometimes are made visible by the spectral illumination of moonshine.

His remark did not seem at all surprising. It was just like Marlow. It was accepted in silence. No one took the trouble to grunt even; and presently he said, very slow —

'I was thinking of very old times, when the Romans first came here, nineteen hundred years ago — the other day. . . . Light came out of this river since — you say Knights? Yes; but it is like a running blaze on a plain, like a flash of lightning in the clouds. We live in the flicker — may it last as long as the old earth keeps rolling! But darkness was here yesterday. Imagine the feelings of a commander of a fine — what d'ye call 'em? — trireme in the Mediterranean, ordered suddenly to the north; run overland across the Gauls in a hurry; put in charge of one of these craft the legionaries — a wonderful lot of handy men they must have been, too — used to build, apparently by the hundred, in a month or two, if we may believe what we read. Imagine him here — the very end of the world, a sea the colour of lead, a sky the colour of smoke, a kind of ship about as rigid as a concertina — and going up this river with stores, or orders, or what you like. Sand-banks, marshes, forests, savages, — precious little to eat fit for a civilized man, nothing but Thames water to drink. No Falernian wine here, no going ashore. Here and there a military camp lost in a wilderness, like a needle in a bundle of hay — cold, fog, tempests, disease, exile, and death, — death skulking in the air, in the water, in the bush. They must have been dying like flies here. Oh, yes — he did it. Did it very well, too, no doubt, and without thinking much about it either, except afterwards to brag of what he had gone through in his time, perhaps. They were men enough to face the darkness. And perhaps he was cheered by keeping his eye on a chance of promotion to the fleet at Ravenna by-and-by, if he had good friends in Rome and survived the awful climate. Or think of a decent young citizen in a toga — perhaps too much dice, you know — coming out here in the train of some prefect, or tax-gatherer, or trader even, to mend his fortunes. Land in a swamp, march through the woods, and in some inland post feel the savagery, the utter savagery, had closed round him, — all that mysterious life of the wilderness that stirs in the forest, in the jungles, in the hearts of wild men. There's no initiation either into such mysteries. He has to live in the midst of the incomprehensible, which is also detestable. And it has a fascination, too, that goes to work upon him. The fascination of the abomination – you know, imagine the growing regrets, the longing to escape, the powerless disgust, the surrender, the hate.'

He paused.

'Mind,' he began again, lifting one arm from the elbow, the palm of the hand outwards, so that, with his legs folded before him, he had the pose of a Buddha preaching in European clothes and without a lotus-flower – 'Mind, none of us would feel exactly like this. What saves us is efficiency – the devotion to efficiency. But these chaps were not much account, really. They were no colonists; their administration was merely a squeeze, and nothing more, I suspect. They were conquerors, and for that you want only brute force – nothing to boast of, when you have it, since your strength is just an accident arising from the weakness of others. They grabbed what they could get for the sake of what was to be got. It was just robbery with violence, aggravated murder on a great scale, and men going at it blind – as is very proper for those who tackle a darkness. The conquest of the earth, which mostly means the taking it away from those who have a different complexion or slightly flatter noses than ourselves, is not a pretty thing when you look into it too much. What redeems it is the idea only. An idea at the back of it; not a sentimental pretence but an idea; and an unselfish belief in the idea – something you can set up, and bow down before, and offer a sacrifice to. . . .'

He broke off. Flames glided in the river, small green flames, red flames, white flames, pursuing, overtaking, joining, crossing each other – then separating slowly or hastily. The traffic of the great city went on in the deepening night upon the sleepless river. We looked on, waiting patiently – there was nothing else to do till the end of the flood; but it was only after a long silence, when he said, in a hesitating voice, 'I suppose you fellows remember I did once turn fresh-water sailor for a bit,' that we knew we were fated, before the ebb began to run, to hear about one of Marlow's inconclusive experiences.

'I don't want to bother you much with what happened to me

personally,' he began, showing in this remark the weakness of many tellers of tales who seem so often unaware of what their audience would best like to hear; 'yet to understand the effect of it on me you ought to know how I got out there, what I saw, how I went up that river to the place where I first met the poor chap. It was the farthest point of navigation and the culminating point of my experience. It seemed somehow to throw a kind of light on everything about me – and into my thoughts. It was sombre enough, too – and pitiful – not extraordinary in any way – not very clear either. No, not very clear. And yet it seemed to throw a kind of light.

'I had then, as you remember, just returned to London after a lot of Indian Ocean, Pacific, China Seas – a regular dose of the East – six years or so, and I was loafing about, hindering you fellows in your work and invading your homes, just as though I had got a heavenly mission to civilize you. It was very fine for a time, but after a bit I did get tired of resting. Then I began to look for a ship – I should think the hardest work on earth. But the ships wouldn't even look at me. And I got tired of that game, too.

'Now when I was a little chap I had a passion for maps. I would look for hours at South America, or Africa, or Australia, and lose myself in all the glories of exploration. At that time there were many blank spaces on the earth, and when I saw one that looked particularly inviting on a map (but they all look that) I would put my finger on it and say, When I grow up I will go there. The North Pole was one of these places, I remember. Well, I haven't been there yet, and shall not try now. The glamour's off. Other places were scattered about the Equator, and in every sort of latitude all over the two hemispheres. I have been in some of them, and . . . well, we won't talk about that. But there was one yet – the biggest, the most blank, so to speak – that I had a hankering after.

'True, by this time it was not a blank space any more. It had got filled since my boyhood with rivers and lakes and names. It had ceased to be a blank space of delightful mystery – a white patch for a boy to dream gloriously over. It had become a place of darkness. But there was in it one river especially, a mighty big river, that you could see on the map, resembling an immense snake uncoiled, with its head in the sea, its body at rest curving afar over a vast country, and its tail lost in the depths of the land.

And as I looked at the map of it in a shop-window, it fascinated me as a snake would a bird – a silly little bird. Then I remembered there was a big concern, a Company for trade on that river. Dash it all! I thought to myself, they can't trade without using some kind of craft on that lot of fresh water – steamboats! Why shouldn't I try to get charge of one? I went on along Fleet Street, but could not shake off the idea. The snake had charmed me.

'You understand it was a Continental concern, that Trading society; but I have a lot of relations living on the Continent, because it's cheap and not so nasty as it looks, they say

'I am sorry to own I began to worry them. This was already a fresh departure for me. I was not used to get things that way, you know. I always went my own road and on my own legs where I had a mind to go. I wouldn't have believed it of myself; but, then – you see – I felt somehow I must get there by hook or by crook. So I worried them. The men said "My dear fellow," and did nothing. Then – would you believe it? – I tried the women. I, Charlie Marlow, set the women to work – to get a job. Heavens! Well, you see, the notion drove me I had an aunt, a dear enthusiastic soul. She wrote: "It will be delightful. I am ready to do anything, anything for you. It is a glorious idea. I know the wife of a very high personage in the Administration, and also a man who has lots of influence with," etc., etc. She was determined to make no end of fuss to get me appointed skipper of a river-steamboat, if such was my fancy.

'I got my appointment – of course; and I got it very quick. It appears the Company had received news that one of their captains had been killed in a scuffle with the natives. This was my chance, and it made me the more anxious to go. It was only months and months afterwards, when I made the attempt to recover what was left of the body, that I heard the original quarrel arose from a misunderstanding about some hens. Yes, two black hens. Fresleven – that was the fellow's name, a Dane – thought himself wronged somehow in the bargain, so he went ashore and started to hammer the chief of the village with a stick. Oh, it didn't surprise me in the least to hear this, and at the same time to be told that Fresleven was the gentlest, quietest creature that ever walked on two legs. No doubt he was; but he had been a couple of years already out there engaged in the noble cause, you know, and he probably felt the need at last of asserting his self-respect in some way. Therefore he whacked the old nigger mercilessly, while a big crowd of his people watched him, thunderstruck, till some man – I was told the chief's son – in desperation at hearing the old chap yell, made a tentative jab with a spear at the white man – and of course it went quite easy between the shoulder-blades. Then the whole population cleared into the forest, expecting all kinds of calamities to happen, while, on the other hand, the steamer Fresleven commanded left also in a bad panic, in charge of the engineer, I believe. Afterwards nobody seemed to trouble much about Fresleven's remains, till I got out and stepped into his shoes. I couldn't let it rest, though; but when an opportunity offered at last to meet my predecessor, the grass growing through his ribs was tall enough to hide his bones. They were all there. The supernatural being had not been touched after he fell. And the village was deserted, the huts gaped black, rotting, all askew within the fallen enclosures. A calamity had come to it, sure enough. The people had vanished. Mad terror had scattered them, men, women, and children, through the bush, and they had never returned. What became of the hens I don't know either. I should think the cause of progress got them, anyhow. However, through this glorious affair I got my appointment, before I had fairly begun to hope for it.

'I flew around like mad to get ready, and before forty-eight hours I was crossing the Channel to show myself to my employers, and sign the contract. In a very few hours I arrived in a city that always makes me think of a whited sepulchre. Prejudice no doubt. I had no difficulty in finding the Company's offices. It was the biggest thing in the town, and everybody I met was full of it. They were going to run an over-sea empire, and make no end of coin by trade.

'A narrow and deserted street in deep shadow, high houses, innumerable windows with venetian blinds, a dead silence, grass sprouting between the stones, imposing carriage archways right and left, immense double doors standing ponderously ajar. I slipped through one of these cracks, went up a swept and ungarnished staircase, as arid as a desert, and opened the first door I came to. Two women, one fat and the other slim, sat on straw-bottomed chairs, knitting black wool. The slim one got up and walked straight to me – still knitting with down-cast eyes – and only just as I began to think of getting out of her way, as you would for a somnambulist, stood still, and looked up. Her dress was as plain as an umbrella-cover, and she turned round without a word and preceded me into a waiting-room. I gave my name, and looked about. Deal table in the middle, plain chairs all round the walls, on one end a large shining map, marked with all the colours of a rainbow. There was a vast amount of red – good to see at any time, because one knows that some real work is done in there, a deuce of a lot of blue, a little green, smears of orange, and, on the East Coast, a purple patch, to show where the jolly pioneers of progress drink the jolly lager-beer. However, I wasn't going into any of these. I was going into the yellow. Dead in the centre. And the river was there – fascinating – deadly – like a snake. Ough! A door opened, a white-haired secretarial head, but wearing a compassionate expression, appeared, and a skinny forefinger beckoned me into the sanctuary. Its light was dim, and a heavy writing-desk squatted in the middle. From behind that structure came out an impression of pale plumpness in a frock-coat. The great man himself. He was five feet six, I should judge, and had his grip on the handle-end of ever so many millions. He shook hands, I fancy, murmured vaguely, was satisfied with my French. *Bon voyage.*

'In about forty-five seconds I found myself again in the waiting-room with the compassionate secretary, who, full of desolation and sympathy, made me sign some document. I believe I undertook amongst other things not to disclose any trade secrets. Well, I am not going to.

'I began to feel slightly uneasy. You know I am not used to such ceremonies, and there was something ominous in the atmosphere. It was just as though I had been let into some conspiracy – I don't know – something not quite right; and I was glad to get out. In the outer room the two women knitted black wool feverishly. People were arriving, and the younger one was walking back and forth introducing them. The old one sat on her chair. Her flat cloth slippers were propped up on a foot-warmer, and a cat reposed on her lap. She wore a starched white affair on her head, had a wart on one cheek, and silver-rimmed spectacles hung on the tip of her nose. She glanced at me above the glasses. The swift and indifferent placidity of that look troubled me. Two youths with foolish and cheery countenances were being piloted over, and she threw at them the same quick glance of unconcerned wisdom. She seemed to know all about them and about me, too. An eerie feeling came over me. She seemed uncanny and fateful. Often far away there I thought of these two, guarding the door of Darkness, knitting black wool as for a warm pall, one introducing, introducing continuously to the unknown, the other scrutinizing the cheery and foolish faces with unconcerned old eyes. *Ave!* Old knitter of black wool. *Morituri te salutant.* Not many of those she looked at ever saw her again — not half, by a long way.

'There was yet a visit to the doctor. "A simple formality," assured me the secretary, with an air of taking an immense part in all my sorrows. Accordingly a young chap wearing his hat over the left eyebrow, some clerk I suppose, — there must have been clerks in the business, though the house was as still as a house in a city of the dead — came from somewhere upstairs, and led me forth. He was shabby and careless, with ink-stains on the sleeves of his jacket, and his cravat was large and billowy, under a chin shaped like the toe of an old boot. It was a little too early for the doctor, so I proposed a drink, and thereupon he developed a vein of joviality. As we sat over our vermouths he glorified the Company's business, and by-and-by I expressed casually my surprise at him not going out there. He became very cool and collected all at once. "I am not such a fool as I look, quoth Plato to his disciples," he said sententiously, emptied his glass with great resolution, and we rose.

'The old doctor felt my pulse, evidently thinking of something else the while. "Good, good for there," he mumbled, and then with a certain eagerness asked me whether I would let him measure my head. Rather surprised, I said Yes, when he produced a thing like calipers and got the dimensions back and front and every way, taking notes carefully. He was an unshaven little man in a threadbare coat like a gaberdine, with his feet in slippers, and I thought him a harmless fool. "I always ask leave, in the interests of science, to measure the crania of those going out there," he said. "And when they come back, too?" I asked. "Oh, I never see them," he remarked; "and, moreover, the changes take place inside, you know." He smiled, as if at some quiet joke. "So you are going out there. Famous. Interesting, too." He gave me a searching glance, and made another note. "Ever any madness in your family?" he asked, in a matter-of-fact tone. I felt very annoyed. "Is that question in the interests of science, too?" "It would be," he said, without taking notice of my irritation, "interesting for science to watch the mental changes of individuals, on the spot, but . . .' "Are you an alienist?" I interrupted. "Every doctor should be – a little," answered that original, imperturbably. "I have a little theory which you Messieurs who go out there must help me to prove. This is my share in the advantages my country shall reap from the possession of such a magnificent dependency. The mere wealth I leave to others. Pardon my questions, but you are the first Englishman coming under my observation . . ." I hastened to assure him I was not in the least typical. "If I were," said I, "I wouldn't be talking like this with you." "What you say is rather profound, and probably erroneous," he said, with a laugh. "Avoid irritation more than exposure to the sun. Adieu. How do you English say, eh? Goodbye. Ah! Goodbye. Adieu. In the tropics one must before everything keep calm." . . . He lifted a warning fore-finger. . . . "*Du calme, du calme. Adieu.*"

'One thing more remained to do – say goodbye to my excellent aunt. I found her triumphant. I had a cup of tea – the last decent cup of tea for many days – and in a room that most soothingly looked just as you would expect a lady's drawing-room to look, we had a long quiet chat by the fireside. In the course of these confidences it became quite plain to me I had been represented to the wife of the high dignitary, and goodness knows to how many more people besides, as an exceptional and gifted creature – a piece of good fortune for the Company – a man you don't get hold of every day. Good heavens! and I was going to take charge of a two-penny-half-penny river-steamboat with a penny whistle attached! It appeared, however, I was also one of the Workers, with a capital – you know. Something like an emissary of light, something like a lower sort of apostle. There had been a lot of such rot let loose in print and talk just about that time, and the excellent woman, living right in the rush of all that humbug, got carried off her feet. She talked about "weaning those ignorant millions from their horrid ways", till, upon my word, she made me quite uncomfortable. I ventured to hint that the Company was run for profit.

'You forget, dear Charlie, that the labourer is worthy of his hire," she said, brightly. It's queer how out of touch with truth women are. They live in a world of their own, and there had never been anything like it, and never can be. It is too beautiful altogether, and if they were to set it up it would go to pieces before the first sunset. Some confounded fact we men have been living contentedly with ever since the day of creation would start up and knock the whole thing over.

'After this I got embraced, told to wear flannel, be sure to write often, and so on – and I left. In the street – I don't know why – a queer feeling came to me that I was an impostor. Odd thing that I, who used to clear out for any part of the world at twenty-four hours' notice, with less thought than most men give to the crossing of a street, had a moment – I won't say of hesitation, but of startled pause, before this commonplace affair. The best way I can explain it to you is by saying that, for a second or two, I felt as though, instead of going to the centre of a continent, I were about to set off for the centre of the earth.

'I left in a French steamer, and she called in every blamed port they have out there, for, as far as I could see, the sole purpose of landing soldiers and custom-house officers. I watched the coast. Watching a coast as it slips by the ship is like thinking about an enigma. There it is before you – smiling, frowning, inviting, grand, mean, insipid, or savage, and always mute with an air of whispering, Come and find out. This one was almost featureless, as if still in the making, with an aspect of monotonous grimness. The edge of a colossal jungle, so dark-green as to be almost black, fringed with white surf, ran straight, like a ruled line, far, far away along a blue sea whose glitter was blurred by a creeping mist. The sun was fierce, the land seemed to glisten and drip with steam. Here and there greyish-whitish specks showed up clustered inside the white surf, with a flag flying above them perhaps. Settlements some centuries old, and still no bigger than pinheads on the untouched expanse of their background. We pounded along, stopped, landed soldiers; went on, landed custom-house clerks to levy toll in what looked like a God-forsaken wilderness, with a tin shed and a flag-pole lost in it; landed more soldiers – to take care

of the custom-house clerks, presumably. Some, I heard, got
drowned in the surf; but whether they did or not, nobody seemed
particularly to care. They were just flung out there, and on we
went. Every day the coast looked the same, as though we had not
moved; but we passed various places — trading places — with
names like Gran' Bassam, Little Popo; names that seemed to
belong to some sordid farce acted in front of a sinister back-cloth.
The idleness of a passenger, my isolation amongst all these men
with whom I had no point of contact, the oily and languid sea, the
uniform sombreness of the coast, seemed to keep me away from
the truth of things, within the toil of a mournful and senseless
delusion. The voice of the surf heard now and then was a positive
pleasure, like the speech of a brother. It was something natural,
that had its reason, that had a meaning. Now and then a boat
from the shore gave one a momentary contact with reality. It was
paddled by black fellows. You could see from afar the white of
their eyeballs glistening. They shouted, sang; their bodies
streamed with perspiration; they had faces like grotesque masks
— these chaps; but they had bone, muscle, a wild vitality, an intense
energy of movement, that was as natural and true as the surf along
their coast. They wanted no excuse for being there. They were a
great comfort to look at. For a time I would feel I belonged still to
a world of straightforward facts; but the feeling would not last
long. Something would turn up to scare it away. Once, I
remember, we came upon a man-of-war anchored off the coast.
There wasn't even a shed there, and she was shelling the bush. It
appears the French had one of their wars going on thereabouts.
Her ensign dropped limp like a rag; the muzzles of the long six-
inch guns stuck out all over the low hull; the greasy, slimy swell
swung her up lazily and let her down, swaying her thin masts. In
the empty immensity of earth, sky, and water, there she was,
incomprehensible, firing into a continent. Pop, would go one of
the six-inch guns; a small flame would dart and vanish, a little
white smoke would disappear, a tiny projectile would give a
feeble screech — and nothing happened. Nothing could happen.
There was a touch of insanity in the proceeding, a sense of
lugubrious drollery in the sight; and it was not dissipated by
somebody on board assuring me earnestly there was a camp of

natives – he called them enemies! – hidden out of sight somewhere.

'We gave her her letters (I heard the men in that lonely ship were dying of fever at the rate of three-a-day) and went on. We called at some more places with farcical names, where the merry dance of death and trade goes on in a still and earthy atmosphere as of an overheated catacomb; all along the formless coast bordered by dangerous surf, as if Nature herself had tried to ward off intruders; in and out of rivers, streams of death in life, whose banks were rotting into mud, whose waters, thickened into slime, invaded the contorted mangroves, that seemed to writhe at us in the extremity of an impotent despair. Nowhere did we stop long enough to get a particularized impresssion, but the general sense of vague and oppressive wonder grew upon me. It was like a weary pilgrimage amongst hints for nightmares.

'It was upward of thirty days before I saw the mouth of the big river. We anchored off the seat of the government. But my work would not begin till some two hundred miles farther on. So as soon as I could I made a start for a place thirty miles higher up.

'I had my passage on a little sea-going steamer. Her captain was a Swede, and knowing me for a seaman, invited me on the bridge. He was a young man, lean, fair, and morose, with lanky hair and a shuffling gait. As we left the miserable little wharf, he tossed his head contemptuously at the shore. "Been living there?" he asked. I said, "Yes." "Fine lot these government chaps – are they not?" he went on, speaking English with great precision and considerable bitterness. "It is funny what some people will do for a few francs a-month. I wonder what becomes of that kind when it goes up country?" I said to him I expected to see that soon. "So-o-o!" he exclaimed. He shuffled athwart, keeping one eye ahead vigilantly. "Don't be too sure," he continued. "The other day I took up a man who hanged himself on the road. He was a Swede, too." "Hanged himself! Why, in God's name?" I cried. He kept on looking out watchfully. "Who knows? The sun too much for him, or the country perhaps."

'At last we opened a reach. A rocky cliff appeared, mounds of turned-up earth by the shore, houses on a hill, others with iron roofs, amongst a waste of excavations, or hanging to the declivity. A continuous noise of the rapids above hovered over this scene of inhabited devastation. A lot of people, mostly black and naked, moved about like ants. A jetty projected into the river. A blinding sunlight drowned all this at times in a sudden recrudescence of glare. "There's your Company's station," said the Swede, pointing to three wooden barrack-like structures on the rocky slope. "I will send your things up. Four boxes did you say? So. Farewell."

'I came upon a boiler wallowing in the grass, then found a path leading up the hill. It turned aside for the boulders, and also for an undersized railway-truck lying there on its back with its wheels in the air. One was off. The thing looked as dead as the carcass of some animal. I came upon more pieces of decaying machinery, a stack of rusty rails. To the left a clump of trees made a shady spot, where dark things seemed to stir feebly. I blinked, the path was steep. A horn tooted to the right, and I saw the black people run. A heavy and dull detonation shook the ground, a puff of smoke came out of the cliff, and that was all. No change appeared on the face of the rock. They were building a railway. The cliff was not in the way of anything; but this objectless blasting was all the work going on.

'A slight clinking behind me made me turn my head. Six black men advanced in a file, toiling up the path. They walked erect and slow, balancing small baskets full of earth on their heads, and the clink kept time with their footsteps. Black rags were wound round their loins, and the short ends behind waggled to and fro like tails. I could see every rib, the joints of their limbs were like knots in a rope; each had an iron collar on his neck, and all were connected together with a chain whose bights swung between them, rhythmically clinking. Another report from the cliff made me think suddenly of that ship of war I had seen firing into a continent. It was the same kind of ominous voice; but these men could by no stretch of imagination be called enemies. They were called criminals, and the outraged law, like the bursting shells, had come to them, an insoluble mystery from the sea. All their meagre breasts panted together, the violently dilated nostrils quivered, the eyes stared stonily uphill. They passed me within six inches, without a glance, with that complete, deathlike indifference of unhappy savages. Behind this raw matter one of the reclaimed, the product of the new forces at work, strolled despondently, carrying a rifle by its middle. He had a uniform jacket with one button off, and seeing a white man on the path, hoisted his weapon to his shoulder with alacrity. This was simple prudence, white men being so much alike at a distance that he could not tell who I might be. He was speedily reassured, and with a large, white, rascally grin, and a glance at his charge, seemed to take me into partnership in his exalted trust. After all, I also was a part of the great cause of these high and just proceedings.

'Instead of going up, I turned and descended to the left. My idea was to let that chain-gang get out of sight before I climbed the hill. You know I am not particularly tender; I've had to strike and to fend off. I've had to resist and to attack sometimes – that's only one way of resisting – without counting the exact cost, according to the demands of such sort of life as I had blundered into. I've seen the devil of violence, and the devil of greed, and the devil of hot desire; but, by all the stars! these were strong, lusty, red-eyed devils, that swayed and drove men – men, I tell you. But as I stood on this hillside, I foresaw that in the blinding sunshine of that land I would become acquainted with a flabby, pretending, weak-eyed devil of a rapacious and pitiless folly. How insidious he could be, too, I was only to find out several months later and a thousand miles farther. For a moment I stood appalled, as though by a warning. Finally I descended the hill, obliquely, towards the trees I had seen.

'I avoided a vast artificial hole somebody had been digging on the slope, the purpose of which I found it impossible to divine. It wasn't a quarry or a sandpit, anyhow. It was just a hole. It might have been connected with the philanthropic desire of giving the criminals something to do. I don't know. Then I nearly fell into a very narrow ravine, almost no more than a scar in the hillside. I discovered that a lot of imported drainage-pipes for the settlement had been tumbled in there. There wasn't one that was not broken. It was a wanton smash-up. At last I got under the trees. My purpose was to stroll into the shade for a moment; but no sooner within than it seemed to me I had stepped into the gloomy circle of some Inferno. The rapids were near, and an uninterrupted, uniform, headlong, rushing noise filled the mournful stillness of the grove, where not a breath stirred, not a leaf moved, with a mysterious sound – as though the tearing pace of the launched earth had suddenly become audible.

'Black shapes crouched, lay, sat between the trees leaning against the trunks, clinging to the earth, half coming out, half effaced within the dim light, in all the attitudes of pain, abandonment, and despair. Another mine on the cliff went off, followed by a slight shudder of the soil under my feet. The work was going on. The work! And this was the place where some of the helpers had withdrawn to die.

'They were dying slowly – it was very clear. They were not enemies, they were not criminals, they were nothing earthly now, – nothing but black shadows of disease and starvation, lying confusedly in the greenish gloom. Brought from all the recesses of the coast in all the legality of time contracts, lost in uncongenial surroundings, fed on unfamiliar food, they sickened, became inefficient, and were then allowed to crawl away and rest. These moribund shapes were free as air – and nearly as thin. I began to distinguish the gleam of the eyes under the trees. Then, glancing down, I saw a face near my hand. The black bones reclined at full length with one shoulder against the tree, and slowly the eyelids rose and the sunken eyes looked up at me, enormous and vacant, a kind of blind, white flicker in the depths of the orbs, which died out slowly. The man seemed young – almost a boy – but you know with them it's hard to tell. I found nothing else to do but to offer him one of my good Swede's ship's biscuits I had in my pocket. The fingers closed slowly on it and held – there was no other movement and no other glance. He had tied a bit of white worsted round his neck – Why? Where did he get it? Was it a badge – an ornament – a charm – a propitiatory act? Was there any idea at all connected with it? It looked startling round his black neck, this bit of white thread from beyond the seas.

'Near the same tree two more bundles of acute angles sat with their legs drawn up. One, with his chin propped on his knees, stared at nothing, in an intolerable and appalling manner: his brother phantom rested its forehead, as if overcome with a great weariness; and all about others were scattered in every pose of contorted collapse, as in some picture of a massacre or a pestilence. While I stood horror-struck, one of these creatures rose to his hands and knees, and went off on all-fours towards the river to drink. He lapped out of his hand, then sat up in the sunlight, crossing his shins in front of him, and after a time let his woolly head fall on his breastbone.

'I didn't want any more loitering in the shade, and I made haste towards the station. When near the buildings I met a white man, in such an unexpected elegance of get-up that in the first moment I took him for a sort of vision. I saw a high starched collar, white cuffs, a light alpaca jacket, snowy trousers, a clear necktie, and varnished boots. No hat. Hair parted, brushed, oiled, under a green-lined parasol held in a big white hand. He was amazing, and had a penholder behind his ear.

'I shook hands with this miracle, and I learned he was the Company's chief accountant, and that all the book-keeping was done at this station. He had come out for a moment, he said, "to get a breath of fresh air". The expression sounded wonderfully odd, with its suggestion of sedentary desk-life. I wouldn't have mentioned the fellow to you at all, only it was from his lips that I first heard the name of the man who is so indissolubly connected with the memories of that time. Moreover, I respected the fellow. Yes; I respected his collars, his vast cuffs, his brushed hair. His appearance was certainly that of a hairdresser's dummy; but in the great demoralization of the land he kept up his appearance. That's backbone. His starched collars and got-up shirt-fronts were achievements of character. He had been out nearly three years; and, later, I could not help asking him how he managed to sport such linen. He had just the faintest blush, and said modestly, "I've been teaching one of the native women about the station. It was difficult. She had a distaste for the work." Thus this man had verily accomplished something. And he was devoted to his books, which were in apple-pie order.

'Everything else in the station was in a muddle, – heads, things, buildings. Strings of dusty niggers with splay feet arrived and departed; a stream of manufactured goods, rubbishy cottons, beads, and brass-wire set into the depths of darkness, and in return came a precious trickle of ivory.

'I had to wait in the station for ten days – an eternity. I lived in a hut in the yard, but to be out of the chaos I would sometimes get into the accountant's office. It was built of horizontal planks, and so badly put together that, as he bent over his high desk, he was barred from neck to heels with narrow strips of sunlight. There was no need to open the big shutter to see. It was hot there, too; big flies buzzed fiendishly , and did not sting, but stabbed. I sat generally on the floor, while, of faultless appearance (and even slightly scented), perching on a high stool, he wrote, he wrote. Sometimes he stood up for exercise. When a truckle-bed with a sick man (some invalid agent from up-country) was put in there, he exhibited a gentle annoyance. "The groans of this sick person," he said, "distract my attention. And without that it is extremely difficult to guard against clerical errors in this climate."

'One day he remarked, without lifting his head, "In the interior you will no doubt meet Mr Kurtz." On my asking who Mr Kurtz was, he said he was a first-class agent; and seeing my disappointment at this information, he added slowly, laying down his pen, "He is a very remarkable person." Further questions elicited from him that Mr Kurtz was at present in charge of a trading-post, a very important one, in the true ivory-country, at "the very bottom of there. Sends in as much ivory as all the others put together. . . ." He began to write again. The sick man was too ill to groan. The flies buzzed in a great peace.

'Suddenly there was a growing murmur of voices and a great tramping of feet. A caravan had come in. A violent babble of uncouth sounds burst out on the other side of the planks. All the carriers were speaking together, and in the midst of the uproar the lamentable voice of the chief agent was heard "giving it up" tearfully for the twentieth time that day. . . . He rose slowly. "What a frightful row," he said. He crossed the room gently to look at the sick man, and returning, said to me, "He does not hear." "What! Dead?" I asked, startled. "No, not yet," he answered, with great composure. Then, alluding with a toss of the head to the tumult in the station-yard, "When one has got to make correct entries, one comes to hate those savages – hate them to the death." He remained thoughtful for a moment. "When you see Mr Kurtz," he went on, "tell him from me that everything here" – he glanced at the desk – "is very satisfactory. I don't like to write to him – with those messengers of ours you never know who may get hold of your letter – at that Central Station." He stared at me for a moment with his mild, bulging eyes. "Oh, he will go far, very far," he began again. "He will be a somebody in the Administration before long. They, above – the Council in Europe, you know – mean him to be."

'He turned to his work. The noise outside had ceased, and presently in going out I stopped at the door. In the steady buzz of flies the homeward-bound agent was lying flushed and insensible; the other, bent over his books, was making correct entries of perfectly correct transactions; and fifty feet below the doorstep I could see the still tree-tops of the grove of death.

'Next day I left that station at last, with a caravan of sixty men, for a two-hundred-mile tramp.

'No use telling you much about that. Paths, paths, everywhere; a stamped-in network of paths spreading over the empty land, through long grass, through burnt grass, through thickets, down and up chilly ravines, up and down stony hills ablaze with heat; and a solitude, a solitude, nobody, not a hut. The population had cleared out a long time ago. Well, if a lot of mysterious niggers armed with all kinds of fearful weapons suddenly took to travelling on the road between Deal and Gravesend, catching the yokels right and left to carry heavy loads for them, I fancy every farm and cottage thereabouts would get empty very soon. Only here the dwellings were gone, too. Still I passed through several abandoned villages. There's something pathetically childish in the ruins of grass walls. Day after day, with the stamp and shuffle of sixty pair of bare feet behind me, each pair under a 60-lb load. Camp, cook, sleep, strike camp, march. Now and then a carrier dead in harness, at rest in the long grass near the path, with an empty water-gourd and his long staff lying by his side. A great silence around and above. Perhaps on some quiet night the tremor of far-off drums, sinking, swelling, a tremor vast, faint; a sound weird, appealing, suggestive, and wild – and perhaps with as profound a meaning as the sound of bells in a Christian country. Once a white man in an unbuttoned uniform, camping on the path with an armed escort of lank Zanzibaris, very hospitable and festive – not to say drunk. Was looking after the upkeep of the road, he declared. Can't say I saw any road or any upkeep, unless the body of a middle-aged negro, with a bullet-hole in the forehead, upon which I absolutely stumbled three miles farther on, may be considered as a permanent improvement. I had a white companion, too, not a bad chap, but rather too fleshy and with the exasperating habit of fainting on the hot hillsides, miles away from the least bit of shade and water. Annoying, you know, to hold your own coat like a parasol over a man's head while he is coming-to. I couldn't help asking him once what he meant by coming there at all. "To make money, of course. What do you think?" he said, scornfully. Then he got fever, and had to be carried in a hammock slung under a pole. As he weighed sixteen stone I had no end of rows with the carriers. They jibbed, ran away, sneaked off with their loads in the night – quite a mutiny. So, one evening, I made a speech in English with gestures, not one of which was lost to the sixty pairs of eyes before me, and the next morning I started the hammock off in front all right. An hour afterwards I came upon the whole concern wrecked in a bush – man, hammock, groans, blankets, horrors. The heavy pole had skinned his poor nose. He was very anxious for me to kill somebody, but there wasn't the shadow of a carrier near. I remember the old doctor, – "It would be interesting for science to watch the mental changes of individuals, on the spot." I felt I was becoming scientifically interesting. However, all that is to no purpose. On the fifteenth day I came in sight of the big river again, and hobbled into the Central Station. It was on a back water surrounded by scrub and forest, with a pretty border of smelly mud on one side, and on the three others enclosed by a crazy fence of rushes. A neglected gap was all the gate it had, and the first glance at the place was enough to let you see the flabby devil was running that show. White men with long staves in their hands appeared languidly from amongst the buildings, strolling up to take a look at me, and then retired out of sight somewhere. One of them, a stout, excitable chap with black moustaches, informed me with great volubility and many digressions, as soon as I told him who I was, that my steamer was at the bottom of the river. I was thunderstruck. What, how, why? Oh, it was "all right". The "manager himself" was there. All quite correct. "Everybody had behaved splendidly! splendidly!" – "you must," he said in agitation, "go and see the general manager at once. He is waiting!"

'I did not see the real significance of that wreck at once. I fancy I see it now, but I am not sure – not at all. Certainly the affair was too stupid – when I think of it – to be altogether natural. Still . . . But at the moment it presented itself simply as a confounded nuisance. The steamer was sunk. They had started two days before in a sudden hurry up the river with the manager on board, in charge of some volunteer skipper, and before they had been out three hours they tore the bottom out of her on stones, and she sank near the south bank. I asked myself what I was to do there, now my boat was lost. As a matter of fact, I had plenty to do in fishing my command out of the river. I had to set about it the very next day. That, and the repairs when I brought the pieces to the station, took some months.

'My first interview with the manager was curious. He did not ask me to sit down after my twenty-mile walk that morning. He was commonplace in complexion, in feature, in manners, and in voice. He was of middle size and of ordinary build. His eyes, of the usual blue, were perhaps remarkably cold, and he certainly could make his glance fall on one as trenchant and heavy as an axe. But even at these times the rest of his person seemed to disclaim the intention. Otherwise there was only an indefinable, faint expression of his lips, something stealthy – a smile – not a smile – I remember it, but I can't explain. It was unconscious, this smile was, though just after he had said something it got intensified for an instant. It came at the end of his speeches like a seal applied on the words to make the meaning of the commonest phrase appear absolutely inscrutable. He was a common trader, from his youth up employed in these parts – nothing more. He was obeyed, yet he inspired neither love nor fear, nor even respect. He inspired uneasiness. That was it! Uneasiness. Not a definite mistrust – just uneasiness – nothing more. You have no idea how effective such a . . . a . . . faculty can be. He had no genius for organizing, for initiative, or for order even. That was evident in such things as the deplorable state of the station. He had no learning, and no intelligence. His position had come to him – why? Perhaps because he was never ill . . . He had served three terms of three years out there . . . Because triumphant health in the general rout of constitutions is a kind of power in itself. When he went home on leave he rioted on a large scale – pompously. Jack ashore – with a difference – in externals only. This one could gather from his casual talk. He originated nothing, he could keep the routine going – that's all. But he was great. He was great by this little thing that it was impossible to tell what could control such a man. He never gave that secret away. Perhaps there was nothing within him. Such a suspicion made one pause – for out there there were no external checks. Once when various tropical diseases had laid low almost every "agent" in the station, he was heard to say, "Men who come out here should have no entrails." He sealed the utterance with that smile of his, as though it had been a door opening into a darkness he had in his keeping. You fancied you had seen things – but the seal was on. When annoyed at meal-times by the constant quarrels of the white men about precedence, he ordered an immense round table to be made, for which a special house had to be built. This was the station's mess-room. Where he sat was the first place – the rest were nowhere. One felt this to be his unalterable conviction. He was neither civil or uncivil. He was quiet. He allowed his "boy" – an overfed young negro from the coast – to treat the white men, under his very eyes, with provoking insolence.

'He began to speak as soon as he saw me. I had been very long on the road. He could not wait. Had to start without me. The up-river stations had to be relieved. There had been so many delays already that he did not know who was dead and who was alive, and how they got on – and so on, and so on. He paid no attention to my explanations, and, playing with a stick of sealing-wax, repeated several times that the situation was "very grave, very grave". There were rumours that a very important station was in jeopardy, and its chief, Mr Kurtz, was ill. Hoped it was not true. Mr Kurtz was . . . I felt weary and irritable. Hang Kurtz, I thought. I interrupted him by saying I had heard of Mr Kurtz on the coast. "Ah! So they talk of him down there," he murmured to himself. Then he began again, assuring me Mr Kurtz was the best agent he had, an exceptional man, of the greatest importance to the Company; therefore, I could understand his anxiety. He was, he said, "very, very uneasy". Certainly he fidgeted on his chair a good deal, exclaimed, "Ah, Mr Kurtz!" broke the stick of sealing-wax and seemed dumbfounded by the accident. Next thing he wanted to know "how long it would take to. . ." I interrupted him again. Being hungry, you know, and kept on my feet, too, I was getting savage. "How could I tell?" I said. "I hadn't even seen the wreck yet – some months, no doubt." All this talk seemed to me so futile. "Some months," he said. "Well, let us say three months before we can make a start. Yes. That ought to do the affair." I flung out of his hut (he lived all alone in a clay hut with a sort of verandah) muttering to myself my opinion of him. He was a chattering idiot. Afterwards I took it back when it was borne in upon me startlingly with what extreme nicety he had estimated the time requisite for the "affair".

'I went to work the next day, turning, so to speak, my back on that station. In that way only it seemed to me I could keep my hold on the redeeming facts of life. Still, one must look about sometimes; and then I saw this station, these men strolling aimlessly about in the sunshine of the yard. I asked myself sometimes what it all meant. They wandered here and there with their absurd long staves in their hands, like a lot of faithless pilgrims bewitched inside a rotten fence. The word "ivory" rang in the air, was whispered, was sighed. You would think they were praying to it. A taint of imbecile rapacity blew through it all, like a whiff from some corpse. By Jove! I've never seen anything so unreal in my life. And outside, the silent wilderness surrounding his cleared speck on the earth struck me as something great and invincible, like evil or truth, waiting patiently for the passing away of this fantastic invasion.

'Oh, those months! Well, never mind. Various things happened. One evening a grass shed full of calico, cotton prints, beads, and I don't know what else, burst into a blaze so suddenly that you would have thought the earth had opened to let an avenging fire consume all that trash. I was smoking my pipe quietly by my dismantled steamer, and saw them all cutting capers in the light, with their arms lifted high, when the stout man with moustaches came tearing down to the river, a tin pail in his hand, assured me that everybody was "behaving splendidly, splendidly", dipped about a quart of water and tore back again. I noticed there was a hole in the bottom of his pail.

'I strolled up. There was no hurry. You see the thing had gone off like a box of matches. It had been hopeless from the very first. The flame had leaped high, driven everybody back, lighted up everything – and collapsed. The shed was already a heap of embers glowing fiercely. A nigger was being beaten near by. They said he had caused the fire in some way; be that as it may, he was screeching most horribly. I saw him, later, for several days, sitting in a bit of shade looking very sick and trying to recover himself:

afterwards he arose and went out – and the wilderness without a sound took him into its bosom again. As I approached the glow from the dark I found myself at the back of two men, talking. I heard the name of Kurtz pronounced, then the words, "take advantage of this unfortunate accident". One of the men was the manager. I wished him a good evening. "Did you ever see anything like it – eh? it is incredible," he said, and walked off. The other man remained. He was a first-class agent, young, gentlemanly, a bit reserved, with a forked little beard and a hooked nose. He was stand-offish with the other agents, and they on their side said he was the manager's spy upon them. As to me, I had hardly ever spoken to him before. We got into talk, and by-and-by we strolled away from the hissing ruins. Then he asked me to his room, which was in the main building of the station. He struck a match, and I perceived that this young aristocrat had not only a silver-mounted dressing-case but also a whole candle all to himself. Just at that time the manager was the only man supposed to have any right to candles. Native mats covered the clay walls; a collection of spears, assegais, shields, knives was hung up in trophies. The business intrusted to this fellow was the making of bricks – so I had been informed; but there wasn't a fragment of a brick anywhere in the station, and he had been there more than a year – waiting. It seems he could not make bricks without something. I don't know what – straw maybe. Anyways, it could not be found there, and as it was not likely to be sent from Europe, it did not appear clear to me what he was waiting for. An act of special creation perhaps. However, they were all waiting – all the sixteen or twenty pilgrims of them – for something; and upon my word it did not seem an uncongenial occupation, from the way they took it, though the only thing that ever came to them was disease – as far as I could see. They beguiled the time by backbiting and intriguing against each other in a foolish kind of way. There was an air of plotting about that station, but nothing came of it, of course. It was as unreal as everything else – as the philanthropic pretence of the whole concern, as their talk, as their government, as their show of work. The only real feeling was a desire to get appointed to a trading-post where ivory was to be had, so that they could earn percentages. They intrigued and slandered and hated each other only on that account, – but as to effectually lifting a little finger –

oh, no. By heavens! there is something after all in the world allowing one man to steal a horse while another must not look at a halter. Steal a horse straight out. Very well. He has done it. Perhaps he can ride. But there is a way of looking at a halter that would provoke the most charitable of saints into a kick.

'I had no idea why he wanted to be sociable, but as we chatted in there it suddenly occurred to me the fellow was trying to get at something – in fact, pumping me. He alluded constantly to Europe, to the people I was supposed to know there – putting leading questions as to my acquaintances in the sepulchral city, and so on. His little eyes glittered like mica discs – with curiosity – though he tried to keep up a bit of superciliousness. At first I was astonished, but very soon I became awfully curious to see what he would find out from me. I couldn't possibly imagine what I had in me to make it worth his while. It was very pretty to see how he baffled himself, for in truth my body was full only of chills, and my head had nothing in it but that wretched steamboat business. It was evident he took me for a perfectly shameless prevaricator. At last he got angry, and, to conceal a movement of furious annoyance, he yawned. I rose. Then I noticed a small sketch in oils, on a panel, representing a woman, draped and blind-folded, carrying a lighted torch. The background was sombre – almost black. The movement of the woman was stately, and the effect of the torch-light on the face was sinister.

'It arrested me, and he stood by civilly, holding an empty half-pint champagne bottle (medical comforts) with the candle stuck in it. To my question he said Mr Kurtz had painted this – in this very station more than a year ago – while waiting for means to go to his trading-post. "Tell me, pray," said I, "who is this Mr Kurtz?"

'"The chief of the Inner Station," he answered in a short tone, looking away. "Much obliged," I said, laughing. "And you are the brickmaker of the Central Station. Everyone knows that." He was silent for a while. "He is a prodigy," he said at last. "He is an emissary of pity, and science, and progress, and devil knows what else. We want," he began to declaim suddenly, "for the guidance of the cause intrusted to us by Europe, so to speak, higher intelligence, wide sympathies, a singleness of purpose." "Who says that?" I asked. "Lots of them," he replied. "Some even write that; and so *he* comes here, a special being, as you ought to know." "Why ought I to know?" I interrupted, really surprised. He paid no attention. "Yes. Today he is chief of the best station, next year he will be assistant-manager, two years more and . . . but I daresay you know what he will be in two years' time. You are of the new gang – the gang of virtue. The same people who sent him specially also recommended you. Oh, don't say no. I've my own eyes to trust.' Light dawned upon me. My dear aunt's influential acquaintances were producing an unexpected effect upon that young man. I nearly burst into a laugh. "Do you read the Company's confidential correspondence?" I asked. He hadn't a word to say. It was great fun. "When Mr Kurtz," I continued, severely, "is General Manager, you won't have the opportunity."

'He blew the candle out suddenly, and we went outside. The moon had risen. Black figures strolled about listlessly, pouring water on the glow, whence proceeded a sound of hissing; steam ascended in the moonlight, the beaten nigger groaned somewhere. "What a row the brute makes!" said the indefatigable man with the moustaches, appearing near us. "Serve him right. Trans-gression – punishment – bang! Pitiless, pitiless. That's the only way. This will prevent all conflagrations for the future. I was just telling the manager. . . ." He noticed my companion, and became crestfallen all at once. "Not in bed yet," he said, with a kind of servile heartiness; "it's so natural. Ha! Danger – agitation." He vanished. I went on to the river-side, and the other followed me. I heard a scathing murmur at my ear, ' Heap of muffs – go to." The pilgrims could be seen in knots gesticulating, discussing. Several had still their staves in their hands. I verily believe they took these sticks to bed with them. Beyond the fence the forest stood up spectrally in the moonlight, and through the dim stir, through the faint sounds of that lamentable courtyard, the silence of the land went home to one's very heart – its mystery, its greatness, the amazing reality of its concealed life. The hurt nigger moaned feebly somewhere near by, and then fetched a deep sigh that made me mend my pace away from there. I felt a hand introducing itself under my arm. "My dear sir," said the fellow, "I don't want to be misunderstood, and especially by you, who will see Mr Kurtz long before I can have that pleasure. I wouldn't like him to get a false idea of my disposition. . . ."

'I let him run on, this papier-mâché Mephistopheles, and it seemed to me that if I tried I could poke my forefinger through him, and would find nothing inside but a little loose dirt, maybe. He, don't you see, had been planning to be assistant-manager by-and-by under the present man, and I could see that the coming of that Kurtz had upset them both not a little. He talked precipitately, and I did not try to stop him. I had my shoulders against the wreck of my steamer, hauled up on the slope like a carcass of some big river animal. The smell of mud, of primeval mud, by Jove! was in my nostrils, the high stillness of primeval forest was before my eyes; there were shiny patches on the black creek. The moon had spread over everything a thin layer of silver – over the rank grass, over the mud, upon the wall of matted vegetation standing higher than the wall of a temple, over the great river I could see through a sombre gap glittering, glittering, as it flowed broadly by without a murmur. All this was great, expectant, mute, while the man jabbered about himself. I wondered whether the stillness on the face of the immensity looking at us two were meant as an appeal or as a menace. What were we who had strayed in here? Could we handle that dumb thing, or would it handle us? I felt how big, how confoundedly big, was that thing that couldn't talk, and perhaps was deaf as well. What was in there? I could see a little ivory coming out from there, and I had heard Mr Kurtz was in there. I had heard enough about it, too – God knows! Yet somehow it didn't bring any image with it – no more than if I had been told an angel or a fiend was in there. I believed it in the same way one of you might believe there are inhabitants in the planet Mars. I knew once a Scotch sailmaker who was certain, dead sure, there were people in Mars. If you asked him for some idea how they looked and behaved, he would get shy and mutter something about "walking on all-fours". If you as much as smiled, he would – though a man of sixty – offer to fight you. I would not have gone so far as to fight for Kurtz, but I went for him near enough to a lie. You know I hate, detest, and can't bear a lie, not because I am straighter than the rest of us, but simply because it appals me. There is a taint of death, a flavour of mortality in lies – which is exactly what I hate and detest in the world – what I want to forget. It makes me miserable and sick, like biting something rotten would do. Temperament, I suppose. Well, I went near enough to it by letting the young fool there believe anything he liked to imagine as to my influence in Europe. I became in an instant as much of a pretence as the rest of the bewitched pilgrims. This simply because I had a notion it somehow would be of help to that Kurtz whom at the time I did not see – you understand. He was just a word for me. I did not see the man in the name any more than you do. Do you see him? Do you see the story? Do you see anything? It seems to me I am trying to tell you a dream – making a vain attempt, because no relation of a dream can convey the dream-sensation, that commingling of absurdity, surprise, and bewilderment in a tremor of struggling revolt, that notion of being captured by the incredible which is of the very essence of dreams. . . .'

He was silent for a while.

'. . . No, it is impossible; it is impossible to convey the life-sensation of any given epoch of one's existence – that which makes its truth, its meaning – its subtle and penetrating essence. It is impossible. We live, as we dream – alone. . . .'

He paused again as if reflecting, then added–

'Of course in this you fellows see more than I could then. You see me, whom you know. . . .'

It had become so pitch dark that we listeners could hardly see one another. For a long time already he, sitting apart, had been no more to us than a voice. There was not a word from anybody. The others might have been asleep, but I was awake. I listened, I listened on the watch for the sentence, for the word, that would give me the clue to the faint uneasiness inspired by this narrative that seemed to shape itself without human lips in the heavy night-air of the river.

'. . . Yes – I let him run on,' Marlow began again, 'and think what he pleased about the powers that were behind me. I did! And there was nothing behind me! There was nothing but that wretched, old, mangled steamboat I was leaning against, while he talked fluently about "the necessity for every man to get on". "And when one comes out here, you conceive, it is not to gaze at the moon." Mr Kurtz was a "universal genius", but even a genius would find it easier to work with "adequate tools – intelligent men". He did not make bricks – why, there was a physical impossibility in the way – as I was well aware; and if he did secretarial work for the manager, it was because "no sensible man rejects wantonly the confidence of his superiors". Did I see it? I saw it. What more did I want? What I really wanted was rivets, by heaven! Rivets. To get on with the work – to stop the hole. Rivets I wanted. There were cases of them down at the coast – cases – piled up – burst – split! You kicked a loose rivet at every second step in that station yard on the hillside. Rivets had rolled into the grove of death. You could fill your pockets with rivets for the trouble of stooping down – and there wasn't one rivet to be found where it was wanted. We had plates that would do, but nothing to fasten them with. And every week the messenger, a lone negro, letter-bag on shoulder and staff in hand, left our station for the coast. And several times a week a coast caravan came in with trade goods – ghastly glazed calico that made you shudder only to look at it, glass beads value about a penny a quart, confounded spotted cotton handkerchiefs. And no rivets. Three carriers could have brought all that was wanted to set that steamboat afloat.

'He was becoming confidential now, but I fancy my unresponsive attitude must have exasperated him at last for he judged it necessary to inform me he feared neither God nor devil, let alone any mere man. I said I could see that very well, but what I wanted was a certain quantity of rivets – and rivets were what really Mr Kurtz wanted, if he had only known it. Now letters went to the coast every week. . . . "My dear sir," he cried, "I write from dictation." I demanded rivets. There was a way – for an intelligent man. He changed his manner; became very cold, and suddenly began to talk about a hippopotamus; wondered whether sleeping on board the steamer (I stuck to my salvage night and day) I wasn't disturbed. There was an old hippo that had the bad habit of getting out on the bank and roaming at night over the station grounds. The pilgrims used to turn out in a body and empty every rifle they could lay hands on at him. Some even had sat up o' nights for him. All this energy was wasted, though. "That animal has a charmed life," he said; "but you can say this only of brutes in this country. No man – you apprehend me? – no man here bears a charmed life." He stood there for a moment in the moonlight with his delicate hooked nose set a little askew, and his mica eyes glittering without a wink, then, with a curt Goodnight, he strode off. I could see he was disturbed and considerably puzzled, which made me feel more hopeful than I had been for days. It was a great comfort to turn from that chap to my influential friend, the battered, twisted, ruined, tin-pot steamboat. I clambered on board. She rang under my feet like an empty Huntley & Palmer biscuit-tin kicked along a gutter; she was nothing so solid in make, and rather less pretty in shape, but I had expended enough hard work on her to make me love her. No influential friend would have served me better. She had given me a chance to come out a bit – to find out what I could do. No, I don't like work. I had rather laze about and think of all the fine things that can be done. I don't like work – no man does – but I like what is in the work, – the chance to find yourself. Your own reality – for yourself, not for others – what no other man can ever know. They can only see the mere show, and never can tell what it really means.

'I was not surprised to see somebody sitting aft, on the deck, with his legs dangling over the mud. You see I rather chummed with the few mechanics there were in that station, whom the other pilgrims naturally despised – on account of their imperfect manners, I suppose. This was the foreman – a boiler-maker by trade – a good worker. He was a lank, bony, yellow-faced man, with big intense eyes. His aspect was worried, and his head was as bald as the palm of my hand; but his hair in falling seemed to have stuck to his chin, and had prospered in the new locality, for his beard hung down to his waist. He was a widower with six young children (he had left them in charge of a sister of his to come out there), and the passion of his life was pigeon-flying. He was an enthusiast and a connoisseur. He would rave about pigeons. After work hours he used sometimes to come over from his hut for a talk about his children and his pigeons; at work, when he had to crawl in the mud under the bottom of the steamboat, he would tie up that beard of his in a kind of white serviette he brought for the purpose. It had loops to go over his ears. In the evening he could be seen squatted on the bank rinsing that wrapper in the creek with great care, then spreading it solemnly on a bush to dry.

'I slapped him on the back and shouted "We shall have rivets!" He scrambled to his feet exclaiming "No! Rivets!" as though he couldn't believe his ears. Then in a low voice, "You . . . eh?" I don't know why we behaved like lunatics. I put my finger to the side of my nose and nodded mysteriously. "Good for you!" he cried, snapped his fingers above his head, lifting one foot. I tried a jig. We capered on the iron deck. A frightful clatter came out of that hulk, and the virgin forest on the other bank of the creek sent it back in a thundering roll upon the sleeping station. It must have made some of the pilgrims sit up in their hovels. A dark figure obscured the lighted doorway of the manager's hut, vanished, then, a second or so after, the doorway itself vanished, too. We stopped, and the silence driven away by the stamping of our feet flowed back again from the recesses of the land. The great wall of vegetation, an exuberant and entangled mass of trunks, branches, leaves, boughs, festoons, motionless in the moonlight, was like a rioting invasion of soundless life, a rolling wave of plants, piled up, crested, ready to topple over the creek, to sweep every little man of us out of his little existence. And it moved not. A deadened burst of mighty splashes and snorts reached us from afar, as though an ichthyosaurus had been taking a bath of glitter in the great river. "After all," said the boiler-maker in a reasonable tone, "why shouldn't we get the rivets?" Why not, indeed! I did not know any reason why we shouldn't. "They'll come in three weeks," I said, confidently.

'But they didn't. Instead of the rivets there came an invasion, an affliction, a visitation. It came in sections during the next three weeks, each section headed by a donkey carrying a white man in new clothes and tan shoes, bowing from that elevation right and left to the impressed pilgrims. A quarrelsome band of footsore sulky niggers trod on the heels of the donkey; a lot of tents, camp-stools, tin boxes, white cases, brown bales would be shot down in the courtyard, and the air of mystery would deepen a little over the muddle of the station. Five such instalments came, with their absurd air of disorderly flight with the loot of innumerable outfit shops and provision stores, that, one would think, they were lugging, after a raid, into the wilderness for equitable division. It was an inextricable mess of things decent in themselves but that human folly made look like spoils of thieving.

'This devoted band called itself the Eldorado Exploring Expedition, and I believe they were sworn to secrecy. Their talk, however, was the talk of sordid buccaneers: it was reckless without hardihood, greedy without audacity, and cruel without courage; there was not an atom of foresight or of serious intention in the whole batch of them, and they did not seem aware these things are wanted for the work of the world. To tear treasure out of the bowels of the land was their desire, with no more moral purpose at the back of it than there is in burglars breaking into a safe. Who paid the expenses of the noble enterprise I don't know; but the uncle of our manager was leader of that lot.

'In exterior he resembled a butcher in a poor neighbourhood, and his eyes had a look of sleepy cunning. He carried his fat paunch with ostentation on his short legs, and during the time his gang infested the station spoke to no one but his nephew. You coud see these two roaming about all day long with their heads close together in an everlasting confab.

'I had given up worrying myself about the rivets. One's capacity for that kind of folly is more limited than you would suppose. I said Hang! – and let things slide. I had plenty of time for meditation, and now and then I would give some thought to Kurtz. I wasn't very interested in him. No. Still, I was curious to see whether this man, who had come out equipped with moral ideas of some sort, would climb to the top after all and how he would set about his work when there.'

II

'ONE evening as I was lying flat on the deck of my steamboat, I heard voices approaching – and there were the nephew and the uncle strolling along the bank. I laid my head on my arm again, and had nearly lost myself in a doze, when somebody said in my ear, as it were: "I am as harmless as a little child, but I don't like to be dictated to. Am I the manager – or am I not? I was ordered to send him there. It's incredible.". . . . I became aware that the two were standing on the shore alongside the forepart of the steamboat, just below my head. I did not move; it did not occur to me to move: I was sleepy. "It *is* unpleasant," grunted the uncle. "He has asked the Administration to be sent there," said the other, "with the idea of showing what he could do; and I was instructed accordingly. Look at the influence that man must have. Is it not frightful?" They both agreed it was frightful, then made several bizarre remarks: "Make rain and fine weather – one man – the Council – by the nose" – bits of absurd sentences that got the better of my drowsiness, so that I had pretty near the whole of my wits about me when the uncle said, "The climate may do away with this difficulty for you. Is he alone there?" "Yes," answered the manager; "he sent his assistant down the river with a note to me in these terms: 'Clear this poor devil out of the country, and don't bother sending more of that sort. I had rather be alone than have the kind of men you can dispose of with me.' It was more than a year ago. Can you imagine such impudence!" "Anything since then?" asked the other, hoarsely. "Ivory," jerked the nephew; "lots of it – prime sort – lots – most annoying, from him." "And with that?" questioned the heavy rumble. "Invoice," was the reply fired out, so to speak. Then silence. They had been talking about Kurtz.

'I was broad awake by this time, but, lying perfectly at ease, remained still, having no inducement to change my position. "How did that ivory come all this way?" growled the elder man, who seemed very vexed. The other explained that it had come with a fleet of canoes in charge of an English half-caste clerk Kurtz had with him; that Kurtz had apparently intended to return himself, the station being by that time bare of goods and stores, but after coming three hundred miles, had suddenly decided to go back, which he started to do alone in a small dugout with four paddlers, leaving the half-caste to continue down the river with the ivory. The two fellows there seemed astounded at anybody attempting such a thing. They were at a loss for an adequate motive. As to me, I seemed to see Kurtz for the first time. It was a distinct glimpse: the dugout, four paddling savages, and the lone white man turning his back suddenly on the headquarters, on relief, on thoughts of home – perhaps; setting his face towards the depths of the wilderness, towards his empty and desolate station. I did not know the motive. Perhaps he was just simply a fine fellow who stuck to his work for its own sake. His name, you understand, had not been pronounced once. He was "that man". The half-caste, who, as far as I could see, had conducted a difficult trip with great prudence and pluck, was invariably alluded to as "that scoundrel". The "scoundrel" had reported that the "man" had been very ill – had recovered imperfectly. . . . The two below me moved away then a few paces, and strolled back and forth at some little distance. I heard: "Military post – doctor – two hundred miles – quite alone now – unavoidable delays – nine months – no news – strange rumours." They approached again, just as the manager was saying, "No one, as far as I know, unless a species of wandering trader – a pestilential fellow, snapping ivory from the natives." Who was it they were talking about now? I gathered in snatches that this was some man supposed to be in Kurtz's district, and of whom the manager did not approve. "We will not be free from unfair competition till one of these fellows is hanged for an example," he said. "Certainly," grunted the other; "get him hanged! Why not? Anything – anything can be done in this country. That's what I say; nobody here, you understand, *here*, can endanger your position. And why? You stand the climate – you outlast them all. The danger is in Europe; but there before I left I took care to –" They moved off and whispered, then their voices rose again. "The extraordinary series of delays is not my fault. I did my best." The fat man sighed. "Very sad." "And the pestiferous absurdity of his talk," continued the other; "he bothered me enough when he was here. 'Each station should be like a beacon on the road towards better things, a centre for trade of course, but also for humanizing, improving, instructing.' Conceive you – that ass! And he wants to be manager! No, it's—" Here he got choked by excessive indignation, and I lifted my head the least bit. I was surprised to see how near they were – right under me. I could have spat upon their hats. They were looking on the ground, absorbed in thought. The manager was switching his leg with a slender twig; his sagacious relative lifted his head. "You have been well since you came out this time?" he asked. The other gave a start. "Who? I? Oh! Like a charm – like a charm. But the rest – oh, my goodness! All sick. They die so quick, too, that I haven't the time to send them out of the country – it's incredible!" "H'm. Just so," grunted the uncle. "Ah! my boy, trust to this – I say, trust to this." I saw him extend his short flipper of an arm for a gesture that took in the forest, the creek, the mud, the river, – seemed to beckon with a dishonouring flourish before the sunlit face of the land a treacherous appeal to the lurking death, to the hidden evil, to the profound darkness of its heart. It was so startling that I leaped to my feet and looked back at the edge of the forest, as though I expected an answer of some sort to that black display of confidence. You know the foolish notions that come to one sometimes. The high stillness confronted these two figures with its ominous patience, waiting for the passing away of a fantastic invasion.

'They swore aloud together – out of sheer fright, I believe – then pretending not to know anything of my existence, turned back to the station. The sun was low; and leaning forward side by side, they seemed to be tugging painfully uphill their two ridiculous shadows of unequal length, that trailed behind them slowly over the tall grass without bending a single blade.

'In a few days the Eldorado Expedition went into the patient wilderness, that closed upon it as the sea closes over a diver. Long afterwards the news came that all the donkeys were dead. I know nothing as to the fate of the less valuable animals. They, no doubt, like the rest of us, found what they deserved. I did not inquire. I was rather excited about the prospect of meeting Kurtz very soon. When I say very soon I mean it comparatively. It was just two months from the day we left the creek when we came to the bank below Kurtz's station.

'Going up that river was like travelling back to the earliest beginnings of the world, when vegetation rioted on the earth and the big trees were kings. An empty stream, a great silence, an impenetrable forest. The air was warm, thick, heavy, sluggish. There was no joy in the brilliance of sunshine. The long stretches of the waterway ran on, deserted, into the gloom of over-shadowed distances. On silvery sandbanks hippos and alligators sunned themselves side by side. The broadening waters flowed through a mob of wooded islands; you lost your way on that river as you would in a desert, and butted all day long against shoals, trying to find the channel, till you thought yourself bewitched and cut off for ever from everything you had known once – somewhere – far away – in another existence perhaps. There were moments when one's past came back to one, as it will sometimes when you have not a moment to spare to yourself; but it came in the shape of an unrestful and noisy dream, remembered with wonder amongst the overwhelming realities of this strange world of plants, and water, and silence. And this stillness of life did not in the least resemble a peace. It was a stillness of an implacable force brooding over an inscrutable intention. It looked at you with a vengeful aspect. I got used to it afterwards; I did not see it any more; I had no time. I had to keep guessing at the channel; I had to discern, mostly by inspiration, the signs of hidden banks; I watched for sunken stones; I was learning to clap my teeth smartly before my heart flew out, when I shaved by a fluke some infernal sly old snag that would have ripped the life out of the tin-pot steamboat and drowned all the pilgrims; I had to keep a look-out for the signs of dead wood we could cut up in the night for next day's steaming. When you have to attend to things of that sort, to the mere incidents of the surface, the reality, – the reality, I tell you – fades. The inner truth is hidden – luckily, luckily. But I felt it all the same; I felt often its mysterious stillness watching me at my monkey tricks, just as it watches you fellows performing on your respective tight-ropes for – what is it? half-a-crown a tumble –'

'Try to be civil, Marlow,' growled a voice, and I knew there was at least one listener awake besides myself.

'I beg your pardon. I forgot the heartache which makes up the rest of the price. And indeed what does the price matter, if the trick be well done? You do your tricks very well. And I didn't do badly either, since I managed not to sink that steamboat on my first trip. It's a wonder to me yet. Imagine a blindfolded man set to drive a van over a bad road. I sweated and shivered over that business considerably, I can tell you. After all, for a seaman, to scrape the bottom of the thing that's supposed to float all the time under his care is the unpardonable sin. No one may know of it, but you never forget the thump – eh? A blow on the very heart. You remember it, you dream of it, you wake up at night and think of it – years after – and go hot and cold all over. I don't pretend to say that steamboat floated all the time. More than once she had to wade for a bit, with twenty cannibals splashing around and pushing. We had enlisted some of these chaps on the way for a crew. Fine fellows – cannibals – in their place. They were men one could work with, and I am grateful to them. And, after all, they did not eat each other before my face: they had brought along provision of hippo-meat which went rotten, and made the mystery of the wilderness stink in my nostrils. Phoo! I can sniff it now. I had the manager on board and three or four pilgrims with their staves – all complete. Sometimes we came upon a station close by the bank, clinging to the skirts of the unknown, and the white men rushing out of a tumbledown hovel, with great gestures of joy and surprise and welcome, seemed very strange – had the appearance of being held there captive by a spell. The word ivory would ring in the air for a while – and on we went again into the silence, along empty reaches, round the still bends, between the high walls of our winding way, reverberating in hollow claps the ponderous beat of the stern-wheel. Trees, trees, millions of trees, massive, immense, running up high; and at their foot, hugging the bank against the stream, crept the little begrimed steamboat, like a sluggish beetle crawling on the floor of a lofty portico. It made you feel very small, very lost, and yet it was not altogether depressing, that feeling. After all, if you were small, the grimy beetle crawled on – which was just what you wanted it to do. Where the pilgrims imagined it crawled to I don't know. To some place where they expected to get something, I bet! For me it crawled towards Kurtz – exclusively; but when the steam-pipes started leaking we crawled very slow. The reaches opened before us and closed behind, as if the forest had stepped leisurely across the water to bar the way for our return. We penetrated deeper and deeper into the heart of darkness. It was very quiet there. At night sometimes the roll of drums behind the curtain of trees would run up the river and remain sustained faintly, as if hovering in the air high over our heads, till the first break of day. Whether it meant war, peace, or prayer we could not tell. The dawns were heralded by the descent of a chill stillness; the wood-cutters slept, their fires burned low; the snapping of a twig would make you start. We were wanderers on prehistoric earth, on an earth that wore the aspect of an unknown planet. We could have fancied ourselves the first men taking possession of an accursed inheritance, to be subdued at the cost of profound anguish and of excessive toil. But suddenly, as we struggled round a bend, there would be a glimpse of rush walls, of peaked grass-roofs, a burst of yells, a whirl of black limbs, a mass of hands clapping, of feet stamping, of bodies swaying, of eyes rolling, under the droop of heavy and motionless foliage. The steamer toiled along slowly on the edge of the black and incomprehensible frenzy. The pre-historic man was cursing us, praying to us, welcoming us – who could tell? We were cut off from the comprehension of our surroundings; we glided past like phantoms, wondering and secretly appalled, as sane men would be before an enthusiastic outbreak in a madhouse. We could not understand because we were too far and could not remember, because we were travelling in the night of first ages, of those ages that are gone, leaving hardly a sign – and no memories.

'The earth seemed unearthly. We are accustomed to look upon the shackled form of a conquered monster, but there – there you could look at a thing monstrous and free. It was unearthly, and the men were— No, they were not inhuman. Well, you know, that was the worst of it – this suspicion of their not being inhuman. It would come slowly to one. They howled and leaped, and spun, and made horrid faces; but what thrilled you was just the thought of their humanity – like yours – the thought of your remote kinship with this wild and passionate uproar. Ugly. Yes, it was ugly enough; but if you were man enough you would admit to yourself that there was in you just the faintest trace of a response to the terrible frankness of that noise, a dim suspicion of there being a meaning in it which you – you so remote from the night of first ages – could comprehend. And why not? The mind of man is capable of anything – because everything is in it, all the past as well as all the future. What was there after all? Joy, fear, sorrow, devotion, valour, rage – who can tell? – but truth – truth stripped of its cloak of time. Let the fool gape and shudder – the man knows, and can look on without a wink. But he must at least be as much of a man as these on the shore. He must meet that truth with his own true stuff – with his own inborn strength. Principles won't do. Acquisitions, clothes, pretty rags – rags that would fly off at the first good shake. No; you want a deliberate belief. An appeal to me in this fiendish row – is there? Very well; I hear; I admit, but I have a voice, too, and for good or evil mine is the speech that cannot be silenced. Of course, a fool, what with sheer fright and fine sentiments, is always safe. Who's that grunting? You wonder I didn't go ashore for a howl and a dance? Well, no – I didn't. Fine sentiments, you say? Fine sentiments, be hanged! I had no time. I had to mess about with white-lead and strips of woollen blanket helping to put bandages on those leaky steam-pipes – I tell you. I had to watch the steering, and circumvent those snags, and get the tin-pot along by hook or by crook. There was surface-truth enough in these things to save a wiser man. And between whiles I had to look after the savage who was fireman. He was an improved specimen; he could fire up a vertical boiler. He was there below me, and, upon my word, to look at him was as edifying as seeing a dog in a parody of breeches and a feather hat, walking on his hind-legs. A few months of training had done for that really fine chap. He squinted at the steam-gauge and at the water-gauge with an evident effort of intrepidity — and he had filed teeth, too, the poor devil, and the wool of his pate shaved into queer patterns, and three ornamental scars on each of his cheeks. He ought to have been clapping his hands and stamping his feet on the bank, instead of which he was hard at work, a thrall to strange witchcraft, full of improving knowledge. He was useful because he had been instructed; and what he knew was this — that should the water in that transparent thing disappear, the evil spirit inside the boiler would get angry through the greatness of his thirst, and take a terrible vengeance. So he sweated and fired up and watched the glass fearfully (with an impromptu charm, made of rags, tied to his arm, and a piece of polished bone, as big as a watch, stuck flatways through his lower lip), while the wooded banks slipped past us slowly, the short noise was left behind, the interminable miles of silence — and we crept on, towards Kurtz. But the snags were thick, the water was treacherous and shallow, the boiler seemed indeed to have a sulky devil in it, and thus neither that fireman nor I had any time to peer into our creepy thoughts.

'Some fifty miles below the Inner Station we came upon a hut of reeds, an inclined and melancholy pole, with the unrecognizable tatters of what had been a flag of some sort flying from it, and a neatly stacked wood-pile. This was unexpected. We came to the bank, and on the stack of firewood found a flat piece of board with some faded pencil-writing on it. When deciphered it said: "Wood for you. Hurry up. Approach cautiously." There was a signature, but it was illegible — not Kurtz — a much longer word. Hurry up. Where? Up the river? "Approach cautiously." We had not done so. But the warning could not have been meant for the place where it could only be found after approach. Something was wrong above. But what — and how much? That was the question. We commented adversely upon the imbecility of that telegraphic style. The bush around said nothing, and would not let us look very far, either. A torn curtain of red twill hung in the doorway of the hut, and flapped sadly in our faces. The dwelling was dismantled; but we could see a white man had lived there not very long ago. There remained a rude table – a plank on two posts; a heap of rubbish reposed in a dark corner, and by the door I picked up a book. It had lost its covers, and the pages had been thumbed into a state of extremely dirty softness; but the back had been lovingly stitched afresh with white cotton thread, which looked clean yet. It was an extraordinary find. Its title was, *An Inquiry into some Points of Seamanship*, by a man Tower, Towson – some such name – Master in his Majesty's Navy. The matter looked dreary reading enough, with illustrative diagrams and repulsive tables of figures, and the copy was sixty years old. I handled this amazing antiquity with the greatest possible tenderness, lest it should dissolve in my hands. Within, Towson or Towser was inquiring earnestly into the breaking strain of ship's chains and tackle, and other such matters. Not a very enthralling book; but at the first glance you could see there a singleness of intention, an honest concern for the right way of going to work, which made these humble pages, thought out so many years ago, luminous with another than a professional light. The simple old sailor, with his talk of chains and purchases, made me forget the jungle and the pilgrims in a delicious sensation of having come upon something unmistakably real. Such a book being there was wonderful enough; but still more astounding were the notes pencilled in the margin, and plainly referring to the text. I couldn't believe my eyes! They were in cipher! Yes, it looked like cipher. Fancy a man lugging with him a book of that description into this nowhere and studying it – and making notes – in cipher at that! It was an extravagant mystery.

'I had been dimly aware for some time of a worrying noise, and when I lifted my eyes I saw the wood-pile was gone, and the manager, aided by all the pilgrims, was shouting at me from the river-side. I slipped the book into my pocket. I assure you to leave off reading was like tearing myself away from the shelter of an old and solid friendship.

'I started the lame engine ahead. "It must be this miserable trader – this intruder," exclaimed the manager, looking back malevolently at the place we had left. "He must be English," I said. "It will not save him from getting into trouble if he is not careful," muttered the manager darkly. I observed with assumed innocence that no man was safe from trouble in this world.

'The current was more rapid now, the steamer seemed at her last gasp, the stern-wheel flogged languidly, and I caught myself listening on tiptoe for the next beat of the boat, for in sober truth I expected the wretched thing to give up every moment. It was like watching the last flickers of life. But still we crawled. Sometimes I would pick out a tree a little way ahead to measure our progress towards Kurtz by, but I lost it invariably before we got abreast. To keep the eyes so long on one thing was too much for human patience. The manager displayed a beautiful resignation. I fretted and fumed and took to arguing with myself whether or no I would talk openly with Kurtz; but before I could come to any conclusion it occurred to me that my speech or my silence, indeed any action of mine, would be a mere futility. What did it matter what any one knew or ignored? What did it matter who was manager? One gets sometimes a flash of insight. The essentials of this affair lay deep under the surface, beyond my reach, and beyond my power of meddling.

'Towards the evening of the second day we judged ourselves about eight miles from Kurtz's station. I wanted to push on; but the manager looked grave, and told me the navigation up there was so dangerous that it would be advisable, the sun being very low already, to wait where we were till next morning. Moreover, he pointed out that if the warning to approach cautiously were to be followed, we must approach in daylight – not at dusk, or in the dark. This was sensible enough. Eight miles meant nearly three hours' steaming for us, and I could also see suspicious ripples at the upper end of the reach. Nevertheless, I was annoyed beyond expression at the delay, and most unreasonably, too, since one night more could not matter much after so many months. As we had plenty of wood, and caution was the word, I brought up in the middle of the stream. The reach was narrow, straight, with high sides like a railway cutting. The dusk came gliding into it long before the sun had set. The current ran smooth and swift, but a dumb immobility sat on the banks. The living trees, lashed together by the creepers and every living bush of the undergrowth, might have been changed into stone, even to the slenderest twig, to the lightest leaf. It was not sleep – it seemed unnatural, like a state of trance. Not the faintest sound of any kind could be heard. You looked on amazed, and began to suspect yourself of being deaf – then the night came suddenly, and struck you blind as well. About three in the morning some large fish leaped, and the loud splash made me jump as though a gun had been fired. When the sun rose there was a white fog, very warm and clammy, and more blinding than the night. It did not shift or drive; it was just there, standing all round you like something solid. At eight or nine, perhaps, it lifted as a shutter lifts. We had a glimpse of the towering multitude of trees, of the immense matted jungle, with the blazing little ball of the sun hanging over it – all perfectly still – and then the white shutter came down again, smoothly, as if sliding in greased grooves. I ordered the chain, which we had begun to heave in, to be paid out again. Before it stopped running with a muffled rattle, a cry, a very loud cry, as of infinite desolation, soared slowly in the opaque air. It ceased. A complaining clamour, modulated in savage discords, filled our ears. The sheer unexpectedness of it made my hair stir under my cap. I don't know how it struck the others: to me it seemed as though the midst itself had screamed, so suddenly, and apparently from all sides at once, did this tumultuous and mournful uproar arise. It culminated in a hurried outbreak of almost intolerably excessive shrieking, which stopped short, leaving us stiffened in a variety of silly attitudes, and obstinately listening to the nearly appalling and excessive silence. "Good God! What is the meaning –" stammered at my elbow one of the pilgrims, – a little fat man, with sandy hair and red whiskers, who wore side-spring boots, and pink pyjamas tucked into his socks. Two others remained openmouthed a whole minute, then dashed into the little cabin, to rush out incontinently and stand darting scared glances, with Winchesters at "ready" in their hands. What we could see was just the steamer we were on, her outlines blurred as though she had been on the point of dissolving, and a misty strip of water, perhaps two feet broad, around her – and that was all. The rest of the world was nowhere, as far as our eyes and ears were concerned. Just nowhere. Gone, disappeared; swept off without leaving a whisper or a shadow behind.

'I went forward, and ordered the chain to be hauled in short, so as to be ready to trip the anchor and move the steamboat at once if necessary. "Will they attack?" whispered an awed voice. "We will be all butchered in this fog," murmured another. The faces twitched with the strain, the hands trembled slightly, the eyes forgot to wink. It was very curious to see the contrast of expressions of the white men and of the black fellows of our crew, who were as much strangers to that part of the river as we, though their homes were only eight hundred miles away. The whites, of course greatly discomposed, had besides a curious look of being painfully shocked by such an outrageous row. The others had an alert, naturally interested expression; but their faces were essentially quiet, even those of the one or two who grinned as they hauled at the chain. Several exchanged short, grunting phrases, which seemed to settle the matter to their satisfaction. Their headman, a young, broad-chested black, severely draped in dark-blue fringed cloths, with fierce nostrils and his hair all done up artfully in oily ringlets, stood near me. "Aha!" I said, just for good fellowship's sake. "Catch 'im," he snapped, with a bloodshot widening of his eyes and a flash of sharp teeth — "catch 'im. Give 'im to us." "To you, eh?" I asked; "what would you do with them?" "Eat 'im!" he said, curtly, and, leaning his elbow on the rail, looked out into the fog in a dignified and profoundly pensive attitude. I would no doubt have been properly horrified, had it not occurred to me that he and his chaps must be very hungry: that they must have been growing increasingly hungry for at least this past month. They had been engaged for six months (I don't think a single one of them had any clear idea of time, as we at the end of countless ages have. They still belonged to the beginnings of time — had no inherited experience to teach them as it were), and of course, as long as there was a piece of paper written over in accordance with some farcical law or other made down the river, it didn't enter anybody's head to trouble how they would live. Certainly they had brought with them some rotten hippo-meat, which couldn't have lasted very long, anyway, even if the pilgrims hadn't, in the midst of a shocking hullabaloo, thrown a considerable quantity of it overboard. It looked like a high-handed proceeding; but it was really a case of legitimate self-defence. You can't breathe dead hippo waking, sleeping, and eating, and at the same time keep your precarious grip on existence. Besides that, they had given them every week three pieces of brass wire, each about nine inches long; and the theory was they were to buy their provisions with that currency in river-side villages. You can see how *that* worked. There were either no villages, or the people were hostile, or the director, who like the rest of us fed out of tins, with an occasional old he-goat thrown in, didn't want to stop the steamer for some more or less recondite reason. So, unless they swallowed the wire itself, or made loops of it to snare the fishes with, I don't see what good their extravagant salary could be to them. I must say it was paid with a regularity worthy of a large and honourable trading company. For the rest, the only thing to eat – though it didn't look eatable in the least – I saw in their possession was a few lumps of some stuff like half-cooked dough, of a dirty lavender colour, they kept wrapped in leaves, and now and then swallowed a piece of, but so small that it seemed done more for the looks of the thing than for any serious purpose of sustenance. Why in the name of all the gnawing devils of hunger they didn't go for us – they were thirty to five – and have a good tuck in for once, amazes me now when I think of it. They were big powerful men, with not much capacity to weigh the consequences, with courage, with strength, even yet, though their skins were no longer glossy and their muscles no longer hard. And I saw that something restraining, one of these human secrets that baffle probability, had come into play there. I looked at them with a swift quickening of interest – not because it occurred to me I might be eaten by them before very long, though I own to you that just then I perceived – in a new light, as it were – how unwholesome the pilgrims looked, and I hoped, yes, I positively hoped, that my aspect was not so – what shall I say? – so – unappetizing: a touch of fantastic vanity which fitted well with the dream-sensation that pervaded all my days at that time. Perhaps I had a little fever, too. One can't live with one's finger everlastingly on one's pulse. I had often "a little fever", or a little touch of other things – the playful paw-strokes of the wilderness, the preliminary trifling before the more serious onslaught which came in due course. Yes; I looked at them as you would on any human being, with a curiosity of their impulses, motives, capacities, weaknesses, when brought to the test of an inexorable physical necessity. Restraint! What possible restraint? Was it superstition, disgust, patience, fear – or some kind of primitive honour? No fear can stand up to hunger, no patience can wear it out, disgust simply does not exist where hunger is; and as to superstition, beliefs, and what you may call principles, they are less than chaff in a breeze. Don't you know the devilry of lingering starvation, its exasperating torment, its black thoughts, its sombre and brooding ferocity? Well, I do. It takes a man all his inborn strength to fight hunger properly. It's really easier to face bereavement, dishonour, and the perdition of one's soul – than this kind of prolonged hunger. Sad, but true. And these chaps, too, had no earthly reason for any kind of scruple. Restraint! I would just as soon have expected restraint from a hyena prowling amongst the corpses of a battlefield. But there was the fact facing me – the fact dazzling, to be seen, like the foam on the depths of the sea, like a ripple on an unfathomable enigma, a mystery greater – when I thought of it – than the curious, inexplicable note of desperate grief in this savage clamour that had swept by us on the river-bank, behind the blind whiteness of fog.

'Two pilgrims were quarrelling in hurried whispers as to which bank. "Left." "No, no; how can you? Right, right, of course." "It is very serious," said the manager's voice behind me; "I would be desolated if anything should happen to Mr Kurtz before we came up." I looked at him, and had not the slightest doubt he was sincere. He was just the kind of man who would wish to preserve appearances. That was his restraint. But when he muttered something about going on at once, I did not even take the trouble to answer him. I knew, and he knew, that it was impossible. Were we to let go our hold of the bottom, we would be absolutely in the air – in space. We wouldn't be able to tell where we were going to – whether up or downstream, or across – till we fetched against one bank or the other, – and then we wouldn't know at first which it was. Of course I made no move. I had no mind for a smash-up. You couldn't imagine a more deadly place for a shipwreck. Whether drowned at once or not, we were sure to perish speedily in one way or another. "I authorize you to take all the risks," he said, after a short silence. "I refuse to take any," I said, shortly; which was just the answer he expected, though its tone might have surprised him. "Well, I must defer to your judgment. You are captain," he said, with marked civility. I turned my shoulder to him in sign of my appreciation, and looked into the fog. How long would it last? It was the most hopeless look-out. The approach to this Kurtz grubbing for ivory in the wretched bush was beset by as many dangers as though he had been an enchanted princess sleeping in a fabulous castle. "Will they attack, do you think?" asked the manager, in a confidential tone.

'I did not think they would attack, for several obvious reasons. The thick fog was one. If they left the bank in their canoes they would get lost in it, as we would be if we attempted to move. Still, I had also judged the jungle of both banks quite impenetrable – and yet eyes were in it, eyes that had seen us. The river-side bushes were certainly very thick; but the undergrowth behind was evidently penetrable. However, during the short lift I had seen no canoes anywhere in the reach – certainly not abreast of the steamer. But what made the idea of attack inconceivable to me was the nature of the noise – of the cries we had heard. They had not the fierce character boding of immediate hostile intention. Unexpected, wild, and violent as they had been, they had given me an irresistible impression of sorrow. The glimpse of the steamboat had for some reason filled those savages with unrestrained grief. The danger, if any, I expounded, was from our proximity to a great human passion let loose. Even extreme grief may ultimately vent itself in violence – but more generally takes the form of apathy. . . .

'You should have seen the pilgrims stare! They had no heart to grin, or even to revile me: but I believe they thought me gone mad – with fright, maybe. I delivered a regular lecture. My dear boys, it was no good bothering. Keep a look-out? Well, you may guess I watched the fog for signs of lifting as a cat watches a mouse; but for anything else our eyes were of no more use to us than if we had been buried miles deep in a heap of cotton-wool. It felt like it, too – choking, warm, stifling. Besides, all I said, though it sounded extravagant, was absolutely true to fact. What we afterwards alluded to as an attack was really an attempt at repulse. The action was very far from being aggressive – it was not even defensive, in the usual sense: it was undertaken under the stress of desperation, and in its essence was purely protective.

'It developed itself, I should say, two hours after the fog lifted, and its commencement was at a spot, roughly speaking, about a mile and a half below Kurtz's station. We had just floundered and

flopped round a bend, when I saw an islet, a mere grassy
hummock of bright green, in the middle of the stream. It was the
only thing of the kind; but as we opened the reach more, I
perceived it was the head of a long sandbank, or rather of a chain
of shallow patches stretching down the middle of the river. They
were discoloured, just awash, and the whole lot was seen just
under the water, exactly as a man's backbone is seen running
down the middle of his back under his skin. Now, as far as I did
see, I could go to the right or to the left of this. I didn't know either
channel, of course. The banks looked pretty well alike, the depth
appeared the same; but as I had been informed the station was on
the west side, I naturally headed for the western passage.

'No sooner had we fairly entered it than I became aware it was
much narrower than I had supposed. To the left of us there was
the long uninterrupted shoal, and to the right a high, steep bank
heavily overgrown with bushes. Above the bush the trees stood in
serried ranks. The twigs overhung the current thickly, and from
distance to distance a large limb of some tree projected rigidly
over the stream. It was then well on in the afternoon, the face of
the forest was gloomy, and a broad strip of shadow had already
fallen on the water. In this shadow we steamed up – very slowly,
as you may imagine. I sheered her well inshore – the water being
deeper near the bank, as the sounding-pole informed me.

'One of my hungry and forbearing friends was sounding in the
bows just below me. This steamboat was exactly like a decked
scow. On the deck, there were two little teak-wood houses, with
doors and windows. The boiler was in the fore-end, and the
machinery right astern. Over the whole there was a light roof,
supported on stanchions. The funnel projected through that roof,
and in front of the funnel a small cabin built of light planks served
for a pilot-house. It contained a couch, two camp-stools, a loaded
Martini-Henry leaning in one corner, a tiny table, and the
steering-wheel. It had a wide door in front and a broad shutter at
each side. All these were always thrown open, of course. I spent
my days perched up there on the extreme fore-end of that roof,
before the door. At night I slept, or tried to, on the couch. An
athletic black belonging to some coast tribe, and educated by my
poor predecessor, was the helmsman. He sported a pair of brass
earrings, wore a blue cloth wrapper from waist to the ankles, and

thought all the world of himself. He was the most unstable kind of fool I had ever seen. He steered with no end of a swagger while you were by; but if he lost sight of you, he became instantly the prey of an abject funk, and would let that cripple of a steamboat get the upper hand of him in a minute.

'I was looking down at the sounding-pole, and feeling much annoyed to see at each try a little more of it stick out of that river, when I saw the poleman give up the business suddenly, and stretch himself flat on the deck, without even taking the trouble to haul his pole in. He kept hold on it though, and it trailed in the water. At the same time the fireman, whom I could see also below me, sat down abruptly before his furnace and ducked his head. I was amazed. Then I had to look at the river mighty quick, because there was a snag in the fairway. Sticks, little sticks, were flying about – thick: they were whizzing before my nose, dropping below me, striking behind me against my pilot-house. All this time the river, the shore, the woods, were very quiet – perfectly quiet. I could only hear the heavy splashing thump of the stern-wheel and the patter of these things. We cleared the snag clumsily. Arrows, by Jove! We were being shot at! I stepped in quickly to close the shutter on the land-side. That fool-helmsman, his hands on the spokes, was lifting his knees high, stamping his feet, champing his mouth, like a reined-in horse. Confound him! And we were staggering within ten feet of the bank. I had to lean right out to swing the heavy shutter, and I saw a face amongst the leaves on the level with my own, looking at me very fierce and steady; and suddenly, as though a veil had been removed from my eyes, I made out, deep in the tangled gloom, naked breasts, arms, legs, glaring eyes, – the bush was swarming with human limbs in movement, glistening, of bronze colour. The twigs shook, swayed, and rustled, the arrows flew out of them, and then the shutter came to. "Steer her straight," I said to the helmsman. He held his head rigid, face forward; but his eyes rolled, he kept on, lifting and setting down his feet gently, his mouth foamed a little. "Keep quiet!' I said in a fury. I might just as well have ordered a tree not to sway in the wind. I darted out. Below me there was a great scuffle of feet on the iron deck; confused exclamations; a voice screamed, "Can you turn back?" I caught sight of a V-shaped ripple on the water ahead. What? Another snag! A fusillade burst out under my feet. The pilgrims had opened with their Winchesters, and were simply squirting lead into that bush. A deuce of a lot of smoke came up and drove slowly forward. I swore at it. Now I couldn't see the ripple or the snag either. I stood in the doorway, peering, and the arrows came in swarms. They might have been poisoned, but they looked as though they wouldn't kill a cat. The bush began to howl. Our wood-cutters raised a warlike whoop; the report of a rifle just at my back deafened me. I glanced over my shoulder, and the pilot-house was yet full of noise and smoke when I made a dash at the wheel. The fool-nigger had dropped everything, to throw the shutter open and let off that Martini-Henry. He stood before the wide opening, glaring, and I yelled at him to come back, while I straightened the sudden twist out of that steamboat. There was no room to turn even if I had wanted to, the snag was somewhere very near ahead in that confounded smoke, there was no time to lose, so I just crowded her into the bank – right into the bank, where I knew the water was deep.

'We tore slowly along the overhanging bushes in a whirl of broken twigs and flying leaves. The fusillade below stopped short, as I had foreseen it would when the squirts got empty. I threw my head back to a glinting whizz that traversed the pilot-house, in at one shutter-hole and out at the other. Looking past that mad helmsman, who was shaking the empty rifle and yelling at the shore, I saw vague forms of men running bent double, leaping, gliding, distinct, incomplete, evanescent. Something big appeared in the air before the shutter, the rifle went overboard, and the man stepped back swiftly, looked at me over his shoulder in an extraordinary, profound, familiar manner, and fell upon my feet. The side of his head hit the wheel twice, and the end of what appeared a long cane clattered round and knocked over a little camp-stool. It looked as though after wrenching that thing from somebody ashore he had lost his balance in the effort. The thin smoke had blown away, we were clear of the snag, and looking ahead I could see that in another hundred yards or so I would be free to sheer off, away from the bank; but my feet felt so very warm and wet that I had to look down. The man had rolled on his back and stared straight up at me; both his hands clutched that cane. It was the shaft of a spear that, either thrown or lunged through the opening, had caught him in the side just below the ribs; the blade had gone in out of sight, after making a frightful gash; my shoes were full; a pool of blood lay very still, gleaming dark-red under the wheel; his eyes shone with an amazing lustre. The fusillade burst out again. He looked at me anxiously, gripping the spear like something precious, with an air of being afraid I would try to take it away from him. I had to make an effort to free my eyes from his gaze and attend to the steering. With one hand I felt above my head for the line of the steam whistle, and jerked out screech after screech hurriedly. The tumult of angry and warlike yells was checked instantly, and then from the depths of the woods went out such a tremulous and prolonged wail of mournful fear and utter despair as may be imagined to follow the flight of the last hope from the earth. There was a great commotion in the bush; the shower of arrows stopped, a few dropping shots rang out sharply – then silence, in which the languid beat of the stern-wheel came plainly to my ears. I put the helm hard a-starboard at the moment when the pilgrim in pink pyjamas, very hot and agitated, appeared in the doorway. "The manager sends me—" he began in an official tone, and stopped short. "Good God!" he said, glaring at the wounded man.

'We two whites stood over him, and his lustrous and inquiring glance enveloped us both. I declare it looked as though he would presently put to us some question in an understandable language; but he died without uttering a sound, without moving a limb, without twitching a muscle. Only in the very last moment, as though in response to some sign we could not see, to some whisper we could not hear, he frowned heavily, and that frown gave to his black death-mask an inconceivably sombre, brooding, and menacing expression. The lustre of inquiring glance faded swiftly into vacant glassiness. "Can you steer?" I asked the agent eagerly. He looked very dubious; but I made a grab at his arm, and he understood at once I meant him to steer whether or no. To tell you the truth, I was morbidly anxious to change my socks and shoes. "He is dead," murmured the fellow, immensely impressed. "No doubt about it," said I, tugging like mad at the shoe-laces. "And by the way, I suppose Mr Kurtz is dead as well by this time."

'For the moment that was the dominant thought. There was a

sense of extreme disappointment, as though I had found out I had been striving after something altogether without a substance. I couldn't have been more disgusted if I had travelled all this way for the sole purpose of talking with Mr Kurtz. Talking with . . . I flung one shoe overboard, and became aware that that was exactly what I had been looking forward to – a talk with Kurtz. I made the strange discovery that I had never imagined him as doing, you know, but as discoursing. I didn't say to myself, "Now I will never see him", or "Now I will never shake him by the hand", but, "Now I will never hear him". The man presented himself as a voice. Not of course that I did not connect him with some sort of action. Hadn't I been told in all the tones of jealousy and admiration that he had collected, bartered, swindled, or stolen more ivory than all the other agents together? That was not the point. The point was in his being a gifted creature, and that of all of his gifts the one that stood out pre-eminently, that carried with it a sense of real presence, was his ability to talk, his words – the gift of expression, the bewildering, the illuminating, the most exalted and the most contemptible, the pulsating stream of light, or the deceitful flow from the heart of an impenetrable darkness.

'The other shoe went flying unto the devil-god of that river. I thought, By Jove! it's all over. We are too late; he has vanished – the gift has vanished, by means of some spear, arrow, or club. I will never hear that chap speak after all, – and my sorrow had a startling extravagence of emotion, even such as I had noticed in the howling sorrow of these savages in the bush. I couldn't have felt more of lonely desolation somehow, had I been robbed of a belief or had missed my destiny in life. . . . Why do you sigh in this beastly way, somebody? Absurd? Well, absurd. Good Lord! musn't a man ever— Here, give me some tobacco.'. .

There was a pause of profound stillness, then a match flared, and Marlow's lean face appeared, worn, hollow, with downward folds and dropped eyelids, with an aspect of concentrated attention; and as he took vigorous draws at his pipe, it seemed to retreat and advance out of the night in the regular flicker of the tiny flame. The match went out.

'Absurd!' he cried. 'This is the worst of trying to tell . . . Here you all are, each moored with two addresses, like a hulk with two anchors, a butcher round one corner, a policeman round another, excellent appetites, and temperature normal – you hear – normal from year's end to year's end. And you say, Absurd! Absurd be – exploded! Absurd! My dear boys, what can you expect from a man who out of sheer nervousness had just flung overboard a pair of new shoes! Now I think of it, it is amazing I did not shed tears. I am, upon the whole, proud of my fortitude. I was cut to the quick at the idea of having lost the inestimable privilege of listening to the gifted Kurtz. Of course I was wrong. The privilege was waiting for me. Oh, yes, I heard more than enough. And I was right, too. A voice. He was very little more than a voice. And I heard – him – it – this voice – other voices – all of them were so little more than voices – and the memory of that time itself lingers around me, impalpable, like a dying vibration of one immense jabber, silly, atrocious, sordid, savage, or simply mean, without any kind of sense. Voices, voices – even the girl herself – now –'

He was silent for a long time.

'I laid the ghost of his gifts at last with a lie,' he began, suddenly. 'Girl! What? Did I mention a girl? Oh, she is out of it – completely. They – the women I mean – are out of it – should be out of it. We must help them to stay in that beautiful world of their own, lest ours gets worse. Oh, she had to be out of it. You should have heard the disinterred body of Mr Kurtz saying, "My Intended." You would have perceived directly then how completely she was out of it. And the lofty frontal bone of Mr Kurtz! They say the hair goes on growing sometimes, but this – ah – specimen, was impressively bald. The wilderness had patted him on the head, and, behold, it was like a ball – an ivory ball; it had caressed him, and – lo! – he had withered; it had taken him, loved him, embraced him, and got into his veins, consumed his flesh, and sealed his soul to its own by the inconceivable ceremonies of some devilish initiation. He was its spoiled and pampered favourite. Ivory? I should think so. Heaps of it, stacks of it. The old mud shanty was bursting with it. You would think there was not a single tusk left either above or below the ground in the whole country. "Mostly fossil," the manager had remarked, disparagingly. It was no more fossil than I am; but they call it fossil when it is dug up. It appears these niggers do bury the tusks sometimes – but evidently they couldn't bury this parcel deep enough to save the gifted Mr Kurtz from his fate. We filled the steamboat with it, and had to pile a lot on the deck. Thus he could see and enjoy as long as he could see, because the appreciation of this favour had remained with him to the last. You should have heard him say, "My ivory." Oh yes, I heard him. "My Intended, my ivory, my station, my river, my —" Everything belonged to him. It made me hold my breath in expectation of hearing the wilderness burst into a prodigious peal of laughter that would shake the fixed stars in their places. Everything belonged to him — but that was a trifle. The thing was to know what he belonged to, how many powers of darkness claimed him for their own. That was the reflection that made you creepy all over. It was impossible — it was not good for one either — trying to imagine. He had taken a high seat amongst the devils of the land — I mean literally. You can't understand. How could you? — with solid pavement under your feet, surrounded by kind neighbours ready to cheer you or to fall on you, stepping delicately between the butcher and the policeman, in the holy terror of scandal and gallows and lunatic asylums — how can you imagine what particular region of the first ages a man's untrammelled feet may take him into by way of solitude — utter solitude without a policeman — by the way of silence — utter silence, where no warning voice of a kind neighbour can be heard whispering of public opinion? These little things make all the great difference. When they are gone you must fall back upon your own innate strength, upon your own capacity for faithfulness. Of course you may be too much of a fool to go wrong — too dull even to know you are being assaulted by the powers of darkness. I take it, no fool ever made a bargain for his soul with the devil: the fool is too much of a fool, or the devil too much of a devil — I don't know which. Or you may be such a thunderingly exalted creature as to be altogether deaf and blind to anything but heavenly sights and sounds. Then the earth for you is only a standing place — and whether to be like this is your loss or your gain I won't pretend to say. But most of us are neither one nor the other. The earth for us is a place to live in, where we must put up with sights, with sounds, with smells, too, by Jove! — breathe dead hippo, so to speak, and not be contaminated. And there, don't you see? your strength comes in, the faith in your ability for the digging of unostentatious holes to bury the stuff in — your power of devotion, not to yourself, but to an obscure, back-breaking business. And that's difficult enough. Mind, I am not trying to excuse or even explain – I am trying to account to myself for – for – Mr Kurtz – for the shade of Mr Kurtz. This initiated wraith from the back of Nowhere honoured me with its amazing confidence before it vanished altogether. This was because it could speak English to me. The original Kurtz had been educated partly in England, and – as he was good enough to say himself – his sympathies were in the right place. His mother was half-English, his father was half-French. All Europe contributed to the making of Kurtz; and by-and-by I learned that, most appropriately, the International Society for the Suppression of Savage Customs had intrusted him with the making of a report, for its future guidance. And he had written it, too. I've seen it. I've read it. It was eloquent, vibrating with eloquence, but too high-strung, I think. Seventeen pages of close writing he had found time for! But this must have been before his – let us say – nerves, went wrong, and caused him to preside at certain midnight dances ending with unspeakable rites, which – as far as I reluctantly gathered from what I heard at various times – were offered up to him – do you understand? – to Mr Kurtz himself. But it was a beautiful piece of writing. The opening paragraph, however, in the light of later information, strikes me now as ominous. He began with the argument that we whites, from the point of development we had arrived at, "must necessarily appear to them [savages] in the nature of supernatural beings – we approach them with the might as of a deity", and so on, and so on. "By the simple exercise of our will we can exert a power for good practically unbounded", etc. etc. From that point he soared and took me with him. The peroration was magnificent, though difficult to remember, you know. It gave me the notion of an exotic Immensity ruled by an august Benevolence. It made me tingle with enthusiasm. This was the unbounded power of eloquence – of words – of burning noble words. There were no practical hints to interrupt the magic current of phrases, unless a kind of note at the foot of the last page, scrawled evidently much later, in an unsteady hand, may be regarded as the exposition of a method. It was very simple, and at the end of that moving appeal to every altruistic sentiment it blazed at you, luminous and terrifying, like a flash of lightning in a serene sky: "Exterminate all the brutes!" The curious part was

that he had apparently forgotten all about that valuable postscrip-
tum, because, later on, when he in a sense came to himself, he
repeatedly entreated me to take good care of "my pamphlet" (he
called it), as it was sure to have in the future a good influence upon
his career. I had full information about all these things, and,
besides, as it turned out, I was to have the care of his memory. I've
done enough for it to give me the indisputable right to lay it, if I
choose, for an everlasting rest in the dust-bin of progress, amongst
all the sweepings and, figuratively speaking, all the dead cats of
civilization. But then, you see, I can't choose. He won't be
forgotten. Whatever he was, he was not common. He had the
power to charm or frighten rudimentary souls into an aggravated
witch-dance in his honour; he could also fill the small souls of the
pilgrims with bitter misgivings: he had one devoted friend at least,
and he had conquered one soul in the world that was neither
rudimentary nor tainted with self-seeking. No; I can't forget him,
though I am not prepared to affirm the fellow was exactly worth
the life we lost in getting to him. I missed my late helmsman
awfully, – I missed him even while his body was still lying in the
pilot-house. Perhaps you will think it passing strange this regret
for a savage who was no more account than a grain of sand in a
black Sahara. Well, don't you see, he had done something, he had
steered; for months I had him at my back – a help – an instrument.
It was a kind of partnership. He steered for me – I had to look after
him, I worried about his deficiencies, and thus a subtle bond had
been created, of which I only became aware when it was suddenly
broken. And the intimate profundity of that look he gave me
when he received his hurt remains to this day in my memory – like
a claim of distant kinship affirmed in a supreme moment.

'Poor fool! If he had only left that shutter alone. He had no
restraint, no restraint – just like Kurtz – a tree swayed by the wind.
As soon as I had put on a dry pair of slippers, I dragged him out,
after first jerking the spear out of his side, which operation I
confess I performed with my eyes shut tight. His heels leaped
together over the little door-step; his shoulders were pressed to
my breast; I hugged him from behind desperately. Oh! he was
heavy, heavy; heavier than any man on earth, I should imagine.
Then without more ado I tipped him overboard. The current
snatched him as though he had been a wisp of grass, and I saw the

body roll over twice before I lost sight of it for ever. All the
pilgrims and the manager were then congregated on the awning-
deck about the pilot-house, chattering at each other like a flock of
excited magpies, and there was a scandalized murmur at my
heartless promptitude. What they wanted to keep that body
hanging about for I can't guess. Embalm it, maybe. But I had also
heard another, and a very ominous, murmur on the deck below.
My friends the wood-cutters were likewise scandalized, and with
a better show of reason – though I admit that the reason itself was
quite inadmissable. Oh, quite! I had made up my mind that if my
late helmsman was to be eaten, the fishes alone should have him.
He had been a very second-rate helmsman while alive, but now he
was dead he might have become a first-class temptation, and
possibly cause some startling trouble. Besides, I was anxious to
take the wheel, the man in pink pyjamas showing himself a
hopeless duffer at the business.

'This I did directly the simple funeral was over. We were going
half-speed, keeping right in the middle of the stream, and I
listened to the talk about me. They had given up Kurtz, they had
given up the station; Kurtz was dead, and the station had been
burnt – and so on – and so on. The red-haired pilgrim was beside
himself with the thought that at least this poor Kurtz had been
properly avenged. "Say! We must have a glorious slaughter of
them in the bush. Eh? What do you think? Say?" He positively
danced, the bloodthirsty little gingery beggar. And he had nearly
fainted when he saw the wounded man! I could not help saying,
"You made a glorious lot of smoke, anyhow." I had seen, from
the way the tops of the bushes rustled and flew, that almost all the
shots had gone too high. You can't hit anything unless you take
aim and fire from the shoulder; but these chaps fired from the hip
with their eyes shut. The retreat, I maintained – and I was right –
was caused by the screeching of the steam-whistle. Upon this they
forgot Kurtz, and began to howl at me with indignant protests.

'The manager stood by the wheel murmuring confidentially
about the necessity of getting well away down the river before
dark at all events, when I saw in the distance a clearing on the
river-side and the outlines of some sort of building. "What's
this?" I asked. He clapped his hands in wonder. "The station!" he
cried. I edged in at once, still going half-speed.

'Through my glasses I saw the slope of a hill interspersed with rare trees and perfectly free from undergrowth. A long decaying building on the summit was half buried in the high grass; the large holes in the peaked roof gaped black from afar; the jungle and the woods made a background. There was no enclosure or fence of any kind; but there had been one apparently, for near the house half-a-dozen slim posts remained in a row, roughly trimmed, and with their upper ends ornamented with round carved balls. The rails, or whatever there had been between, had disappeared. Of course the forest surrounded all that. The river-bank was clear, and on the water-side I saw a white man under a hat like a cart-wheel beckoning persistently with his whole arm. Examining the edge of the forest above and below, I was almost certain I could see movements – human forms gliding here and there. I steamed past prudently, then stopped the engines and let her drift down. The man on the shore began to shout, urging us to land. "We have been attacked," screamed the manager. "I know – I know. It's all right," yelled back the other, as cheerful as you please. "Come along. It's all right. I am glad."

'His aspect reminded me of something I had seen – something funny I had seen somewhere. As I manoeuvred to get alongside, I was asking myself, "What does this fellow look like?" Suddenly I got it. He looked like a harlequin. His clothes had been made of some stuff that was brown holland probably, but it was covered with patches all over, with bright patches, blue, red, and yellow, – patches on the back, patches on the front, patches on elbows, on knees; coloured binding around his jacket, scarlet edging at the bottom of his trousers; and the sunshine made him look extremely gay and wonderfully neat withal, because you could see how beautifully all this patching had been done. A beardless, boyish face, very fair, no features to speak of, nose peeling, little blue eyes, smiles and frowns chasing each other over that open countenance like sunshine and shadow on a wind-swept plain. "Look out, captain!" he cried, "there's a snag lodged in here last night." What! Another snag? I confess I swore shamefully. I had nearly holed my cripple, to finish off that charming trip. The harlequin on the bank turned his little pug-nose up to me. "You English?" he asked, all smiles. "Are you?" I shouted from the wheel. The smiles vanished, and he shook his head as if sorry for my disappointment. Then he brightened up. "Never mind!" he cried, encouragingly. "Are we in time?" I asked. "He is up there," he replied, with a toss of the head up the hill, and becoming gloomy all of a sudden. His face was like the autumn sky, overcast one moment and bright the next.

'When the manager, escorted by the pilgrims, all of them armed to the teeth, had gone to the house this chap came on board. "I say, I don't like this. These natives are in the bush," I said. He assured me earnestly it was all right. "They are simple people," he added; "well, I am glad you came. It took me all my time to keep them off." "But you said it was all right," I cried. "Oh, they meant no harm," he said; and as I stared he corrected himself. "Not exactly." Then vivaciously, "My faith, your pilot-house wants a clean up!" In the next breath he advised me to keep enough steam on the boiler to blow the whistle in case of any trouble. "One good screech will do more for you than all your rifles. They are simple people," he repeated. He rattled away at such a rate he quite overwhelmed me. He seemed to be trying to make up for lots of silence, and actually hinted, laughing, that such was the case. "Don't you talk with Mr Kurtz?" I said. "You don't talk with that man – you listen to him," he exclaimed with severe exaltation. "But now—" He waved his arm, and in the twinkling of an eye was in the uttermost depths of despondency. In a moment he came up again with a jump, possessed himself of both my hands, shook them continuously, while he gabbled: "Brother sailor . . . honour . . . pleasure . . . delight . . . introduce myself . . . Russian . . . son of an arch-priest . . . Government of Tambov . . . What? Tobacco! English tobacco; the excellent English tobacco! Now, that's brotherly. Smoke? Where's a sailor that does not smoke?"

'The pipe soothed him, and gradually I made out he had run away from school, had gone to sea in a Russian ship; ran away again; served some time in English ships; was now reconciled with the arch-priest. He made a point of that. "But when one is young one must see things, gather experience, ideas; enlarge the mind." "Here!" I interrupted. "You can never tell! Here I met Mr Kurtz," he said, youthfully solemn and reproachful. I held my tongue after that. It appears he had persuaded a Dutch trading-house on the coast to fit him out with stores and goods, and had started for the interior with a light heart, and no more idea of what would

happen to him than a baby. He had been wandering about that
river for nearly two years alone, cut off from everybody and
everything. "I am not so young as I look. I am twenty-five," he
said. "At first old Van Shuyten would tell me to go to the devil,"
he narrated with keen enjoyment; "but I stuck to him, and talked
and talked, till at last he got afraid I would talk the hind-leg off his
favourite dog, so he gave me some cheap things and a few guns,
and told me he hoped he would never see my face again. Good old
Dutchman, Van Shuyten. I've sent him one small lot of ivory a
year ago, so that he can't call me a little thief when I get back. I
hope he got it. And for the rest I don't care. I had some wood
stacked for you. That was my old house. Did you see?"

'I gave him Towson's book. He made as though he would kiss
me, but restrained himself. "The only book I had left, and I
thought I had lost it," he said, looking at it ecstatically. "So many
accidents happen to a man going about alone, you know. Canoes
get upset sometimes – and sometimes you've got to clear out so
quick when the people get angry." He thumbed the pages. "You
made notes in Russian?" I asked. He nodded. "I thought they
were written in cipher," I said. He laughed, then became serious.
"I had lots of trouble to keep these people off," he said. "Did they
want to kill you?" I asked. "Oh, no!" he cried, and checked
himself. "Why did they attack us?" I pursued. He hesitated, then
said shamefacedly, "They don't want him to go." "Don't they?" I
said, curiously. He nodded a nod full of mystery and wisdom. "I
tell you," he cried, "this man has enlarged my mind." He opened
his arms wide, staring at me with his little blue eyes that were
perfectly round.'

III

'I LOOKED at him, lost in astonishment. There he was before me,
in motley, as though he had absconded from a troupe of mimes,
enthusiastic, fabulous. His very existence was improbable, inexplicable, and altogether bewildering. He was an insoluble
problem. It was inconceivable how he had existed, how he had
succeeded in getting so far, how he had managed to remain – why

he did not instantly disappear. "I went a little farther," he said, "then still a little farther – till I had gone so far that I don't know how I'll ever get back. Never mind. Plenty time. I can manage. You take Kurtz away quick – quick – I tell you." The glamour of youth enveloped his particoloured rags, his destitution, his loneliness, the essential desolation of his futile wanderings. For months – for years – his life hadn't been worth a day's purchase; and there he was gallantly, thoughtlessly alive, to all appearance indestructible solely by the virtue of his few years and of his unreflecting audacity. I was seduced into something like admiration – like envy. Glamour urged him on, glamour kept him unscathed. He surely wanted nothing from the wilderness but space to breathe in and to push on through. His need was to exist, and to move onwards at the greatest possible risk, and with a maximum of privation. If the absolutely pure, uncalculating, unpractical spirit of adventure had ever ruled a human being, it ruled this be-patched youth. I almost envied him the possession of this modest and clear flame. It seemed to have consumed all thought of self so completely, that even while he was talking to you, you forgot that it was he – the man before your eyes – who had gone through these things. I did not envy him his devotion to Kurtz, though. He had not meditated over it. It came to him, and he accepted it with a sort of eager fatalism. I must say that to me it appeared about the most dangerous thing in every way he had come upon so far.

'They had come together unavoidably, like two ships becalmed near each other, and lay rubbing sides at last. I suppose Kurtz wanted an audience, because on a certain occasion, when encamped in the forest, they had talked all night, or more probably Kurtz had talked. "We talked of everything," he said, quite transported at the recollection. "I forgot there was such a thing as sleep. The night did not seem to last an hour. Everything! Everything! . . . Of love, too." "Ah, he talked to you of love!" I said, much amused. "It isn't what you think," he cried, almost passionately. "It was in general. He made me see things – things."

'He threw his arms up. We were on deck at the time, and the headman of my wood-cutters, lounging near by, turned upon him his heavy and glittering eyes. I looked around, and I don't know why, but I assure you that never, never before, did this land, this river, this jungle, the very arch of this blazing sky, appear to me so hopeless and so dark, so impenetrable to human thought, so pitiless to human weakness. "And, ever since, you have been with him, of course?" I said.

'On the contrary. It appears their intercourse had been very much broken by various causes. He had, as he informed me proudly, managed to nurse Kurtz through two illnesses (he alluded to it as you would to some risky feat), but as a rule Kurtz wandered alone, far in the depths of the forest. "Very often coming to this station, I had to wait days and days before he would turn up," he said. "Ah, it was worth waiting for! – sometimes." "What was he doing? exploring or what?" I asked. "Oh, yes, of course"; he had discovered lots of villages, a lake, too – he did not know exactly in what direction; it was dangerous to inquire too much – but mostly his expeditions had been for ivory. "But he had no goods to trade with by that time," I objected. "There's a good lot of cartridges left even yet," he answered, looking away. "To speak plainly, he raided the country," I said. He nodded. "Not alone, surely!" He muttered something about the villages round that lake. "Kurtz got the tribe to follow him, did he?" I suggested. He fidgeted a little. "They adored him," he said. The tone of these words was so extraordinary that I looked at him searchingly. It was curious to see his mingled eagerness and reluctance to speak of Kurtz. The man filled his life, occupied his thoughts, swayed his emotions. "What can you expect?" he burst out; "he came to them with thunder and lightning, you know – and they had never seen anything like it – and very terrible. He could be very terrible. You can't judge Mr Kurtz as you would an ordinary man. No, no no! Now – just to give you an idea – I don't mind telling you, he wanted to shoot me, too, one day – but I don't judge him." "Shoot you!" I cried. "What for?" "Well, I had a small lot of ivory the chief of that village near my house gave me. You see I used to shoot game for them. Well, he wanted it, and wouldn't hear reason. He declared he would shoot me unless I gave him the ivory and then cleared out of the country, because he could do so, and had a fancy for it, and there was nothing on earth to prevent him killing whom he jolly well pleased. And it was true, too. I gave him the ivory. What did I care! But I didn't clear out. No, no. I couldn't leave him. I had to be careful, of course, till we got friendly again for a time. He had his second illness then. Afterwards I had to keep out of the way; but I didn't mind. He was living for the most part in those villages on the lake. When he came down to the river, sometimes he would take to me, and sometimes it was better for me to be careful. This man suffered too much. He hated all this, and somehow he couldn't get away. When I had a chance I begged him to try and leave while there was time; I offered to go back with him. And he would say yes, and then he would remain; go off on another ivory hunt; disappear for weeks; forget himself amongst these people – forget himself – you know." "Why! he's mad," I said. He protested indignantly. Mr Kurtz couldn't be mad. If I had heard him talk, only two days ago, I wouldn't dare hint at such a thing . . . I had taken up my binoculars while we talked, and was looking at the shore, sweeping the limit of the forest at each side and at the back of the house. The consciousness of there being people in that bush, so silent, so quiet – as silent and quiet as the ruined house on the hill – made me uneasy. There was no sign on the face of nature of this amazing tale that was not so much told as suggested to me in desolate exclamations, completed by shrugs, in interrupted phrases, in hints ending in deep sighs. The woods were unmoved, like a mask – heavy, like the closed door of a prison – they looked with their air of hidden knowledge, of patient expectation, of unapproachable silence. The Russian was explaining to me that it was only lately that Mr Kurtz had come down to the river, bringing along with him all the fighting men of that lake tribe. He had been absent for several months – getting himself adored, I suppose – and had come down unexpectedly, with the intention to all appearance of making a raid either across the river or down stream. Evidently the appetite for more ivory had got the better of the – what shall I say? – less material aspirations. However he had got much worse suddenly. "I heard he was lying helpless, and so I came up – took my chance," said the Russian. "Oh, he is bad, very bad." I directed my glass to the house. There were no signs of life, but there was the ruined roof, the long mud wall peeping above the grass, with three little square window-holes, no two of the same size; all this brought within reach of my hand, as it were. And then I made a brusque movement, and one of the remaining posts of that vanished fence leaped up in the field of my glass. You remember I told you I had been struck at the distance by certain attempts at ornamentation, rather remarkable in the ruinous aspect of the place. Now I had suddenly a nearer view, and its first result was to make me throw my head back as if before a blow. Then I went carefully from post to post with my glass, and I saw my mistake. These round knobs were not ornamental but symbolic; they were expressive and puzzling, striking and disturbing – food for thought and also for the vultures if there had been any looking down from the sky; but at all events for such ants as were industrious enough to ascend the pole. They would have been even more impressive, those heads on the stakes, if their faces had not been turned to the house. Only one, the first I had made out, was facing my way. I was not so shocked as you may think. The start back I had given was really nothing but a movement of surprise. I had expected to see a knob of wood there, you know. I returned deliberately to the first I had seen – and there it was, black, dried, sunken, with closed eyelids, – a head that seemed to sleep at the top of that pole, and with the shrunken dry lips showing a narrow white line of the teeth, was smiling, too, smiling continuously at some endless and jocose dream of that eternal slumber.

'I am not disclosing any trade secrets. In fact, the manager said afterwards that Mr Kurtz's methods had ruined the district. I have no opinion on that point, but I want you clearly to understand that there was nothing exactly profitable in these heads being there. They only showed that Mr Kurtz lacked restraint in the gratification of his various lusts, that there was something wanting in him – some small matter which, when the pressing need arose, could not be found under his magnificent eloquence. Whether he knew of this deficiency himself I can't say. I think the knowledge came to him at last – only at the very last. But the wilderness had found him out early, and had taken on him a terrible vengeance for the fantastic invasion. I think it had whispered to him things about himself which he did not know, things of which he had no conception till he took counsel with this great solitude – and the whisper had proved irresistibly fascinating. It echoed loudly within him because he was hollow at the core. . . . I put down the glass, and the head that had appeared near enough to be spoken to seemed at once to have leaped away from me into inaccessible distance.

'The admirer of Mr Kurtz was a bit crestfallen. In a hurried, indistinct voice he began to assure me he had not dared to take these – say, symbols – down. He was not afraid of the natives; they would not stir till Mr Kurtz gave the word. His ascendancy was extraordinary. The camps of these people surrounded the place, and the chiefs came every day to see him. They would crawl. . . . "I don't want to know anything of the ceremonies used when approaching Mr Kurtz," I shouted. Curious, this feeling that came over me that such details would be more intolerable than those heads drying on the stakes under Mr Kurtz's windows. After all, that was only a savage sight, while I seemed at one bound to have been transported into some lightless region of subtle horrors, where pure, uncomplicated savagery was a positive relief, being something that had a right to exist – obviously – in the sunshine. The young man looked at me with surprise. I suppose it did not occur to him that Mr Kurtz was no idol of mine. He forgot that I hadn't heard any of these splendid monologues on, what was it? on love, justice, conduct of life – or what not. If it had come to crawling before Mr Kurtz, he crawled as much as the veriest savage of them all. I had no idea of the conditions, he said: these heads were the heads of rebels. I shocked him excessively by laughing. Rebels! What would be the next definition I was to hear? There had been enemies, criminals, workers – and these were rebels. Those rebellious heads looked very subdued to me on their sticks. "You don't know how such a life tries a man like Kurtz," cried Kurtz's last disciple. "Well, and you?" I said. "I! I! I am a simple man. I have no great thoughts. I want nothing from anybody. How can you compare me to? . . ." His feelings were too much for speech, and suddenly he broke down. "I don't understand," he groaned. "I've been doing my best to keep him alive, and that's enough. I had no hand in all this. I have no abilities. There hasn't been a drop of medicine or a mouthful of invalid food for months here. He was shamefully abandoned. A man like this, with such ideas. Shamefully! Shamefully! I – I – haven't slept for the last ten nights. . . ."

'His voice lost itself in the calm of the evening. The long shadows of the forest had slipped downhill while we talked, had gone far beyond the ruined hovel, beyond the symbolic row of stakes. All this was in the gloom, while we down there were yet in the sunshine, and the stretch of the river abreast of the clearing glittered in a still and dazzling splendour, with a murky and overshadowed bend above and below. Not a living soul was seen on the shore. The bushes did not rustle.

'Suddenly round the corner of the house a group of men appeared, as though they had come up from the ground. They waded waist-deep in the grass, in a compact body, bearing an improvised stretcher in their midst. Instantly, in the emptiness of the landscape, a cry arose whose shrillness pierced the still air like a sharp arrow flying straight to the very heart of the land; and, as if by enchantment, streams of human beings – of naked human beings – with spears in their hands, with bows, with shields, with wild glances and savage movements, were poured into the clearing by the dark-faced and pensive forest. The bushes shook, the grass swayed for a time, and then everything stood still in attentive immobility.

'"Now, if he does not say the right thing to them we are all done for," said the Russian at my elbow. The knot of men with the stretcher had stopped, too, half-way to the steamer, as if petrified. I saw the man on the stretcher sit up, lank and with an uplifted arm, above the shoulders of the bearers. "Let us hope that the man who can talk so well of love in general will find some particular reason to spare us this time," I said. I resented bitterly the absurd danger of our situation, as if to be at the mercy of that atrocious phantom had been a dishonouring necessity. I could not hear a sound, but through my glasses I saw the thin arm extended commandingly, the lower jaw moving, the eyes of that apparition shining darkly far in its bony head that nodded with grotesque jerks. Kurtz – Kurtz – that means short in German – don't it? Well, the name was as true as everything else in his life – and death. He looked at least seven feet long. His covering had fallen off, and his body emerged from it pitiful and appalling as from a winding-sheet. I could see the cage of his ribs all astir, the bones of his arm waving. It was as though an animated image of death carved out of old ivory had been shaking its hand with menaces at a motionless crowd of men made of dark and glittering bronze. I saw him open his mouth wide – it gave him a weirdly voracious aspect, as though he had wanted to swallow all the air, all the earth, all the men before him. A deep voice reached me faintly. He must have been shouting. He fell back suddenly. The stretcher shook as the bearers staggered forward again, and almost at the same time I noticed that the crowd of savages was vanishing without any perceptible movement of retreat, as if the forest that had ejected these beings so suddenly had drawn them in again as the breath is drawn in a long aspiration.

'Some of the pilgrims behind the stretcher carried his arms – two shot-guns, a heavy rifle, and a light revolver-carbine – the thunderbolts of that pitiful Jupiter. The manager bent over him murmuring as he walked beside his head. They laid him down in one of the little cabins – just room for a bedplace and a camp-stool or two, you know. We had brought his belated correspondence, and a lot of torn envelopes and open letters littered his bed. His hand roamed feebly amongst these papers. I was struck by the fire of his eyes and the composed languor of his expression. It was not such much the exhaustion of disease. He did not seem in pain. This shadow looked satiated and calm, as though for the moment it had had its fill of all the emotions.

'He rustled one of the letters, and looking straight in my face said, "I am glad." Somebody had been writing to him about me. These special recommendations were turning up again. The volume of tone he emitted without effort, almost without the trouble of moving his lips, amazed me. A voice! a voice! It was grave, profound, vibrating, while the man did not seem capable of a whisper. However, he had enough strength in him – factitious no doubt – to very nearly make an end of us, as you shall hear directly.

'The manager appeared silently in the doorway; I stepped out at once and he drew the curtain after me. The Russian, eyed curiously by the pilgrims, was staring at the shore. I followed the direction of his glance.

'Dark human shapes could be made out in the distance, flitting indistinctly against the gloomy border of the forest, and near the river two bronze figures, leaning on tall spears, stood in the sunlight under fantastic head-dresses of spotted skins, warlike and still in statuesque repose. And from right to left along the lighted shore moved a wild and gorgeous apparition of a woman.

'She walked with measured steps, draped in striped and fringed cloths, treading the earth proudly, with a slight jingle and flash of barbarous ornaments. She carried her head high; her hair was done in the shape of a helmet; she had brass leggings to the knee, brass wire gauntlets to the elbow, a crimson spot on her tawny cheek, innumerable necklaces of glass beads on her neck; bizarre things, charms, gifts of witch-men, that hung about her, glittered and trembled at every step. She must have had the value of several elephant tusks upon her. She was savage and superb, wild-eyed and magnificent; there was something ominous and stately in her deliberate progress. And in the hush that had fallen suddenly upon the whole sorrowful land, the immense wilderness, the colossal body of the fecund and mysterious life seemed to look at her, pensive, as though it had been looking at the image of its own tenebrous and passionate soul.

'She came abreast of the steamer, stood still, and faced us. Her long shadow fell to the water's edge. Her face had a tragic and fierce aspect of wild sorrow and of dumb pain mingled with the fear of some struggling, half-shaped resolve. She stood looking at us without a stir, and like the wilderness itself, with an air of brooding over an inscrutable purpose. A whole minute passed, and then she made a step forward. There was a low jingle, a glint of yellow metal, a sway of fringed draperies, and she stopped as if her heart had failed her. The young fellow by my side growled. The pilgrims murmured at my back. She looked at us all as if her life had depended upon the unswerving steadiness of her glance. Suddenly she opened her bared arms and threw them rigid above her head, as though in an uncontrollable desire to touch the sky, and at the same time the swift shadows darted out on the earth, swept around on the river, gathering the steamer into a shadowy embrace. A formidable silence hung over the scene.

'She turned away slowly, walked on, following the bank, and passed into the bushes on the left. Once only her eyes gleamed back at us in the dusk of the thickets before she disappeared.

'"If she had offered to come aboard I really think I would have tried to shoot her," said the man of patches, nervously. "I had been risking my life every day for the last fortnight to keep her out of the house. She got in one day and kicked up a row about those miserable rags I picked up in the storeroom to mend my clothes with. I wasn't decent. At least it must have been that, for she talked like a fury to Kurtz for an hour, pointing at me now and then. I don't understand the dialect of this tribe. Luckily for me, I fancy Kurtz felt too ill that day to care, or there would have been mischief. I don't understand. . . . No – it's too much for me. Ah, well, it's all over now."

'At this moment I heard Kurtz's deep voice behind the curtain: "Save me! – save the ivory, you mean. Don't tell me. Save *me!* Why, I've had to save you. You are interrupting my plans now. Sick! Sick! Not so sick as you would like to believe. Never mind. I'll carry out my ideas yet – I will return. I'll show you what can be done. You with your little peddling notions – you are interfering with me. I will return. I. . . ."

'The manager came out. He did me the honour to take me under the arm and lead me aside. "He is very low, very low," he said. He considered it necessary to sigh, but neglected to be consistently sorrowful. "We have done all we could for him – haven't we? But there is no disguising the fact, Mr Kurtz has done more harm than good to the Company. He did not see the time was not ripe for vigorous action. Cautiously, cautiously – that's my principle. We must be cautious yet. The district is closed to us for a time. Deplorable! Upon the whole, the trade will suffer. I don't deny there is a remarkable quantity of ivory – mostly fossil. We must save it, at all events – but look how precarious the position is – and why? Because the method is unsound." "Do you," said I, looking at the shore, "call it, 'unsound method'?" "Without doubt," he exclaimed, hotly. "Don't you?" . . .

"No method at all," I murmured after a while. "Exactly," he exulted. "I anticipated this. Shows a complete want of judgment. It is my duty to point it out in the proper quarter." "Oh," said I, "that fellow – what's his name? – the brickmaker, will make a readable report for you." He appeared confounded for a moment. It seemed to me I had never breathed an atmosphere so vile, and I turned mentally to Kurtz for relief – positively for relief. "Nevertheless I think Mr Kurtz is a remarkable man," I said with emphasis. He started, dropped on me a cold heavy glance, said very quietly, "he *was*", and turned his back on me. My hour of favour was over; I found myself lumped along with Kurtz as a partisan of methods for which the time was not ripe: I was unsound! Ah! but it was something to have at least a choice of nightmares.

'I had turned to the wilderness really, not to Mr Kurtz, who, I was ready to admit, was as good as buried. And for a moment it seemed to me as if I also were buried in a vast grave full of unspeakable secrets. I felt an intolerable weight oppressing my breast, the smell of the damp earth, the unseen presence of victorious corruption, the darkness of an impenetrable night. . . . The Russian tapped me on the shoulder. I heard him mumbling and stammering something about "brother seaman — couldn't conceal — knowledge of matters that would affect Mr Kurtz's reputation". I waited. For him evidently Mr Kurtz was not in his grave; I suspect that for him Mr Kurtz was one of the immortals. "Well!" said I at last, "speak out. As it happens, I am Mr Kurtz's friend — in a way."

'He stated with a good deal of formality that had we not been "of the same profession", he would have kept the matter to himself without regard to consequences. "He suspected there was an active ill will towards him on the part of these white men that—" "You are right," I said, remembering a certain conversation I had overheard. "The manager thinks you ought to be hanged." He showed a concern at this intelligence which amused me at first. "I had better get out of the way quietly," he said, earnestly. "I can do no more for Kurtz now, and they would soon find some excuse. What's to stop them? There's a military post three hundred miles from here." "Well, upon my word," said I, "perhaps you had better go if you have any friends amongst the savages near by." "Plenty," he said. "They are simple people —and I want nothing, you know." He stood biting his lip, then: "I don't want any harm to happen to these whites here, but of course I was thinking of Mr Kurtz's reputation — but you are a brother seaman and—" "All right," said I, after a time. "Mr Kurtz's reputation is safe with me." I did not know how truly I spoke.

'He informed me, lowering his voice, that it was Kurtz who had ordered the attack to be made on the steamer. "He hated sometimes the idea of being taken away — and then again. . . . But I don't understand these matters. I am a simple man. He thought it would scare you away — that you would give it up, thinking him dead. I could not stop him. Oh, I had an awful time of it this last month." "Very well," I said. "He is all right now." "Ye-e-es," he muttered, not very convinced apparently. "Thanks," said I; "I shall keep my eyes open." "But quiet – eh?" he urged, anxiously. "It would be awful for his reputation if anybody here—" I promised a complete discretion with great gravity. "I have a canoe and three black fellows waiting not very far. I am off. Could you give me a few Martini-Henry cartridges?" I could, and did, with proper secrecy. He helped himself, with a wink at me, to a handful of my tobacco. "Between sailors – you know – good English tobacco." At the door of the pilot-house he turned round – "I say, haven't you a pair of shoes you could spare?" He raised one leg. "Look." The soles were tied with knotted strings sandal-wise under his bare feet. I rooted out an old pair, at which he looked with admiration before tucking it under his left arm. One of his pockets (bright red) was bulging with cartridges, from the other (dark blue) peeped "Towson's Inquiry", etc., etc. He seemed to think himself excellently well equipped for a renewed encounter with the wilderness. "Ah! I'll never, never meet such a man again. You ought to have heard him recite poetry – his own, too, it was, he told me. Poetry!" He rolled his eyes at the recollection of these delights. "Oh, he enlarged my mind!" "Good-bye," said I. He shook hands and vanished in the night. Sometimes I ask myself whether I had ever really seen him – whether it was possible to meet such a phenomenon! . . .

'When I woke up shortly after midnight his warning came to my mind with its hint of danger that seemed, in the starred darkness, real enough to make me get up for the purpose of having a look round. On the hill a big fire burned, illuminating fitfully a crooked corner of the station-house. One of the agents with a picket of a few of our blacks, armed for the purpose, was keeping guard over the ivory; but deep within the forest, red gleams that wavered, that seemed to sink and rise from the ground amongst confused columnar shapes of intense blackness, showed the exact position of the camp where Mr Kurtz's adorers were keeping their uneasy vigil. The monotonous beating of a big drum filled the air with muffled shocks and a lingering vibration. A steady droning sound of many men chanting each to himself some weird incantation came out from the black, flat wall of the woods as the humming of bees comes out of a hive, and had a strange narcotic effect upon my half-awake senses. I believe I dozed off leaning over the rail, till an abrupt burst of yells, an overwhelming outbreak of a pent-up and mysterious frenzy, woke me up in a bewildered wonder. It was cut short all at once, and the low droning went on with an effect of audible and soothing silence. I glanced casually into the little cabin. A light was burning within, but Mr Kurtz was not there.

'I think I would have raised an outcry if I had believed my eyes. But I didn't believe them at first – the thing seemed so impossible. The fact is I was completely unnerved by a sheer blank fright, pure abstract terror, unconnected with any distinct shape of physical danger. What made this emotion so overpowering was – how shall I define it? – the moral shock I received, as if something altogether monstrous, intolerable to thought and odious to the soul, had been thrust upon me unexpectedly. This lasted of course the merest fraction of a second, and then the usual sense of commonplace, deadly danger, the possibility of a sudden onslaught and massacre, or something of the kind, which I saw impending, was positively welcome and composing. It pacified me, in fact, so much, that I did not raise an alarm.

'There was an agent buttoned up inside an ulster and sleeping on a chair on deck within three feet of me. The yells had not awakened him; he snored very slightly; I left him to his slumbers and leaped ashore. I did not betray Mr Kurtz – it was ordered I should never betray him – it was written I should be loyal to the nightmare of my choice. I was anxious to deal with this shadow by myself alone, – and to this day I don't know why I was so jealous of sharing with anyone the peculiar blackness of that experience.

'As soon as I got on the bank I saw a trail – a broad trail through the grass. I remember the exultation with which I said to myself, "He can't walk – he is crawling on all-fours – I've got him." The grass was wet with dew. I strode rapidly with clenched fists. I fancy I had some vague notion of falling upon him and giving him a drubbing. I don't know. I had some imbecile thoughts. The knitting old woman with the cat obtruded herself upon my memory as a most improper person to be sitting at the other end of such an affair. I saw a row of pilgrims squirting lead in the air out of Winchesters held to the hip. I thought I would never get back to the steamer, and imagined myself living alone and unarmed in the woods to an advanced age. Such silly things – you know. And I remember I confounded the beat of the drum with the beating of my heart, and was pleased at its calm regularity.

'I kept to the track though – then stopped to listen. The night was very clear; a dark-blue space, sparkling with dew and starlight, in which black things stood very still. I thought I could see a kind of motion ahead of me. I was strangely cocksure of everything that night. I actually left the track and ran in a wide semicircle (I verily believe chuckling to myself) so as to get in front of that stir, of that motion I had seen – if indeed I had seen anything. I was circumventing Kurtz as though it had been a boyish game.

'I came upon him, and, if he had not heard me coming, I would have fallen over him, too, but he got up in time. He rose, unsteady, long, pale, indistinct, like a vapour exhaled by the earth, and swayed slightly, misty and silent before me; while at my back the fires loomed between the trees, and the murmur of many voices issued from the forest. I had cut him off cleverly; but when actually confronting him I seemed to come to my senses, I saw the danger in its right proportion. It was by no means over yet. Suppose he began to shout? Though he could hardly stand, there was still plenty of vigour in his voice. "Go away – hide yourself," he said, in that profound tone. It was very awful. I glanced back. We were within thirty yards from the nearest fire. A black figure stood up, strode on long black legs, waving long black arms, across the glow. It had horns – antelope horns, I think – on its head. Some sorcerer, some witch-man, no doubt: it looked fiend-like enough. "Do you know what you are doing?" I whispered. "Perfectly," he answered, raising his voice for that single word: it sounded to me far off and yet loud, like a hail through a speaking-trumpet. If he makes a row we are lost, I thought to myself. This clearly was not a case for fisticuffs, even apart from the very natural aversion I had to beat that Shadow – this wandering and tormented thing. "You will be lost," I said – "utterly lost." One gets sometimes such a flash of inspiration, you know. I did say the right thing, though indeed he could not have been more irretrievably lost than he was at this very moment, when the foundations of our intimacy were being laid – to endure – to endure – even to the end – even beyond.

'"I had immense plans," he muttered irresolutely. "Yes," said I; "but if you try to shout I'll smash your head with—" There was not a stick or stone near. "I will throttle you for good," I corrected myself. "I was on the threshold of great things," he pleaded, in a voice of longing, with a wistfulness of tone that made my blood run cold. "And now for this stupid scoundrel—" "Your success in Europe is assured in any case," I affirmed, steadily. I did not want to have the throttling of him, you understand – and indeed it would have been very little use for any practical purpose. I tried to break the spell – the heavy, mute spell of the wilderness – that seemed to draw him to its pitiless breast by the awakening of forgotten and brutal instincts, by the memory of gratified and monstrous passions. This alone, I was convinced, had driven him out to the edge of the forest, to the bush, towards the gleam of fires, the throb of drums, the drone of weird incantations; this alone had beguiled his unlawful soul beyond the bounds of permitted aspirations. And, don't you see, the terror of the position was not in being knocked on the head – though I had a very lively sense of that danger, too – but in this, that I had to deal with a being to whom I could not appeal in the name of anything high or low. I had, even like the niggers, to invoke him – himself – his own exalted and incredible degradation. There was nothing either above or below him, and I knew it. He had kicked himself loose of the earth. Confound the man! he had kicked the very earth to pieces. He was alone, and I before him did not know whether I stood on the ground or floated in the air. I've been telling you what we said – repeating the phrases we pronounced – but what's the good? They were common everyday words – the familiar, vague sounds exchanged on every waking day of life. But what of that? They had behind them, to my mind, the terrific suggestiveness of words heard in dreams, of phrases spoken in nightmares. Soul! If anybody has ever struggled with a soul, I am the man. And I wasn't arguing with a lunatic either. Believe me or not, his intelligence was perfectly clear – concentrated, it is true, upon himself with horrible intensity, yet clear: and therein was my only chance – barring, of course, the killing him there and then, which wasn't so good, on account of unavoidable noise. But his soul was mad. Being alone in the wilderness, it had looked within itself, and, by heavens! I tell you, it had gone mad. I had – for my sins, I suppose – to go through the ordeal of looking into it myself. No eloquence could have been so withering to one's belief in mankind as his final burst of sincerity. He struggled with himself, too. I saw it, – I heard it. I saw the inconceivable mystery of a soul that knew no restraint, no faith, and no fear, yet struggling blindly with itself. I kept my head pretty well; but when I had him at last stretched on the couch, I wiped my forehead, while my legs shook under me as though I had carried half a ton on my back down that hill. And yet I had only supported him, his bony arm clasped round my neck – and he was not much heavier than a child.

'When next day we left at noon, the crowd, of whose presence behind the curtain of trees I had been acutely conscious all the time, flowed out of the woods again, filled the clearing, covered the slope with a mass of naked, breathing, quivering bronze bodies. I steamed up a bit, then swung downstream, and two thousand eyes followed the evolutions of the splashing, thumping, fierce river-demon beating the water with its terrible tail and breathing black smoke into the air. In front of the first rank, along the river, three men, plastered with bright red earth from head to foot, strutted to and fro restlessly. When we came abreast again, they faced the river, stamped their feet, nodded their horned heads, swayed their scarlet bodies; they shook towards the fierce river-demon a bunch of black feathers, a mangy skin with a pendent tail – something that looked like a dried gourd; they shouted periodically together strings of amazing words that resembled no sounds of human language; and the deep murmurs of the crowd, interrupted suddenly, were like the responses of some satanic litany.

'We had carried Kurtz into the pilot-house: there was more air there. Lying on the couch, he stared through the open shutter. There was an eddy in the mass of human bodies, and the woman with helmeted head and tawny cheeks rushed out to the very brink of the stream. She put out her hands, shouted something, and all that wild mob took up the shout in a roaring chorus of articulated, rapid, breathless utterance.

'"Do you understand this?" I asked.

'He kept on looking out past me with fiery, longing eyes, with a mingled expression of wistfulness and hate. He made no answer, but I saw a smile, a smile of indefinable meaning, appear on his colourless lips that a moment after twitched convulsively. "Do I not?" he said slowly, gasping, as if the words had been torn out of him by a supernatural power.

'I pulled the string of the whistle, and I did this because I saw the pilgrims on deck getting out their rifles with an air of anticipating a jolly lark. At the sudden screech there was a movement of abject terror through that wedged mass of bodies. "Don't! don't you frighten them away," cried someone on deck disconsolately. I pulled the string time after time. They broke and ran, they leaped, they crouched, they swerved, they dodged the flying terror of the sound. The three red chaps had fallen flat, face down on the shore, as though they had been shot dead. Only the barbarous and superb woman did not so much as flinch, and stretched tragically her bare arms after us over the sombre and glittering river.

'And then that imbecile crowd down on the deck started their little fun, and I could see nothing more for smoke.

*

'The brown current ran swiftly out of the heart of darkness, bearing us down towards the sea with twice the speed of our upward progress; and Kurtz's life was running swiftly, too, ebbing, ebbing out of his heart into the sea of inexorable time. The manager was very placid, he had no vital anxieties now, he took us both in with a comprehensive and satisfied glance: the "affair" had come off as well as could be wished. I saw the time approaching when I would be left alone of the party of "unsound method". The pilgrims looked upon me with disfavour. I was, so to speak, numbered with the dead. It is strange how I accepted this unforeseen partnership, this choice of nightmares forced upon me in the tenebrous land invaded by these mean and greedy phantoms.

'Kurtz discoursed. A voice! a voice! It rang deep to the very last. It survived his strength to hide in the magnificent folds of eloquence the barren darkness of his heart. Oh, he struggled! he struggled! The wastes of his weary brain were haunted by shadowy images now — images of wealth and fame revolving obsequiously round his unextinguishable gift of noble and lofty expression. My Intended, my station, my career, my ideas — these were the subjects for the occasional utterances of elevated sentiments. The shade of the original Kurtz frequented the bedside of the hollow sham, whose fate it was to be buried presently in the mould of primeval earth. But both the diabolic love and the unearthly hate of the mysteries it had penetrated fought for the possession of that soul satiated with primitive emotions, avid of lying fame, of sham distinction, of all the appearances of success and power.

'Sometimes he was contemptibly childish. He desired to have kings meet him at railway-stations on his return from some ghastly Nowhere, where he intended to accomplish great things. "You show them you have in you something that is really profitable, and then there will be no limits to the recognition of your ability," he would say. "Of course you must take care of the motives – right motives – always." The long reaches that were like one and the same reach, monotonous bends that were exactly alike, slipped past the steamer with their multitude of secular trees looking patiently after this grimy fragment of another world, the forerunner of change, of conquest, of trade, of massacres, of blessings. I looked ahead – piloting. "Close the shutter," said Kurtz suddenly one day; "I can't bear to look at this." I did so. There was a silence. "Oh, but I will wring your heart yet!" he cried at the invisible wilderness.

'We broke down – as I had expected – and had to lie up for repairs at the head of an island. This delay was the first thing that shook Kurtz's confidence. One morning he gave me a packet of papers and a photograph – the lot tied together with a shoe-string. "Keep this for me," he said. "This noxious fool" (meaning the manager) "is capable of prying into my boxes when I am not looking." In the afternoon I saw him. He was lying on his back with closed eyes, and I withdrew quietly, but I heard him mutter, "Live rightly, die, die . . ." I listened. There was nothing more. Was he rehearsing some speech in his sleep, or was it a fragment of a phrase from some newspaper article? He had been writing for the papers and meant to do so again, "for the furthering of my ideas. It's a duty."

'His was an impenetrable darkness. I looked at him as you peer down at a man who is lying at the bottom of a precipice where the sun never shines. But I had not much time to give him, because I was helping the engine-driver to take to pieces the leaky cylinders, to straighten a bent connecting-rod, and in other such matters. I lived in an infernal mess of rust, filings, nuts, bolts, spanners, hammers, ratchet-drills – things I abominate, because I don't get on with them. I tended the little forge we fortunately had aboard; I toiled wearily in a wretched scrap-heap – unless I had the shakes too bad to stand.

'One evening coming in with a candle I was startled to hear him say a little tremulously, "I am lying here in the dark waiting for death." The light was within a foot of his eyes. I forced myself to murmur, "Oh, nonsense!" and stood over him as if transfixed.

'Anything approaching the change that came over his features I have never seen before, and hope never to see again. Oh, I wasn't touched. I was fascinated. It was as though a veil had been rent. I saw on that ivory face the expression of sombre pride, of ruthless power, of craven terror – of an intense and hopeless despair. Did he live his life again in every detail of desire, temptation, and surrender during that supreme moment of complete knowledge? He cried in a whisper at some image, at some vision – he cried out twice, a cry that was no more than a breath –

'"The horror! The horror!"

'I blew the candle out and left the cabin. The pilgrims were dining in the mess-room, and I took my place opposite the manager, who lifted his eyes to give me a questioning glance, which I successfully ignored. He leaned back, serene, with that peculiar smile of his sealing the unexpressed depths of his meanness. A continuous shower of small flies streamed upon the lamp, upon the cloth, upon our hands and faces. Suddenly the manager's boy put his insolent black head in the doorway, and said in a tone of scathing contempt –

'"Mistah Kurtz – he dead."

'All the pilgrims rushed out to see. I remained, and went on with my dinner. I believe I was considered brutally callous. However, I did not eat much. There was a lamp in there – light, don't you know – and outside it was so beastly, beastly dark. I went no more near the remarkable man who had pronounced a judgment upon the adventures of his soul on this earth. The voice was gone. What else had been there? But I am of course aware that next day the pilgrims buried something in a muddy hole.

'And then they very nearly buried me.

'However, as you see, I did not go to join Kurtz there and then. I did not. I remained to dream the nightmare out to the end, and to show my loyalty to Kurtz once more. Destiny. My destiny! Droll thing life is – that mysterious arrangement of merciless logic for a futile purpose. The most you can hope from it is some knowledge of yourself – that comes too late – a crop of unextinguishable regrets. I have wrestled with death. It is the most unexciting contest you can imagine. It takes place in an impalpable greyness, with nothing underfoot, with nothing around, without spectators, without clamour, without glory, without the great desire of victory, without the great fear of defeat, in a sickly atmosphere of tepid scepticism, without much belief in your own right, and still less in that of your adversary. If such is the form of ultimate wisdom, then life is a greater riddle than some of us think it to be. I was within a hair's-breadth of the last opportunity for pronouncement, and I found with humiliation that probably I would have nothing to say. This is the reason why I affirm that Kurtz was a remarkable man. He had something to say. He said it. Since I had peeped over the edge myself, I understand better the meaning of his stare, that could not see the flame of the candle, but was wide enough to embrace the whole universe, piercing enough to penetrate all the hearts that beat in the darkness. He had summed up – he had judged. "The horror!" He was a remarkable man. After all, this was the expression of some sort of belief; it had candour, it had conviction, it had a vibrating note of revolt in its whisper, it had the appalling face of a glimpsed truth – the strange commingling of desire and hate. And it is not my own extremity I remember best – a vision of greyness without form filled with physical pain, and a careless contempt for the evanescence of all things – even of this pain itself. No! It is his extremity that I seem to have lived through. True, he had made that last stride, he had stepped over the edge, while I had been permitted to draw back my hesitating foot. And perhaps in this is the whole difference; perhaps all the wisdom, and all truth, and all sincerity, are just compressed into that inappreciable moment of time in which we step over the threshold of the invisible. Perhaps! I like to think my summing-up would not have been a word of careless contempt. Better his cry – much better. It was an affirmation, a moral victory paid for by innumerable defeats, by abominable terrors, by abominable satisfactions. But it was a victory! That is why I have remained loyal to Kurtz to the last, and even beyond, when a long time after I heard once more, not his own voice, but the echo of his magnificent eloquence thrown to me from a soul as translucently pure as a cliff of crystal.

'No, they did not bury me, though there is a period of time which I remember mistily, with a shuddering wonder, like a passage through some inconceivable world that had no hope in it and no desire. I found myself back in the sepulchral city resenting the sight of people hurrying through the streets to filch a little money from each other, to devour their infamous cookery, to gulp their unwholesome beer, to dream their insignificant and silly dreams. They trespassed upon my thoughts. They were intruders whose knowledge of life was to me an irritating pretence, because I felt so sure they could not possibly know the things I knew. Their bearing, which was simply the bearing of commonplace individuals going about their business in the assurance of perfect safety, was offensive to me like the outrageous flauntings of folly in the face of a danger it is unable to comprehend. I had no particular desire to enlighten them, but I had some difficulty in restraining myself from laughing in their faces, so full of stupid importance. I daresay I was not very well at that time. I tottered about the streets – there were various affairs to settle – grinning bitterly at perfectly respectable persons. I admit my behaviour was inexcusable, but then my temperature was seldom normal in these days. My dear aunt's endeavours to "nurse up my strength" seemed altogether beside the mark. It was not my strength that wanted nursing, it was my imagination that wanted soothing. I kept the bundle of papers given me by Kurtz, not knowing exactly what to do with it. His mother had died lately, watched over, as I was told, by his Intended. A clean-shaved man, with an official manner and wearing gold-rimmed spectacles, called on me one day and made inquiries, at first circuitous, afterwards suavely pressing, about what he was pleased to denominate certain "documents". I was not surprised, because I had had two rows with the manager on the subject out there. I had refused to give up the smallest scrap out of that package, and I took the same attitude with the spectacled man. He became darkly menacing at last, and with much heat argued that the Company had the right to every bit of information about its "territories". And said he, "Mr Kurtz's knowledge of unexplored regions must have been necessarily extensive and peculiar – owing to his great abilities and to the deplorable circumstances in which he had been placed: therefore –". I assured him Mr Kurtz's knowledge, however extensive, did not bear upon the problems of commerce or administration. He invoked then the name of science. "It would be an incalculable loss if," etc., etc. I offered him the report on the "Suppression of Savage Customs", with the postcriptum torn off. He took it up eagerly, but ended by sniffing at it with an air of contempt. "This is not what we had a right to expect," he remarked. "Expect nothing else," I said. "There are only private letters." He withdrew upon some threat of legal proceedings, and I saw him no more; but another fellow, calling himself Kurtz's cousin, appeared two days later, and was anxious to hear all the details about his dear relative's last moments. Incidentally he gave me to understand that Kurtz had been essentially a great musician. "There was the making of an immense success," said the man, who was an organist, I believe, with lank grey hair flowing over a greasy coat-collar. I had no reason to doubt his statement; and to this day I am unable to say what was Kurtz's profession, whether he ever had any – which was the greatest of his talents. I had taken him for a painter who wrote for the papers, or else for a journalist who could paint – but even the cousin (who took snuff during the interview) could not tell me what he had been – exactly. He was a universal genius – on that point I agreed with the old chap, who thereupon blew his nose noisily into a large cotton handkerchief and withdrew in senile agitation, bearing off some family letters and memoranda without importance. Ultimately a journalist anxious to know something of the fate of his "dear colleague" turned up. This visitor informed me Kurtz's proper sphere ought to have been politics "on the popular side". He had furry straight eyebrows, bristly hair cropped short, an eye-glass on a broad ribbon, and, becoming expansive, confessed his opinion that Kurtz really couldn't write a bit – "but heavens! how that man could talk. He electrified large meetings. He had faith – don't you see? – he had the faith. He could get himself to believe anything – anything. He would have been a splendid leader of an extreme party." "What party?" I asked. "Any party," answered the other. "He was an – an – extremist." Did I not think so? I assented. Did I know, he asked, with a sudden flash of curiosity, "what it was that had induced him to go out there?" "Yes," said I, and forthwith handed him the famous Report for publication, if he thought fit. He glanced through it hurriedly, mumbling all the time, judged "it would do," and took himself off with this plunder.

'Thus I was left at last with a slim packet of letters and the girl's portrait. She struck me as beautiful – I mean she had a beautiful expression. I know that the sunlight can be made to lie, too, yet one felt that no manipulation of light and pose could have conveyed the delicate shade of truthfulness upon those features. She seemed ready to listen without mental reservation, without suspicion, without a thought for herself. I concluded I would go and give her back her portrait and those letters myself. Curiosity? Yes; and also some other feelings perhaps. All that had been Kurtz's had passed out of my hands: his soul, his body, his station, his plans, his ivory, his career. There remained only his memory and his Intended – and I wanted to give that up, too, to the past, in a way – to surrender personally all that remained of him with me to that oblivion which is the last word of our common fate. I don't defend myself. I had no clear perception of what it was I really wanted. Perhaps it was an impulse of unconscious loyalty, or the fulfilment of one of these ironic necessities that lurk in the facts of human existence. I don't know. I can't tell. But I went.

'I thought his memory was like the other memories of the dead that accumulate in every man's life – a vague impress on the brain of shadows that had fallen on it in their swift and final passage; but before the high and ponderous door, between the tall houses of a street as still and decorous as a well-kept alley in a cemetery, I had a vision of him on the stretcher, opening his mouth voraciously, as if to devour all the earth with all its mankind. He lived then before me; he lived as much as he had ever lived – a shadow insatiable of splendid appearances, of frightful realities; a shadow darker than the shadow of the night, and draped nobly in the folds of a gorgeous eloquence. The vision seemed to enter the house with me – the stretcher, the phantom-bearers, the wild crowd of obedient worshippers, the gloom of the forests, the glitter of the reach between the murky bends, the beat of the drum, regular and muffled like the beating of a heart – the heart of a conquering darkness. It was a moment of triumph for the wilderness, an invading and vengeful rush which, it seemed to me, I would have to keep back alone for the salvation of another soul. And the memory of what I had heard him say afar there, with the horned shapes stirring at my back, in the glow of fires, within the patient woods, those broken phrases came back to me, were heard again in their ominous and terrifying simplicity. I remembered his abject pleading, his abject threats, the colossal scale of his vile desires, the meanness, the torment, the tempestuous anguish of his soul. And later on I seemed to see his collected languid manner, when he said one day, "This lot of ivory now is really mine. The Company did not pay for it. I collected it myself at a very great personal risk. I am afraid they will try to claim it at theirs though. H'm. It is a difficult case. What do you think I ought to do – resist? Eh? I want no more than justice." . . . He wanted no more than justice – no more than justice. I rang the bell before a mahogany door on the first floor, and while I waited he seemed to stare at me out of the glassy panel – stare with that wide and immense stare embracing, condemning, loathing all the universe. I seemed to hear the whispered cry, "The horror! The horror!"

'The dusk was falling. I had to wait in a lofty drawing-room with three long windows from floor to ceiling that were like three luminous and bedraped columns. The bent gilt legs and backs of the furniture shone in indistinct curves. The tall marble fireplace had a cold and monumental whiteness. A grand piano stood massively in a corner; with dark gleams on the flat surfaces like a sombre and polished sarcophagus. A high door opened – closed. I rose.

'She came forward, all in black, with a pale head, floating towards me in the dusk. She was in mourning. It was more than a year since his death, more than a year since the news came; she seemed as though she would remember and mourn for ever. She took both my hands in hers and murmured, "I had heard you were coming." I noticed she was not very young – I mean not girlish. She had a mature capacity for fidelity, for belief, for suffering. The room seemed to have grown darker, as if all the sad light of the cloudy evening had taken refuge on her forehead. This fair hair, this pale visage, this pure brow, semed surrounded by an ashy halo from which the dark eyes looked out at me. Their glance was guileless, profound, confident, and trustful. She carried her sorrowful head as though she were proud of that sorrow, as though she would say, I – I alone know how to mourn for him as he deserves. But while we were still shaking hands, such a look of awful desolation came upon her face that I perceived she was one of those creatures that are not the playthings of Time. For her he had died only yesterday. And, by Jove! the impression was so powerful that for me, too, he seemed to have died only yesterday – nay, this very minute. I saw her and him in the same instant of time – his death and her sorrow – I saw her sorrow in the very moment of his death. Do you understand? I saw them together – I heard them together. She had said, with a deep catch of the breath, "I have survived" while my strained ears seemed to hear distinctly, mingled with her tone of despairing regret, the summing up whisper of his eternal condemnation. I asked myself what I was doing there, with a sensation of panic in my heart as though I had blundered into a place of cruel and absurd mysteries not fit for a human being to behold. She motioned me to a chair. We sat down. I laid the packet gently on the little table, and she put her hand over it. . . . "You knew him well," she murmured, after a moment of mourning silence.

' "Intimacy grows quickly out there," I said. "I knew him as well as it is possible for one man to know another."

' "And you admired him," she said. "It was impossible to know him and not to admire him. Was it?"

' "He was a remarkable man," I said, unsteadily. Then before the appealing fixity of her gaze, that seemed to watch for more words on my lips, I went on. "It was impossible not to—"

' "Love him," she finished eagerly, silencing me into an appalled dumbness. "How true! how true! But when you think that no one knew him so well as I! I had all his noble confidence. I knew him best."

' "You knew him best," I repeated. And perhaps she did. But with every word spoken the room was growing darker, and only her forehead, smooth and white, remained illumined by the unextinguishable light of belief and love.

' "You were his friend," she went on. "His friend," she repeated, a little louder. "You must have been, if he had given you this, and sent you to me. I feel I can speak to you – and oh! I must speak. I want you – you who have heard his last words – to know I have been worthy of him. . . . It is not pride. . . . Yes! I am proud to know I understood him better than anyone on earth – he told me so himself. And since his mother died I have had no one – no one – to – to—"

'I listened. The darkness deepened. I was not even sure whether he had given me the right bundle. I rather suspect he wanted me to take care of another batch of his papers which, after his death, I saw the manager examining under the lamp. And the girl talked, easing her pain in the certitude of my sympathy; she talked as thirsty men drink. I had heard that her engagement with Kurtz had been disapproved by her people. He wasn't rich enough or something. And indeed I don't know whether he had not been a pauper all his life. He had given me some reason to infer that it was his impatience of comparative poverty that drove him out there.

' ". . . Who was not his friend who had heard him speak once?" she was saying. "He drew men towards him by what was best in them." She looked at me with intensity. "It is the gift of the great," she went on, and the sound of her low voice seemed to have the accompaniment of all the other sounds, full of mystery, desolation, and sorrow, I had ever heard – the ripple of the river, the soughing of the trees by the wind, the murmurs of the crowds, the faint ring of incomprehensible words cried from afar, the whisper of a voice speaking from beyond the threshold of an eternal darkness. "But you have heard him! You know!" she cried.

' "Yes, I know," I said with something like despair in my heart, but bowing my head before the faith that was in her, before that great and saving illusion that shone with an unearthly glow in the darkness, in the triumphant darkness from which I could not have defended her – from which I could not even defend myself.

' "What a loss to me – to us!" – she corrected herself with beautiful generosity; then added in a murmur, "To the world." By the last gleams of twilight I could see the glitter of her eyes, full of tears – of tears that would not fall.

' "I have been very happy – very fortunate – very proud," she went on. "Too fortunate. Too happy for a little while. And now I am unhappy for – for life."

'She stood up; her fair hair seemed to catch all the remaining light in a glimmer of gold. I rose, too.

' "And of all this," she went on, mournfully, "of all his promise, and of all his greatness, of his generous mind, of his noble heart, nothing remains – nothing but his memory. You and I—"

' "We shall always remember him," I said, hastily.

' "No!" she cried. "It is impossible that all this should be lost —
that such a life should be sacrificed to leave nothing — but sorrow.
You know what vast plans he had. I knew of them, too — I could
not perhaps understand — but others knew them too. Something
must remain. His words, at least, have not died."

' "His words will remain," I said.

' "And his example," she whispered to herself. "Men looked up
to him — his goodness shone in every act. His example—"

' "True," I said; "his example, too. Yes, his example. I forgot
that."

' "But I do not. I cannot — I cannot believe — not yet. I cannot
believe that I shall never see him again, that nobody will see him
again, never, never, never."

'She put out her arms as if after a retreating figure, stretching
them black and with clasped pale hands across the fading and
narrow sheen of the window. Never see him! I saw him clearly
enough then. I shall see this eloquent phantom as long as I live,
and I shall see her, too, a tragic and familiar Shade, resembling in
this gesture another one, tragic also, and bedecked with powerless
charms, stretching bare brown arms over the glitter of the infernal
stream, the stream of darkness. She said suddenly very low, "He
died as he lived."

' "His end," said I, with dull anger stirring in me, "was in every
way worthy of his life."

' "And I was not with him," she murmured. My anger subsided
before a feeling of infinite pity.

' "Everything that could be done—" I mumbled.

' "Ah, but I believed in him more than anyone on earth — more
than his own mother, more than — himself. He needed me! Me! I
would have treasured every sigh, every word, every sign, every
glance."

'I felt a chill grip on my chest. "Don't," I said in a muffled voice.

' "Forgive me. I – I – have mourned so long in silence – in
silence. . . . You were with him — to the last? I think of his
loneliness. Nobody near to understand him as I would have
understood. Perhaps no one to hear . . ."

' "To the very end," I said, shakily. "I heard his very last
words . . ." I stopped in a fright.

' "Repeat them," she murmured in a heart-broken tone. "I want
— I want — something — something — to — to live with."

'I was on the point of crying at her, "Don't you hear them?" The dusk was repeating them in a persistent whisper all around us, in a whisper that seemed to swell menacingly like the first whisper of a rising wind. "The horror! the horror!"

'"His last word – to live with," she insisted. "Don't you understand I loved him – I loved him – I loved him!"

'I pulled myself together and spoke slowly.

'"The last word he pronounced was – your name."

'I heard a light sigh and then my heart stood still, stopped dead short by an exulting and terrible cry, by the cry of inconceivable triumph and of unspeakable pain. "I knew it – I was sure!" . . . She knew. She was sure. I heard her weeping; she had hidden her face in her hands. It seemed to me that the house would collapse before I could escape, that the heavens would fall upon my head. But nothing happened. The heavens do not fall for such a trifle. Would they have fallen, I wonder, if I had rendered Kurtz that justice which was his due? Hadn't he said he wanted only justice? But I couldn't. I could not tell her. It would have been too dark – too dark altogether . . .'

Marlow ceased, and sat apart, indistinct and silent, in the pose of a meditating Buddha. Nobody moved for a time. 'We have lost the first of the ebb,' said the Director, suddenly. I raised my head. The offing was barred by a black bank of clouds, and the tranquil waterway leading to the uttermost ends of the earth flowed sombre under an overcast sky – seemed to lead into the heart of an immense darkness.

The End of the Tether

THE END OF THE TETHER

I

FOR a long time after the course of the steamer *Sofala* had been altered for the land, the low swampy coast had retained its appearance of a mere smudge of darkness beyond a belt of glitter. The sunrays fell violently upon the calm sea — seemed to shatter themselves upon an adamantine surface into sparkling dust, into a dazzling vapour of light that blinded the eye and wearied the brain with its unsteady brightness.

Captain Whalley did not look at it. When his Serang, approaching the roomy cane arm-chair which he filled capably, had informed him in a low voice that the course was to be altered, he had risen at once and had remained on his feet, face forward, while the head of his ship swung through a quarter of a circle. He had not uttered a single word, not even the word to steady the helm. It was the Serang, an elderly, alert, little Malay, with a very dark skin, who murmured the order to the helmsman. And then slowly Captain Whalley sat down again in the arm-chair on the bridge and fixed his eyes on the deck between his feet.

He could not hope to see anything new upon this lane of the sea. He had been on these coasts for the last three years. From Low Cape to Malantan the distance was fifty miles, six hours' steaming for the old ship with the tide, or seven against. Then you steered straight for the land, and by-and-by three palms would appear on the sky, tall and slim, and with their dishevelled heads in a bunch, as if in confidential criticism of the dark mangroves. The *Sofala* would be headed towards the sombre strip of the coast, which at a given moment, as the ship closed with it obliquely, would show several clean shining fractures — the brimful estuary of a river.

Then on through a brown liquid, three parts water and one part black earth, on and on between the low shores, three parts black earth and one part brackish water, the *Sofala* would plough her way upstream, as she had done once every month for these seven years or more, long before he was aware of her existence, long before he had ever thought of having anything to do with her and her invariable voyages. The old ship ought to have known the road better than her men, who had not been kept so long at it without a change; better than the faithful Serang, whom he had brought over from his last ship to keep the captain's watch; better than he himself, who had been her captain for the last three years only. She could always be depended upon to make her courses. Her compasses were never out. She was no trouble at all to take about, as if her great age had given her knowledge, wisdom, and steadiness. She made her landfalls to a degree of the bearing, and almost to a minute of her allowed time. At any moment, as he sat on the bridge without looking up, or lay sleepless in his bed, simply by reckoning the days and the hours he could tell where he was — the precise spot of the beat. He knew it well, too, this monotonous huckster's round, up and down the Straits; he knew its order and its sights and its people. Malacca to begin with, in at daylight and out at dusk, to cross over with a rigid phosphorescent wake this highway of the Far East. Darkness and gleams on the water, clear stars on a black sky, perhaps the lights of a home steamer keeping her unswerving course in the middle, or maybe the elusive shadow of a native craft with her mat sails flitting by silently — and low land on the other side in sight at daylight. At noon the three palms of the next place of call, up a sluggish river. The only white man residing there was a retired young sailor, with whom he had become friendly in the course of many voyages. Sixty miles farther on there was another place of call, a deep bay with only a couple of houses on the beach. And so on, in and out, picking up coastwise cargo here and there, and finishing with a hundred miles' steady steaming through the maze of an archipelago of small islands up to a large native town at the end of the beat. There was a three days' rest for the old ship before he started her again in inverse order, seeing the same shores from another bearing, hearing the same voices in the same places, back again to the *Sofala*'s port of registry on the great highway to the

East, where he would take up a berth nearly opposite the big stone pile of the harbour office till it was time to start again on the old round of 1,600 miles and thirty days. Not a very enterprising life, this, for Captain Whalley, Henry Whalley, otherwise Dare-devil Harry Whalley, of the *Condor*, a famous clipper in her day. No. Not a very enterprising life for a man who had served famous firms, who had sailed famous ships (more than one or two of them his own); who had made famous passages, had been the pioneer of new routes and new trades; who had steered across the unsurveyed tracts of the South Seas, and had seen the sun rise on uncharted islands. Fifty years at sea, and forty out in the East ('a pretty thorough apprenticeship', he used to remark smilingly), had made him honourably known to a generation of shipowners and merchants in all the ports from Bombay clear over to where the East merges into the West upon the coast of the two Americas. His fame remained writ, not very large but plain enough, on the Admiralty charts. Was there not somewhere between Australia and China a Whalley Island and a Condor Reef? On that dangerous coral formation the celebrated clipper had hung stranded for three days, her captain and crew throwing her cargo overboard with one hand and with the other, as it were, keeping off her a flotilla of savage war-canoes. At that time neither the island nor the reef had any official existence. Later the officers of Her Majestry's steam-vessel *Fusilier*, despatched to make a survey of the route, recognized in the adoption of these two names the enterprise of the man and the solidity of the ship. Besides, as any-one who cares may see, the *General Directory* vol. ii. p. 410, begins the description of the 'Malotuor Whalley Passage' with the words: 'This advantageous route, first discovered in 1850 by Captain Whalley in the ship *Condor*,' etc., and ends by recom-mending it warmly to sailing vessels leaving the China ports for the south in the months from December to April inclusive.

This was the clearest gain he had out of life. Nothing could rob him of this kind of fame. The piercing of the Isthmus of Suez, like the breaking of a dam, had let in upon the East a flood of new ships, new men, new methods of trade. It had changed the face of the Eastern seas and the very spirit of their life; so that his early experiences meant nothing whatever to the new generation of seamen.

In those bygone days he had handled many thousands of pounds of his employers' money and of his own; he had attended faithfully, as by law a shipmaster is expected to do, to the conflicting interests of owners, charterers, and underwriters. He had never lost a ship or consented to a shady transaction; and he had lasted well, outlasting in the end the conditions that had gone to the making of his name. He had buried his wife (in the Gulf of Pe-tchi-li), had married off his daughter to the man of her unlucky choice, and had lost more than an ample competence in the crash of the notorious Travancore and Deccan Banking Corporation, whose downfall had shaken the East like an earthquake. And he was sixty-seven years old.

II

HIS AGE sat lightly enough on him; and of his ruin he was not ashamed. He had not been alone to believe in the stability of the Banking Corporation. Men whose judgment in matters of finance was as expert as his seamanship had commended the prudence of his investments, and had themselves lost much money in the great failure. The only difference between him and them was that he had lost his all. And yet not his all. There had remained to him from his lost fortune a very pretty little barque, *Fair Maid*, which he had bought to occupy his leisure of a retired sailor – 'to play with', as he expressed it himself.

He had formally declared himself tired of the sea the year preceding his daughter's marriage. But after the young couple had gone to settle in Melbourne he found out that he could not make himself happy on shore. He was too much of a merchant sea-captain for mere yachting to satisfy him. He wanted the illusion of affairs; and his acquisition of the *Fair Maid* preserved the continuity of his life. He introduced her to his acquaintances in various ports as 'my last command'. When he grew too old to be trusted with a ship, he would lay her up and go ashore to be buried, leaving directions in his will to have the barque towed out and scuttled decently in deep water on the day of the funeral. His daughter would not grudge him the satisfaction of knowing that no stranger would handle his last command after him. With the fortune he was able to leave her, the value of a 500-ton barque was neither here nor there. All this would be said with a jocular twinkle in his eye: the vigorous old man had too much vitality for the sentimentalism of regret; and a little wistfully withal, because he was at home in life, taking a genuine pleasure in its feelings and its possessions; in the dignity of his reputation and his wealth, in his love for his daughter, and in his satisfaction with the ship — the plaything of his lonely leisure.

He had the cabin arranged in accordance with his simple ideal of comfort at sea. A big bookcase (he was a great reader) occupied one side of his stateroom; the portrait of his late wife, a flat bituminous oil-painting representing the profile and one long black ringlet of a young woman, faced his bedplace. Three chronometers ticked him to sleep and greeted him on waking with the tiny competition of their beats. He rose at five every day. The officer of the morning watch, drinking his early cup of coffee aft by the wheel, would hear through the wide orifice of the copper ventilators all the splashings, blowings, and splutterings of his captain's toilet. These noises would be followed by a sustained deep murmur of the Lord's Prayer recited in a loud earnest voice. Five minutes afterwards the head and shoulders of Captain Whalley emerged out of the companion-hatchway. Invariably he paused for a while on the stairs, looking all round at the horizon, upwards at the trim of the sails; inhaling deep draughts of the fresh air. Only then he would step out on the poop, acknowledging the hand raised to the peak of the cap with a majestic and benign 'Good morning to you.' He walked the deck till eight scrupulously. Sometimes, not above twice a year, he had to use a thick cudgel-like stick on account of a stiffness in the hip — a slight touch of rheumatism, he supposed. Otherwise he knew nothing of the ills of the flesh. At the ringing of the breakfast bell he went below to feed his canaries, wind up the chronometers, and take the head of the table. From there he had before his eyes the big carbon photographs of his daughter, her husband, and two fat-legged babies — his grandchildren — set in black frames into the maple-wood bulkheads of the cuddy. After breakfast he dusted the glass over these portraits himself with a cloth, and brushed the oil painting of his wife with a plummet kept suspended from a small brass hook by the side of the heavy gold frame. Then with the door of his stateroom shut, he would sit down on the couch under the portrait to read a chapter out of a thick pocket Bible – her Bible. But on some days he only sat there for half an hour with his finger between the leaves and the closed book resting on his knees. Perhaps he had remembered suddenly how fond of boat-sailing she used to be.

She had been a real shipmate and a true woman, too. It was like an article of faith with him that there never had been, and never could be, a brighter, cheerier home anywhere afloat or ashore than his home under the poop-deck of the *Condor*, with the big main cabin all white and gold, garlanded as if for a perpetual festival with an unfading wreath. She had decorated the centre of every panel with a cluster of home flowers. It took her a twelvemonth to go round the cuddy with this labour of love. To him it had remained a marvel of painting, the highest achievement of taste and skill; and as to old Swinburne, his mate, every time he came down to his meals he stood transfixed with admiration before the progress of the work. You could almost smell these roses, he declared, sniffing the faint flavour of turpentine which at that time pervaded the saloon, and (as he confessed afterwards) made him somewhat less hearty than usual in tackling his food. But there was nothing of the sort to interfere with his enjoyment of her singing. 'Mrs Whalley is a regular out-and-out nightingale, sir,' he would pronounce with a judicial air after listening profoundly over the skylight to the very end of the piece. In fine weather, in the second dog-watch, the two men could hear her trills and roulades going on to the accompaniment of the piano in the cabin. On the very day they got engaged he had written to London for the instrument; but they had been married for over a year before it reached them, coming out round the Cape. The big case made part of the first direct general cargo landed in Hongkong harbour – an event that to the men who walked the busy quays of to-day seemed as hazily remote as the dark ages of history. But Captain Whalley could in a half-hour of solitude live again all his life, with its romance, its idyll, and its sorrow. He had to close her eyes himself. She went away from under the ensign like a sailor's wife, a sailor herself at heart. He had read the service over her, out of her own prayer-book, without a break in his

voice. When he raised his eyes he could see old Swinburne facing
him with his cap pressed to his breast, and his rugged, weather-
beaten, impassive face streaming with drops of water like a lump
of chipped red granite in a shower. It was all very well for that old
sea-dog to cry. He had to read on to the end; but after the splash
he did not remember much of what happened for the next few
days. An elderly sailor of the crew, deft at needlework, put
together a mourning frock for the child out of one of her black
skirts.

He was not likely to forget; but you cannot dam up life like a
sluggish stream. It will break out and flow over a man's troubles,
it will close upon a sorrow like the sea upon a dead body, no
matter how much love has gone to the bottom. And the world is
not bad. People had been very kind to him; especially Mrs
Gardner, the wife of the senior partner in Gardner, Patteson &
Co., the owners of the *Condor*. It was she who volunteered to
look after the little one, and in due course took her to England
(something of a journey in those days, even by the overland mail
route) with her own girls to finish her education. It was ten years
before he saw her again.

As a little child she had never been frightened of bad weather;
she would beg to be taken up on deck in the bosom of his oilskin
coat to watch the big seas hurling themselves upon the *Condor*.
The swirl and crash of the waves seemed to fill her small soul with
a breathless delight. 'A good boy spoiled', he used to say of her in
joke. He had named her Ivy because of the sound of the word, and
obscurely fascinated by a vague association of ideas. She had
twined herself tightly round his heart, and he intended her to cling
close to her father as to a tower of strength; forgetting while she
was little, that in the nature of things she would probably elect to
cling to someone else. But he loved life well enough for even that
event to give him a certain satisfaction, apart from his more
intimate feeling of loss.

After he had purchased the *Fair Maid* to occupy his loneliness,
he hastened to accept a rather unprofitable freight to Australia
simply for the opportunity of seeing his daughter in her own
home. What made him dissatisfied there was not to see that she
clung now to somebody else, but that the prop she had selected
seemed on closer examination 'a rather poor stick' – even in the

matter of health. He disliked his son-in-law's studied civility perhaps more than his method of handling the sum of money he had given Ivy at her marriage. But of his apprehensions he said nothing. Only on the day of his departure, with the hall-door open all ready, holding her hands and looking steadily into her eyes, he had said, 'You know, my dear, all I have is for you and the chicks. Mind you write to me openly.' She had answered him by an almost imperceptible movement of her head. She resembled her mother in the colour of her eyes, and in character – and also in this, that she understood him without many words.

Sure enough she had to write; and some of these letters made Captain Whalley lift his white eyebrows. For the rest he considered he was reaping the true reward of his life by being thus able to produce on demand whatever was needed. He had not enjoyed himself so much in a way since his wife had died. Characteristically enough his son-in-law's punctuality in failure caused him at a distance to feel a sort of kindness towards the man. The fellow was so perpetually being jammed on a lee shore that to charge it all to his reckless navigation would be manifestly unfair. No, no! He knew well what that meant. It was bad luck. His own had been simply marvellous, but he had seen in his life too many good men – seamen and others – go under with the sheer weight of bad luck not to recognize the fatal signs. For all that, he was cogitating on the best way of tying up very strictly every penny he had to leave, when with a preliminary rumble of rumours (whose first sound reached him in Shanghai as it happened), the shock of the big failure came; and, after passing through the phases of stupor, of incredulity, of indignation, he had to accept the fact that he had nothing to speak of to leave.

Upon that, as if he had only waited for this catastrophe, the unlucky man, away there in Melbourne, gave up his unprofitable game, and sat down – in an invalid's bath-chair at that, too. 'He will never walk again,' wrote the wife. For the first time in his life Captain Whalley was a bit staggered.

The *Fair Maid* had to go to work in bitter earnest now. It was no longer a matter of preserving alive the memory of Dare-devil Harry Whalley in the Eastern Seas, or of keeping an old man in pocket-money and clothes, with, perhaps, a bill for a few hundred first-class cigars thrown in at the end of the year. He would have to buckle-to, and keep her going hard on a scant allowance of gilt for the ginger-bread scrolls at her stem and stern.

This necessity opened his eyes to the fundamental changes of the world. Of his past only the familiar names remained, here and there, but the things and the men, as he had known them, were gone. The name of Gardner, Patteson & Co. was still displayed on the walls of warehouses by the waterside, on the brass plates and window-panes in the business quarters of more than one Eastern port, but there was no longer a Gardner or a Patteson in the firm. There was no longer for Captain Whalley an arm-chair and a welcome in the private office, with a bit of business ready to be put in the way of an old friend, for the sake of bygone services. The husbands of the Gardner girls sat behind the desks in that room where, long after he had left the employ, he had kept his right of entrance in the old man's time. Their ships now had yellow funnels with black tops, and a time-table of appointed routes like a confounded service of tramways. The winds of December and June were all one to them; their captains (excellent young men he doubted not) were, to be sure, familiar with Whalley Island, because of late years the Government had established a white fixed light on the north end (with a red danger sector over the Condor Reef), but most of them would have been extremely surprised to hear that a flesh-and-blood Whalley still existed – an old man going about the world trying to pick up a cargo here and there for his little barque.

And everywhere it was the same. Departed the men who would have nodded appreciatively at the mention of his name, and would have thought themselves bound in honour to do something for Dare-devil Harry Whalley. Departed the opportunities which he would have known how to seize; and gone with them the white-winged flock of clippers that lived in the boisterous uncertain life of the winds, skimming big fortunes out of the foam of the sea. In a world that pared down the profits to an irreducible minimum, in a world that was able to count its disengaged tonnage twice over every day and in which lean charters were snapped up by cable three months in advance, there were no chances of fortune for an individual wandering haphazard with a little barque – hardly indeed any room to exist.

He found it more difficult from year to year. He suffered greatly from the smallness of remittances he was able to send his daughter. Meantime he had given up good cigars, and even in the matter of inferior cheroots limited himself to six a day. He never told her of his difficulties, and she never enlarged upon her struggle to live. Their confidence in each other needed no explanations, and their perfect understanding endured without protestations of gratitude or regret. He would have been shocked if she had taken it into her head to thank him in so many words, but he found it perfectly natural that she should tell him she needed two hundred pounds.

He had come in with the *Fair Maid* in ballast to look for a freight in the *Sofala*'s port of registry, and her letter met him there. Its tenor was that it was no use mincing matters. Her only resource was in opening a boarding-house, for which the prospects, she judged, were good. Good enough, at any rate, to make her tell him frankly that with two hundred pounds she could make a start. He had torn the envelope open, hastily, on deck, where it was handed to him by the ship-chandler's runner, who had brought his mail at the moment of anchoring. For the second time in his life he was appalled, and remained stock-still at the cabin door with the paper trembling between his fingers. Open a boarding-house! Two hundred pounds for a start! The only resource! And he did not know where to lay his hands on two hundred pence.

All that night Captain Whalley walked the poop of his anchored ship, as though he had been about to close with the land in thick weather, and uncertain of his position after a run of many grey days without a sight of sun, moon, or stars. The black night twinkled with the guiding lights of seamen and the steady straight lines of lights on shore; and all around the *Fair Maid* the riding lights of ships cast trembling trails upon the water of the roadstead. Captain Whalley saw not a gleam anywhere till the dawn broke and he found out that his clothing was soaked through with the heavy dew.

His ship was awake. He stopped short, stroked his wet beard, and descended the poop ladder backwards, with tired feet. At the sight of him the chief officer, lounging about sleepily on the quarterdeck, remained open-mouthed in the middle of a great early-morning yawn.

'Good morning to you,' pronounced Captain Whalley, solemnly, passing into the cabin. But he checked himself in the doorway, and without locking back. 'By the bye,' he said, 'there should be an empty wooden case put away in the lazarette. It has not been broken up – has it?'

The mate shut his mouth, and then asked as if dazed, 'What empty case, sir?'

'A big flat packing-case belonging to that painting in my room. Let it be taken up on deck and tell the carpenter to look it over. I may want to use it before long.'

The chief officer did not stir a limb till he had heard the door of the captain's stateroom slam within the cuddy. Then he beckoned aft the second mate with his forefinger to tell him that there was something 'in the wind'.

When the bell rang Captain Whalley's authoritative voice boomed out through a closed door, 'Sit down and don't wait for me.' And his impressed officers took their places, exchanging looks and whispers across the table. What! No breakfast? And after apparently knocking about all night on deck, too! Clearly, there was something in the wind. In the skylight above their heads, bowed earnestly over the plates, three wire cages rocked and rattled to the restless jumping of the hungry canaries; and they could detect the sounds of their 'old man's' deliberate movements within his stateroom. Captain Whalley was methodically winding up the chronometers, dusting the portrait of his late wife, getting a clean white shirt out of the drawers, making himself ready in his punctilious, unhurried manner to go ashore. He could not have swallowed a single mouthful of food that morning. He had made up his mind to sell the *Fair Maid*.

III

JUST at that time the Japanese were casting far and wide for ships of European build, and he had no difficulty in finding a purchaser, a speculator who drove a hard bargain, but paid cash down for the *Fair Maid*, with a view to a profitable resale. Thus it came about that Captain Whalley found himself on a certain afternoon

descending the steps of one of the most important post-offices of
the East with a slip of bluish paper in his hand. This was the
receipt of a registered letter enclosing a draft for two hundred
pounds, and addressed to Melbourne. Captain Whalley pushed
the paper into his waistcoat-pocket, took his stick from under his
arm, and walked down the street.

It was a recently opened and untidy thoroughfare with
rudimentary side-walks and a soft layer of dust cushioning the
whole width of the road. One end touched the slummy street of
Chinese shops near the harbour, the other drove straight on,
without houses, for a couple of miles, through patches of jungle-
like vegetation, to the yard gates of the new Consolidated Docks
Company. The crude frontages of the new Government buildings
alternated with the blank fencing of vacant plots, and the view of
the sky seemed to give an added spaciousness to the broad vista. It
was empty and shunned by natives after business hours, as though
they had expected to see one of the tigers from the neighbourhood
of the New Waterworks on the hill coming at a loping canter
down the middle to get a Chinese shopkeeper for supper. Captain
Whalley was not dwarfed by the solitude of the grandly planned
street. He had too fine a presence for that. He was only a lonely
figure walking purposefully, with a great white beard like a
pilgrim, and with a thick stick that resembled a weapon. On one
side the new Courts of Justice had a low and unadorned portico of
squat columns half concealed by a few old trees left in the
approach. On the other the pavilion wings of the new Colonial
Treasury came out to the line of the street. But Captain Whalley,
who had now no ship and no home, remembered in passing that
on that very site when he first came out from England there had
stood a fishing village, a few mat huts erected on piles between a
muddy tidal creek and a miry pathway that went writhing into a
tangled wilderness without any docks or waterworks.

No ship – no home. And his poor Ivy away there had no home
either. A boarding-house is no sort of home though it may get you
a living. His feelings were horribly rasped by the idea of the
boarding-house. In his rank of life he had that truly aristocratic
temperament characterized by a scorn of vulgar gentility and by
prejudiced views as to the derogatory nature of certain occupations. For his own part he had always preferred sailing merchant

ships (which is a straightforward occupation) to buying and selling merchandise of which the essence is to get the better of somebody in a bargain – an undignified trial of wits at best. His father had been Colonel Whalley (retired) of the H.E.I. Company's service, with very slender means besides his pension, but with distinguished connections. He could remember as a boy how frequently waiters at the inns, country tradesmen and small people of that sort, used to 'My lord' the old warrior on the strength of his appearance.

Captain Whalley himself (he would have entered the Navy if his father had not died before he was fourteen) had something of a grand air which would have suited an old and glorious admiral; but he became lost like a straw in the eddy of a brook amongst the swarm of brown and yellow humanity filling a thoroughfare, that by contrast with the vast and empty avenue he had left seemed as narrow as a lane and absolutely riotous with life. The walls of the houses were blue; the shops of the Chinamen yawned like cavernous lairs; heaps of nondescript merchandise overflowed the gloom of the long range of arcades, and the fiery serenity of sunset took the middle of the street from end to end with a glow like the reflection of a fire. It fell on the bright colours and the dark faces of the bare-footed crowd, on the pallid yellow backs of the half-naked jostling coolies, on the accoutrements of a tall Sikh trooper with a parted beard and fierce moustaches on sentry before the gate of the police compound. Looming very big above the heads in a red haze of dust, the tightly packed car of the cable tramway navigated cautiously up the human stream, with the incessant blare of its horn, in the manner of a steamer groping in a fog.

Captain Whalley emerged like a diver on the other side, and in the desert shade between the walls of closed warehouses removed his hat to cool his brow. A certain disrepute attached to the calling of a landlady of a boarding-house. These women were said to be rapacious, unscrupulous, untruthful; and though he condemned no class of his fellow-creatures – God forbid! – these were suspicions to which it was unseemly that a Whalley should lay herself open. He had not expostulated with her, however. He was confident she shared his feelings; he was sorry for her; he trusted her judgment; he considered it a merciful dispensation that he could help her once more – but in his aristocratic heart of hearts

he would have found it more easy to reconcile himself to the idea
of her turning seamstress. Vaguely he remembered reading years
ago a touching piece called the 'Song of the Shirt'. It was all very
well making songs about poor women. The granddaughter of
Colonel Whalley, the landlady of a boarding-house! Pooh! He
replaced his hat, dived into two pockets, and stopping a moment
to apply a flaring match to the end of a cheap cheroot, blew an
embittered cloud of smoke at a world that could hold such
surprises.

Of one thing he was certain – that she was the own child of a
clever mother. Now he had got over the wrench of parting with
his ship, he perceived clearly that such a step had been unavoidable. Perhaps he had been growing aware of it all along with an
unconfessed knowledge. But she, far away there, must have had
an intuitive perception of it, with the pluck to face that truth and
the courage to speak out – all the qualities which had made her
mother a woman of such excellent counsel.

It would have had to come to that in the end! It was fortunate
she had forced his hand. In another year or two it would have been
an utterly barren sale. To keep the ship going he had been
involving himself deeper every year. He was defenceless before the
insidious work of adversity, to whose more open assaults he could
present a firm front; like a cliff that stands unmoved the open
battering of the sea, with a lofty ignorance of the treacherous
backwash undermining its base. As it was, every liability satisfied,
her request answered, and owing no man a penny, there remained
to him from the proceeds a sum of five hundred pounds put away
safely. In addition he had upon his person some forty odd dollars
– enough to pay his hotel bill, providing he did not linger too long
in the modest bedroom where he had taken refuge.

Scantily furnished, and with a waxed floor, it opened into one
of the side-verandahs. The straggling building of bricks, as airy as
a bird-cage, resounded with the incessant flapping of rattan
screens worried by the wind between the whitewashed square
pillars of the sea-front. The rooms were lofty, a ripple of sunshine
flowed over the ceilings; and the periodical invasions of tourists
from some passenger steamer in the harbour flitted through the
wind-swept dusk of the apartments with the tumult of their
unfamiliar voices and impermanent presences, like relays of

migratory shades condemned to speed headlong round the earth without leaving a trace. The babble of their irruptions ebbed out as suddenly as it had arisen; the draughty corridors and the long chairs of the verandahs knew their sightseeing hurry or their prostrate repose no more; and Captain Whalley, substantial and dignified, left well nigh alone in the vast hotel by each light-hearted scurry, felt more and more like a stranded tourist with no aim in view, like a forlorn traveller without a home. In the solitude of his room he smoked thoughtfully, gazing at the two sea-chests which held all that he could call his own in this world. A thick roll of charts in a sheath of sailcloth leaned in a corner; the flat packing-case containing the portrait in oils and the three carbon photographs had been pushed under the bed. He was tired of discussing terms, of assisting at surveys, of all the routine of the business. What to the other parties was merely the sale of a ship was to him a momentous event involving a radically new view of existence. He knew that after this ship there would be no other; and the hopes of his youth, the exercise of his abilities, every feeling and achievement of his manhood, had been indissolubly connected with ships. He had served on ships; he had owned ships; and even the years of his actual retirement from the sea had been made bearable by the idea that he had only to stretch out his hand full of money to get a ship. He had been at liberty to feel as though he were the owner of all the ships in the world. The selling of this one was weary work; but when she passed from him at last, when he signed the last receipt, it was as though all the ships had gone out of the world together, leaving him on the shore of inaccessible oceans with seven hundred pounds in his hands.

Striding firmly, without haste, along the quay, Captain Whalley averted his glances from the familiar roadstead. Two generations of seamen born since his first day at sea stood between him and all these ships at the anchorage. His own was sold, and he had been asking himself, What next?

From the feeling of loneliness, of inward emptiness – and of loss, too, as if his very soul had been taken out of him forcibly – there had sprung at first a desire to start right off and join his daughter. 'Here are the last pence,' he would say to her; 'take them, my dear. And here's your old father: you must take him, too.'

His soul recoiled, as if afraid of what lay hidden at the bottom of this impulse. Give up! Never! When one is thoroughly weary all sorts of nonsense come into one's head. A pretty gift it would have been for a poor woman – this seven hundred pounds with the incumbrance of a hale old fellow more than likely to last for years and years to come. Was he not as fit to die in harness as any of the youngsters in charge of these anchored ships out yonder? He was as solid now as ever he had been. But as to who would give him work to do, that was another matter. Were he, with his appearance and antecedents, to go about looking for a junior's berth, people, he was afraid, would not take him seriously; or else if he succeeded in impressing them, he would maybe obtain their pity, which would be like stripping yourself naked to be kicked. He was not anxious to give himself away for less than nothing. He had no use for anybody's pity. On the other hand, a command – the only thing he could try for with due regard for common decency – was not likely to be lying in wait for him at the corner of the next street. Commands don't go a-begging nowadays. Ever since he had come ashore to carry out the business of the sale he had kept his ears open, but had heard no hint of one being vacant in the port. And even if there had been one, his successful past itself stood in his way. He had been his own employer too long. The only credential he could produce was the testimony of his whole life. What better recommendation could anyone require? But vaguely he felt that the unique document would be looked upon as an archaic curiosity of the Eastern waters, a screed traced in obsolete words – in a half-forgotten language.

IV

REVOLVING these thoughts, he strolled on near the railings of the quay, broad-chested, without a stoop, as though his big shoulders had never felt the burden of the loads that must be carried between the cradle and the grave. No single betraying fold or line of care disfigured the reposeful modelling of his face. It was full and untanned; and the upper part emerged, massively quiet, out of the downward flow of silvery hair, with the striking delicacy of its clear complexion and the powerful width of the forehead. The first cast of his glance fell on you candid and swift, like a boy's; but because of the ragged snowy thatch of the eyebrows the affability of his attention acquired the character of a keen and searching scrutiny. With age he had put on flesh a little, had increased his girth like an old tree presenting no symptoms of decay; and even the opulent, lustrous ripple of white hairs upon his chest seemed an attribute of unquenchable vitality and vigour.

Once rather proud of his great bodily strength, and even of his personal appearance, conscious of his worth, and firm in his rectitude, there had remained to him, like the heritage of departed prosperity, the tranquil bearing of a man who had proved himself fit in every sort of way for the life of his choice. He strode on squarely under the projecting brim of an ancient Panama hat. It had a low crown, a crease through its whole diameter, a narrow black ribbon. Imperishable and a little discoloured, this headgear made it easy to pick him out from afar on thronged wharves and in the busy streets. He had never adopted the comparatively modern fashion of pipeclayed cork helmets. He disliked the form; and he hoped he could manage to keep a cool head to the end of his life without all these contrivances for hygienic ventilation. His hair was cropped close, his linen always of immaculate whiteness; a suit of thin grey flannel, worn threadbare but scrupulously brushed, floated about his burly limbs, adding to his bulk by the looseness of its cut. The years had mellowed the good-humoured, imperturbable audacity of his prime into a temper carelessly serene; and the leisurely tapping of his iron-shod stick accompanied his footfalls with a self-confident sound on the flagstones. It was impossible to connect such a fine presence and this unruffled aspect with the belittling troubles of poverty; the man's whole existence appeared to pass before you, facile and large, in the freedom of means as ample as the clothing of his body.

The irrational dread of having to break into his five hundred pounds for personal expenses in the hotel disturbed the steady poise of his mind. There was no time to lose. The bill was running up. He nourished the hope that this five hundred would perhaps be the means, if everything else failed, of obtaining some work which, keeping his body and soul together (not a matter of great outlay), would enable him to be of use to his daughter. To his mind it was her own money which he employed, as it were, in backing her father and solely for her benefit. Once at work, he would help her with the greater part of his earnings; he was good for many years yet, and this boarding-house business, he argued to himself, whatever the prospects, could not be much of a gold-mine from the first start. But what work? He was ready to lay hold of anything in an honest way so that it came quickly to his hand; because the five hundred pounds must be preserved intact for eventual use. That was the great point. With the entire five hundred one felt a substance at one's back; but it seemed to him that should he let it dwindle to four-fifty or even four-eighty, all the efficiency would be gone out of the money, as though there were some magic power in the round figure. But what sort of work?

Confronted by that haunting question as by an uneasy ghost, for whom he had no exorcizing formula, Captain Whalley stopped short on the apex of a small bridge spanning steeply the bed of a canalized creek with granite shores. Moored between the square blocks a sea-going Malay prau floated half hidden under the arch of masonry, with her spars lowered down, without a sound of life on board, and covered from stem to stern with a ridge of palm-leaf mats. He had left behind him the overheated pavements bordered by the stone frontages that, like the sheer face of cliffs, followed the sweep of the quays; and an unconfined spaciousness of orderly and sylvan aspect opened before him its wide plots of rolled grass, like pieces of green carpet smoothly pegged out, its long ranges of trees lined up in colossal porticos of dark shafts roofed with a vault of branches.

Some of these avenues ended at the sea. It was a terraced shore; and beyond, upon the level expanse, profound and glistening like the gaze of a dark-blue eye, an oblique band of stippled purple lengthened itself indefinitely through the gap between a couple of verdant twin islets. The masts and spars of a few ships far away, hull down in the outer roads, sprang straight from the water in a fine maze of rosy lines pencilled on the clear shadow of the eastern board. Captain Whalley gave them a long glance. The ship, once his own, was anchored out there. It was staggering to think that it was open to him no longer to take a boat at the jetty and get himself pulled off to her when the evening came. To no ship.

Perhaps never more. Before the sale was concluded, and till the purchase-money had been paid, he had spent daily some time on board the *Fair Maid*. The money had been paid this very morning, and now, all at once, there was positively no ship that he could go on board of when he liked; no ship that would need his presence in order to do her work — to live. It seemed an incredible state of affairs, something too bizarre to last. And the sea was full of craft of all sorts. There was that prau lying so still swathed in her shroud of sewn palm-leaves — she, too, had her indispensable man. They lived through each other, this Malay he had never seen, and this high-sterned thing of no size that seemed to be resting after a long journey. And of all the ships in sight, near and far, each was provided with a man, the man without whom the finest ship is a dead thing, a floating and purposeless log.

After his one glance at the roadstead he went on since there was nothing to turn back for, and the time must be got through somehow. The avenues of big trees ran straight over the Esplanade, cutting each other at diverse angles, columnar below and luxuriant above. The interlaced boughs high up there seemed to slumber; not a leaf stirred overhead: and the reedy cast-iron lamp-posts in the middle of the road, gilt like sceptres diminished in a long perspective, with their globes of white porcelain atop, resembling a barbarous decoration of ostriches' eggs displayed in a row. The flaming sky kindled a tiny crimson spark upon the glistening surface of each glassy shell.

With his chin sunk a little, his hands behind his back, and the end of his stick marking the gravel with a faint wavering line at his heels, Captain Whalley reflected that if a ship without a man was like a body without a soul, a sailor without a ship was of not much more account in this world than an aimless log adrift upon the sea. The log might be sound enough by itself, tough of fibre, and hard to destroy — but what of that! And a sudden sense of irremediable idleness weighted his feet like a great fatigue.

A succession of open carriages came bowling along the newly opened sea-road. You could see across the wide grass-plots the discs of vibration made by the spokes. The bright domes of the parasols swayed lightly outwards like full-blown blossoms on the rim of a vase; and the quiet sheet of dark-blue water, crossed by a bar of purple, made a background for the spinning wheels and the high action of the horses, whilst the turbaned heads of the Indian servants elevated above the line of the sea horizon glided rapidly on the paler blue of the sky. In an open space near the little bridge each turn-out trotted smartly in a wide curve away from the sunset; then pulling up sharp, entered the main alley in a long slow-moving file with the great red stillness of the sky at the back. The trunks of mighty trees stood all touched with red on the same side, the air seemed aflame under the high foliage, the very ground under the hoofs of the horses was red. The wheels turned solemnly; one after another the sunshades drooped, folding their colours like gorgeous flowers shutting their petals at the end of the day. In the whole half-mile of human beings no voice uttered a distinct word, only a faint thudding noise went on mingled with slight jingling sounds, and the motionless heads and shoulders of men and women sitting in couples emerged stolidly above the lower hoods – as if wooden. But one carriage and pair coming late did not join the line.

It fled along in a noiseless roll; but on entering the avenue one of the dark bays snorted, arching his neck and shying against the steel-tipped pole; a flake of foam fell from the bit upon the point of a satiny shoulder, and the dusky face of the coachman leaned forward at once over the hands taking a fresh grip of the reins. It was a long dark-green landau, having a dignified and buoyant motion between the sharply curved C-springs, and a sort of strictly official majesty in its supreme elegance. It seemed more roomy than is usual, its horses seemed slightly bigger, the appointments a shade more perfect, the servants perched somewhat higher on the box. The dresses of three women – two young and pretty, and one, handsome, large, of mature age – seemed to fill completely the shallow body of the carriage. The fourth face was that of a man, heavy lidded, distinguished and sallow, with a sombre, thick, iron-grey imperial and moustaches, which somehow had the air of solid appendages. His Excellency—

The rapid motion of that one equipage made all the others appear utterly inferior, blighted, and reduced to crawl painfully at a snail's pace. The landau distanced the whole file in a sort of sustained rush; the features of the occupants whirling out of sight left behind an impression of fixed stares and impassive vacancy; and after it had vanished in full flight as it were, notwithstanding the long line of vehicles hugging the curb at a walk, the whole lofty vista of the avenue seemed to lie open and emptied of life in the enlarged impression of an august solitude.

Captain Whalley had lifted his head to look, and his mind, disturbed in its meditation, turned with wonder (as men's minds will do) to matters of no importance. It struck him that it was to this port, where he had just sold his last ship, that he had come with the very first he had ever owned, and with his head full of a plan for opening a new trade with a distant part of the Archipelago. The then governor had given him no end of encouragement. No Excellency he – this Mr Denham – this governor with his jacket off; a man who tended night and day, so to speak, the growing prosperity of the settlement with the self-forgetful devotion of a nurse for a child she loves; a lone bachelor who lived as in a camp with the few servants and his three dogs in what was called then the Government Bungalow: a low-roofed structure on the half-cleared slope of a hill, with a new flagstaff in front and a police orderly on the verandah. He remembered toiling up that hill under a heavy sun for his audience; the unfurnished aspect of the cool shaded room; the long table covered at one end with piles of papers, and with two guns, a brass telescope, a small bottle of oil with a feather stuck in the neck at the other – and the flattering attention given to him by the man in power. It was an undertaking full of risk he had come to expound, but a twenty minutes' talk in the Government Bungalow on the hill had made it go smoothly from the start. And as he was retiring Mr Denham, already seated before the papers, called out after him, 'Next month the *Dido* starts for a cruise that way, and I shall request her captain officially to give you a look in and see how you get on.' The *Dido* was one of the smart frigates on the China station – and five-and-thirty years make a big slice of time. Five-and-thirty years ago an enterprise like his had for the colony enough importance to be looked after by a Queen's ship. A big slice of time. Individuals were of some account then. Men like himself; men, too, like poor Evans, for instance, with his red face, his coal-black whiskers, and his restless eyes, who had set up the first patent slip for repairing small ships, on the edge of the forest, in a lonely bay three miles up the coast. Mr Denham had encouraged that enterprise, too, and yet somehow poor Evans had ended by dying at home deucedly hard up. His son, they said, was squeezing oil out of cocoanuts for a living on some God-forsaken islet of the Indian Ocean; but it was from that patent slip in a lonely wooded bay that had sprung the workshops of the Consolidated Docks Company, with its three graving basins carved out of solid rock, its wharves, its jetties, its electric-light plant, its steam-power houses – with its gigantic sheer-legs, fit to lift the heaviest weight ever carried afloat, and whose head could be seen like the top of a queer white monument peeping over busy points of land and sandy promontories, as you approached the New Harbour from the west.

There had been a time when men counted: there were not so many carriages in the colony then, though Mr Denham, he fancied, had a buggy. And Captain Whalley seemed to be swept out of the great avenue by the swirl of a mental backwash. He remembered muddy shores, a harbour without quays, the one solitary wooden pier (but that was a public work) jutting out crookedly, the first coal-sheds erected on Monkey Point, that caught fire mysteriously and smouldered for days, so that amazed ships came into a roadstead full of sulphurous fog, and the sun hung blood-red at midday. He remembered the things, the faces, and something more besides – like the faint flavour of a cup quaffed to the bottom, like a subtle sparkle of the air that was not to be found in the atmosphere of today.

In this evocation, swift and full of detail like a flash of magnesium light into the niches of a dark memorial hall, Captain Whalley contemplated things once important, the efforts of small men, the growth of a great place, but now robbed of all consequence by the greatness of accomplished facts, by hopes greater still; and they gave him for a moment such an almost physical grip upon time, such a comprehension of our unchange-able feelings, that he stopped short, struck the ground with his stick, and ejaculated mentally, 'What the devil am I doing here!' He seemed lost in a sort of surprise; but he heard his name called out in wheezy tones once, twice – and turned on his heels slowly.

He beheld then, waddling towards him autocratically, a man of an old-fashioned and gouty aspect, with hair as white as his own, but with shaved, florid cheeks, wearing a necktie – almost a neckcloth – whose stiff ends projected far beyond his chin; with round legs, round arms, a round body, a round face – generally producing the effect of his short figure having been distended by means of an air-pump as much as the seams of his clothing would stand. This was the Master-Attendant of the port. A master-attendant is a superior sort of harbour-master; a person, out in the East, of some consequence in his sphere, a Government official, a magistrate for the waters of the port, and possessed of vast but ill-defined disciplinary authority over seamen of all classes. This particular Master-Attendant was reported to consider it miserably inadequate, on the ground that it did not include the power of life and death. This was a jocular exaggeration. Captain Eliott was fairly satisfied with his position, and nursed no inconsiderable sense of such power as he had. His conceited and tyrannical disposition did not allow him to let it dwindle in his hands for want of use. The uproarious, choleric frankness of his comments on people's character and conduct caused him to be feared at bottom. Though in conversation many pretended not to mind him in the least, others would only smile sourly at the mention of his name, and there were even some who dared to pronounce him 'a meddlesome old ruffian'. But for almost all of them one of Captain Eliott's outbreaks was nearly as distasteful to face as a chance of annihilation.

V

As soon as he had come up quite close he said, mouthing in a growl –

'What's this I hear, Whalley? Is it true you're selling the *Fair Maid*?'

Captain Whalley, looking away, said the thing was done – money had been paid that morning; and the other expressed at once his approbation of such an extremely sensible proceeding. He had got out of his trap to stretch his legs, he explained, on his way home to dinner. Sir Frederick looked well at the end of his time. Didn't he?

Captain Whalley could not say; had only noticed the carriage going past.

The Master-Attendant, plunging his hands into the pockets of an alpaca jacket inappropriately short and tight for a man of his age and appearance, strutted with a slight limp, and with his head reaching only to the shoulder of Captain Whalley, who walked easily, staring straight before him. They had been good comrades years ago, almost intimates. At the time when Whalley commanded the renowned *Condor*, Eliott had charge of the nearly as famous *Ringdove* for the same owners; and when the appointment of Master-Attendant was created, Whalley would have been the only other serious candidate. But Captain Whalley, then in the prime of life, was resolved to serve no one but his own auspicious Fortune. Far away, tending his hot irons, he was glad to hear the other had been successful. There was a worldly suppleness in bluff Ned Eliott that would serve him well in that sort of official appointment. And they were so dissimilar at bottom that as they came slowly to the end of the avenue before the Cathedral, it had never come into Whalley's head that he might have been in that man's place – provided for to the end of his days.

The sacred edifice, standing in solemn isolation amongst the converging avenues of enormous trees, as if to put grave thoughts of heaven into the hours of ease, presented a closed Gothic portal to the light and glory of the west. The glass of the rosace above the ogive glowed like fiery coal in the deep carvings of a wheel of stone. The two men faced about.

'I'll tell you what they ought to do next, Whalley,' growled Captain Eliott suddenly.

'Well?'

'They ought to send a real live lord out here when Sir Frederick's time is up. Eh?'

Captain Whalley perfunctorily did not see why a lord of the right sort should not do as well as anyone else. But this was not the other's point of view.

'No, no. Place runs itself. Nothing can stop it now. Good enough for a lord,' he growled in short sentences. 'Look at the changes in our own time. We need a lord here now. They have got a lord in Bombay.'

He dined once or twice every year at the Government House – a many-windowed, arcaded palace upon a hill laid out in roads and gardens. And lately he had been taking about a duke in his

Master-Attendant's steam-launch to visit the harbour improvements. Before that he had 'most obligingly' gone out in person to pick out a good berth for the ducal yacht. Afterwards he had an invitation to lunch on board. The duchess herself lunched with them. A big woman with a big red face. Complexion quite sunburnt. He should think ruined. Very gracious manners. They were going on to Japan. . . .

He ejaculated these details for Captain Whalley's edification, pausing to blow out his cheeks as if with a pent-up sense of importance, and repeatedly protruding his thick lips till the blunt crimson end of his nose seemed to dip into the milk of his moustache. The place ran itself; it was fit for any lord; it gave no trouble except in its Marine department – in its Marine department, he repeated twice, and after a heavy snort began to relate how the other day Her Majesty's Consul-General in French Cochin-China had cabled to him – in his official capacity – asking for a qualified man to be sent over to take charge of a Glasgow ship whose master had died in Saigon.

'I sent word of it to the officers' quarters in the Sailors' Home,' he continued, while the limp in his gait seemed to grow more accentuated with the increasing irritation of his voice. 'Place's full of them. Twice as many men as there are berths going in the local trade. All hungry for an easy job. Twice as many – and – What d'you think, Whalley? . . .'

He stopped short; his hands, clenched and thrust deeply downwards, seemed ready to burst the pockets of his jacket. A slight sigh escaped Captain Whalley.

'Hey? You would think they would be falling over each other. Not a bit of it. Frightened to go home. Nice and warm out here to lie about a verandah waiting for a job. I sit and wait in my office. Nobody. What did they suppose? That I was going to sit there like a dummy with the Consul-General's cable before me? Not likely. So I looked up a list of them I keep by me and sent word for Hamilton – the worst loafer of them all – and just made him go. Threatened to instruct the steward of the Sailors' Home to have him turned out neck and crop. He did not think the berth was good enough – if you – please. "I've your little record by me," said I. "You came ashore here eighteen months ago, and you haven't done six months' work since. You are in debt for your board now

at the Home, and I suppose you reckon the Marine Office will pay
in the end. Eh? So it shall; but if you don't take this chance, away
you go to England, assisted passage, by the first homeward
steamer that comes along. You are no better than a pauper. We
don't want any white paupers here." I scared him. But look at the
trouble all this gave me.'

'You would not have had any trouble,' Captain Whalley said
almost involuntarily, 'if you had sent for me.'

Captain Eliott was immensely amused; he shook with laughter
as he walked. But suddenly he stopped laughing. A vague
recollection had crossed his mind. Hadn't he heard it said at the
time of the Travancore and Deccan smash that poor Whalley had
been cleaned out completely. 'Fellow's hard up, by heavens!' he
thought; and at once he cast a sidelong upwards glance at his
companion. But Captain Whalley was smiling austerely straight
before him, with a carriage of the head inconceivable in a
penniless man – and he became reassured. Impossible. Could not
have lost everything. That ship had been only a hobby of his. And
the reflection that a man who had confessed to receiving that very
morning a presumably large sum of money was not likely to
spring upon him a demand for a small loan put him entirely at his
ease again. There had come a long pause in their talk, however,
and not knowing how to begin again, he growled out soberly, 'We
old fellows ought to take a rest now.'

'The best thing for some of us would be to die at the oar,'
Captain Whalley said, negligently.

'Come, now. Aren't you a bit tired by this time of the whole
show?' muttered the other, sullenly.

'Are you?'

Captain Eliott was. Infernally tired. He only hung on to his
berth so long in order to get his pension on the highest scale before
he went home. It would be no better than poverty, anyhow; still, it
was the only thing between him and the workhouse. And he had a
family. Three girls, as Whalley knew. He gave 'Harry, old boy', to
understand that these three girls were a source of the greatest
anxiety and worry to him. Enough to drive a man distracted.

'Why? What have they been doing now?' asked Captain
Whalley with a sort of amused absent-mindedness.

'Doing! Doing nothing. That's just it. Lawn-tennis and silly
novels from morning to night. . . .'

If one of them at least had been a boy! But all three! And, as ill-luck would have it, there did not seem to be any decent young fellows left in the world. When he looked around in the club he saw only a lot of conceited popinjays too selfish to think of making a good woman happy. Extreme indigence stared him in the face with all that crowd to keep at home. He had cherished the idea of building himself a little house in the country – in Surrey –to end his days in, but he was afraid it was out of the question . . . and his staring eyes rolled upwards with such a pathetic anxiety that Captain Whalley charitably nodded down at him, restraining a sort of sickening desire to laugh.

'You must know what it is yourself, Harry. Girls are the very devil for worry and anxiety.'

'Ay! But mine is doing well,' Captain Whalley pronounced slowly, staring to the end of the avenue.

The Master-Attendant was glad to hear this. Uncommonly glad. He remembered her well. A pretty girl she was.

Captain Whalley, stepping out carelessly, assented as if in a dream:

'She was pretty.'

The procession of carriages was breaking up.

One after another they left the file to go off at a trot, animating the vast avenue with their scattered life and movement; but soon the aspect of dignified solitude returned and took possession of the straight wide road. A syce in white stood at the head of a Burmah pony harnessed to a varnished two-wheel cart; and the whole thing waiting by the curb seemed no bigger than a child's toy forgotten under the soaring trees. Captain Eliott waddled up to it and made as if to clamber in, but refrained; and keeping one hand resting easily on the shaft, he changed the conversation from his pension, his daughters, and his poverty back again to the only other topic in the world – the Marine Office, the men and the ships of the port.

He proceeded to give instances of what was expected of him; and his thick voice drowsed in the still air like the obstinate droning of an enormous bumble-bee. Captain Whalley did not know what was the force or the weakness that prevented him from saying Good night and walking away. It was as though he had been too tired to make the effort. How queer. More queer than any of Ned's instances. Or was it that overpowering sense of idleness alone that made him stand there and listen to these stories? Nothing very real had ever troubled Ned Eliott; and gradually he seemed to detect deep in, as if wrapped up in the gross wheezy rumble, something of the clear hearty voice of the young captain of the *Ringdove*. He wondered if he, too, had changed to the same extent; and it seemed to him that the voice of his old chum had not changed so very much — that the man was the same. Not a bad fellow the pleasant, jolly Ned Eliott, friendly, well up to his business — and always a bit of a humbug. He remembered how he used to amuse his poor wife. She could read him like an open book. When the *Condor* and the *Ringdove* happened to be in port together, she would frequently ask him to bring Captain Eliott to dinner. They had not met often since those old days. Not once in five years, perhaps. He regarded from under his white eyebrows this man he could not bring himself to take into his confidence at this juncture; and the other went on with his intimate outpourings, and as remote from his hearer as though he had been talking on a hill-top a mile away.

He was in a bit of a quandary now as to the steamer *Sofala*. Ultimately every hitch in the port came into his hands to undo. They would miss him when he was gone in another eighteen months, and most likely some retired naval officer had been pitchforked into the appointment — a man that would understand nothing and care less. That steamer was a coasting craft having a steady trade connection as far north as Tenasserim; but the trouble was she could get no captain to take her on her regular trip. Nobody would go in her. He really had no power, of course, to order a man to take a job. It was all very well to stretch a point on the demand of a consul-general, but. . . .

'What's the matter with the ship?' Captain Whalley interrupted in measured tones.

'Nothing's the matter. Sound old steamer. Her owner has been in my office this afternoon tearing his hair.'

'Is he a white man?' asked Whalley in an interested voice.

'He calls himself a white man,' answered the Master-Attendant scornfully; 'but if so, it's just skin-deep and no more. I told him that to his face, too.'

'But who is he, then?'

'He's the chief engineer of her. See *that*, Harry?'

'I see,' Captain Whalley said, thoughtfully. 'The engineer. I see.'

How the fellow came to be a shipowner at the same time was quite a tale. He came out third in a home ship nearly fifteen years ago, Captain Eliott remembered, and got paid off after a bad sort of row both with his skipper and his chief. Anyway, they seemed jolly glad to get rid of him at all costs. Clearly a mutinous sort of chap. Well, he remained out here, a perfect nuisance, everlastingly shipped and unshipped, unable to keep a berth very long, pretty nigh went through every engine-room afloat belonging to the colony. Then suddenly, 'What do you think happened, Harry?'

Captain Whalley, who seemed lost in a mental effort as of doing a sum in his head, gave a slight start. He really couldn't imagine. The Master-Attendant's voice vibrated dully with hoarse emphasis. The man actually had the luck to win the second great prize in the Manila lottery. All these engineers and officers of ships took tickets in that gamble. It seemed to be a perfect mania with them all.

Everybody expected now that he would take himself off home with his money, and go to the devil in his own way. Not at all. The *Sofala*, judged too small and not quite modern enough for the sort of trade she was in, could be got for a moderate price from her owners, who had ordered a new steamer from Europe. He rushed in and bought her. This man had never given any signs of that sort of mental intoxication the mere fact of getting hold of a large sum of money may produce – not till he got a ship of his own; but then he went off his balance all at once: came bouncing into the Marine Office on some transfer business, with his hat hanging over his left eye and switching a little cane in his hand, and told each one of the clerks separately that 'Nobody could put him out now. It was his turn. There was no one over him on earth, and there never would be either.' He swaggered and strutted between the desks, talking at the top of his voice, and trembling like a leaf all the while, so that the current business of the office was suspended for the time he was in there, and everybody in the big room stood open-mouthed looking at his antics. Afterwards he could be seen during the hottest hours of the day with his face as red as fire rushing along up and down the quays to look at his ship from different points of view: he seemed inclined to stop every stranger he came

across just to let them know 'that there would be no longer anyone over him; he had bought a ship; nobody on earth could put
him out of his engine-room now'.

Good bargain as she was, the price of the *Sofala* took up pretty
near all the lottery-money. He had left himself no capital to work
with. That did not matter so much, for these were the halcyon
days of steam coasting trade, before some of the home shipping
firms had thought of establishing local fleets to feed their main
lines. These, when once organized, took the biggest slices out of
that cake, of course; and by-and-by a squad of confounded
German tramps turned up east of Suez Canal and swept up all the
crumbs. They prowled on the cheap to and fro along the coast and
between the islands, like a lot of sharks in the water ready to snap
up anything you let drop. And then the high old times were over
for good; for years the *Sofala* had made no more, he judged, than
a fair living. Captain Eliott looked upon it as his duty in every way
to assist an English ship to hold her own; and it stood to reason
that if for want of a captain the *Sofala* began to miss her trips she
would very soon lose her trade. There was the quandary. The man
was too impracticable. 'Too much of a beggar on horseback from
the first,' he explained. 'Seemed to grow worse as the time went
on. In the last three years he's run through eleven skippers; he had
tried every single man here, outside of the regular lines. I had
warned him before that this would not do. And now, of course, no
one will look at the *Sofala*. I had one or two men up at my office
and talked to them; but, as they said to me, what was the good of
taking the berth to lead a regular dog's life for a month and then
get the sack at the end of the first trip? The fellow, of course, told
me it was all nonsense; there has been a plot hatching for years
against him. And now it had come. All the horrid sailors in the
port had conspired to bring him to his knees, because he was an
engineer.' Captain Eliott emitted a throaty chuckle.

'And the fact is, that if he misses a couple more trips he need
never trouble himself to start again. He won't find any cargo in his
old trade. There's too much competition nowadays for people to
keep their stuff lying about for a ship that does not turn up when
she's expected. It's a bad look-out for him. He swears he will shut
himself on board and starve to death in his cabin rather than sell
her — even if he could find a buyer. And that's not likely in the

least. Not even the Japs would give her insured value for her. It isn't like selling sailing-ships. Steamers *do* get out of date, besides getting old.'

'He must have laid by a good bit of money though,' observed Captain Whalley, quietly.

The Harbour-Master puffed out his purple cheeks to an amazing size.

'Not a stiver, Harry. Not – a – single sti-ver.'

He waited; but as Captain Whalley, stroking his beard slowly, looked down on the ground without a word, he tapped him on the forearm, tiptoed, and said in a hoarse whisper –

'The Manila lottery has been eating him up.'

He frowned a little, nodding in tiny affirmative jerks. They all were going in for it; a third of the wages paid to ships' officers ('in my port,' he snorted) went to Manila. It was a mania. That fellow Massy had been bitten by it like the rest of them from the first; but after winning once he seemed to have persuaded himself he had only to try again to get another big prize. He had taken dozens and scores of tickets for every drawing since. What with this vice and his ignorance of affairs, ever since he had improvidently bought that steamer he had been more or less short of money.

This, in Captain Eliott's opinion, gave an opening for a sensible sailor-man with a few pounds to step in and save that fool from the consequences of his folly. It was his craze to quarrel with his captains. He had had some really good men, too, who would have been too glad to stay if he would only let them. But no. He seemed to think he was no owner unless he was kicking somebody out in the morning and having a row with the new man in the evening. What was wanted for him was a master with a couple of hundred or so to take an interest in the ship on proper conditions. You don't discharge a man for no fault, only because of the fun of telling him to pack up his traps and go ashore, when you know that in that case you are bound to buy back his share. On the other hand, a fellow with an interest in the ship is not likely to throw up his job in a huff about a trifle. He had told Massy that. He had said: ' "This won't do, Mr Massy. We are getting very sick of you here in the Marine Office. What you must do now is to try whether you could get a sailor to join you as partner. That seems to be the only way." And that was sound advice, Harry.'

Captain Whalley, leaning on his stick, was perfectly still all over, and his hand, arrested in the act of stroking, grasped his whole beard. And what did the fellow say to that?

The fellow had the audacity to fly out at the Master-Attendant. He had received the advice in a most impudent manner. 'I didn't come here to be laughed at,' he had shrieked. 'I appeal to you as an Englishman and a shipowner brought to the verge of ruin by an illegal conspiracy of your beggarly sailors, and all you condescend to do for me is to tell me to go and get a partner!'. . . The fellow had presumed to stamp with rage on the floor of the private office. Where was he going to get a partner? Was he being taken for a fool? Not a single one of that contemptible lot ashore at the 'Home' had twopence in his pocket to bless himself with. The very native curs in the bazaar knew that much. . . . 'And it's true enough, Harry,' rumbled Captain Eliott, judicially. 'They are much more likely one and all to owe money to the Chinamen in Denham Road for the clothes on their backs. "Well," said I, "you make too much noise over it for my taste, Mr Massy. Good morning." He banged the door after him; he dared to bang my door, confound his cheek!'

The head of the Marine department was out of breath with indignation; then recollecting himself as it were, 'I'll end by being late to dinner – yarning with you here . . . wife doesn't like it.'

He clambered ponderously into the trap; leaned out sideways, and only then wondered wheezily what on earth Captain Whalley could have been doing with himself of late. They had had no sight of each other for years and years till the other day when he had seen him unexpectedly in the office.

What on earth. . . .

Captain Whalley seemed to be smiling to himself in his white beard.

'The earth is big,' he said, vaguely.

The other, as if to test the statement, stared all round from his driving-seat. The Esplanade was very quiet; only from afar, from very far, a long way from the sea-shore, across the stretches of grass, through the long ranges of trees, came faintly the toot – toot – toot of the cable car beginning to roll before the empty peristyle of the Public Library on its three-mile journey to the New Harbour Docks.

'Doesn't seem to be so much room on it,' growled the Master-Attendant, 'since these Germans came along shouldering us at every turn. It was not so in our time.'

He fell into deep thought, breathing stertorously, as though he had been taking a nap open-eyed. Perhaps he, too, on his side, had detected in the silent pilgrim-like figure, standing there by the wheel, like an arrested wayfarer, the buried lineaments of the features belonging to the young captain of the *Condor*. Good fellow – Harry Whalley – never very talkative. You never knew what he was up to – a bit too off-hand with people of consequence, and apt to take a wrong view of a fellow's actions. Fact was he had a too good opinion of himself. He would have liked to tell him to get in and drive him home to dinner. But one never knew. Wife would not like it.

'And it's funny to think, Harry,' he went on in a big subdued drone, 'that of all the people on it there seems only you and I left to remember this part of the world as it used to be. . . .'

He was ready to indulge in the sweetness of a sentimental mood had it not struck him suddenly that Captain Whalley, unstirring and without a word, seemed to be awaiting something – perhaps expecting. . . . He gathered the reins at once and burst out in bluff hearty growls –

'Ha! My dear boy. The men we have known – the ships we've sailed – ay! and the things we've done. . . .'

The pony plunged – the syce skipped out of the way. Captain Whalley raised his arm.

'Good bye.'

VI

THE sun had set. And when, after drilling a deep hole with his stick, he moved from that spot the night had massed its army of shadows under the trees. They filled the eastern ends of the avenue as if only waiting the signal for a general advance upon the open spaces of the world; they were gathering low between the deep stone-faced banks of the canal. The Malay prau, half concealed under the arch of the bridge, had not altered its position a quarter of an inch. For a long time Captain Whalley stared down over the parapet, till at last the floating immobility of that beshrouded thing seemed to grow upon him into something inexplicable and alarming. The twilight abandoned the zenith; its reflected gleams left the world below, and the water of the canal seemed to turn into pitch. Captain Whalley crossed it.

The turning to the right, which was his way to his hotel, was only a very few steps farther. He stopped again (all the houses of the sea-front were shut up, the quayside was deserted, but for one or two figures of natives walking in the distance) and began to reckon the amount of his bill. So many days in the hotel at so many dollars a day. To count the days he used his fingers: plunging one hand into his pocket, he jingled a few silver coins. All right for three days more; and then, unless something turned up, he must break into the five hundred – Ivy's money – invested in her father. It seemed to him that the first meal coming out of that reserve would choke him – for certain. Reason was of no use. It was a matter of feeling. His feelings had never played him false.

He did not turn to the right. He walked on, as if there still had been a ship in the roadstead to which he could get himself pulled off in the evening. Far away, beyond the houses, on the slope of an indigo promontory closing the view of the quays, the slim column of a factory-chimney smoked quietly straight up into the clear air. A Chinaman, curled down in the stern of the half-dozen sampans floating off the end of the jetty, caught sight of a beckoning hand. He jumped up, rolled his pigtail round his head swiftly, tucked in two rapid movements his wide dark trousers high up his yellow thighs, and by a single, noiseless, finlike stir of the oars, sheered the sampan alongside the steps with the ease and precision of a swimming fish.

'*Sofala*,' articulated Captain Whalley from above; and the Chinaman, a new emigrant probably, stared upwards with a tense attention as if waiting to see the queer word fall visibly from the white man's lips. '*Sofala*,' Captain Whalley repeated; and suddenly his heart failed him. He paused. The shores, the islets, the high ground, the low points, were dark: the horizon had grown sombre; and across the eastern sweep of the shore the white obelisk, marking the landing-place of the telegraph-cable, stood like a pale ghost on the beach before the dark spread of uneven roofs, intermingled with palms, of the native town. Captain Whalley began again:

'*Sofala*. Savee *So-fa-la*, John?'

This time the Chinaman made out that bizarre sound, and grunted his assent uncouthly, low down in his bare throat. With the first yellow twinkle of a star that appeared like the head of a pin stabbed deep into the smooth, pale, shimmering fabric of the sky, the edge of a keen chill seemed to cleave through the warm air of the earth. At the moment of stepping into the sampan to go and try for the command of the *Sofala* Captain Whalley shivered a little.

When on his return he landed on the quay again, Venus, like a choice jewel set low on the hem of the sky, cast a faint gold trail behind him upon the roadstead, as level as a floor made of one dark and polished stone. The lofty vaults of the avenues were black – all black overhead – and the porcelain globes on the lamp-posts resembled egg-shaped pearls, gigantic and luminous, displayed in a row whose farther end seemed to sink in the distance, down to the level of his knees. He put his hands behind his back. He would now consider calmly the discretion of it before saying the final word to-morrow. His feet scrunched the gravel loudly – the discretion of it. It would have been easier to appraise had there been a workable alternative. The honesty of it was indubitable: he meant well by the fellow; and periodically his shadow leaped up intense by his side on the trunks of the trees, to lengthen itself, oblique and dim, far over the grass – repeating his stride.

The discretion of it. Was there a choice? He seemed already to have lost something of himself; to have given up to a hungry spectre something of his truth and dignity in order to live. But his life was necessary. Let poverty do its worst in exacting its toll of humiliation. It was certain that Ned Eliott had rendered him, without knowing it, a service for which it would have been impossible to ask. He hoped Ned would not think there had been something underhand in his action. He supposed that now when he heard of it he would understand – or perhaps he would only think Whalley an eccentric old fool. What would have been the good of telling him – any more than of blurting the whole tale to that man Massy? Five hundred pounds ready to invest. Let him make the best of that. Let him wonder. You want a captain – I want a ship. That's enough. B-r-r-r-r. What a disagreeable impression that empty, dark, echoing steamer had made upon him. . . .

A laid-up steamer was a dead thing and no mistake; a sailing-ship somehow seems always ready to spring into life with the breath of incorruptible heaven; but a steamer, thought Captain Whalley, with her fires out, without the warm whiffs from below meeting you on her decks, without the hiss of steam, the clangs of iron in her breast – lies there as cold and still and pulseless as a corpse.

In the solitude of the avenue, all black above and lighted below, Captain Whalley, considering the discretion of his course, met, as it were incidentally, the thought of death. He pushed it aside with dislike and contempt. He almost laughed at it; and in the unquenchable vitality of his age only thought with a kind of exultation how little he needed to keep body and soul together. Not a bad investment for the poor woman this solid carcass of her father. And for the rest – in case of anything – the agreement should be clear: the whole five hundred to be paid back to her integrally within three months. Integrally. Every penny. He was not to lose any of her money whatever else had to go – a little dignity – some of his self-respect. He had never before allowed anybody to remain under any sort of false impression as to himself. Well, let that go – for her sake. After all, he had never *said* anything misleading – and Captain Whalley felt himself corrupt to the marrow of his bones. He laughed a little with the intimate scorn of his worldly prudence. Clearly, with a fellow of that sort, and in the peculiar relation they were to stand to each other, it would not have done to blurt out everything. He did not like the fellow. He did not like his spells of fawning loquacity and bursts of resentfulness. In the end – a poor devil. He would not have liked to stand in his shoes. Men were not evil, after all. He did not like his sleek hair, his queer way of standing at right angles, with his nose in the air, and glancing along his shoulder at you. No. On the whole, men were not bad – they were only silly or unhappy.

Captain Whalley had finished considering the discretion of that step – and there was the whole long night before him. In the full light his long beard would glisten like a silver breastplate covering his heart; in the spaces between the lamps his burly figure passed less distinct, loomed very big, wandering, and mysterious. No; there was not much real harm in men: and all the time a shadow marched with him, slanting on his left hand – which in the East is a presage of evil.

*

'Can you make out the clump of palms yet, Serang?' asked Captain Whalley from his chair on the bridge of the *Sofala* approaching the bar of Batu Beru.

'No, Tuan. By-and-by see.' The old Malay, in a blue dungaree suit, planted on his bony dark feet under the bridge awning, put his hands behind his back and stared ahead out of the innumerable wrinkles at the corners of his eyes.

Captain Whalley sat still, without lifting his head to look for himself. Three years – thirty-six times. He had made these palms thirty-six times from the southward. They would come into view at the proper time. Thank God, the old ship made her courses and distances trip after trip, as correct as clockwork. At last he murmured again –

'In sight yet?'

'The sun makes a very great glare, Tuan.'

'Watch well, Serang.'

'Ya, Tuan.'

A white man had ascended the ladder from the deck noiselessly, and had listened quietly to this short colloquy. Then he stepped out on the bridge and began to walk from end to end, holding up the long cherrywood stem of a pipe. His black hair lay plastered in long lanky wisps across the bald summit of his head; he had a furrowed brow, a yellow complexion, and a thick shapeless nose. A scanty growth of whisker did not conceal the contour of his jaw. His aspect was of brooding care; and sucking at a curved black mouthpiece, he presented such a heavy overhanging profile that even the Serang could not help reflecting sometimes upon the extreme unloveliness of some white men.

Captain Whalley seemed to brace himself up in his chair, but gave no recognition whatever to his presence. The other puffed jets of smoke; then suddenly –

'I could never understand that new mania of yours of having this Malay here for your shadow, partner.'

Captain Whalley got up from the chair in all his imposing stature and walked across to the binnacle, holding such an unswerving course that the other had to back away hurriedly, and remained as if intimidated, with the pipe trembling in his hand. 'Walk over me now,' he muttered in a sort of astounded and discomfited whisper. Then slowly and distinctly he said –

'I – am – not – dirt.' And then added defiantly, 'As you seem to think.'

The Serang jerked out –

'See the palms now, Tuan.'

Captain Whalley strode forward to the rail; but his eyes, instead of going straight to the point, with the assured keen glance of a sailor, wandered irresolutely in space, as though he, the discoverer of new routes, had lost his way upon this narrow sea.

Another white man, the mate, came up on the bridge. He was tall, young, lean, with a moustache like a trooper, and something malicious in the eye. He took up a position beside the engineer. Captain Whalley, with his back to them, inquired –

'What's on the log?'

'Eighty-five,' answered the mate quickly, and nudged the engineer with his elbow.

Captain Whalley's muscular hands squeezed the iron rail with an extraordinary force; his eyes glared with an enormous effort; he knitted his eyebrows, the perspiration fell from under his hat – and in a faint voice he murmured, 'Steady her, Serang – when she is on the proper bearing.'

The silent Malay stepped back, waited a little, and lifted his arm warningly to the helmsman. The wheel revolved rapidly to meet the swing of the ship. Again the mate nudged the engineer. But Massy turned upon him.

'Mr Sterne,' he said, violently, 'let me tell you – as a shipowner – that you are no better than a confounded fool.'

VII

STERNE went down smirking and apparently not at all disconcerted, but the engineer Massy remained on the bridge, moving about with uneasy self-assertion. Everybody on board was his inferior – everyone without exception. He paid their wages and found them in their food. They ate more of his bread and pocketed more of his money than they were worth; and they had no care in the world, while he alone had to meet all the difficulties of shipowning. When he contemplated his position in all its menacing entirety, it seemed to him that he had been for years the prey of a band of parasites; and for years he had scowled at everybody connected with the *Sofala* except, perhaps, at the Chinese firemen who served to get her along. Their use was manifest: they were an indispensable part of the machinery of which he was the master.

When he passed along his decks he shouldered those he came across brutally; but the Malay deck hands had learned to dodge out of his way. He had to bring himself to tolerate them because of the necessary manual labour of the ship which must be done. He had to struggle and plan and scheme to keep the *Sofala* afloat – and what did he get for it? Not even enough respect. They could not have given him enough of that if all their thoughts and all their actions had been directed to that end. The vanity of possession, the vainglory of power, had passed away by this time, and there remained only the material embarrassments, the fear of losing that position which had turned out not worth having, and an anxiety of thought which no abject subservience of men could repay.

He walked up and down. The bridge was his own after all. He had paid for it; and with the stem of the pipe in his hand he would stop short at times as if to listen with a profound and concentrated attention to the deadened beat of the engines (his own engines) and the slight grinding of the steering chains upon the continuous low wash of water alongside. But for these sounds, the ship might have been lying as still as if moored to a bank, and as silent as if abandoned by every living soul; only the coast, the low coast of mud and mangroves with the three palms in a bunch at the back, grew slowly more distinct in its long straight line; without a single feature to arrest attention. The native passengers of the *Sofala* lay about on mats under the awnings; the smoke of her funnel seemed the only sign of her life and connected with her gliding motion in a mysterious manner.

Captain Whalley on his feet, with a pair of binoculars in his hand and the little Malay Serang at his elbow, like an old giant attended by a wizened pigmy, was taking her over the shallow water of the bar.

This submarine ridge of mud, scoured by the stream out of the soft bottom of the river and heaped up far out on the hard bottom of the sea, was difficult to get over. The alluvial coast having no distinguishing marks, the bearings of the crossing-place had to be taken from the shape of the mountains inland. The guidance of a form flattened and uneven at the top like a grinder tooth, and of another smooth, saddle-backed summit, had to be searched for within the great unclouded glare that seemed to shift and float like a dry fiery mist, filling the air, ascending from the water, shrouding the distances, scorching to the eye. In this veil of light the near edge of the shore alone stood out almost coal-black with an opaque and motionless solidity. Thirty miles away the serrated range of the interior stretched across the horizon, its outlines and shades of blue, faint and tremulous like a background painted on airy gossamer on the quivering fabric of an impalpable curtain let down to the plain of alluvial soil; and the openings of the estuary appeared, shining white, like bits of silver let into the square pieces snipped clean and sharp out of the body of the land bordered with mangroves.

On the forepart of the bridge the giant and the pigmy muttered to each other frequently in quiet tones. Behind them Massy stood sideways with an expression of disdain and suspense on his face. His globular eyes were perfectly motionless, and he seemed to have forgotten the long pipe he held in his hand.

On the foredeck below the bridge, steeply roofed with the white slopes of the awnings, a young lascar seaman had clambered outside the rail. He adjusted quickly a broad band of sail canvas under his armpits, and throwing his chest against it, leaned out far over the water. The sleeve of his thin cotton shirt, cut off close to the shoulder, bared his brown arm of full rounded form and with a satiny skin like a woman's. He swung it rigidly with the rotary and menacing action of a slinger: the 14-lb weight hurtled circling in the air, then suddenly flew ahead as far as the curve of the bow. The wet thin line swished like scratched silk running through the dark fingers of the man, and the plunge of the lead close to the ship's side made a vanishing silvery scar upon the golden glitter; then after an interval the voice of the young Malay uplifted and long-drawn declared the depth of the water in his own language.

'Tiga stengah,' he cried after each splash and pause, gathering the line busily for another cast. 'Tiga stengah', which means three fathom and a half. For a mile or so from seaward there was a uniform depth of water right up to the bar. 'Half-three. Half-three. Half-three,' – and his modulated cry, returned leisurely and monotonous, like the repeated call of a bird, seemed to float away in sunshine and disappear in the spacious silence of the empty sea and of a lifeless shore lying open, north and south, east and west, without the stir of a single cloud-shadow or the whisper of any other voice.

The owner-engineer of the *Sofala* remained very still behind the two seamen of different race, creed, and colour; the European with the time-defying vigour of his old frame, the little Malay, old, too, but slight and shrunken like a withered brown leaf blown by a chance wind under the mighty shadow of the other. Very busy looking forward at the land, they had not a glance to spare; and Massy, glaring at them from behind, seemed to resent their attention to their duty like a personal slight upon himself.

This was unreasonable; but he had lived in his own world of unreasonable resentments for many years. At last, passing his moist palm over the rare lanky wisps of coarse hair on the top of his yellow head, he began to talk slowly.

'A leadsman, you want! I suppose that's your correct mail-boat style. Haven't you enough judgment to tell where you are by looking at the land? Why, before I had been a twelvemonth in the trade I was up to that trick – and I am only an engineer. I can point to you from here where the bar is, and I could tell you besides that you are likely as not to stick her in the mud in about five minutes from now; only you would call it interfering, I suppose. And there's that written agreement of ours, that says I mustn't interfere.'

His voice stopped. Captain Whalley, without relaxing the set severity of his features, moved his lips to ask in a quick mumble –

'How near, Serang?'

'Very near now, Tuan,' the Malay muttered, rapidly.

'Dead slow,' said the captain aloud in a firm tone.

The Serang snatched at the handle of the telegraph. A gong clanged down below. Massy with a scornful snigger walked off and put his head down the engine-room skylight.

'You may expect some rare fooling with the engines, Jack,' he bellowed. The space into which he stared was deep and full of gloom; and the grey gleams of steel down there seemed cool after the intense glare of the sea around the ship. The air, however, came up clammy and hot on his face. A short hoot on which it would have been impossible to put any sort of interpretation came from the bottom cavernously. This was the way in which the second engineer answered his chief.

He was a middle-aged man with an inattentive manner, and apparently wrapped up in such a taciturn concern for his engines that he seemed to have lost the use of speech. When addressed directly his only answer would be a grunt or a hoot, according to the distance. For all the years he had been in the *Sofala* he had never been known to exchange as much as a frank good morning with any of his shipmates. He did not seem aware that men came and went in the world; he did not seem to see them at all. Indeed he never recognized his shipmates on shore. At table (the four white men of the *Sofala* messed together) he sat looking into his plate dispassionately, but at the end of the meal would jump up and bolt down below as if a sudden thought had impelled him to rush and see whether somebody had not stolen the engines while he dined. In port at the end of the trip he went ashore regularly, but no one knew where he spent his evenings or in what manner. The local coasting fleet had preserved a wild and incoherent tale of his infatuation for the wife of a sergeant in an Irish infantry regiment. The regiment, however, had done its turn of garrison duty there ages before, and was gone somewhere to the other side of the earth, out of men's knowledge. Twice or perhaps three times in the course of the year he would take too much to drink. On these occasions he returned on board at an earlier hour than usual; ran across the deck balancing himself with his spread arms like a tight-rope walker; and locking the door of his cabin, he would converse and argue with himself the livelong night in an amazing variety of tones; storm, sneer and whine with an inexhaustible persistence. Massy in his berth next door, raising himself on his elbow, would discover that his second had remembered the name of every white man that had passed through the *Sofala* for years and years back. He remembered the names of men that had died, that had gone home, that had gone to America: he remembered in his cups the names of men whose connection with the ship had been so short that Massy had almost forgotten its circumstances and could barely recall their faces. The inebriated voice on the other side of the bulkhead commented upon them all with an extraordinary and ingenious venom of scandalous inventions. It seems they had all offended him in some way, and in return he had found them all out. He muttered darkly; he laughed sardonically; he crushed them one after another; but of his chief, Massy, he babbled with an envious and naïve admiration. Clever scoundrel! Don't meet the likes of him every day. Just look at him. Ha! Great! Ship of his own. Wouldn't catch *him* going wrong. No fear – the beast! And Massy, after listening with a gratified smile to these artless tributes to his greatness, would begin to shout, thumping at the bulkhead with both fists –

'Shut up, you lunatic! Won't you let me go to sleep, you fool!'

But a half smile of pride lingered on his lips; outside the solitary lascar told off for night duty in harbour, perhaps a youth fresh from a forest village, would stand motionless in the shadows of the deck listening to the endless drunken gabble. His heart would be thumping with breathless awe of white men: the arbitrary and obstinate men who pursue inflexibly their incomprehensible purposes – beings with weird intonations in the voice, moved by unaccountable feelings, actuated by inscrutable motives.

VIII

FOR a while after his second's answering hoot Massy hung over the engine-room gloomily. Captain Whalley who, by the power of five hundred pounds, had kept his command for three years, might have been suspected of never having seen that coast before. He seemed unable to put down his glasses, as though they had been glued under his contracted eyebrows. This settled frown gave to his face an air of invincible and just severity; but his raised elbow trembled slightly, and the perspiration poured from under his hat as if a second sun had suddenly blazed up at the zenith by the side of the ardent still globe already there, in whose blinding white heat the earth whirled and shone like a mote of dust.

From time to time, still holding up his glasses, he raised his other hand to wipe his streaming face. The drops rolled down his cheeks, fell like rain upon the white hairs of his beard, and brusquely, as if guided by an uncontrollable and anxious impulse, his arm reached out to the stand of the engine-room telegraph.

The gong clanged down below. The balanced vibration of the dead-slow speed ceased together with every sound and tremor in the ship, as if the great stillness that reigned upon the coast had stolen in through her sides of iron and taken possession of her innermost recesses. The illusion of perfect immobility seemed to fall upon her from the luminous blue dome without a stain arching over a flat sea without a stir. The faint breeze she had made for herself expired, as if all at once the air had become too thick to budge; even the slight hiss of the water on her stem died out. The narrow, long hull, carrying its way without a ripple, seemed to approach the shoal water of the bar by stealth. The plunge of the lead with the mournful, mechanical cry of the lascar came at longer and longer intervals; and the men on her bridge seemed to hold their breath. The Malay at the helm looked fixedly at the compass card, the captain and the Serang stared at the coast.

Massy had left the skylight, and, walking flat-footed, had returned softly to the very spot on the bridge he had occupied before. A slow, lingering grin exposed his set of big white teeth: they gleamed evenly in the shade of the awning like the keyboard of a piano in a dusky room.

At last, pretending to talk to himself in excessive astonishment, he said not very loud —

'Stop the engines now. What next, I wonder?'

He waited, stooping from the shoulders, his head bowed, his glance oblique. Then raising his voice a shade —

'If I dared make an absurd remark I would say that you haven't the stomach to. . . .'

But a yelling spirit of excitement, like some frantic soul wandering unsuspected in the vast stillness of the coast, had seized upon the body of the lascar at the lead. The languid monotony of his sing-song changed to a swift, sharp clamour. The weight flew after a single whirr, the line whistled, splash followed splash in haste. The water had shoaled, and the man, instead of the drowsy tale of fathoms, was calling out the soundings in feet.

'Fifteen feet. Fifteen, fifteen! Fourteen, fourteen. . . .'

Captain Whalley lowered the arm holding the glasses. It descended slowly as if by its own weight; no other part of his towering body stirred; and the swift cries with their eager warning note passed him by as though he had been deaf.

Massy, very still, and turning an attentive ear, had fastened his eyes upon the silvery, close-cropped back of the steady old head. The ship herself seemed to be arrested but for the gradual decrease of depth under her keel.

'Thirteen feet . . . thirteen! Twelve!' cried the leadsman anxiously below the bridge. And suddenly the barefooted Serang stepped away noiselessly to steal a glance over the side.

Narrow of shoulder, in a suit of faded blue cotton, an old grey felt hat rammed down on his head, with a hollow in the nape of his dark neck, and with his slender limbs, he appeared from the back no bigger than a boy of fourteen. There was a childlike impulsiveness in the curiosity with which he watched the spread of the voluminous, yellowish convolutions rolling up from below to the surface of the blue water like massive clouds driving slowly upwards on the unfathomable sky. He was not startled at the sight in the least. It was not doubt, but the certitude that the keel of the *Sofala* must be stirring the mud now, which made him peep over the side.

His peering eyes, set aslant in a face of the Chinese type, a little old face, immovable, as if carved in old brown oak, had informed him long before that the ship was not headed at the bar properly. Paid off from the *Fair Maid*, together with the rest of the crew, after the completion of the sale, he had hung, in his faded blue suit and floppy grey hat, about the doors of the Harbour Office, till one day, seeing Captain Whalley coming along to get a crew for the *Sofala*, he had put himself quietly in the way, with his bare feet in the dust and an upward mute glance. The eyes of his old commander had fallen on him favourably – it must have been an auspicious day – and in less than half an hour the white men in the

'Ofiss' had written his name on a document as Serang of the fire-ship *Sofala*. Since that time he had repeatedly looked at that estuary, upon that coast, from this bridge and from this side of the bar. The record of the visual world fell through his eyes upon his unspeculating mind as on a sensitized plate through the lens of a camera. His knowledge was absolute and precise; nevertheless, had he been asked his opinion, and especially if questioned in the downright, alarming manner of white men, he would have displayed the hesitation of ignorance. He was certain of his facts – but such a certitude counted for little against the doubt what answer would be pleasing. Fifty years ago, in a jungle village, and before he was a day old, his father (who died without ever seeing a white face) had had his nativity cast by a man of skill and wisdom in astrology, because in the arrangement of the stars may be read the last word of human destiny. His destiny had been to thrive by the favour of various white men on the sea. He had swept the decks of ships, had tended their helms, had minded their stores, had risen at last to be a Serang; and his placid mind had remained as incapable of penetrating the simplest motives of those he served as they themselves were incapable of detecting through the crust of the earth the secret nature of its heart, which may be fire or may be stone. But he had no doubt whatever that the *Sofala* was out of the proper track for crossing the bar at Batu Beru.

It was a slight error. The ship could not have been more than twice her own length too far to the northward; and a white man at a loss for a cause (since it was impossible to suspect Captain Whalley of blundering ignorance, of want of skill, or of neglect) would have been incined to doubt the testimony of his senses. It was some such feeling that kept Massy motionless, with his teeth laid bare by an anxious grin. Not so the Serang. He was not troubled by any intellectual mistrust of his senses. If his captain chose to stir the mud it was well. He had known in his life white men indulge in outbreaks equally strange. He was only genuinely interested to see what would come of it. At last, apparently satisfied, he stepped back from the rail.

He had made no sound: Captain Whalley, however, seemed to have observed the movements of his Serang. Holding his head rigidly, he asked with a mere stir of his lips –

'Going ahead still, Serang?'

'Still going a little, Tuan,' answered the Malay. Then added casually, 'She is over.'

The lead confirmed his words; the depth of water increased at every cast, and the soul of excitement departed suddenly from the lascar swung in the canvas belt over the *Sofala*'s side. Captain Whalley ordered the lead in, set the engines ahead without haste, and averting his eyes from the coast directed the Serang to keep a course for the middle of the entrance.

Massy brought the palm of his hand with a loud smack against his thigh.

'You grazed on the bar. Just look astern and see if you didn't. Look at the track she left. You can see it plainly. Upon my soul, I thought you would! What made you do that? What on earth made you do that? I believe you are trying to scare me.'

He talked slowly, as it were circumspectly, keeping his prominent black eyes on his captain. There was also a slight plaintive note in his rising choler, for, primarily, it was the clear sense of a wrong suffered undeservedly that made him hate the man who, for a beggarly five hundred pounds, claimed a sixth part of the profits under the three years' agreement. Whenever his resentment got the better of the awe the person of Captain Whalley inspired he would positively whimper with fury.

'You don't know what to invent to plague my life out of me. I would not have thought that a man of your sort would condescend . . .'

He paused, half hopefully, half timidly, whenever Captain Whalley made the slightest movement in the deck-chair, as though expecting to be conciliated by a soft speech or else rushed upon and hunted off the bridge.

'I am puzzled,' he went on again, with the watchful, unsmiling baring of his big teeth. 'I don't know what to think. I do believe you are trying to frighten me. You very nearly planted her on the bar for at least twelve hours, besides getting the engines choked with mud. Ships can't afford to lose twelve hours on a trip nowadays — as you ought to know very well, and do know very well to be sure, only . . .'

His slow volubility, the sideways cranings of his neck, the black glances out of the very corners of his eyes, left Captain Whalley unmoved. He looked at the deck with a severe frown. Massy waited for some little time, then began to threaten plaintively.

'You think you've got me bound hand and foot in that agreement. You think you can torment me in any way you please. Ah! But remember it has another six weeks to run yet. There's time for me to dismiss you before the three years are out. You will do yet something that will give me the chance to dismiss you, and make you wait a twelvemonth for your money before you can take yourself off and pull out your five hundred, and leave me without a penny to get the new boilers for her. You gloat over that idea – don't you? I do believe you sit here gloating. It's as if I had sold my soul for five hundred pounds to be everlastingly damned in the end. . . .'

He paused, without apparent exasperation, then continued evenly –

'. . . With the boilers worn out and the survey hanging over my head, Captain Whalley – Captain Whalley, I say, what do you do with your money? You must have stacks of money somewhere – a man like you must. It stands to reason. I am not a fool, you know, Captain Whalley – partner.'

Again he paused, as though he had done for good. He passed his tongue over his lips, gave a backward glance at the Serang conning the ship with quiet whispers and slight signs of the hand. The wash of the propeller sent a swift ripple, crested with dark froth, upon a long flat spit of black slime. The *Sofala* had entered the river; the trail she had stirred up over the bar was a mile astern of her now, out of sight, had disappeared utterly; and the smooth, empty sea along the coast was left behind in the glittering desolation of sunshine. On each side of her, low down, the growth of sombre twisted mangroves covered the semi-liquid banks; and Massy continued in his old tone, with an abrupt start, as if his speech had been ground out of him, like the tune of a music-box, by turning a handle.

'Though if anybody ever got the best of me, it is you. I don't mind saying this. I've said it – there! What more can you want? Isn't that enough for your pride, Captain Whalley? You got over me from the first. It's all of a piece, when I look back at it. You allowed me to insert that clause about intemperance without saying anything, only looking very sick when I made a point of it going in black on white. How could I tell what was wrong about you? There's generally something wrong somewhere. And, lo and behold! when you come on board it turns out that you've been in the habit of drinking nothing but water for years and years.'

His dogmatic, reproachful whine stopped. He brooded profoundly, after the manner of crafty and unintelligent men. It seemed inconceivable that Captain Whalley should not laugh at the expression of disgust that overspread the heavy, yellow countenance. But Captain Whalley never raised his eyes – sitting in his arm-chair, outraged, dignified, and motionless.

'Much good it was to me,' Massy remonstrated, monotonously, 'to insert a clause of dismissal for intemperance against a man who drinks nothing but water. And you looked so upset, too, when I read my draft in the lawyer's office that morning, Captain Whalley – you looked so crestfallen, that I made sure I had gone home on your weak spot. A shipowner can't be too careful as to the sort of skipper he gets. You must have been laughing at me in your sleeve all the blessed time. . . . Eh? What are you going to say?'

Captain Whalley had only shuffled his feet slightly. A dull animosity became apparent in Massy's sideways stare.

'But recollect that there are other grounds of dismissal. There's habitual carelessness, amounting to incompetence – there's gross and persistent neglect of duty. I am not quite as big a fool as you try to make me out to be. You have been careless of late – leaving everything to that Serang. Why! I've seen you letting that old fool of a Malay take bearings for you, as if you were too big to attend to your work yourself. And what do you call that silly touch-and-go manner in which you took the ship over the bar just now? You expect me to put up with that?'

Leaning on his elbow against the ladder abaft the bridge, Sterne, the mate, tried to hear, blinking the while from the distance at the second engineer, who had come up for a moment, and stood in the engine-room companion. Wiping his hands on a bunch of cotton waste, he looked about with indifference to the right and left at the river-banks slipping astern of the *Sofala* steadily.

Massy turned full at the chair. The character of his whine became again threatening.

'Take care. I may yet dismiss you and freeze to your money for a year. I may. . . .'

But before the silent, rigid immobility of the man whose money had come in the nick of time to save him from utter ruin, his voice died out in his throat.

'Not that I want you to go,' he resumed after a silence, and in an absurdly insinuating tone. 'I want nothing better than to be friends and renew the agreement, if you will consent to find another couple of hundred to help with the new boilers, Captain Whalley. I've told you before. She must have new boilers; you know it as well as I do. Have you thought this over?'

He waited. The slender stem of the pipe with its bulky lump of a bowl at the end hung down from his thick lips. It had gone out. Suddenly he took it from between his teeth and wrung his hands slightly.

'Don't you believe me?' He thrust the pipe bowl into the pocket of his shiny black jacket.

'It's like dealing with the devil,' he said. 'Why don't you speak? At first you were so high and mighty with me I hardly dared to creep about my own deck. Now I can't get a word from you. You don't seem to see me at all. What does it mean? Upon my soul, you terrify me with this deaf and dumb trick. What's going on in that head of yours? What are you plotting against me there so hard that you can't say a word? You will never make me believe that you – you – don't know where to lay your hands on a couple of hundred. You have made me curse the day I was born. . . .'

'Mr Massy,' said Captain Whalley, suddenly, without stirring.

The engineer started violently.

'If that is so I can only beg you to forgive me.'

'Starboard,' muttered the Serang to the helmsman; and the *Sofala* began to swing round the bend into the second reach.

'Ough!' Massy shuddered. 'You make my blood run cold. What made you come here? What made you come aboard that evening all of a sudden, with your high talk and your money – tempting me? I always wondered what was your motive? You fastened yourself on me to have easy times and grow fat on my life blood, I tell you. Was that it? I believe you are the greatest miser in the world, or else why. . . .'

'No. I am only poor,' interrupted Captain Whalley, stonily.

'Steady,' murmured the Serang. Massy turned away with his chin on his shoulder.

'I don't believe it,' he said in his dogmatic tone. Captain Whalley made no movement. 'There you sit like a gorged vulture – exactly like a vulture.'

He embraced the middle of the reach and both the banks in one blank, unseeing, circular glance, and left the bridge slowly.

IX

ON TURNING to descend Massy perceived the head of Sterne the mate loitering, with his sly, confident smile, his red moustaches and blinking eyes, at the foot of the ladder.

Sterne had been a junior in one of the larger shipping concerns before joining the *Sofala*. He had thrown up his berth, he said, 'on general principles'. The promotion in the employ was very slow, he complained, and he thought it was time for him to try and get on a bit in the world. It seemed as though nobody would ever die or leave the firm; they all stuck fast in their berths till they got mildewed; he was tired of waiting; and he feared that when a vacancy did occur the best servants were by no means sure of being treated fairly. Besides, the captain he had to serve under – Captain Provost – was an unaccountable sort of man and had taken a dislike to him for some reason or other. For doing rather more than his bare duty as likely as not. When he had done anything wrong he could take a talking to, like a man; but he expected to be treated like a man, too, and not to be addressed invariably as though he were a dog. He had asked Captain Provost plump and plain to tell him where he was at fault, and Captain Provost, in a most scornful way, had told him that he was a perfect officer, and that if he disliked the way he was being spoken to there was the gangway – he could take himself off ashore at once. But everybody knew what sort of man Captain Provost was. It was no use appealing to the office. Captain Provost had too much influence in the employ. All the same, they had to give him a good character. He made bold to say there was nothing in the world against him, and, as he had happened to hear that the mate of the *Sofala* had been taken to the hospital that morning with a sunstroke, he thought there would be no harm in seeing whether he would not do. . . .

He had come to Captain Whalley freshly shaved, red-faced, thin-flanked, throwing out his lean chest; and had recited his little tale with an open and manly assurance. Now and then his eyelids quivered slightly, his hand would steal up to the end of the flaming moustache; his eyebrows were straight, furry, of a chestnut colour, and the directness of his gaze seemed to tremble on the verge of impudence. Captain Whalley had engaged him temporarily; then, the other man having been ordered home by the doctors, he had remained for the next trip, and then the next. He had now attained permanency, and the performance of his duties was marked by an air of serious, single-minded application. Directly he was spoken to, he began to smile attentively, with a great deference expressed in his whole attitude; but there was in the rapid winking which went on all the time something quizzical, as though he had possessed the secret of some universal joke cheating all creation and impenetrable to other mortals.

Grave and smiling he watched Massy come down step by step; when the chief engineer had reached the deck he swung about, and they found themselves face to face. Matched as to height and utterly dissimilar, they confronted each other as if there had been something between them – something else than the bright strip of sunlight that, falling through the wide lacing of two awnings, cut crosswise the narrow planking of the deck and separated their feet as it were a stream; something profound and subtle and incalculable, like an unexpressed understanding, a secret mistrust, or some sort of fear.

At last Sterne, blinking his deep-set eyes and sticking forward his scraped, clean-cut chin, as crimson as the rest of his face, murmured –

'You've seen? He grazed! You've seen?'

Massy, contemptuous, and without raising his yellow, fleshy countenance, replied in the same pitch –

'Maybe. But if it had been you we would have been stuck fast in the mud.'

'Pardon me, Mr Massy. I beg to deny it. Of course a shipowner may say what he jolly well pleases on his own deck. That's all right; but I beg to. . . .'

'Get out of my way!'

The other had a slight start, the impulse of suppressed

indignation perhaps, but held his ground. Massy's downward glance wandered right and left, as though the deck all round Sterne had been bestrewn with eggs that must not be broken, and he had looked irritably for places where he could set his feet in flight. In the end he, too, did not move, though there was plenty of room to pass on.

'I heard you say up there,' went on the mate – 'and a very just remark it was, too – that there's always something wrong . . .'

'Eavesdropping is what's wrong with *you*, Mr Sterne.'

'Now, if you would only listen to me for a moment, Mr Massy, sir, I could. . . .'

'You are a sneak,' interrupted Massy in a great hurry, and even managed to get so far as to repeat, 'a common sneak', before the mate had broken in argumentatively –

'Now, sir, what is it you want? You want. . . .'

'I want – I want,' stammered Massy, infuriated and astonished – 'I want? How do you know that I want anything? How dare you? . . . What do you mean? . . . What are you after – you. . . .'

'Promotion.' Sterne silenced him with candid bravado. The engineer's round soft cheeks quivered still, but he said quietly enough –

'You are only worrying my head off,' and Sterne met him with a confident little smile.

'A chap in business I know (well up in the world he is now) used to tell me that this was the proper way. "Always push on to the front," he would say. "Keep yourself well before your boss. Interfere whenever you get a chance. Show him what you know. Worry him into seeing you." That was his advice. Now I know no other boss than you here. You are the owner, and no one else counts for *that* much in my eyes. See, Mr Massy? I want to get on. I make no secret of it that I am one of the sort that means to get on. These are the men to make use of, sir. You haven't arrived at the top of the tree, sir, without finding that out – I daresay.'

'Worry your boss in order to get on,' repeated Massy, as if awestruck by the irreverent originality of the idea. 'I shouldn't wonder if this was just what the Blue Anchor people kicked you out of their employ for. Is that what you call getting on? You shall get on in the same way here if you aren't careful – I can promise you.'

At this Sterne hung his head, thoughtful, perplexed, winking hard at the deck. All his attempts to enter into confidential relations with his owner had led of late to nothing better than these dark threats of dismissal; and a threat of dismissal would check him at once into a hesitating silence as though he were not sure that the proper time for defying it had come. On this occasion he seemed to have lost his tongue for a moment, and Massy, getting in motion, heavily passed him by with an abortive attempt at shouldering. Sterne defeated it by stepping aside. He turned then swiftly, opening his mouth very wide as if to shout something after the engineer, but seemed to think better of it.

Always — as he was ready to confess — on the look-out for an opening to get on, it had become an instinct with him to watch the conduct of his immediate superiors for something 'that one could lay hold of'. It was his belief that no skipper in the world would keep his command for a day if only the owners could be 'made to know'. This romantic and naïve theory had led him into trouble more than once, but he remained incorrigible; and his character was so instinctively disloyal that whenever he joined a ship the intention of ousting his commander out of the berth and taking his place was always present at the back of his head, as a matter of course. It filled the leisure of his waking hours with the reveries of careful plans and compromising discoveries — the dreams of his sleep with images of lucky turns and favourable accidents. Skippers had been known to sicken and die at sea, than which nothing could be better to give a smart mate a chance of showing what he's made of. They also would tumble overboard sometimes: he had heard of one or two such cases. Others again . . . But, as it were constitutionally, he was faithful to the belief that the conduct of no single one of them would stand the test of careful watching by a man who 'knew what's what' and who kept his eyes 'skinned pretty well' all the time.

After he had gained a permanent footing on board the *Sofala* he allowed his perennial hope to rise high. To begin with, it was a great advantage to have an old man for captain: the sort of man besides who in the nature of things was likely to give up the job before long from one cause or another. Sterne was greatly chagrined, however, to notice that he did not seem anyway near being past his work yet. Still, these old men go to pieces all at once sometimes. Then there was the owner-engineer close at hand to be impressed by his zeal and steadiness. Sterne never for a moment doubted the obvious nature of his own merits (he was really an excellent officer); only, nowadays, professional merit alone does not take a man along fast enough. A chap must have some push in him, and must keep his wits at work, too, to help him forward. He made up his mind to inherit the charge of this steamer if it was to be done at all; not indeed estimating the command of the *Sofala* as a very great catch, but for the reason that, out East especially, to make a start is everything, and one command leads to another.

He began by promising himself to behave with great circumspection; Massy's sombre and fantastic humours intimidated him as being outside one's usual sea experience; but he was quite intelligent enough to realize almost from the first that he was there in the presence of an exceptional situation. His peculiar prying imagination penetrated it quickly; the feeling that there was in it an element which eluded his grasp exasperated his impatience to get on. And so one trip came to an end, then another, and he had begun his third before he saw an opening by which he could step in with any sort of effect. It had all been very queer and very obscure; something had been going on near him, as if separated by a chasm from the common life and the working routine of the ship, which was exactly like the life and the routine of any other coasting steamer of that class.

Then one day he made his discovery.

It came to him after all these weeks of watchful observation and puzzled surmises, suddenly, like the long-sought solution of a riddle that suggests itself to the mind in a flash. Not with the same authority, however. Great heavens! Could it be that? And after remaining thunderstruck for a few seconds he tried to shake it off with self-contumely, as though it had been the product of an unhealthy bias toward the Incredible, the Inexplicable, the Unheard-of – the Mad!

This – the illuminating moment – had occurred the trip before, on the return passage. They had just left a place of call on the mainland called Pangu; they were steaming straight out of a bay. To the east a massive headland closed the view, with the tilted edges of the rocky strata showing through its ragged clothing of rank bushes and thorny creepers. The wind had begun to sing in the rigging; the sea along the coast, green and as if swollen a little above the line of the horizon, seemed to pour itself over, time after time, with a slow and thundering fall, into the shadow of the leeward cape; and across the wide opening the nearest of a group of small islands stood enveloped in the hazy yellow light of a breezy sunrise; still farther out the hummocky tops of other islets peeped out motionless above the water of the channels between, scoured tumultuously by the breeze.

The usual track of the *Sofala* both going and returning on every trip led her for a few miles along this reef-infested region. She followed a broad lane of water, dropping astern, one after another, these crumbs of the earth's crust resembling a squadron of dismasted hulks run in disorder upon a foul ground of rocks and shoals. Some of these fragments of land appeared, indeed, no bigger than a stranded ship; others, quite flat, lay awash like anchored rafts, like ponderous, black rafts of stone; several, heavily timbered and round at the base, emerged in squat domes of deep green foliage that shuddered darkly all over to the flying touch of cloud shadows driven by the sudden gusts of the squally season. The thunderstorms of the coast broke frequently over that cluster; it turned then shadowy in its whole extent; it turned more dark, and as if more still in the play of fire; as if more impenetrably silent in the peals of thunder; its blurred shapes vanished – dissolving utterly at times in the thick rain – to reappear clear-cut and black in the stormy light against the grey sheet of the cloud – scattered on the slaty round table of the sea. Unscathed by storms, resisting the work of years, unfretted by the strife of the world, there it lay unchanged as on that day, four hundred years ago, when first beheld by Western eyes from the deck of a high-pooped caravel.

It was one of these secluded spots that may be found on the busy sea, as on land you come sometimes upon the clustered houses of a hamlet untouched by men's restlessness, untouched by their need, by their thought, and as if forgotten by time itself. The lives of uncounted generations had passed it by, and the multitudes of seafowl, urging their way from all the points of the horizon to sleep on the outer rocks of the group, unrolled the converging evolutions of their flight in long, sombre streamers upon the glow of the sky. The palpitating cloud of their wings soared and stooped over the pinnacles of the rocks, over the rocks slender like spires, squat like martello towers; over the pyramidal heaps like fallen ruins, over the lines of bald boulders showing like a wall of stones battered to pieces and scorched by lightning – with the sleepy, clear glimmer of water in every breach. The noise of their continous and violent screaming filled the air.

This great noise would meet the *Sofala* coming up from Batu Beru; it would meet her on quiet evenings, a pitiless and savage clamour enfeebled by distance, the clamour of seabirds settling to rest, and struggling for a footing at the end of the day. No one noticed it especially on board; it was the voice of their ship's unerring landfall, ending the steady stretch of a hundred miles. She had made good her course, she had run her distance till the punctual islets began to emerge one by one, the points of rocks, the hummocks of earth . . . and the cloud of birds hovered – the restless cloud emitting a strident and cruel uproar, the sound of the familiar scene, the living part of the broken land beneath, of the outspread sea, and of the high sky without a flaw.

But when the *Sofala* happened to close with the land after sunset she would find everything very still there under the mantle of the night. All would be still, dumb, almost invisible – but for the blotting out of the low constellations occulted in turns behind the vague masses of the islets whose true outlines eluded the eye amongst the dark spaces of the heaven: and the ship's three lights, resembling three stars – the red and the green with the white above – her three lights, like three companion stars wandering on the earth, held their unswerving course for the passage at the southern end of the group. Sometimes there were human eyes open to watch them come nearer, travelling smoothly in the sombre void; the eyes of a naked fisherman in his canoe floating over a reef. He thought drowsily: 'Ha! The fire-ship that once in every moon goes in and comes out of Pangu Bay.' More he did not know of her. And just as he had detected the faint rhythm of the propeller beating the calm water a mile and a half away, the time would come for the *Sofala* to alter her course, the lights would swing off him their triple beam – and disappear.

A few miserable, half-naked families, a sort of outcast tribe of long-haired, lean, and wild-eyed people, strove for their living in this lonely wilderness of islets, lying like an abandoned outwork

of the land at the gates of the bay. Within the knots and loops of
the rocks the water rested more transparent than crystal under
their crooked and leaky canoes, scooped out of the trunk of a tree:
the forms of the bottom undulated slightly to the dip of a paddle;
and the men seemed to hang in the air, they seemed to hang
enclosed within the fibres of a dark, sodden log, fishing patiently
in a strange, unsteady, pellucid, green air above the shoals.

Their bodies stalked brown and emaciated as if dried up in the
sunshine; their lives ran out silently; the homes where they were
born, went to rest, and died – flimsy sheds of rushes and coarse
grass eked out with a few ragged mats – were hidden out of sight
from the open sea. No glow of their household fires ever kindled
for a seaman a red spark upon the blind night of the group; and
the calms of the coast, the flaming long calms of the equator, the
unbreathing, concentrated calms like the deep introspection of a
passionate nature, brooded awfully for days and weeks together
over the unchangeable inheritance of their children; till at last the
stones, hot like live embers, scorched the naked sole, till the water
clung warm, and sickly, and as if thickened about the legs of lean
men with girded loins, wading thigh-deep in the pale blaze of the
shallows. And it would happen now and then that the *Sofala*,
through some delay in one of the ports of call, would heave in
sight making for Pangu Bay as late as noonday.

Only a blurring cloud at first, the thin mist of her smoke would
arise mysteriously from an empty point on the clear line of sea and
sky. The taciturn fishermen within the reefs would extend their
lean arms toward the offing; and the brown figures stooping on
the tiny beaches, the brown figures of men, women, and children
grubbing in the sand in search of turtles' eggs, would rise up,
crooked elbow aloft and hand over the eyes, to watch this
monthly apparition glide straight on, swerve on – and go by.
Their ears caught the panting of that ship; their eyes followed her
till she passed between the two capes of the mainland going at full
speed as though she hoped to make her way unchecked into the
very bosom of the earth.

On such days the luminous sea would give no sign of the
dangers lurking on both sides of her path. Everything remained
still, crushed by the overwhelming power of the light; and the
whole group, opaque in the sunshine, – the rocks resembling

pinnacles, the rocks resembling spires, the rocks resembling ruins; the forms of islets resembling beehives, resembling mole-hills; the islets recalling the shapes of haystacks, the contours of ivy-clad towers – would stand reflected together upside down in the unwrinkled water, like carved toys of ebony disposed on the silvered plate-glass of a mirror.

The first touch of blowing weather would envelop the whole at once in the spume of the windward breakers, as if in a sudden cloudlike burst of steam; and the clear water seemed fairly to boil in all the passages. The provoked sea outlined exactly in a design of angry foam the wide base of the group; the submerged level of broken waste and refuse left over from the building of the coast near by, projecting its dangerous spurs, all awash, far into the channel, and bristling with wicked long spits often a mile long: with deadly spits made of froth and stones.

And even nothing more than a brisk breeze – as on that morning, the voyage before, when the *Sofala* left Pangu Bay early, and Mr Sterne's discovery was to blossom out like a flower of incredible and evil aspect from the tiny seed of instinctive suspicion – even such a breeze had enough strength to tear the placid mask from the face of the sea. To Sterne, gazing with indifference, it had been like a revelation to behold for the first time the dangers marked by the hissing livid patches on the water as distinctly as on the engraved paper of a chart. It came into his mind that this was the sort of day most favourable for a stranger attempting the passage: a clear day, just windy enough for the sea to break on every ledge, buoying, as it were, the channel plainly to the sight; whereas during a calm you had nothing to depend on but the compass and the practised judgment of your eye. And yet the successive captains of the *Sofala* had had to take her through at night more than once. Nowadays you could not afford to throw away six or seven hours of a steamer's time. That you couldn't. But then use is everything, and with proper care . . . The channel was broad and safe enough; the main point was to hit upon the entrance correctly in the dark – for if a man got himself involved in that stretch of broken water over yonder he would never get out with a whole ship – if he ever got out at all.

This was Sterne's last train of thought independent of the great discovery. He had just seen to the securing of the anchor, and had remained forward idling away a moment or two. The captain was in charge on the bridge. With a slight yawn he had turned away from his survey of the sea and had leaned his shoulders against the fish davit.

These, properly speaking, were the very last moments of ease he was to know on board the *Sofala*. All the instants that came after were to be pregnant with purpose and intolerable with perplexity. No more idle, random thoughts; the discovery would put them on the rack, till sometimes he wished to goodness he had been fool enough not to make it at all. And yet, if his chance to get on rested on the discovery of 'something wrong', he could not have hoped for a greater stroke of luck.

X

THE knowledge was too disturbing, really. There was 'something wrong' with a vengeance, and the moral certitude of it was at first simply frightful to contemplate. Sterne had been looking aft in a mood so idle, that for once he was thinking no harm of any one. His captain on the bridge presented himself naturally to his sight. How insignificant, how casual was the thought that had started the train of discovery – like an accidental spark that suffices to ignite the charge of a tremendous mine!

Caught under by the breeze, the awnings of the fore-deck bellied upwards and collapsed slowly, and above their heavy flapping the grey stuff of Captain Whalley's roomy coat fluttered incessantly around his arms and trunk. He faced the wind in full light, with his great silvery beard blown forcibly against his chest; the eyebrows overhung heavily the shadows whence his glance appeared to be staring ahead piercingly. Sterne could just detect the twin gleam of the whites shifting under the shaggy arches of the brow. At short range these eyes, for all the man's affable manner, seemed to look you through and through. Sterne never could defend himself from that feeling when he had occasion to speak with his captain. He did not like it. What a big heavy man he appeared up there, with that little shrimp of a Serang in close attendance – as was usual in this extraordinary steamer! Confounded absurd custom that. He resented it. Surely the old fellow could have looked after his ship without that loafing native at his elbow. Sterne wriggled his shoulders with disgust. What was it? Indolence or what?

That old skipper must have been growing lazy for years. They all grew lazy out East here (Sterne was very conscious of his own unimpaired activity); they got slack all over. But he towered very erect on the bridge; and quite low by his side, as you see a small child looking over the edge of a table, the battered soft hat and the brown face of the Serang peeped over the white canvas screen of the rail.

No doubt the Malay was standing back, nearer to the wheel; but the great disparity of size in close association amused Sterne like the observation of a bizarre fact in nature. There were as queer fish out of the sea as any in it.

He saw Captain Whalley turn his head quickly to speak to his Serang; the wind whipped the whole white mass of the beard sideways. He would be directing the chap to look at the compass for him, or what not. Of course. Too much trouble to step over and see for himself. Sterne's scorn for that bodily indolence which overtakes white men in the East increased on reflection. Some of them would be utterly lost if they hadn't all these natives at their beck and call; they grew perfectly shameless about it, too. He was not of that sort, thank God! It wasn't in him to make himself dependent for his work on any shrivelled-up little Malay like that. As if one could ever trust a silly native for anything in the world! But that fine old man thought differently, it seems. There they were together, never far apart; a pair of them, recalling to the mind an old whale attended by a little pilot-fish.

The fancifulness of the comparison made him smile. A whale with an inseparable pilot-fish! That's what the old man looked like; for it could not be said he looked like a shark, though Mr Massy had called him that very name. But Mr Massy did not mind what he said in his savage fits. Sterne smiled to himself — and gradually the ideas evoked by the sound, by the imagined shape of the word pilot-fish; the ideas of aid, of guidance needed and received, came uppermost in his mind: the word pilot awakened the idea of trust, of dependence, the idea of the welcome, clear-eyed help brought to the seaman groping for the land in the dark:

groping blindly in fogs: feeling his way in the thick weather of the gales that, filling the air with a salt mist blown up from the sea, contract the range of sight on all sides to a shrunken horizon that seems within reach of the hand.

A pilot sees better than a stranger, because his local knowledge, like a sharper vision, completes the shapes of things hurriedly glimpsed; penetrates the veils of mist spread over the land by the storms of the sea; defines with certitude the outlines of a coast lying under the pall of fog, the forms of landmarks half buried in a starless night as in a shallow grave. He recognizes because he already knows. It is not to his far-reaching eye but to his more extensive knowledge that the pilot looks for certitudes; for this certitude of the ship's position on which may depend a man's good fame and the peace of his conscience, the justification of the trust deposited in his hands, with his own life, too, which is seldom wholly his to throw away, and the humble lives of others rooted in distant affections, perhaps, and made as weighty as the lives of kings by the burden of the awaiting mystery. The pilot's knowledge brings relief and certitude to the commander of a ship; the Serang, however, in his fanciful suggestion of a pilot-fish attending a whale, could not in any way be credited with a superior knowledge. Why should he have it? These two men had come on that run together — the white and the brown — on the same day: and of course a white man would learn more in a week than the best native would in a month. He was made to stick to the skipper as though he were of some use — as the pilot-fish, they say, is to the whale. But how — it was very marked — how? A pilot-fish — a pilot — a . . . But if not superior knowledge then. . .

Sterne's discovery was made. It was repugnant to his imagination, shocking to his ideas of honesty, shocking to his conception of mankind. This enormity affected one's outlook on what was possible in this world: it was as if for instance the sun had turned blue, throwing a new and sinister light on men and nature. Really in the first moment he had felt sickish, as though he had got a blow below the belt: for a second the very colour of the sea seemed changed — appeared queer to his wandering eye; and he had a passing, unsteady sensation in all his limbs as though the earth had started turning the other way.

A very natural incredulity succeeding this sense of upheaval brought a measure of relief. He had gasped; it was over. But afterwards, during all that day, sudden paroxysms of wonder would come over him in the midst of his occupations. He would stop and shake his head. The revolt of his incredulity had passed away almost as quick as the first emotion of discovery, and for the next twenty-four hours he had no sleep. That would never do. At meal-times (he took the foot of the table set up for the white men on the bridge) he could not help losing himself in a fascinated contemplation of Captain Whalley opposite. He watched the deliberate upward movements of the arm; the old man put his food to his lips as though he never expected to find any taste in his daily bread, as though he did not know anything about it. He fed himself like a somnambulist. 'It's an awful sight,' thought Sterne; and he watched the long period of mournful, silent immobility, with a big brown hand lying loosely closed by the side of the plate, till he noticed the two engineers to the right and left looking at him in astonishment. He would close his mouth in a hurry then, and lowering his eyes, wink rapidly at his plate. It was awful to see the old chap sitting there: it was even awful to think that with three words he could blow him up sky-high. All he had to do was to raise his voice and pronounce a single short sentence, and yet that simple act seemed as impossible to attempt as moving the sun out of its place in the sky. The old chap could eat in his terrific mechanical way; but Sterne, from mental excitement, could not – not that evening, at any rate.

He had had ample time since to get accustomed to the strain of the meal-hours. He would never have believed it. But then use is everything; only the very potency of his success prevented anything resembling elation. He felt like a man who, in his legitimate search for a loaded gun to help him on his way through the world, chances to come upon a torpedo – upon a live torpedo with a shattering charge in its head and a pressure of many atmospheres in its tail. It is the sort of weapon to make its possessor careworn and nervous. He had no mind to be blown up himself; and he could not get rid of the notion that the explosion was bound to damage him, too, in some way.

This vague apprehension had restrained him at first. He was able now to eat and sleep with that fearful weapon by his side, with the conviction of its power always in his mind. It had not been arrived at by any reflective process; but once the idea had entered his head, the conviction had followed overwhelmingly in a multitude of observed little facts to which before he had given only a languid attention. The abrupt and faltering intonations of the deep voice; the taciturnity put on like an armour; the deliberate, as if guarded, movements; the long immobilities, as if the man he watched had been afraid to disturb the very air: every familiar gesture, every word uttered in his hearing, every sigh overheard, had acquired a special significance, a confirmatory import.

Every day that passed over the *Sofala* appeared to Sterne simply crammed full with proofs – with incontrovertible proofs. At night, when off duty, he would steal out of his cabin in pyjamas (for more proofs) and stand a full hour, perhaps, on his bare feet below the bridge, as absolutely motionless as the awning stanchion in its deck socket near by. On the stretches of easy navigation it is not usual for a coasting captain to remain on deck all the time of his watch. The Serang keeps it for him as a matter of custom; in open water, on a straight course, he is usually trusted to look after the ship by himself. But this old man seemed incapable of remaining quietly down below. No doubt he could not sleep. And no wonder. This was also a proof. Suddenly in the silence of the ship panting upon the still, dark sea, Sterne would hear a low voice above him exclaiming nervously –

'Serang!'

'Tuan!'

'You are watching the compass well?'

'Yes, I am watching, Tuan.'

'The ship is making her course?'

'She is, Tuan. Very straight.'

'It is well; and remember, Serang, that the order is, that you are to mind the helmsmen and keep a look-out with care, the same as if I were not on deck.'

Then, when the Serang had made his answer, the low tones on the bridge would cease, and everything round Sterne seemed to become more still and more profoundly silent. Slightly chilled and with his back aching a little from long immobility, he would steal away to his room on the port side of the deck. He had long since parted with the last vestige of incredulity; of the original emotions, set into a tumult by the discovery, some trace of the first awe alone remained. Not the awe of the man himself – he could blow him up sky-high with six words – rather it was an awestruck indignation at the reckless perversity of avarice (what else could it be?), at the mad and sombre resolution that for the sake of a few dollars more seemed to set at nought the common rule of conscience and pretended to struggle against the very decree of Providence.

You could not find another man like this one in the whole round world – thank God. There was something devilishly dauntless in the character of such a deception which made you pause.

Other considerations occurring to his prudence had kept him tongue-tied from day to day. It seemed to him now that it would yet have been easier to speak out in the first hour of discovery. He almost regretted not having made a row at once. But then the very monstrosity of the disclosure. . . . Why! he could hardly face it himself, let alone pointing it out to somebody else. Moreover, with a desperado of that sort one never knew. The object was not to get him out (that was as well as done already), but to step into his place. Bizarre as the thought seemed he might have shown fight. A fellow up to working such a fraud would have enough cheek for anything; a fellow that, as it were, stood up against God Almighty Himself. He was a horrid marvel – that's what he was: he was perfectly capable of brazening out the affair scandalously till he got him (Sterne) kicked out of the ship and everlastingly damaged his prospects in this part of the East. Yet if you want to get on something must be risked. At times Sterne thought he had been unduly timid of taking action in the past; and what was worse, it had come to this, that in the present he did not seem to know what action to take.

Massy's savage moroseness was too disconcerting. It was an incalculable factor of the situation. You could not tell what there was behind that insulting ferocity. How could one trust such a temper? It did not put Sterne in bodily fear for himself, but it frightened him exceedingly as to his prospects.

Though of course inclined to credit himself with exceptional powers of observation, he had by now lived too long with his discovery. He had gone on looking at nothing else, till at last one day it occurred to him that the thing was so obvious that no one could miss seeing it. There were four white men in all on board the *Sofala*. Jack, the second engineer, was too dull to notice anything that took place out of his engine-room. Remained Massy — the owner — the interested person — nearly going mad with worry. Sterne had heard and seen more than enough on board to know what ailed him; but his exasperation seemed to make him deaf to cautious overtures. If he had only known it, there was the very thing he wanted. But how could you bargain with a man of that sort? It was like going into a tiger's den with a piece of raw meat in your hand. He was as likely as not to rend you for your pains. In fact, he was always threatening to do that very thing; and the urgency of the case, combined with the impossibility of handling it with safety, made Sterne in his watches below toss and mutter open-eyed in his bunk, for hours, as though he had been burning with fever.

Occurrences like the crossing of the bar just now were extremely alarming to his prospects. He did not want to be left behind by some swift catastrophe. Massy being on the bridge, the old man had to brace himself up, and make a show, he supposed. But it was getting very bad with him, very bad indeed, now. Even Massy had been emboldened to find fault this time; Sterne, listening at the foot of the ladder, had heard the other's whimpering and artless denunciations. Luckily the beast was very stupid and could not see the why of all this. However, small blame to him; it took a clever man to hit upon the cause. Nevertheless, it was high time to do something. The old man's game could not be kept up for many days more.

'I may yet lose my life at this fooling — let alone my chance,' Sterne mumbled angrily to himself, after the stooping back of the chief engineer had disappeared round the corner of the skylight. Yes, no doubt — he thought; but to blurt out his knowledge would not advance his prospects. On the contrary, it would blast them utterly as likely as not. He dreaded another failure. He had a vague consciousness of not being much liked by his fellows in this part of the world; inexplicably enough, for he had done nothing to them. Envy, he supposed. People were always down on a clever chap who made no bones about his determination to get on. To do your duty and count on the gratitude of that brute Massy would be sheer folly. He was a bad lot. Unmanly! A vicious man! Bad! Bad! A brute! A brute without a spark of anything human about him; without so much as simple curiosity even, or else surely he would have responded in some way to all these hints he had been given. . . . Such insensibility was almost mysterious. Massy's state of exasperation seemed to Sterne to have made him stupid beyond the ordinary silliness of shipowners.

Sterne, meditating on the embarrassments of that stupidity, forgot himself completely. His stony, unwinking stare was fixed on the planks of the deck.

The slight quiver agitating the whole fabric of the ship was more perceptible in the silent river, shaded and still like a forest path. The *Sofala*, gliding with an even motion, had passed beyond the coast-belt of mud and mangroves. The shores rose higher, in firm sloping banks, and the forest of big trees came down to the brink. Where the earth had been crumbled by the floods it showed a steep brown cut, denuding a mass of roots intertwined as if wrestling underground; and in the air, the interlaced boughs, bound and loaded with creepers, carried on the struggle for life, mingled their foliage in one solid wall of leaves, with here and there the shape of an enormous dark pillar soaring, or a ragged opening, as if torn by the flight of a cannon-ball, disclosing the impenetrable gloom within, the secular inviolable shade of the virgin forest. The thump of the engines reverberated regularly like the strokes of a metronome beating the measure of the vast silence, the shadow of the western wall had fallen across the river, and the smoke pouring backwards from the funnel eddied down behind the ship, spread a thin dusky veil over the sombre water, which, checked by the flood-tide, seemed to lie stagnant in the whole straight length of the reaches.

Sterne's body, as if rooted on the spot, trembled slightly from top to toe with the internal vibration of the ship; from under his feet came sometimes a sudden clang of iron, the noisy burst of a shout below; to the right the leaves of the tree-tops caught the rays of the low sun, and seemed to shine with a golden green light of their own shimmering around the highest boughs which stood out black against a smooth blue sky that seemed to droop over the bed of the river like the roof of a tent. The passengers for Batu Beru, kneeling on the planks, were engaged in rolling their bedding of mats busily; they tied up bundles, they snapped the locks of wooden chests. A pockmarked pedlar of small wares threw his head back to drain into his throat the last drops out of an earthenware bottle before putting it away in a roll of blankets. Knots of travelling traders standing about the deck conversed in low tones; the followers of a small Rajah from down the coast, broad-faced simple young fellows in white drawers and round white cotton caps with their coloured sarongs twisted across their bronze shoulders, squatted on their hams on the hatch, chewing betel with bright red mouths as if they had been tasting blood. Their spears, lying piled up together within the circle of their bare toes, resembled a casual bundle of dry bamboos; a thin, livid Chinaman, with a bulky package wrapped up in leaves already thrust under his arm, gazed ahead eagerly; a wandering King rubbed his teeth with a bit of wood, pouring over the side a bright stream of water out of his lips; the fat Rajah dozed in a shabby deck-chair – and at the turn of every bend the two walls of leaves reappeared running parallel along the banks, with their impenetrable solidity fading at the top to a vaporous mistiness of countless slender twigs growing free, of young delicate branches shooting from the topmost limbs of hoary trunks, of feathery heads of climbers like delicate silver sprays standing up without a quiver. There was not a sign of a clearing anywhere; not a trace of human habitation, except when in one place, on the bare end of a low point under an isolated group of slender tree-ferns, the jagged, tangled remnants of an old hut on piles appeared with that peculiar aspect of ruined bamboo walls that look as if smashed with a club. Farther on, half hidden under the drooping bushes, a canoe containing a man and a woman together with a dozen green cocoanuts in a heap, rocked helplessly after the *Sofala* had passed, like a navigating contrivance of venturesome insects, of travelling ants; while two glassy folds of water streaming away from each bow of the steamer across the whole width of the river ran with her upstream smoothly, fretting their outer ends into a brown whispering tumble of froth against the miry foot of each bank.

'I must,' thought Sterne, 'bring that brute Massy to his bearings. It's getting too absurd in the end. Here's the old man up there buried in his chair – he may just as well be in his grave for all the use he'll ever be in the world – and the Serang's in charge.

Because that's what he is. In charge. In the place that's mine by rights. I must bring that savage brute to his bearings. I'll do it at once, too. . . .'

When the mate made an abrupt start, a little brown, half-naked boy, with large black eyes, and the string of a written charm round his neck, became panic-struck at once. He dropped the banana he had been munching, and ran to the knee of a grave dark Arab in flowing robes, sitting like a Biblical figure, incongruously, on a yellow tin trunk corded with a rope of twisted rattan. The father, unmoved, put out his hand to pat the little shaven poll protectingly.

XI

STERNE crossed the deck upon the track of the chief engineer. Jack, the second, retreating backwards down the engine-room ladder, and still wiping his hands, treated him to an incomprehensible grin of white teeth out of his grimy hard face; Massy was nowhere to be seen. Sterne scratched at the door softly, then, putting his lips to the rose of the ventilator, said –

'I must speak to you, Mr Massy. Just give me a minute or two.'

'I am busy. Go away from my door.'

'But pray, Mr Massy. . . .'

'You go away. D'you hear? Take yourself off altogether – to the other end of the ship – quite away. . . .' The voice inside dropped low. 'To the devil.'

Sterne paused: then very quietly –

'It's rather pressing. When do you think you will be at liberty, sir?'

The answer to this was an exasperated 'Never'; and at once Sterne, with a very firm expression of face, turned the handle.

Mr Massy's stateroom – a narrow, one-berth cabin – smelt strongly of soap, and presented to view a swept, dusted, unadorned neatness, not so much bare as barren, not so much severe as starved and lacking in humanity, like the ward of a public hospital, or rather (owing to the small size) like the clean retreat of a desperately poor but exemplary person. Not a single photograph frame ornamented the bulkheads; not a single article of clothing, not as much as a spare cap, hung from the brass hooks. All the inside was painted in one plain tint of pale blue; two big sea-chests in sailcloth covers and with iron padlocks fitted exactly in the space under the bunk. One glance was enough to embrace all the strip of scrubbed planks within the four unconcealed corners. The absence of the usual settee was striking; the teak-wood top of the washing-stand seemed hermetically closed, and so was the lid of the writing-desk, which protruded from the partition at the foot of the bed place, containing a mattress as thin as a pancake under a threadbare blanket with a faded red stripe, and a folded mosquito-net against the nights spent in harbour. There was not a scrap of paper anywhere in sight, no boots on the floor, no litter of any sort, not a speck of dust anywhere; no traces of pipe-ash even, which, in a heavy smoker, was morally revolting, like a manifestation of extreme hypocrisy; and the bottom of the old wooden arm-chair (the only seat there), polished with much use, shone as if its shabbiness had been waxed. The screen of leaves on the bank, passing as if unrolled endlessly in the round opening of the port, sent a wavering network of light and shade into the place.

Sterne, holding the door open with one hand, had thrust in his head and shoulders. At this amazing intrusion Massy, who was doing absolutely nothing, jumped up speechless.

'Don't call names,' murmured Sterne, hurriedly. 'I won't be called names. I think of nothing but your good, Mr Massy.'

A pause as of extreme astonishment followed. They both seemed to have lost their tongues. Then the mate went on with discreet glibness:

'You simply couldn't conceive what's going on on board your ship. It wouldn't enter your head for a moment. You are too good – too – too upright, Mr Massy, to suspect anybody of such a. . . . It's enough to make your hair stand on end.'

He watched for the effect: Massy seemed dazed, uncomprehending. He only passed the palm of his hand on the coal-black wisps plastered across the top of his head. In a tone suddenly changed to confidential audacity Sterne hastened on:

'Remember that there's only six weeks left to run . . .' The other was looking at him stonily. . . . 'So anyhow you will require a captain for the ship before long.'

Then only, as if that suggestion had scarified his flesh in the manner of red-hot iron, Massy gave a start and seemed ready to shriek. He contained himself by a great effort.

'Require – a – captain,' he repeated with scathing slowness. 'Who requires a captain? You dare tell me that I need any of you humbugging sailors to run my ship. You and your likes have been fattening on me for years. It would have hurt me less to throw my money overboard. Pam – pe – red us – e – less f-f-f-frauds. The old ship knows as much as the best of you.' He snapped his teeth audibly and growled through them. 'The silly law requires a captain.'

Sterne had taken heart of grace meantime.

'And the silly insurance people, too, as well,' he said, lightly. 'But never mind that. What I want to ask is: Why shouldn't *I* do, sir? I don't say but you could take a steamer about the world as well as any of us sailors. I don't pretend to tell *you* that it is a very great trick . . .' He emitted a short, hollow guffaw, familiarly . . . 'I didn't make the law – but there it is; and I am an active young fellow; I quite hold with your ideas; I know your ways by this time, Mr Massy. I wouldn't try to give myself airs like that – that – er – lazy specimen of an old man up there.'

He put a marked emphasis on the last sentence, to lead Massy away from the track in case . . . but he did not doubt of now holding his success. The chief engineer seemed nonplussed, like a slow man invited to catch hold of a whirligig of some sort.

'What you want, sir, is a chap with no nonsense about him, who would be content to be your sailing-master. Quite right, too. Well, I am fit for the work as much as that Serang. Because that's what it amounts to. Do you know, sir, that a dam' Malay like a monkey is in charge of your ship – and no one else? Just listen to his feet pit-patting above us on the bridge – real officer in charge. He's taking her up the river while the great man is wallowing in the chair – perhaps asleep; and if he is, that would not make it much worse either – take my word for it.'

He tried to thrust himself farther in. Massy, with lowered forehead, one hand grasping the back of the arm-chair, did not budge.

'You think, sir, that the man has got you tight in his agreement . . .' Massy raised a heavy snarling face at this . . . 'Well, sir, one can't help hearing of it on board. It's no secret. And it has been the talk on shore for years; fellows have been making bets about it. No, sir! It's *you* who have got him at your mercy. You will say that you can't dismiss him for indolence. Difficult to prove in court, and so on. Why, yes. But if you say the word, sir, I can tell you something about his indolence that will give you the clear right to fire him out on the spot and put me in charge for the rest of this very trip – yes, sir, before we leave Batu Beru – and make him pay a dollar a day for his keep till we get back, if you like. Now, what do you think of that? Come, sir. Say the word. It's really well worth your while, and I am quite ready to take your bare word. A definite statement from you would be as good as a bond.'

His eyes began to shine. He insisted. A simple statement – and he thought to himself that he would manage somehow to stick in his berth as long as it suited him. He would make himself indispensable; the ship had a bad name in her port; it would be easy to scare the fellows off. Massy would have to keep him.

'A definite statement from me would be enough,' Massy repeated, slowly.

'Yes, sir. It would.' Sterne stuck out his chin cheerily and blinked at close quarters with that unconscious impudence which had the power to enrage Massy beyond anything.

The engineer spoke very distinctly:

'Listen well to me, then, Mr Sterne: I wouldn't – d'ye hear? – I wouldn't promise you the value of two pence for anything *you* can tell me.'

He struck Sterne's arm away with a smart blow, and catching hold of the handle pulled the door to. The terrific slam darkened the cabin instantaneously to his eyes as if after the flash of an explosion. At once he dropped into the chair. 'Oh, no! You don't!' he whispered faintly.

The ship had in that place to shave the bank so close that the gigantic wall of leaves came gliding like a shutter against the port; the darkness of the primeval forest seemed to flow into that bare cabin with the odour of rotting leaves, of sodden soil – the strong muddy smell of the living earth steaming uncovered after the passing of a deluge. The bushes swished loudly alongside; above there was a series of crackling sounds, with a sharp rain of small broken branches falling on the bridge; a creeper with a great rustle snapped on the head of a boat davit, and a long, luxuriant green twig actually whipped in and out of the open port, leaving behind a few torn leaves that remained suddenly at rest on Mr Massy's blanket. Then, the ship sheering out in the stream, the light began to return, but did not augment beyond a subdued clearness: for the sun was very low already, and the river, wending its sinuous course through a multitude of secular trees as if at the bottom of a precipitous gorge, had been already invaded by a deepening gloom – the swift precursor of the night.

'Oh, no, you don't!' murmured the engineer again. His lips trembled almost imperceptibly; his hands, too, a little: and to calm himself he opened the writing-desk, spread out a sheet of thin greyish paper covered with a mass of printed figures and began to scan them attentively for the twentieth time this trip at least.

With his elbows propped, his head between his hands, he seemed to lose himself in the study of an abstruse problem in mathematics. It was the list of the winning numbers from the last drawing of the great lottery which had been the one inspiring fact of so many years of his existence. The conception of a life deprived of that periodical sheet of paper had slipped away from him entirely, as another man, according to his nature, would not have been able to conceive a world without fresh air, without activity, or without affection. A great pile of flimsy sheets had been growing for years in his desk, while the *Sofala*, driven by the faithful Jack, wore out her boilers in tramping up and down the Straits, from cape to cape, from river to river, from bay to bay; accumulating by that hard labour of an overworked, starved ship the blackened mass of these documents. Massy kept them under lock and key like a treasure. There was in them, as in the experience of life, the fascination of hope, the excitement of a half-penetrated mystery, the longing of a half-satisfied desire.

For days together, on a trip, he would shut himself up in his berth with them: the thump of the toiling engines pulsated in his ear; and he would weary his brain poring over the rows of disconnected figures, bewildering by their senseless sequence,

resembling the hazards of destiny itself. He nourished a conviction that there must be some logic lurking somewhere in the
results of chance. He thought he had seen its very form. His head
swam; his limbs ached; he puffed at his pipe mechanically; a
contemplative stupor would soothe the fretfulness of his temper,
like the passive bodily quietude precured by a drug, while the
intellect remains tensely on the stretch. Nine, nine, nought, four,
two. He made a note. The next winning number of the great prize
was forty-seven thousand and five. These numbers of course
would have to be avoided in the future when writing to Manila for
the tickets. He mumbled, pencil in hand . . . 'and five. Hm . . .
hm.' He wetted his finger: the papers rustled. Ha! But what's this?
Three years ago, in the September drawing, it was number nine,
nought, four, two that took the first prize. Most remarkable.
There was a hint there of a definite rule! He was afraid of missing
some recondite principle in the overwhelming wealth of his
material. What could it be? And for half an hour he would remain
dead still, bent low over the desk, without twitching a muscle. At
his back the whole berth would be thick with a heavy body of
smoke, as if a bomb had burst in there, unnoticed, unheard.

At last he would lock up the desk with the decision of unshaken
confidence, jump up and go out. He would walk swiftly back and
forth on that part of the foredeck which was kept clear of the
lumber and of the bodies of the native passengers. They were a
great nuisance, but they were also a source of profit that could not
be disdained. He needed every penny of profit the *Sofala* could
make. Little enough it was, in all conscience! The incertitude of
chance gave him no concern, since he had somehow arrived at the
conviction that, in the course of years, every number was bound
to have its winning turn. It was simply a matter of time and of
taking as many tickets as he could afford for every drawing. He
generally took rather more; all the earnings of the ship went that
way, and also the wages he allowed himself as chief engineer. It
was the wages he paid to others that he begrudged with a reasoned
and at the same time a passionate regret. He scowled at the lascars
with their deck brooms, at the quartermasters rubbing the brass
rails with greasy rags; he was eager to shake his fist and roar abuse
in bad Malay at the poor carpenter – a timid, sickly, opium-
fuddled Chinaman, in loose blue drawers for all costume, who

invariably dropped his tools and fled below, with streaming tail and shaking all over, before the fury of that 'devil'. But it was when he raised up his eyes to the bridge where one of these sailor frauds was always planted by law in charge of his ship that he felt almost dizzy with rage. He abominated them all; it was an old feud, from the time he first went to sea, an unlicked cub with a great opinion of himself, in the engine-room. The slights that had been put upon him. The persecutions he had suffered at the hands of skippers – of absolute nobodies in a steamship after all. And now that he had risen to be a shipowner they were still a plague to him: he had absolutely to pay away precious money to the conceited useless loafers: – As if a fully qualified engineer – who was the owner as well – were not fit to be trusted with the whole charge of a ship. Well! he made it pretty warm for them; but it was a poor consolation. He had come in time to hate the ship, too, for the repairs she required, for the coal-bills he had to pay, for the poor beggarly freights she earned. He would clench his hand as he walked and hit the rail a sudden blow, viciously, as though she could be made to feel pain. And yet he could not do without her; he needed her; he must hang on to her tooth and nail to keep his head above water till the expected flood of fortune came sweeping up and landed him safely on the high shore of his ambition.

It was now to do nothing, nothing whatever, and have plenty of money to do it on. He had tasted of power, the highest form of it his limited experience was aware of – the power of shipowning. What a deception! Vanity of vanities! He wondered at his folly. He had thrown away the substance for the shadow. Of the gratification of wealth he did not know enough to excite his imagination with any visions of luxury. How could he – the child of a drunken boiler-maker – going straight from the workshop into the engine-room of a north-country collier! But the notion of the absolute idleness of wealth he could very well conceive. He revelled in it, to forget his present troubles; he imagined himself walking about the streets of Hull (he knew their gutters well as a boy) with his pockets full of sovereigns. He would buy himself a house; his married sisters, their husbands, his old workshop chums, would render him infinite homage. There would be nothing to think of. His word would be law. He had been out of work for a long time before he won his prize, and he remembered how Carlo Mariani (commonly known as Paunchy Charley), the Maltese hotel-keeper at the slummy end of Denham Street, had cringed joyfully before him in the evening, when the news had come. Poor Charley, though he made his living by ministering to various abject vices, gave credit for the food to many a piece of white wreckage. He was naïvely overjoyed at the idea of his old bills being paid, and he reckoned confidently on a spell of festivities in the cavernous grog-ship downstairs. Massy remembered the curious, respectful looks of the 'trashy' white men in the place. His heart had swelled within him. Massy had left Charley's infamous den directly he had realized the possibilities open to him, with his nose in the air. Afterwards the memory of these adulations was a great sadness.

This was the true power of money – and no trouble with it, nor any thinking required either. He thought with difficulty and felt vividly; to his blunt brain the problems offered by any ordered scheme of life seemed in their cruel toughness to have been put in his way by the obvious malevolence of men. As a shipowner everyone had conspired to make him a nobody. How could he have been such a fool as to purchase that accursed ship? He had been abominably swindled; there was no end to this swindling, and as the difficulties of his improvident ambition gathered thicker round him, he really came to hate everybody he had ever come in contact with. A temper naturally irritable and an amazing sensitiveness to the claims of his own personality had ended by making of life for him a sort of inferno – a place where his lost soul had been given up to the torment of savage brooding.

But he had never hated anyone so much as that old man who turned up one evening to save him from an utter disaster, – from the conspiracy of the wretched sailors. He seemed to have fallen on board from the sky. His footsteps echoed on the empty steamer, and the strange deep-toned voice on deck repeating interrogatively the words, 'Mr Massy, Mr Massy there?' had been startling like a wonder. And coming up from the depths of the cold engine-room, where he had been pottering dismally with a candle amongst the enormous shadows, thrown on all sides by the skeleton limbs of machinery. Massy had been struck dumb by astonishment in the presence of that imposing old man with a beard like a silver plate, towering in the dusk rendered lurid by the expiring flames of sunset.

'Want to see me on business? What business? I am doing no business. Can't you see that this ship is laid up?' Massy had turned at bay before the pursuing irony of his disaster. Afterwards he could not believe his ears. What was that old fellow getting at? Things don't happen that way. It was a dream. He would presently wake up and find the man vanished like a shape of mist. The gravity, the dignity, the firm and courteous tone of that athletic old stranger impressed Massy. He was almost afraid. But it was no dream. Five hundreds pounds are no dream. At once he became suspicious. What did it mean? Of course it was an offer to catch hold of for dear life. But what could there be behind?

Before they had parted, after appointing a meeting in a solicitor's office early on the morrow, Massy was asking himself, What is his motive? He spent the night in hammering out the clauses of the agreement – a unique instrument of its sort whose tenor got bruited abroad somehow and became the talk and wonder of the port.

Massy's object had been to secure for himself as many ways as possible of getting rid of his partner without being called upon at once to pay back his share. Captain Whalley's efforts were directed to making the money secure. Was it not Ivy's money – a part of her fortune whose only other asset was the time-defying body of her old father? Sure of his forbearance in the strength of his love for her, he accepted, with stately serenity, Massy's stupidly cunning paragraphs against his incompetence, his dishonesty, his drunkenness, for the sake of other stringent stipulations. At the end of three years he was at liberty to withdraw from the partnership, taking his money with him. Provision was made for forming a fund to pay him off. But if he left the *Sofala* before the term, from whatever cause (barring death), Massy was to have a whole year for paying. 'Illness?' the lawyer had suggested: a young man fresh from Europe and not overburdened with business, who was rather amused. Massy began to whine unctuously, 'How could he be expected? . .'

'Let that go,' Captain Whalley had said with a superb confidence in his body. 'Acts of God,' he added. In the midst of life we are in death, but he trusted his Maker with a still greater fearlessness – his Maker who knew his thoughts, his human affections, and his motives. His Creator knew what use he was making of his health – how much he wanted it. . . . 'I trust my first illness will be my last. I've never been ill that I can remember,' he had remarked. 'Let it go.'

But at this early stage he had already awakened Massy's hostility by refusing to make it six hundred instead of five. 'I cannot do that,' was all he had said, simply, but with so much decision that Massy desisted at once from pressing the point, but had thought to himself, 'Can't! Old curmudgeon. *Won't!* He must have lots of money, but he would like to get hold of a soft berth and the sixth part of my profits for nothing if he only could.'

And during these years Massy's dislike grew under the restraint of something resembling fear. The simplicity of that man appeared dangerous. Of late he had changed, however, had appeared less formidable and with a lessened vigour of life, as though he had received a secret wound. But still he remained incomprehensible in his simplicity, fearlessness, and rectitude. And when Massy learned that he meant to leave him at the end of the time, to leave him confronted with the problem of the boilers, his dislike blazed up secretly into hate.

It had made him so clear-eyed that for a long time now Mr Sterne could have told him nothing he did not know. He had much ado in trying to terrorize that mean sneak into silence; he wanted to deal alone with the situation; and – incredible as it might have appeared to Mr Sterne – he had not yet given up the desire and the hope of inducing that hated old man to stay. Why! there was nothing else to do, unless he were to abandon his chances of fortune. But now, suddenly, since the crossing of the bar at Batu Beru things seemed to be coming rapidly to a point. It disquieted him so much that the study of the winning numbers failed to soothe his agitation: and the twilight in the cabin deepened, very sombre.

He put the list away, muttering once more, 'Oh, no, my boy, you don't. Not if I know it.' He did not mean the blinking, eavesdropping humbug to force his action. He took his head again into his hands; his immobility confined in the darkness of this shut-up little place seemed to make him a thing apart infinitely removed from the stir and the sounds of the deck.

He heard them: the passengers were beginning to jabber excitedly; somebody dragged a heavy box past his door. He heard Captain Whalley's voice above –

'Stations, Mr Sterne.' And the answer from somewhere on deck forward –

'Ay, ay, sir.'

'We shall moor head upstream this time; the ebb has made.'

'Head upstream, sir.'

'You will see to it, Mr Sterne.'

The answer was covered by the autocratic clang of the engine-room gong. The propeller went on beating slowly: one, two, three; one, two three – with pauses as if hesitating on the turn. The gong clanged time after time, and the water churned this way and that by the blades was making a great noisy commotion alongside. Mr Massy did not move. A shore-light on the other bank, a quarter of a mile across the river, drifted, no bigger than a tiny star, passing slowly athwart the circle of the port. Voices from Mr Van Wyk's jetty answered the hails from the ship; ropes were thrown and missed and thrown again; the swaying flame of a torch carried in a large sampan coming to fetch away in state the Rajah from down the coast cast a sudden ruddy glare into his cabin, over his very person. Mr Massy did not move. After a few last ponderous turns the engines stopped, and the prolonged clanging of the gong signified that the captain had done with them. A great number of boats and canoes of all sizes boarded the off-side of the *Sofala*. Then after a time the tumult of splashing, of cries, of shuffling feet, of packages dropped with a thump, the noise of the native passengers going away, subsided slowly. On the shore, a voice, cultivated, slightly authoritative, spoke very close alongside –

'Brought any mail for me this time?'

'Yes, Mr Van Wyk.' This was from Sterne, answering over the rail in a tone of respectful cordiality. 'Shall I bring it up to you?'

But the voice asked again –

'Where's the captain?'

'Still on the bridge, I believe. He hasn't left his chair. Shall I. . . .'

The voice interrupted negligently—

'I will come on board.'

'Mr Van Wyk,' Sterne suddenly broke out with an eager effort, 'will you do me the favour. . . .'

The mate walked away quickly towards the gangway. A silence fell. Mr Massy in the dark did not move.

He did not move even when he heard slow shuffling footsteps pass his cabin lazily. He contented himself to bellow out through the closed door –

'You – Jack!'

The footsteps came back without haste; the door-handle rattled, and the second engineer appeared in the opening, shadowy in the sheen of the skylight at his back, with his face apparently as black as the rest of his figure.

'We have been very long coming up this time,' Mr Massy growled, without changing his attitude.

'What do you expect with half the boiler tubes plugged up for leaks.' The second defended himself loquaciously.

'None of your lip,' said Massy.

'None of your rotten boilers – I say,' retorted his faithful subordinate without animation, huskily.

'Go down there and carry a head of steam on them yourself – if you dare. I don't.'

'You aren't worth your salt then', Massy said. The other made a faint noise which resembled a laugh but might have been a snarl.

'Better go slow than stop the ship altogether,' he admonished his admired superior. Mr Massy moved at last. He turned in his chair, and grinding his teeth –

'Dam' you and the ship! I wish she were at the bottom of the sea. Then you would have to starve.'

The trusty second engineer closed the door gently.

Massy listened. Instead of passing on to the bathroom where he should have gone to clean himself, the second entered his cabin, which was next door. Mr Massy jumped up and waited. Suddenly he heard the lock snap in there. He rushed out and gave a violent kick to the door.

'I believe you are locking yourself up to get drunk,' he shouted.

A muffled answer came after a while.

'My own time.'

'If you take to boozing on the trip I'll fire you out,' Massy cried.

An obstinate silence followed that threat. Massy moved away, perplexed. On the bank two figures appeared, approaching the gangway. He heard a voice tinged with contempt –

'I would rather doubt your word. But I shall certainly speak to him of this.'

The other voice, Sterne's, said with a regretful formality —

'Thanks. That's all I want. I must do my duty.'

Mr Massy was surprised. A short, dapper figure leaped lightly on the deck and nearly bounded into him where he stood beyond the circle of light from the gangway lamp. When it had passed towards the bridge, after exchanging a hurried 'Good evening,' Massy said surlily to Sterne, who followed with slow steps —

'What is it you're making up to Mr Van Wyk for, now?'

'Far from it, Mr Massy. I am not good enough for Mr Van Wyk. Neither are you, sir, in his opinion, I am afraid. Captain Whalley is, it seems. He's gone to ask him to dine up at the house this evening.'

Then he murmured to himself darkly —

'I hope he will like it.'

XII

MR VAN WYK, the white man of Batu Beru, an ex-naval officer who, for reasons best known to himself, had thrown away the promise of a brilliant career to become the pioneer of tobacco-planting on that remote part of the coast, had learned to like Captain Whalley. The appearance of the new skipper had attracted his attention. Nothing more unlike all the diverse types he had seen succeeding each other on the bridge of the *Sofala* could be imagined.

At that time Batu Beru was not what it has become since: the centre of a prosperous tobacco-growing district, a tropically suburban-looking little settlement of bungalows in one long street shaded with two rows of trees, embowered by the flowering and trim luxuriance of the gardens, with a three-mile-long carriage-road for the afternoon drives and a first-class Resident with a fat, cheery wife to lead the society of married estate-managers and unmarried young fellows in the service of the big companies.

All this prosperity was not yet; and Mr Van Wyk prospered alone on the left bank on his deep clearing carved out of the forest, which came down above and below to the water's edge. His lonely bungalow faced across the river the houses of the Sultan: a restless and melancholy old ruler who had done with love and war, for whom life no longer held any savour (except of evil forebodings) and time never had any value. He was afraid of death, and hoped he would die before the white men were ready to take his country from him. He crossed the river frequently (with never less than ten boats crammed full of people), in the wistful hope of extracting some information on the subject from his own white man. There was a certain chair on the verandah he always took: the dignitaries of the court squatted on the rugs and skins between the furniture: the inferior people remained below on the grass-plot between the house and the river in rows three or four deep all along the front. Not seldom the visit began at daybreak. Mr Van Wyk tolerated these inroads. He would nod out of his bedroom window, toothbrush or razor in hand, or pass through the throng of courtiers in his bathing robe. He appeared and disappeared humming a tune, polished his nails with attention, rubbed his shaved face with eau-de-Cologne, drank his early tea, went out to see his coolies at work; returned, looked through some papers on his desk, read a page or two in a book or sat before his cottage piano leaning back on the stool, his arms extended, fingers on the keys, his body swaying slightly from side to side. When absolutely forced to speak he gave evasive, vaguely soothing answers out of pure compassion: the same feeling perhaps made him so lavishly hospitable with the aerated drinks that more than once he left himself without soda-water for a whole week. That old man had granted him as much land as he cared to have cleared: it was neither more nor less than a fortune.

Whether it was fortune or seclusion from his kind that Mr Van Wyk sought, he could not have pitched upon a better place. Even the mail-boats of the subsidized company calling on the veriest clusters of palm-thatched hovels along the coast steamed past the mouth of Batu Beru river far away in the offing. The contract was old: perhaps in a few years' time, when it had expired, Batu Beru would be included in the service; meantime all Mr Van Wyk's mail was addressed to Malacca, whence his agent sent it across once a month by the *Sofala*. It followed that whenever Massy had run short of money (through taking too many lottery tickets), or got into a difficulty about a skipper, Mr Van Wyk was deprived of his letters and newspapers. In so far he had a personal interest in the fortunes of the *Sofala*. Though he considered himself a hermit (and for no passing whim evidently, since he had stood eight years of it already), he liked to know what went on in the world.

Handy on the verandah upon a walnut *étagére* (it had come last year by the *Sofala*— everything came by the *Sofala*) there lay, piled up under bronze weights, a pile of *The Times* weekly edition, the large sheets of the *Rotterdam Courant*, the *Graphic* in its world-wide green wrappers, an illustrated Dutch publication without a cover, the numbers of a German magazine with covers of the 'Bismarck malade' colour. There were also parcels of new music – though the piano (it had come years ago by the *Sofala*) in the damp atmosphere of the forests was generally out of tune. It was vexing to be cut off from everything for sixty days at a stretch sometimes, without any means of knowing what was the matter. And when the *Sofala* reappeared Mr Van Wyk would descend the steps of the verandah and stroll over the grass-plot in front of his house, down to the water-side, with a frown on his white brow.

'You've been laid up after an accident, I presume.'

He addressed the bridge, but before anybody could answer Massy was sure to have scrambled ashore over the rail and pushed in, squeezing the palms of his hands together, bowing his sleek head as if gummed all over the top with black threads and tapes. And he would be so enraged at the necessity of having to offer such an explanation that his moaning would be positively pitiful, while all the time he tried to compose his big lips into a smile.

'No, Mr Van Wyk. You would not believe it. I couldn't get one of those wretches to take the ship out. Not a single one of the lazy beasts could be induced, and the law, you know, Mr Van Wyk. . . .'

He moaned at great length apologetically; the words conspiracy, plot, envy, came out prominently, whined with greater energy. Mr Van Wyk, examining with a faint grimace his polished fingernails, would say, 'H'm. Very unfortunate,' and turn his back on him.

Fastidious, clever, slightly sceptical, accustomed to the best society (he had held a much-envied shore appointment at the Ministry of Marine for a year preceding his retreat from his profession and from Europe), he possessed a latent warmth of feeling and a capacity for sympathy which were concealed by a sort of haughty, arbitrary indifference of manner arising from his early training; and by a something an enemy might have called foppish, in his aspect – like a distorted echo of past elegancies. He managed to keep an almost military discipline amongst the coolies of the estate he had dragged into the light of day out of the tangle and shadows of the jungle; and the white shirt he put on every evening with its glossy front and high collar looked as if he had meant to preserve the decent ceremony of evening-dress, but had wound a thick crimson sash above his hips as a concession to the wilderness, once his adversary, now his vanquished companion. Moreover, it was a hygienic precaution. Worn wide open in front, a short jacket of some airy silken stuff floated from his shoulders. His fluffy, thin hair, thin at the top, curled slightly at the sides; a carefully arranged moustache, an ungarnished forehead, the gleam of low patent shoes peeping under the wide bottom of trousers cut straight from the same stuff as the gossamer coat, completed a figure recalling, with its sash, a pirate chief of romance, and at the same time the elegance of a slightly bald dandy indulging, in seclusion, a taste for unorthodox costume.

It was his evening get-up. The proper time for the *Sofala* to arrive at Batu Beru was an hour before sunset, and he looked picturesque, and somehow quite correct, too, walking at the water's edge on the background of grassy slope crowned with a low, long bungalow with an immensely steep roof of palm thatch, and clad to the eaves in flowering creepers. While the *Sofala* was being made fast he strolled in the shade of the few trees left near the landing-place, waiting till he could go on board. Her white men were not of his kind. The old Sultan (though his wistful invasions were a nuisance) was really much more acceptable to his fastidious taste. But still they were white; the periodical visits of the ship made a break in the well-filled sameness of the day without disturbing his privacy. Moreover, they were necessary from a business point of view; and through a strain of preciseness in his nature he was irritated when she failed to appear at the appointed time.

The cause of the irregularity was too absurd, and Massy, in his opinion, was a contemptible idiot. The first time the *Sofala* reappeared under the new agreement swinging out of the bend below, after he had almost given up all hope of ever seeing her again, he felt so angry that he did not go down at once to the landing-place. His servants had come running to him with the news, and he had dragged a chair close against the front rail of the verandah, spread his elbows out, rested his chin on his hands, and went on glaring at her fixedly while she was being made fast opposite his house. He could make out easily all the white faces on board. Who on earth was that kind of patriarch they had got there on the bridge now?

At last he sprang up and walked down the gravel path. It was a fact that the very gravel for his paths had been imported by the *Sofala*. Exasperated out of his quiet superciliousness, without looking at any one right or left, he accosted Massy straightway in so determined a manner that the engineer, taken aback, began to stammer unintelligibly. Nothing could be heard but the words: 'Mr Van Wyk . . . Indeed, Mr Van Wyk . . . For the future, Mr Van Wyk' – and by the suffusion of blood Massy's vast bilious face acquired an unnatural orange tint, out of which the disconcerted coal-black eyes shone in an extraordinary manner.

'Nonsense. I am tired of this. I wonder you have the impudence to come alongside my jetty as if I had made it for your convenience alone.'

Massy tried to protest earnestly. Mr Van Wyk was very angry. He had a good mind to ask that German firm – those people in Malacca – what was their name? – boats with green funnels. They would be only too glad of the opening to put one of their small steamers on the run. Yes; Schnitzler, Jacob Schnitzler, would in a moment. Yes. He had decided to write without delay.

In his agitation Massy caught up his falling pipe.

'You don't mean it, sir!' he shrieked.

'You shouldn't mismanage your business in this ridiculous manner.'

Mr Van Wyk turned on his heel. The other three whites on the bridge had not stirred, during the scene. Massy walked hastily from side to side, puffed out his cheeks, suffocated.

'Stuck-up Dutchman!'

And he moaned out feverishly a long tale of griefs. The efforts

he had made for all these years to please that man. This was the
return you got for it, heh? Pretty. Write to Schnitzler – let in the
green-funnel boats – get an old Hamburg Jew to ruin him. No,
really he could laugh . . . He laughed sobbingly . . . Ha! ha! ha!
And make him carry the letter in his own ship presumably.

He stumbled across a grating and swore. He would not hesitate
to fling the Dutchman's correspondence overboard – the whole
confounded bundle. He had never, never made any charge for that
accommodation. But Captain Whalley, his new partner, would
not let him probably; besides, it would be only putting off the evil
day. For his own part he would make a hole in the water rather
than look on tamely at the green funnels overrunning his trade.

He raved aloud. The China boys hung back with the dishes at
the foot of the ladder. He yelled from the bridge down at the deck,
'Aren't we going to have any chow this evening at all?' then turned
violently to Captain Whalley, who waited, grave and patient, at
the head of the table, smoothing his beard in silence now and then
with a forbearing gesture.

'You don't seem to care what happens to me. Don't you see that
this affects your interests as much as mine? It's no joking matter.'

He took the foot of the table growling between his teeth.

'Unless you have a few thousand pounds put away somewhere.
I haven't.'

Mr Van Wyk dined in his thoroughly lit-up bungalow, putting
a point of splendour in the night of his clearing above the dark
bank of the river. Afterwards he sat down to his piano, and in a
pause he became aware of slow footsteps passing on the path
along the front. A plank or two creaked under a heavy tread; he
swung half round on the music-stool; listening with his finger-tips
at rest on the keyboard. His little terrier barked violently, backing
in from the verandah. A deep voice apologized gravely for 'this
intrusion'. He walked out quickly.

At the head of the steps the patriarchal figure, who was the new
captain of the *Sofala* apparently (he had seen a round dozen of
them, but not one of that sort), towered without advancing. The
little dog barked unceasingly, till a flick of Mr Van Wyk's
handkerchief made him spring aside into silence. Captain
Whalley, opening the matter, was met by a punctiliously polite
but determined opposition.

They carried on their discussion standing where they had come face to face. Mr Van Wyk observed his visitor with attention. Then at last, as if forced out of his reserve —

'I am surprised that you should intercede for such a confounded fool.'

This outbreak was almost complimentary, as if its meaning had been, 'That such a man as you should intercede!' Captain Whalley let it pass by without flinching. One would have thought he had heard nothing. He simply went on to state that he was personally interested in putting things straight between them. Personally. . . .

But Mr Van Wyk, really carried away by his disgust with Massy, became very incisive —

'Indeed — if I am to be frank with you — his whole character does not seem to me particularly estimable or trustworthy . . .'

Captain Whalley, always straight, seemed to grow an inch taller and broader, as if the girth of his chest had suddenly expanded under his beard.

'My dear sir, you don't think I came here to discuss a man with whom I am — I am — h'm — closely associated.'

A sort of solemn silence lasted for a moment. He was not used to asking favours, but the importance he attached to this affair had made him willing to try . . . Mr Van Wyk, favourably impressed, and suddenly mollified by a desire to laugh, interrupted —

'That's all right if you make it a personal matter; but you can do no less than sit down and smoke a cigar with me.'

A slight pause, then Captain Whalley stepped forward heavily. As to the regularity of the service, for the future he made himself responsible for it; and his name was Whalley — perhaps to a sailor (he was speaking to a sailor, was he not?) not altogether unfamiliar. There was a lighthouse now, on an island. Maybe Mr Van Wyk himself . . .

'Oh, yes. Oh, indeed.' Mr Van Wyk caught on at once. He indicated a chair. How very interesting. For his own part he had seen some service in the last Acheen War, but had never been so far East. Whalley Island? Of course. Now that was very interesting. What changes his guest must have seen since.

'I can look further back even — on a whole half-century.'

Captain Whalley expanded a bit. The flavour of a good cigar (it was a weakness) had gone straight to his heart, also the civility of that young man. There was something in that accidental contact of which he had been starved in his years of struggle.

The front wall retreating made a square recess furnished like a room. A lamp with a milky glass shade, suspended below the slope of the high roof at the end of a slender brass chain, threw a bright round of light upon a little table bearing an open book and an ivory paper-knife. And, in the translucent shadows beyond, other tables could be seen, a number of easy-chairs of various shapes, with a great profusion of skin rugs strewn on the teak-wood planking all over the verandah. The flowering creepers scented the air. Their foliage clipped out between the uprights made as if several frames of thick, unstirring leaves reflecting the lamplight in a green glow. Through the opening at his elbow Captain Whalley could see the gangway lantern of the *Sofala* burning dim by the shore, the shadowy masses of the town beyond the open lustrous darkness of the river, and, as if hung along the straight edge of the projecting eaves, a narrow black strip of the night sky full of stars – resplendent. The famous cigar in hand, he had a moment of complacency.

'A trifle. Somebody must lead the way. I just showed that the thing could be done; but you men brought up to the use of steam cannot conceive the vast importance of my bit of venturesomeness to the Eastern trade of the time. Why, that new route reduced the average time of a southern passage by eleven days for more than half the year. Eleven days! It's on record. But the remarkable thing – speaking to a sailor – I should say was . . .'

He talked well, without egotism, professionally. The powerful voice, produced without effort, filled the bungalow even into the empty rooms with a deep and limpid resonance, seemed to make a stillness outside; and Mr Van Wyk was surprised by the serene quality of its tone, like the perfection of manly gentleness. Nursing one small foot, in a silk sock and a patent leather shoe, on his knee, he was immensely entertained. It was as if nobody could talk like this now, and the over-shadowed eyes, the flowing white beard, the big frame, the serenity, the whole temper of the man, were an amazing survival from the prehistoric times of the world coming up to him out of the sea.

Captain Whalley had been also the pioneer of the early trade in the Gulf of Pe-tchi-li. He even found occasion to mention that he had buried his 'dear wife' there six-and-twenty years ago. Mr Van Wyk, impassive, could not help speculating in his mind swiftly as to the sort of woman that would mate with such a man. Did they make an adventurous and well-matched pair? No. Very possibly she had been small, frail, no doubt very feminine – or most likely commonplace with domestic instincts, utterly insignificant. But Captain Whalley was no garrulous bore, and shaking his head as if to dissipate the momentary gloom that had settled on his handsome old face, he alluded conversationally to Mr Van Wyk's solitude.

Mr Van Wyk affirmed that sometimes he had more company than he wanted. He mentioned smilingly some of the peculiarities of his intercourse with 'My Sultan'. He made his visits in force. Those people damaged his grass-plot in front (it was not easy to obtain some approach to a lawn in the tropics), and the other day had broken down some rare bushes he had planted over there. And Captain Whalley remembered immediately that, in 'forty-seven, the then Sultan, 'this man's grandfather', had been notorious as a great protector of the piratical fleets of praus from farther East. They had a safe refuge in the river at Batu Beru. He financed more especially a Balinini chief called Haji Daman. Captain Whalley, nodding significantly his bushy white eye-brows, had very good reason to know something of that. The world had progressed since that time.

Mr Van Wyk demurred with unexpected acrimony. Progressed in what? he wanted to know.

Why, in knowledge of truth, in decency, in justice, in order – in honesty, too, since men harmed each other mostly from ignorance. It was, Captain Whalley concluded quaintly, more pleasant to live in.

Mr Van Wyk whimsically would not admit that Mr Massy, for instance, was more pleasant naturally than the Balinini pirates.

The river had not gained much by the change. They were in their way every bit as honest. Massy was less ferocious than Haji Daman no doubt, but . . .

'And what about you, my good sir?' Captain Whalley laughed a deep soft laugh. '*You* are an improvement, surely.'

He continued in a vein of pleasantry. A good cigar was better than a knock on the head – the sort of welcome he would have found on this river forty or fifty years ago. Then leaning forward slightly, he became earnestly serious. It seems as if, outside their own sea-gipsy tribes, these rovers had hated all mankind with an incomprehensible, bloodthirsty hatred. Meantime their depredations had been stopped, and what was the consequence? The new generation was orderly, peaceable, settled in prosperous villages. He could speak from personal knowledge. And even the few survivors of that time – old men now – had changed so much, that it would have been unkind to remember against them that they had ever slit a throat in their lives. He had one especially in his mind's eye: a dignified, venerable headman of a certain large coast village about sixty miles sou'west of Tampasuk. It did one's heart good to see him – to hear that man speak. He might have been a ferocious savage once. What men wanted was to be checked by superior intelligence, by superior knowledge, by superior force, too – yes, by force held in trust from God and sanctified by its use in accordance with His declared will. Captain Whalley believed a disposition for good existed in every man, even if the world were not a very happy place as a whole. In the wisdom of men he had not so much confidence.

The disposition had to be helped up pretty sharply sometimes, he admitted. They might be silly, wrong-headed, unhappy; but naturally evil – no. There was at bottom a complete harmlessness at least . . .

'Is there?' Mr Van Wyk snapped acrimoniously.

Captain Whalley laughed at the interjection, in the good humour of large, tolerating certitude. He could look back at half a century, he pointed out. The smoke oozed placidly through the white hairs hiding his kindly lips.

'At all events,' he resumed after a pause, 'I am glad that they've had no time to do you much harm as yet.'

This allusion to his comparative youthfulness did not offend Mr Van Wyk, who got up and wriggled his shoulders with an enigmatic half-smile. They walked out together amicably into the starry night towards the river-side. Their footsteps resounded unequally on the dark path. At the shore end of the gangway the lantern, hung low to the handrail, threw a vivid light on the white legs and the big black feet of Mr Massy waiting about anxiously.

From the waist upwards he remained shadowy, with a row of buttons gleaming up to the vague outline of his chin.

'You may thank Captain Whalley for this,' Mr Van Wyk said, curtly, to him before turning away.

The lamps on the verandah flung three long squares of light between the uprights far over the grass. A bat flitted before his face like a circling flake of velvety blackness. Along the jasmine hedge the night air seemed heavy with the fall of perfumed dew; flowerbeds bordered the path; the clipped bushes uprose in dark, rounded clumps here and there before the house; the dense foliage of creepers filtered the sheen of the lamplight within in a soft glow all along the front; and everything near and far stood still in a great immobility, in a great sweetness.

Mr Van Wyk (a few years before he had had occasion to imagine himself treated more badly than anybody alive had ever been by a woman) felt for Captain Whalley's optimistic views the disdain of a man who had once been credulous himself. His disgust with the world (the woman for a time had filled it for him completely) had taken the form of activity in retirement, because, though capable of great depth of feeling, he was energetic and essentially practical. But there was in that uncommon old sailor, drifting on the outskirts of his busy solitude, something that fascinated his scepticism. His very simplicity (amusing enough) was like a delicate refinement of an upright character. The striking dignity of manner could be nothing else, in a man reduced to such a humble position, but the expression of something essentially noble in the character. With all his trust in mankind he was no fool; the serenity of his temper at the end of so many years, since it could not obviously have been appeased by success, wore an air of profound wisdom. Mr Van Wyk was amused at it sometimes. Even the very physical traits of the old captain of the *Sofala*, his powerful frame, his reposeful mien, his intelligent, handsome face, the big limbs, the benign courtesy, the touch of rugged severity in the shaggy eyebrows, made up a seductive personality. Mr Van Wyk disliked littleness of every kind, but there was nothing small about that man, and in the exemplary regularity of many trips an intimacy had grown up between them, a warm feeling at bottom under a kindly stateliness of forms agreeable to his fastidiousness.

They kept their respective opinions on all worldly matters. His other convictions Captain Whalley never intruded. The difference of their ages was like another bond between them. Once, when twitted with the uncharitableness of his youth, Mr Van Wyk, running his eye over the vast proportions of his interlocuter, retorted in friendly banter –

'Oh. You'll come to my way of thinking yet. You'll have plenty of time. Don't call yourself old: you look good for a round hundred.'

But he could not help his stinging incisiveness, and though moderating it by an almost affectionate smile, he added –

'And by then you will probably consent to die from sheer disgust.'

Captain Whalley, smiling, too, shook his head. 'God forbid!'

He thought that perhaps on the whole he deserved something better than to die in such sentiments. The time of course would have to come, and he trusted to his Maker to provide a manner of going out of which he need not be ashamed. For the rest he hoped he would live to a hundred if need be; other men had been known; it would be no miracle. He expected no miracles.

The pronounced, argumentative tone caused Mr Van Wyk to raise his head and look at him steadily. Captain Whalley was gazing fixedly with a rapt expression, as though he had seen his Creator's favourable decree written in mysterious characters on the wall. He kept perfectly motionless for a few seconds, then got his vast bulk on to his feet so impetuously that Mr Van Wyk was startled.

He struck first a heavy blow on his inflated chest: and, throwing out horizontally a big arm that remained steady, extened in the air like the limb of a tree on a windless day –

'Not a pain or an ache there. Can you see this shake in the least?'

His voice was low, in an awing, confident contrast with the headlong emphasis of his movements. He sat down abruptly.

'This isn't to boast of it, you know. I am nothing,' he said in his effortless strong voice, that seemed to come out as naturally as a river flows. He picked up the stump of the cigar he had laid aside, and added peacefully, with a slight nod, 'As it happens, my life is necessary; it isn't my own, it isn't – God knows.'

He did not say much for the rest of the evening, but several times Mr Van Wyk detected a faint smile of assurance flitting under the heavy moustache.

Later on Captain Whalley would now and then consent to dine 'at the house'. He could even be induced to drink a glass of wine. 'Don't think I'm afraid of it, my good sir,' he explained. 'There was a very good reason why I should give it up.'

On another occasion, leaning back at ease, he remarked, 'You have treated me most – most humanely, my dear Mr Van Wyk, from the very first.'

'You'll admit there was some merit,' Mr Van Wyk hinted, slily. 'An associate of that excellent Massy . . . Well, well, my dear captain, I won't say a word against him.'

'It would be no use your saying anything against him,' Captain Whalley affirmed a little moodily. 'As I've told you before, my life – my work, is necessary, not for myself alone. I can't choose . . .' He paused, turned the glass before him right round . . . 'I have an only child – a daughter.'

The ample downward sweep of his arm over the table seemed to suggest a small girl at a vast distance. 'I hope to see her once more before I die. Meantime it's enough to know that she has me sound and solid, thank God. You can't understand how one feels. Bone of my bone, flesh of my flesh; the very image of my poor wife. Well, she . . .'

Again he paused, then pronounced stoically the words, 'She has a hard struggle.'

And his head fell on his breast, his eyebrows remained knitted, as by an effort of meditation. But generally his mind seemed steeped in the serenity of boundless trust in a higher power. Mr Van Wyk wondered sometimes how much of it was due to the splendid vitality of the man, to the bodily vigour which seems to impart something of its force to the soul. But he had learned to like him very much.

XIII

THIS was the reason why Mr Sterne's confidential communication, delivered hurriedly on the shore alongside the dark silent ship, had disturbed his equanimity. It was the most incomprehensible and unexpected thing that could happen; and the perturbation of his spirit was so great that, forgetting all about his letters, he ran rapidly up the bridge ladder.

The portable table was being put together for dinner to the left of the wheel by two pig-tailed 'boys', who as usual snarled at each other over the job, while another, a doleful, burly, very yellow Chinaman, resembling Mr Massy, waited apathetically with the cloth over his arm and a pile of thick dinner-plates against his chest. A common cabin lamp with its globe missing, brought up from below, had been hooked to the wooden framework of the awning; the sidescreens had been lowered all round; Captain Whalley, filling the depths of the wicker-chair, seemed to sit benumbed in a canvas tent crudely lighted, and used for the storing of nautical objects; a shabby steering-wheel, a battered brass binnacle on a stout mahogany stand, two dingy life-buoys, an old cork fender lying in a corner, dilapidated deck-lockers with loops of tin rope instead of door-handles.

He shook off the appearance of numbness to return Mr Van Wyk's unusually brisk greeting, but relapsed directly afterwards. To accept a pressing invitation to dinner 'up at the house' cost him another very visible physical effort. Mr Van Wyk, perplexed, folded his arms, and leaning back against the rail, with his little, black, shiny feet well out, examined him covertly.

'I've noticed of late that you are not quite yourself, old friend.'

He put an affectionate gentleness into the last two words. The real intimacy of their intercourse had never been so vividly expressed before.

'Tut, tut, tut!'

The wicker-chair creaked heavily.

'Irritable,' commented Mr Van Wyk to himself; and aloud, 'I'll expect to see you in half an hour, then,' he said, negligently, moving off.

'In half an hour,' Captain Whalley's rigid silvery head repeated behind him as if out of a trance.

Amidships, below, two voices, close against the engine-room, could be heard answering each other – one angry and slow, the other alert.

'I tell you the beast has locked himself in to get drunk.'

'Can't help it now, Mr Massy. After all, a man has a right to shut himself up in his cabin in his own time.'

'Not to get drunk.'

'I heard him swear that the worry with the boilers was enough to drive any man to drink,' Sterne said, maliciously.

Massy hissed out something about bursting the door in. Mr Van Wyk, to avoid them, crossed in the dark to the other side of the deserted deck. The planking of the little wharf rattled faintly under his hasty feet.

'Mr Van Wyk! Mr Van Wyk!'

He walked on: somebody was running on the path. 'You've forgotten to get your mail.'

Sterne, holding a bundle of papers in his hand, caught up with him.

'Oh, thanks.'

But, as the other continued at his elbow, Mr Van Wyk stopped short. The overhanging eaves, descending low upon the lighted front of the bungalow, threw their black straight-edged shadow into the great body of the night on that side. Everything was very still. A tinkle of cutlery and a slight jingle of glasses were heard. Mr Van Wyk's servants were laying the table for two on the verandah.

'I am afraid you give me no credit whatever for my good intentions on the matter I've spoken to you about,' said Sterne.

'I simply don't understand you.'

'Captain Whalley is a very audacious man, but he will understand that his game is up. That's all that anybody need ever know of it from me. Believe me, I am very considerate in this, but duty is duty. I don't want to make a fuss. All I ask you, as his friend, is to tell him from me that the game's up. That will be sufficient.'

Mr Van Wyk felt a loathsome dismay at this queer privilege of friendship. He would not demean himself by asking for the slightest explanation; to drive the other away with contumely he did not think prudent – as yet, at any rate. So much assurance staggered him. Who could tell what there could be in it? he thought. His regard for Captain Whalley had the tenacity of a disinterested sentiment, and his practical instinct coming to his aid, he concealed his scorn.

'I gather, then, that this is something grave.'

'Very grave,' Sterne assented, solemnly, delighted at having produced an effect at last. He was ready to add some effusive protestations of regret at the 'unavoidable necessity', but Mr Van Wyk cut him short — very civilly, however.

Once on the verandah Mr Van Wyk put his hands in his pockets, and, straddling his legs, stared down at a black panther skin lying on the floor before a rocking-chair. 'It looks as if the fellow had not the pluck to play his own precious game openly,' he thought.

This was true enough. In the face of Massy's last rebuff Sterne dared not declare his knowledge. His object was simply to get charge of the steamer and keep it for some time. Massy would never forgive him for forcing himself on; but if Captain Whalley left the ship of his own accord, the command would devolve upon him for the rest of the trip; so he hit upon the brilliant idea of scaring the old man away. A vague menace, a mere hint, would be enough in such a brazen case; and, with a strange admixture of compassion, he thought that Batu Beru was a very good place for throwing up the sponge. The skipper could go ashore quietly, and stay with that Dutchman of his. Weren't these two as thick as thieves together? And on reflection he seemed to see that there was a way to work the whole thing through that great friend of the old man's. This was another brilliant idea. He had an inborn preference for circuitous methods. In this particular case he desired to remain in the background as much as possible, to avoid exasperating Massy needlessly. No fuss! Let it all happen naturally.

Mr Van Wyk all through the dinner was conscious of a sense of isolation that invades sometimes the closeness of human inter-course. Captain Whalley failed lamentably and obviously in his attempts to eat something. He seemed overcome by a strange absent-mindedness. His hand would hover irresolutely, as if left without guidance by a preoccupied mind. Mr Van Wyk had heard him coming up from a long way off in the profound stillness of the river-side, and had noticed the irresolute character of the footfalls. The toe of his boot had struck the bottom stair as though he had come along mooning with his head in the air right up to the steps of the verandah. Had the captain of the *Sofala* been another sort of man he would have suspected the work of age there. But one glance at him was enough. Time – after, indeed, marking him for its own – had given him up to his usefulness, in which his simple faith would see a proof of divine mercy. 'How could I contrive to warn him?' Mr Van Wyk wondered, as if Captain Whalley had been miles and miles away, out of sight and earshot of all evil. He was sickened by an immense disgust of Sterne. To even mention his threat to a man like Whalley would be positively indecent. There was something more vile and insulting in its hint than in a definite charge of crime – the debasing taint of blackmailing. 'What could anyone bring against him?' he asked himself. This was a limpid personality. 'And for what object?' The Power that man trusted had thought fit to leave him nothing on earth that envy could lay hold of, except a bare crust of bread.

'Won't you try some of this?' he asked, pushing a dish slightly. Suddenly it occurred to Mr Van Wyk that Sterne might possibly be coveting the command of the *Sofala*. His cynicism was quite startled by what looked like a proof that no man may count himself safe from his kind unless in the very abyss of misery. An intrigue of that sort was hardly worth troubling about, he judged; but still, with such a fool as Massy to deal with, Whalley ought to and must be warned.

At this moment Captain Whalley, bolt upright, the deep cavities of the eyes overhung by a bushy frown, and one large brown hand resting on each side of his empty plate, spoke across the table-cloth abruptly –

'Mr Van Wyk, you've always treated me with the most humane consideration.'

'My dear Captain, you make too much of the simple fact that I am not a savage.' Mr Van Wyk, utterly revolted by the thought of Sterne's obscure attempt, raised his voice incisively, as if the mate had been hiding somewhere within earshot. 'Any consideration I have been able to show was no more than the rightful due of a character I've learned to regard by this time with an esteem than nothing can shake.'

A slight ring of glass made him lift his eyes from the slice of pineapple he was cutting into small pieces on his plate. In changing his position Captain Whalley had contrived to upset an empty tumbler.

Without looking that way, leaning sideways on his elbow, his other hand shading his brow, he groped shadily for it, then desisted. Van Wyk stared blankly, as if something momentous had happened all at once. He did not know why he should feel so startled; but he forgot Sterne utterly for the moment.

'Why, what's the matter?'

And Captain Whalley, half-averted, in a deadened, agitated voice, muttered –

'Esteem!'

'And I may add something more,' Mr Van Wyk, very steady-eyed, pronounced slowly.

'Hold! Enough!' Captain Whalley did not change his attitude or raise his voice. 'Say no more! I can make you no return. I am too poor even for that now. Your esteem is worth having. You are not a man that would stoop to deceive the poorest sort of devil on earth, or make a ship unseaworthy every time he takes her to sea.'

Mr Van Wyk, leaning forward, his face gone pink all over, with the starched table-napkin over his knees, was inclined to mistrust his senses, his power of comprehension, the sanity of his guest.

'Where? Why? In the name of God! – what's this? What ship? I don't understand who . . .'

'Then, in the name of God, it is I! A ship's unseaworthy when her captain can't see. I am going blind.'

Mr Van Wyk made a slight movement, and sat very still afterwards for a few seconds; then, with the thought of Sterne's, 'The game's up', he ducked under the table to pick up the napkin which had slipped off his knees. This was the game that was up. And at the same time the muffled voice of Captain Whalley passed over him –

'I've deceived them all. Nobody knows.'

He emerged flushed to the eyes. Captain Whalley, motionless under the full blaze of the lamp, shaded his face with his hand.

'And you had that courage?'

'Call it by what name you like. But you are a humane man – a – a – gentleman, Mr Van Wyk. You may have asked me what I had done with my conscience.'

He seemed to muse, profoundly silent, very still in his mournful pose.

'I began to tamper with it in my pride. You begin to see a lot of things when you are going blind. I could not be frank with an old chum even. I was not frank with Massy – no, not altogether. I knew he took me for a wealthy sailor fool, and I let him. I wanted to keep up my importance – because there was poor Ivy away there – my daughter. What did I want to trade on his misery for? I did trade on it – for her. And now, what mercy could I expect from him? He would trade on mine if he knew it. He would hunt the old fraud out, and stick to the money for a year. Ivy's money. And I haven't kept a penny for myself. How am I going to live for a year. A year! In a year there will be no sun in the sky for her father.'

His deep voice came out, awfully veiled, as though he had been overwhelmed by the earth of a landslide and talking of the thoughts that haunt the dead in their graves. A cold shudder ran down Mr Van Wyk's back.

'And how long is it since you have . . ?' he began.

'It was a long time before I could bring myself to believe in this – this – visitation.' Captain Whalley spoke with gloomy patience from under his hand.

He had not thought he had deserved it. He had begun by deceiving himself from day to day, from week to week. He had the Serang at hand there – an old servant. It came on gradually, and when he could no longer deceive himself. . .

His voice died out almost.

'Rather than give her up I set myself to deceive you all.'

'It's incredible,' whispered Mr Van Wyk. Captain Whalley's appalling murmur flowed on.

'Not even the sign of God's anger could make me forget her. How could I forsake my child, feeling my vigour all the time – the blood warm within me? Warm as yours. It seems to me that, like the blinded Samson, I would find the strength to shake down a temple upon my head. She's a struggling woman – my own child that we used to pray over together, my poor wife and I. Do you remember that day I as well as told you that I believed God would let me live to a hundred for her sake? What sin is there in loving your child? Do you see it? I was ready for her sake to live for ever. I half believed I would. I've been praying for death since. Ha! Presumptuous man – you wanted to live. . .'

A tremendous, shuddering upheaval of that big frame, shaken by a gasping sob, set the glasses jingling all over the table, seemed

to make the whole house tremble to the roof-tree. And Mr Van
Wyk, whose feeling of outraged love had been translated into a
form of struggle with nature, understood very well that, for that
man whose whole life had been conditioned by action, there could
exist no other expression for all the emotions; that, to voluntarily
cease venturing, doing, enduring, for his child's sake, would have
been exactly like plucking his warm love for her out of his living
heart. Something too monstrous, too impossible, even to
conceive.

Captain Whalley had not changed his attitude, that seemed to
express something of shame, sorrow, and defiance.

'I have even deceived you. If it had not been for that word
"esteem". These are not the words for me. I would have lied to
you. Haven't I lied to you? Weren't you going to trust your
property on board this very trip?'

'I have a floating yearly policy,' Mr Van Wyk said almost
unwittingly, and was amazed at the sudden cooping up of a
commercial detail.

'The ship is unseaworthy, I tell you. The policy would be invalid
if it were known. . . .'

'We shall share the guilt, then.'

'Nothing could make mine less,' said Captain Whalley.

He had not dared to consult a doctor; the man would have
perhaps asked who he was, what he was doing; Massy might have
heard something. He had lived on without any help, human or
divine. The very prayers stuck in his throat. What was there to
pray for? and death seemed as far as ever. Once he got into his
cabin he dared not come out again; when he sat down he dared
not get up; he dared not raise his eyes to anybody's face, he felt
reluctant to look upon the sea or up to the sky. The world was
fading before his great fear of giving himself away. The old ship
was his last friend; he was not afraid of her; he knew every inch of
her deck; but at her, too, he hardly dared to look, for fear of
finding he could see less than the day before. A great incertitude
enveloped him. The horizon was gone; the sky mingled darkly
with the sea. Who was this figure standing over yonder? what was
this thing lying down there? And a frightful doubt of the reality of
what he could see made even the remnant of sight that remained
to him an added torment, a pitfall always open for his miserable

pretence. He was afraid to stumble inexcusably over something – to say a fatal Yes or No to a question. The hand of God was upon him, but it could not tear him away from his child. And, as if in a nightmare of humiliation, every featureless man seemed an enemy.

He let his hand fall heavily on the table. Mr Van Wyk, arms down, chin on breast, with a gleam of white teeth pressing on the lower lip, meditated on Sterne's 'The game's up.'

'The Serang of course does not know.'

'Nobody,' said Captain Whalley, with assurance.

'Ah, yes. Nobody. Very well. Can you keep it up to the end of the trip? That is the last under the agreement with Massy.'

Captain Whalley got up and stood erect, very stately, with the great white beard lying like a silver breastplate over the awful secret of his heart. Yes; that was the only hope there was for him of ever seeing her again, of securing the money, the last he could do for her, before he crept away somewhere – useless, a burden, a reproach to himself. His voice faltered.

'Think of it! Never to see her any more: the only human being besides myself now on earth that can remember my wife. She's just like her mother. Lucky the poor woman is where there are no tears shed over those they loved on earth and that remain to pray not to be led into temptation – because, I suppose, the blessed know the secret of grace in God's dealings with His created children.'

He swayed a little, said with austere dignity –

'I don't. I know only the child He has given me.'

And he began to walk. Mr Van Wyk, jumping up, saw the full meaning of the rigid head, the hesitating feet, the vaguely extended hand. His heart was beating fast; he moved a chair aside, and instinctively advanced as if to offer his arm. But Captain Whalley passed him by, making for the stairs quite straight.

'He could not see me at all out of his line,' Van Wyk thought, with a sort of awe. Then going to the head of the stairs, he asked a little tremulously –

'What is it like – like a mist – like. . .' Captain Whalley, half-way down, stopped, and turned round undismayed to answer:

'It is as if the light were ebbing out of the world. Have you ever watched the ebbing sea on an open stretch of sands withdrawing farther and farther away from you? It is like this – only there will be no flood to follow. Never. It is as if the sun were growing smaller, the stars going out one by one. There can't be many left that I can see by this. But I haven't had the courage to look of late. . . .' He must have been able to make out Mr Van Wyk, because he checked him by an authoritative gesture and a stoical –

'I can get about alone yet.'

It was as if he had taken his line, and would accept no help from men, after having been cast out, like a presumptuous Titan, from his heaven. Mr Van Wyk, arrested, seemed to count the footsteps right out of earshot. He walked between the tables, tapping smartly with his heels, took up a paper-knife, dropped it after a vague glance along the blade; then happening upon the piano, struck a few chords, standing up before the keyboard with an attentive poise of the head like a piano-tuner; closing it, he pivoted on his heels brusquely, avoided the little terrier sleeping trustfully on crossed forepaws, came upon the stairs next, and, as though he had lost his balance on the top step, ran down headlong out of the house. His servants, beginning to clear the table, heard him mutter to himself (evil words no doubt) down there, and then after a pause go away with a strolling gait in the direction of the wharf.

The bulwarks of the *Sofala* lying alongside the bank made a low, black wall on the undulating contour of the shore. Two masts and a funnel uprose from behind it with a great rake, as if about to fall: a solid, square elevation in the middle bore the ghostly shapes of white boats, the curves of davits, lines of rail and stanchions, all confused and mingling darkly everywhere; but low down, amidships, a single lighted port stared out on the night, perfectly round, like a small, full moon, whose yellow beam caught a patch of wet mud, the edge of trodden grass, two turns of heavy cable wound round the foot of a thick wooden post in the ground.

Mr Van Wyk, peering alongside, heard a muzzy boastful voice apparently jeering at a person called Prendergast. It mouthed abuse thickly, choked; then pronounced very distinctly the word

'Murphy', and chuckled. Glass tinkled tremulously. All these sounds came from the lighted port. Mr Van Wyk hesitated, stooped; it was impossible to look through unless he went down into the mud.

'Sterne – of course. Look at him blink. Look at him! Sterne, Whalley, Massy. Massy, Whalley, Sterne. But Massy's the best. You can't come over him. He would just love to see you starve.'

Mr Van Wyk moved away, made out farther forward a shadowy head stuck out from under the awnings as if on the watch, and spoke quietly in Malay, 'Is the mate asleep?'

'No. Here, at your service.'

In a moment Sterne appeared, walking as noiselessly as a cat on the wharf.

'It's so jolly dark, and I had no idea you would be down to-night.'

'What's this horrible raving?' asked Mr Van Wyk, as if to explain the cause of a shudder that ran over him audibly.

'Jack's broken out on a drunk. That's our second. It's his way. He will be right enough by tomorrow afternoon, only Mr Massy will keep on worrying up and down the deck. We had better get away.'

He muttered suggestively of a talk 'up at the house'. He had long desired to effect an entrance there, but Mr Van Wyk nonchalantly demurred: it would not, he feared, be quite prudent, perhaps; and the opaque black shadow under one of the two big trees left at the landing-place swallowed them up, impenetrably dense by the side of the wide river, that seemed to spin into threads of glitter the light of a few big stars dropped here and there upon its outspread and flowing stillness.

'The situation is grave beyond doubt,' Mr Van Wyk said. Ghost-like in their white clothes they could not distinguish each other's features, and their feet made no sound on the soft earth. A sort of purring was heard. Mr Sterne felt gratified by such a beginning.

'I thought, Mr Van Wyk, a gentleman of your sort would see at once how awkwardly I was situated.'

'Yes, very. Obviously his health is bad. Perhaps he's breaking up. I see, and he himself is well aware – I assume I am speaking to a man of sense – he is well aware that his legs are giving out.'

'His legs – ah!' Mr Sterne was disconcerted, and then turned sulky. 'You may call it his legs if you like; what I want to know is whether he intends to clear out quietly. That's a good one, too! His legs! Pooh!'

'Why, yes. Only look at the way he walks,' Van Wyk took him up in a perfectly cool and undoubting tone. 'The question, however, is whether your sense of duty does not carry you too far from your true interest. After all, I, too, could do something to serve you. You know who I am.'

'Everybody along the Straits has heard of you, sir.'

Mr Van Wyk presumed that this meant something favourable. Sterne had a soft laugh at this pleasantry. He should think so! To the opening statement, that the partnership agreement was to expire at the end of this very trip, he gave an attentive assent. He was aware. One heard of nothing else on board all the blessed day long. As to Massy, it was no secret that he was in a jolly deep hole with these worn-out boilers. He would have to borrow somewhere a couple of hundred first of all to pay off the Captain; and then he would have to raise money on mortgage upon the ship for the new boilers – that is, if he could find a lender at all. At best it meant loss of time, a break in the trade, short earnings for the year – and there was always the danger of having his connection filched away from him by the Germans. It was whispered about that he had already tried two firms. Neither would have anything to do with him. Ship too old, and the man too well known in the place. . . . Mr Sterne's final rapid winking remained buried in the deep darkness sibilating with his whispers.

'Supposing, then, he got the loan,' Mr Van Wyk resumed in a deliberate undertone, 'on your own showing he's more than likely to get a mortgagee's man thrust upon him as captain. For my part, I know that I would make that very stipulation myself if I had to find the money. And as a matter of fact I am thinking of doing so. It would be worth my while in many ways. Do you see how this would bear on the case under discussion?'

'Thank you, sir. I am sure you couldn't get anybody that would care more for your interests.'

'Well, it suits my interest that Captain Whalley should finish his time. I shall probably take a passage with you down the Straits. If that can be done, I'll be on the spot when all these changes take place, and in a position to look after *your* interests.'

'Mr Van Wyk, I want nothing better. I am sure I am infinitely. . .'

'I take it, then, that this may be done without any trouble.'

'Well, sir, what risk there is can't be helped; but (speaking to you as my employer now) the thing is more safe than it looks. If anybody had told me of it I wouldn't have believed it, but I have been looking on myself. That old Serang has been trained up to the game. There's nothing the matter with his – his – limbs, sir. He's got used to do things on his own in a remarkable way. And let me tell you, sir, that Captain Whalley, poor man, is by no means useless. Fact. Let me explain to you, sir. He stiffens up that old monkey of a Malay, who knows well enough what to do. Why, he must have kept captain's watches in all sorts of country ships off and on for the last five-and-twenty years. These natives, sir, as long as they have a white man close at the back, will go on doing the right thing most surprisingly well – even if left quite to themselves. Only the white man must be of the sort to put starch into them, and the Captain is just the one for that. Why, sir, he has drilled him so well that now he needs hardly speak at all. I have seen that little wrinkled ape made to take the ship out of Pangu Bay on a blowy morning and on all through the islands; take her out first-rate, sir, dodging under the old man's elbow, and in such quiet style that you could not have told for the life of you which of the two was doing the work up there. That's where our poor friend would be still of use to the ship even if – if – he could no longer lift a foot, sir. Providing the Serang does not know that there's anything wrong.'

'He doesn't.'

'Naturally not. Quite beyond his apprehension. They aren't capable of finding out anything about us, sir.'

'You seem to be a shrewd man,' said Mr Van Wyk in a choked mutter, as though he were feeling sick.

'You'll find me a good enough servant, sir.'

Mr Sterne hoped now for a handshake at least, but unexpectedly with a 'What's this? Better not to be seen together,' Mr Van Wyk's white shape wavered, and instantly seemed to melt away in the black air under the roof of boughs. The mate was startled. Yes. There was that faint thumping clatter.

He stole out silently from under the shade. The lighted port-

hole shone from afar. His head swam with the intoxication of
sudden success. What a thing it was to have a gentleman to deal
with! He crept aboard, and there was something weird in the
shadowy stretch of empty decks, echoing with shouts and blows
proceeding from a darker part amidships. Mr Massy was raging
before the door of the berth: the drunken voice within flowed on
undisturbed in the violent racket of kicks.

'Shut up! Put your light out and turn in, you confounded
swilling pig – you! D'you hear me, you beast?'

The kicking stopped, and in the pause the muzzy oracular voice
announced from within –

'Ah! Massy, now – that's another thing. Massy's deep.'

'Who's that aft there? You, Sterne? He'll drink himself into a fit
of horrors.' The chief engineer appeared vague and big at the
corner of the engine-room skylight.

'He will be good enough for duty tomorrow. I would let him
be, Mr Massy.'

Sterne slipped away into his berth, and at once had to sit down.
His head swam with exultation. He got into his bunk as if in a
dream. A feeling of profound peace, of pacific joy, came over him.
On deck all was quiet.

Mr Massy, with his ear against the door of Jack's cabin, listened
critically to a deep, stertorous breathing within. This was a dead-
drunk sleep. The bout was over: tranquillized on that score, he, too,
went in, and with slow wriggles got out of his old tweed jacket. It
was a garment with many pockets, which he used to put on at odd
times of the day, being subject to sudden chilly fits, and when he felt
warmed he would take it off and hang it about anywhere all over the
ship. It would be seen swinging on belaying-pins, thrown over the
heads of winches, suspended on people's very door-handles for that
matter. Was he not the owner? But his favourite place was a hook on
a wooden awning stanchion on the bridge, almost against the
binnacle. He had even in the early days more than one tussle on that
point with Captain Whalley, who desired the bridge to be kept tidy.
He had been overawed then. Of late, though, he had been able to
defy his partner with impunity. Captain Whalley never seemed to
notice anything now. As to the Malays, in their awe of that scowling
man not one of the crew would dream of laying a hand on the thing,
no matter where or what it swung from.

With an unexpectedness which made Mr Massy jump and drop the coat at his feet, there came from the next berth the crash and thud of a headlong, jingling, clattering fall. The faithful Jack must have dropped to sleep suddenly as he sat at his revels, and now had gone over chair and all, breaking, as it seemed by the sound, every single glass and bottle in the place. After the terrific smash all was still for a time in there, as though he had killed himself on the spot. Mr Massy held his breath. At last a sleepy, uneasy groaning sigh was exhaled slowly on the other side of the bulkhead.

'I hope to goodness he's too drunk to wake up now,' muttered Mr Massy.

The sound of a softly knowing laugh nearly drove him to despair. He swore violently under his breath. The fool would keep him awake all night now for certain. He cursed his luck. He wanted to forget his maddening troubles in sleep sometimes. He could detect no movements. Without apparently making the slightest attempt to get up, Jack went on sniggering to himself where he lay; then began to speak, where he had left off as it were –

'Massy! I love the dirty rascal. He would like to see his poor old Jack starve – but just you look where he has climbed to. . .' He hiccoughed in a superior, leisurely manner. . . 'Shipowning it with the best. A lottery ticket you want. Ha! ha! I will give you lottery tickets, my boy. Let the old ship sink and the old chum starve – that's right. He don't go wrong – Massy don't. Not he. He's a genius – that man is. That's the way to win your money. Ship and chum must go.'

'The silly fool has taken it to heart,' muttered Massy to himself. And, listening with a softened expression of face for any slight sign of returning drowsiness, he was discouraged profoundly by a burst of laughter full of joyful irony.

'Would like to see her at the bottom of the sea! Oh, you clever, clever devil! Wish her sunk, eh? I should think you would, my boy; the damned old thing and all your troubles with her. Rake in the insurance money – turn your back on your old chum – all's well – gentleman again.'

A grim stillness had come over Massy's face. Only his big black eyes rolled uneasily. The raving fool. And yet it was all true. Yes.

Lottery tickets, too. All true. What? Beginning again? He wished he wouldn't. . .

But it was even so. The imaginative drunkard on the other side of the bulkhead shook off the deathlike stillness that after his last words had fallen on the dark ship moored to a silent shore.

'Don't you dare to say anything against George Massy, Esquire. When he's tired of waiting he will do away with her. Look out! Down she goes – chum and all. He'll know how to. . .'

The voice hesitated, weary, dreamy, lost, as if dying away in a vast open space.

'. . . Find a trick that will work. He's up to it – never fear. . .'

He must have been very drunk, for at last the heavy sleep gripped him with the suddenness of a magic spell, and the last word lengthened itself into an interminable, noisy, indrawn snore. And then even the snoring stopped, and all was still.

But it seemed as though Mr Massy had suddenly come to doubt the efficacy of sleep as against a man's troubles; or perhaps he had found the relief he needed in the stillness of a calm contemplation that may contain the vivid thoughts of wealth, of a stroke of luck, of long idleness, and may bring before you the imagined form of every desire; for, turning about and throwing his arms over the edge of his bunk, he stood there with his feet on his favourite old coat, looking out through the round port into the night over the river. Sometimes a breath of wind would enter and touch his face, a cool breath charged with the damp, fresh feel from a vast body of water. A glimmer here and there was all he could see of it; and once he might after all suppose he had dozed off, since there appeared before his vision, unexpectedly and connected with no dream, a row of flaming and gigantic figures – three nought seven one two – making up a number such as you may see on a lottery ticket. And then all at once the port was no longer black: it was pearly grey, framing a shore crowded with houses, thatched roof beyond thatched roof, walls of mats and bamboo, gables of carved teak timber. Rows of dwellings raised on a forest of piles lined the steely bank of the river, brimful and still, with the tide on the turn. This was Batu Beru – and the day had come.

Mr Massy shook himself, put on the tweed coat, and, shivering nervously as if from some great shock, made a note of the number. A fortunate, rare hint that. Yes; but to pursue fortune one wanted money – ready cash.

Then he went out and prepared to descend into the engine-room. Several small jobs had to be seen to, and Jack was lying dead drunk on the floor of his cabin, with the door locked at that. His gorge rose at the thought of work. Ay! But if you wanted to do nothing you had to get first a good bit of money. A ship won't save you. True, all true. He was tired of waiting for some chance that would rid him at last of that ship that had turned out a curse on his life.

XIV

THE deep, interminable hoot of the steam-whistle had, in its grave, vibrating note, something intolerable, which sent a slight shudder down Mr Van Wyk's back. It was the early afternoon; the *Sofala* was leaving Batu Beru for Pangu, the next place of call. She swung in the stream, scantily attended by a few canoes, and, gliding on the broad river, became lost to view from the Van Wyk bungalow.

Its owner had not gone this time to see her off. Generally he came down to the wharf, exchanged a few words with the bridge while she cast off, and waved his hand to Captain Whalley at the last moment. This day he did not even go as far as the balustrade of the verandah. 'He couldn't see me if I did,' he said to himself. 'I wonder whether he can make out the house at all.' And this thought somehow made him feel more alone than he had ever felt for all these years. What was it? six or seven? Seven. A long time.

He sat on the verandah with a closed book on his knee, and, as it were, looked out upon his solitude, as if the fact of Captain Whalley's blindness had opened his eyes to his own. There were many sorts of heartaches and troubles, and there was no place where they could not find a man out. And he felt ashamed, as though he had for six years behaved like a peevish boy.

His thought followed the *Sofala* on her way. On the spur of the moment he had acted impulsively, turning to the thing most pressing. And what else could he have done? Later on he should see. It seemed necessary that he should come out into the world, for a time at least. He had money – something could be arranged; he would grudge no time, no trouble, no loss of his solitude. It

weighed on him now – and Captain Whalley appeared to him as
he had sat shading his eyes, as if, being deceived in the trust of his
faith, he were beyond all the good and evil that can be wrought by
the hands of men.

Mr Van Wyk's thoughts followed the *Sofala* down the river,
winding about through the belt of the coast forest, between the
buttressed shafts of the big trees, through the mangrove strip, and
over the bar. The ship crossed it easily in broad daylight, piloted,
as it happened, by Mr Sterne, who took the watch from four to
six, and then went below to hug himself with delight at the
prospect of being virtually employed by a rich man – like Mr Van
Wyk. He could not see how any hitch could occur now. He did not
seem able to get over the feeling of being 'fixed up at last'. From
six to eight, in the course of duty, the Serang looked alone after the
ship. She had a clear road before her now till about three in the
morning, when she would close with the Pangu group. At eight
Mr Sterne came out cheerily to take charge again till midnight. At
ten he was still chirruping and humming to himself on the bridge,
and about the time Mr Van Wyk's thought abandoned the *Sofala*.
Mr Van Wyk had fallen asleep at last.

Massy, blocking the engine-room companion, jerked himself
into his tweed jacket surlily, while the second waited with a scowl.

'Oh. You came out! You sot! Well, what have you got to say for
yourself?'

He had been in charge of the engines till then. A sombre fury
darkened his mind: a hot anger against the ship, against the facts
of life, against the men for their cheating, against himself, too –
because of an inward tremor in his heart.

An incomprehensible growl answered him.

'What? Can't you open your mouth now? You yelp out your
infernal rot loud enough when you are drunk. What do you mean
by abusing people in that way? – you old useless boozer, you!'

'Can't help it. Don't remember anything about it. You
shouldn't listen.'

'You dare to tell me! What do you mean by going on a drunk
like this?'

'Don't ask me. Sick of the dam' boilers – you would be. Sick of
Life.'

'I wish you were dead, then. You've made me sick of you. Don't you remember the uproar you made last night? You miserable old soaker!'

'No; I don't. Don't want to. Drink is drink.'

'I wonder what prevents me from kicking you out. What do you want here?'

'Relieve you. You've been long enough down there, George.'

'Don't you George me – you tippling old rascal, you! If I were to die tomorrow you would starve. Remember that. Say Mr Massy.'

'Mr Massy,' repeated the other, stolidly.

Dishevelled, with dull blood-shot eyes, a snuffy, grimy shirt, greasy trousers, naked feet thrust into ragged slippers, he bolted in head down directly Massy had made way for him.

The chief engineer looked around. The deck was empty as far as the taffrail. All the native passengers had left in Batu Beru this time, and no others had joined. The dial of the patent log tinkled periodically in the dark at the end of the ship. It was a dead calm, and, under the clouded sky, through the still air that seemed to cling warm, with a seaweed smell, to her slim hull, on a sea of sombre grey and unwrinkled, the ship moved on an even keel, as if floating detached in empty space. But Mr Massy slapped his forehead, tottered a little, and caught hold of a belaying-pin at the foot of the mast.

'I shall go mad,' he muttered, walking across the deck unsteadily. A shovel was scraping loose coal down below – a fire-door clanged. Sterne on the bridge began whistling a new tune.

Captain Whalley, sitting on the couch, awake and fully dressed, heard the door of his cabin open. He did not move in the least, waiting to recognize the voice, with an appalling strain of prudence.

A bulkhead lamp blazed on the white paint, the crimson plush, the brown varnish of mahogany tops. The white wood packing-case under the bedplace had remained unopened for three years now, as though Captain Whalley had felt that, after the *Fair Maid* was gone, there could be no abiding-place on earth for his affections. His hands rested on his knees; his handsome head with big eyebrows presented a rigid profile to the doorway. The expected voice spoke out at last.

'Once more, then. What am I to call you?'

Ha! Massy. Again. The weariness of it crushed his heart – and the pain of shame was almost more than he could bear without crying out.

'Well. It is to be "partner" still?'

'You don't know what you ask.'

'I know what I want. . . .'

Massy stepped in and closed the door.

'. . . And I am going to have a try for it with you once more.'

His whine was half persuasive, half menacing.

'For it's no manner of use to tell me that you are poor. You don't spend anything on yourself, that's true enough; but there's another name for that. You think you are going to have what you want out of me for three years, and then cast me off without hearing what I think of you. You think I would have submitted to your airs if I had known you had only a beggarly five hundred pounds in the world. You ought to have told me.'

'Perhaps,' said Captain Whalley, bowing his head. 'And yet it has saved you. . . .' Massy laughed scornfully. . . . 'I have told you often enough since.'

'And I don't believe you now. When I think how I let you lord it over my ship! Do you remember how you used to bullyrag me about my coat and *your* bridge? It was in his way. *His* bridge! "And I won't be a party to this – and I couldn't think of doing that." Honest man! And now it all comes out. "I am poor, and I can't. I have only this five hundred in the world." '

He contemplated the immobility of Captain Whalley, that seemed to present an inconquerable obstacle in his path. His face took on a mournful cast.

'You are a hard man.'

'Enough,' said Captain Whalley, turning upon him. 'You shall get nothing from me, because I have nothing of mine to give away now.'

'Tell that to the marines!'

Mr Massy, going out, looked back once; then the door closed, and Captain Whalley, alone, sat as still as before. He had nothing of his own – even his own past of honour, of truth, of just pride, was gone. All his spotless life had fallen into the abyss. He had said his last good bye to it. But what belonged to *her*, that he meant to save. Only a little money. He would take it to her in his own hands – this last gift of a man that had lasted too long. And an immense and fierce impulse, the very passion of paternity, flamed up with all the unquenched vigour of his worthless life in a desire to see her face.

Just across the deck Massy had gone straight to his cabin, struck a light, and hunted up the note of the dreamed number whose figures had flamed up also with the fierceness of another passion. He must contrive somehow not to miss a drawing. That number meant something. But what expedient could he contrive to keep himself going?

'Wretched miser!' he mumbled.

If Mr Sterne could at no time have told him anything new about his parter, he could have told Mr Sterne that another use could be made of a man's affliction than just to kick him out, and thus defer the term of a difficult payment for a year. To keep the secret of the affliction and induce him to stay was a better move. If without means, he would be anxious to remain; and that settled the question of refunding him his share. He did not know exactly how much Captain Whalley was disabled; but if it so happened that he put the ship ashore somewhere for good and all, it was not the owner's fault – was it? He was not obliged to know that there was anything wrong. But probably nobody would raise such a point, and the ship was fully insured. He had had enough self-restraint to pay up the premiums. But this was not all. He could not believe Captain Whalley to be so confoundedly destitute as not to have some more money put away somewhere. If he, Massy, could get hold of it, that would pay for the boilers, and everything went on as before. And if she got lost in the end, so much the better. He hated her: he loathed the troubles that took his mind off the chances of fortune. He wished her at the bottom of the sea, and the insurance money in his pocket. And as, baffled, he left Captain Whalley's cabin, he enveloped in the same hatred the ship with the worn-out boilers and the man with the dimmed eyes.

And our conduct after all is so much a matter of outside suggestion, that had it not been for his Jack's drunken gabble he would have there and then had it out with this miserable man, who would neither help, nor stay, nor yet lose the ship. The old fraud! He longed to kick him out. But he restrained himself. Time enough for that – when he liked. There was a fearful new thought put into his head. Wasn't he up to it after all? How that beast Jack had raved! 'Find a safe trick to get rid of her.' Well, Jack was not so far wrong. A very clever trick had occurred to him. Ay! But what of the risk?

A feeling of pride – the pride of superiority to common prejudices – crept into his breast, made his heart beat fast, his mouth turn dry. Not everybody would dare; but he was Massy, and he was up to it!

Six bells were struck on deck. Eleven! He drank a glass of water, and sat down for ten minutes or so to calm himself. Then he got out of his chest a small bull's-eye lantern of his own and lit it.

Almost opposite his berth, across the narrow passage under the bridge, there was, in the iron deck-structure covering the stoke-hold fiddle and the boiler-space, a storeroom with iron sides, iron roof, iron-plated floor, too, on account of the heat below. All sorts of rubbish was shot there: it had a mound of scrap-iron in a corner; rows of empty oil-cans; sacks of cotton-waste, with a heap of charcoal, a deck-forge, fragments of an old hen-coop, winch-covers all in rags, remnants of lamps, and a brown felt hat, discarded by a man dead now (of a fever on the Brazil coast), who had been once mate of the *Sofala*, had remained for years jammed forcibly behind a length of burst copper pipe, flung at some time or other out of the engine-room. A complete and impervious blackness pervaded that Capharnaum of forgotten things. A small shaft of light from Mr Massy's bull's-eye fell slanting right through it.

His coat was unbuttoned; he shot the bolt of the door (there was no other opening), and, squatting before the scrap-heap, began to pack his pockets with pieces of iron. He packed them carefully, as if the rusty nuts, the broken bolts, the links of cargo chain, had been so much gold he had that one chance to carry away. He packed his side-pockets till they bulged, the breast-pocket, the pockets inside. He turned over the pieces. Some he rejected. A small mist of powdered rust began to rise about his busy hands. Mr Massy knew something of the scientific basis of his clever trick. If you want to deflect the magnetic needle of a ship's compass, soft iron is the best; likewise many small pieces in the pockets of a jacket would have more effect than a few large ones, because in that way you obtain a greater amount of surface for weight in your iron, and it's surface that tells.

He slipped out swiftly – two strides sufficed – and in his cabin he perceived that his hands were all red – red with rust. It disconcerted him, as though he had found them covered with blood: he looked himself over hastily. Why, his trousers, too! He had been rubbing his rusty palms on his legs.

He tore off the waistband button in his haste, brushed his coat, washed his hands. Then the air of guilt left him, and he sat down to wait.

He sat bolt upright and weighted with iron in his chair. He had a hard, lumpy bulk against each hip, felt the scrappy iron in his pockets touch his ribs at every breath, the downward drag of all these pounds hanging upon his shoulders. He looked very dull, too, sitting idly there, and his yellow face, with motionless black eyes, had something passive and sad in its quietness.

When he heard eight bells struck above his head, he rose and made ready to go out. His movements seemed aimless, his lower lip had dropped a little, his eyes roamed about the cabin, and the tremendous tension of his will had robbed them of every vestige of intelligence.

With the last stroke of the bell the Serang appeared noiselessly on the bridge to relieve the mate. Sterne overflowed with good nature, since he had nothing more to desire.

'Got your eyes well open yet, Serang? It's middling dark; I'll wait till you get your sight properly.'

The old Malay murmured, looked up with his worn eyes, sidled away into the light of the binnacle, and, clasping his hands behind his back, fixed his eyes on the compass-card.

'You'll have to keep a good lookout ahead for land, about half-past three. It's fairly clear, though. You have looked in on the captain as you came along – eh? He knows the time? Well, then, I am off.'

At the foot of the ladder he stood aside for the captain. He watched him go up with an even, certain tread, and remained thoughtful for a moment. 'It's funny,' he said to himself, 'but you can never tell whether that man has seen you or not. He might have heard me breathe this time.'

He was a wonderful man when all was said and done. They said he had had a name in his day. Mr Sterne could well believe it; and he concluded serenely that Captain Whalley must be able to see people more or less – as himself just now, for instance – but not being certain of anybody, had to keep up that unnoticing silence of manner for fear of giving himself away. Mr Sterne was a shrewd guesser.

This necessity of every moment brought home to Captain Whalley's heart the humiliation of his falsehood. He had drifted into it from paternal love, from incredulity, from boundless trust in divine justice meted out to men's feelings on this earth. He would give his poor Ivy the benefit of another month's work; perhaps the affliction was only temporary. Surely God would not rob his child of his power to help, and cast him naked into a night without end. He had caught at every hope; and when the evidence of his misfortune was stronger than hope, he tried not to believe the manifest thing.

In vain. In the steadily darkening universe a sinister clearness fell upon his ideas. In the illuminating moments of suffering he saw life, men, all things, the whole earth with all her burden of created nature, as he had never seen them before.

Sometimes he was seized with a sudden vertigo and an overwhelming terror; and then the image of his daughter appeared. Her, too, he had never seen so clearly before. Was it possible that he should ever be unable to do anything whatever for her? Nothing. And not see her any more? Never.

Why? The punishment was too great for a little presumption, for a little pride. And at last he came to cling to his deception with a fierce determination to carry it out to the end, to save her money intact, and behold her once more with his own eyes. Afterwards – what? The idea of suicide was revolting to the vigour of his manhood. He had prayed for death till the prayers had stuck in his throat. All the days of his life he had prayed, for daily bread, and not to be led into temptation, in a childlike humility of spirit. Did words mean anything? Whence did the gift of speech come? The violent beating of his heart reverberated in his head – seemed to shake his brain to pieces.

He sat down heavily in the deck-chair to keep the pretence of his watch. The night was dark. All the nights were dark now.

'Serang,' he said, half aloud.

'Ada, Tuan. I am here.'

'There are clouds on the sky?'

'There are, Tuan.'

'Let her be steered straight. North.'

'She is going north, Tuan.'

The Serang stepped back. Captain Whalley recognized Massy's footfalls on the bridge.

The engineer walked over to port and returned, passing behind the chair several times. Captain Whalley detected an unusual character as of prudent care in this prowling. The near presence of that man brought with it always a recrudescence of moral suffering for Captain Whalley. It was not remorse. After all, he had done nothing but good to the poor devil. There was also a sense of danger – the necessity of a greater care.

Massy stopped and said –

'So you still say you must go?'

'I must indeed.'

'And you couldn't at least leave the money for a term of years?'

'Impossible.'

'Can't trust it with me without your care, eh?'

Captain Whalley remained silent. Massy sighed deeply over the back of the chair.

'It would just do to save me,' he said in a tremulous voice.

'I've saved you once.'

The chief engineer took off his coat with careful movements, and proceeded to feel for the brass hook screwed into the wooden stanchion. For this purpose he placed himself right in front of the binnacle, thus hiding completely the compass-card from the quartermaster at the wheel. 'Tuan!' the lascar at last murmured softly, meaning to let the white man know that he could not see to steer.

Mr Massy had accomplished his purpose. The coat was hanging from the nail, within six inches of the binnacle. And directly he had stepped aside the quartermaster, a middle-aged, pock-marked, Sumatra Malay, almost as dark as a negro, perceived with amazement that in that short time, in this smooth water, with no wind at all, the ship had gone swinging far out of her course. He had never known her get away like this before. With a slight grunt of astonishment he turned the wheel hastily to bring her head back north, which was the course. The grinding of the steering-chains, the chiding murmurs of the Serang, who had

come over to the wheel, made a slight stir, which attracted
Captain Whalley's anxious attention. He said, 'Take better care.'
Then everything settled to the usual quiet on the bridge. Mr
Massy had disappeared.

But the iron in the pockets of the coat had done its work; and
the *Sofala*, heading north by the compass made untrue by this
simple device, was no longer making a safe course for Pangu Bay.

The hiss of water parted by her stem, the throb of her engines,
all the sounds of her faithful and laborious life, went on
uninterrupted in the great calm of the sea joining on all sides the
motionless layer of cloud over the sky. A gentle stillness as vast as
the world seemed to wait upon her path, enveloping her lovingly
in a supreme caress. Mr Massy thought there could be no better
night for an arranged shipwreck.

Run up high and dry on one of the reefs east of Pangu – wait for
daylight – hole in the bottom – out boats – Pangu Bay same
evening. That's about it. As soon as she touched he would hasten
on the bridge, get hold of the coat (nobody would notice in the
dark), and shake it upside down over the side, or even fling it into
the sea. A detail. Who could guess? Coat been seen hanging there
from that hook hundreds of times. Nevertheless, when he sat
down on the lower step of the bridge-ladder his knees knocked
together a little. The waiting part was the worst of it. At times he
would begin to pant quickly, as though he had been running, and
then breathe largely, swelling with the intimate sense of a
mastered fate. Now and then he would hear the shuffle of the
Serang's bare feet up there: quiet, low voices would exchange a
few words, and lapse almost at once into silence. . .

'Tell me directly you see any land, Serang.'

'Yes, Tuan. Not yet.'

'No, not yet,' Captain Whalley would agree.

The ship had been the best friend of his decline. He had sent all
the money he had made by and in the *Sofala* to his daughter. His
thought lingered on the name. How often he and his wife had
talked over the cot of the child in the big stern-cabin of the
Condor; she would grow up, she would marry, she would love
them, they would live near her and look at her happiness – it
would go on without end. Well, his wife was dead, to the child he
had given all he had to give; he wished he could come near her, see

her, see her face once, live in the sound of her voice, that could make the darkness of the living grave ready for him supportable. He had been starved of love too long. He imagined her tenderness.

The Serang had been peering forward, and now and then glancing at the chair. He fidgeted restlessly, and suddenly burst out close to Captain Whalley –

'Tuan, do you see anything of the land?'

The alarmed voice brought Captain Whalley to his feet at once. He! See! And at the question, the curse of his blindness seemed to fall on him with a hundredfold force.

'What's the time?' he cried.

'Half-past three, Tuan.'

'We are close. You *must* see. Look, I say. Look.'

Mr Massy, awakened by the sudden sound of talking from a short doze on the lowest step, wondered why he was there. Ah! A faintness came over him. It is one thing to sow the seed of an accident and another to see the monstrous fruit hanging over your head ready to fall in the sound of agitated voices. 'There's no danger,' he muttered thickly to himself.

The horror of incertitude had seized upon Captain Whalley, the miserable mistrust of men, of things – of the very earth. He had steered that very course thirty-six times by the same compass – if anything was certain in this world it was its absolute, unerring correctness. Then what had happened? Did the Serang lie? Why lie? Why? Was he going blind, too?

'Is there a mist? Look low on the water. Low down, I say.'

'Tuan, there's no mist. See for yourself.'

Captain Whalley steadied the trembling of his limbs by an effort. Should he stop the engines at once and give himself away? A gust of irresolution swayed all sorts of bizarre notions in his mind. The unusual had come, and he was not fit to deal with it. In this passage of inexpressible anguish he saw her face – the face of a young girl – with an amazing strength of illusion. No, he must not give himself away after having gone so far for her sake. 'You steered the course? You made it? Speak the truth.'

'Ya, Tuan. On the course now. Look.'

Captain Whalley strode to the binnacle, which to him made such a dim spot of light in an infinity of shapeless shadow. By

bending his face right down to the glass he had been able
before . . .

Having to stoop so low, he put out, instinctively, his arm to
where he knew there was a stanchion to steady himself against.
His hand closed on something that was not wood but cloth. The
slight pull adding to the weight, the loop broke, and Mr Massy's
coat falling, struck the deck heavily with a dull thump, accompanied by a lot of clicks.

'What's this?'

Captain Whalley fell on his knees, with groping hands extended
in a frank gesture of blindness. They trembled, these hands feeling
for the truth. He saw it. Iron near the compass. Wrong course.
Wreck her! His ship. Oh, no. Not that.

'Jump and stop her!' he roared out in a voice not his own.

He ran himself – hands forward, a blind man, and while the
clanging of the gong echoed still all over the ship, she seemed to
butt full tilt into the side of a mountain.

It was low water along the north side of the strait. Mr Massy
had not reckoned on that. Instead of running aground for half her
length, the *Sofala* butted the sheer ridge of a stone reef which
would have been awash at high water. This made the shock
absolutely terrific. Everybody in the ship that was standing was
thrown down headlong: the shaken rigging made a great rattling
to the very trucks. All the lights went out; several chain-guys,
snapping, clattered against the funnel; there were crashes, pings
of parted wire-rope, splintering sounds, loud cracks; the mast-
head lamp flew over the bows, and all the doors about the deck
began to bang heavily. Then, after having hit, she rebounded, hit
the second time the very same spot like a battering-ram. This
completed the havoc: the funnel, with all the guys gone, fell over
with a hollow sound of thunder, smashing the wheel to bits,
crushing the frame of the awnings, breaking the lockers, filling the
bridge with a mass of broken wood. Captain Whalley picked
himself up and stood knee-deep in wreckage, torn, bleeding,
knowing the nature of the danger he had escaped mostly by the
sound, and holding Mr Massy's coat in his arms.

By this time Sterne (he had been flung out of his bunk) had set
the engines astern. They worked for a few turns, then a voice
bawled out, 'Get out of the damned engine-room, Jack!' – and

they stopped; but the ship had gone clear of the reef and lay still, with a heavy cloud of steam issuing from the broken deck-pipes, and vanishing in wispy shapes into the night. Notwithstanding the suddenness of the disaster there was no shouting, as if the very violence of the shock had half-stunned the shadowy lot of people swaying here and there about her decks. The voice of the Serang pronounced distinctly above the confused murmurs –

'No bottom.' He had heaved the lead.

Mr Sterne cried out next in a strained pitch –

'Where the devil has she got to? Where are we?'

Captain Whalley replied in a calm bass –

'Amongst the reefs to the eastward.'

'You know it, sir? Then she will never get out again.'

'She will be gone in five minutes. Boats, Sterne. Even one will save you all in this calm.'

The Chinaman stokers went in a disorderly rush for the port boats. Nobody tried to check them. The Malays, after a moment of confusion, became quiet, and Mr Sterne showed a good countenance. Captain Whalley had not moved. His thoughts were darker than this night in which he had lost his first ship.

'He made me lose a ship.'

Another tall figure standing before him amongst the litter of the smash on the bridge whispered insanely –

'Say nothing of it.'

Massy stumbled closer. Captain Walley heard the chattering of his teeth.

'I have the coat.'

'Throw it down and come along,' urged the chattering voice. 'B-b-b-b-boat!'

'You will get five years for this.'

Mr Massy had lost his voice. His speech was a mere dry rustling in his throat.

'Have mercy!'

'Had you any when you made me lose my ship? Mr Massy, you shall get five years for this!'

'I wanted money! Money! My own money! I will give you some money. Take half of it. You love money yourself.'

'There's a justice . . .'

Massy made an awful effort, and in a strange, half-choked utterance –

'You blind devil! It's you that drove me to it.'

Captain Whalley, hugging the coat to his breast, made no sound. The light had ebbed for ever from the world – let everything go. But this man should not escape scot-free.

Sterne's voice commanded –

'Lower away!'

The blocks rattled.

'Now then,' he cried, 'over with you. This way. You, Jack, here. Mr Massy! Mr Massy! Captain! Quick, sir! Let's get—'

'I shall go to prison for trying to cheat the insurance, but you'll get exposed; you, honest man, who has been cheating me. You are poor. Aren't you? You've nothing but the five hundred pounds. Well, you have nothing at all now. The ship's lost, and the insurance won't be paid.'

Captain Whalley did not move. True! Ivy's money. Gone in this wreck. Again he had a flash of insight. He was indeed at the end of his tether.

Urgent voices cried out together alongside. Massy did not seem able to tear himself away from the bridge. He chattered and hissed despairingly –

'Give it up to me! Give it up!'

'No,' said Captain Whalley; 'I could not give it up. You had better go. Don't wait, man, if you want to live. She's settling down by the head fast. No; I shall keep it, but I shall stay on board.'

Massy did not seem to understand; but the love of life, awakened suddenly, drove him away from the bridge.

Captain Whalley laid the coat down, and stumbled amongst the heaps of wreckage to the side.

'Is Mr Massy with you?' he called out into the night.

Sterne from the boat shouted –

'Yes; we've got him. Come along, sir. It's madness to stay longer.'

Captain Whalley felt along the rail carefully, and, without a word, cast off the painter. They were expecting him still down there. They were waiting, till a voice suddenly exclaimed –

'We are adrift! Shove off!'

'Captain Whalley! Leap! . . pull up a little . . . leap! You can swim.'

In that old heart, in that vigorous body, there was, that nothing should be wanting, a horror of death that apparently could not be overcome by the horror of blindness. But after all, for Ivy he had carried his point, walking in his darkness to the very verge of a crime. God had not listened to his prayers. The light had finished ebbing out of the world; not a glimmer. It was a dark waste; but it was unseemly that a Whalley who had gone so far to carry a point should continue to live. He must pay the price.

'Leap as far as you can, sir; we will pick you up.'

They did not hear him answer. But their shouting seemed to remind him of something. He groped his way back, and sought for Mr Massy's coat. He could swim indeed; people sucked down by the whirlpool of a sinking ship do come up sometimes to the surface, and it was unseemly that a Whalley, who had made up his mind to die, should be beguiled by chance into a struggle. He would put all these pieces of iron into his own pockets.

They, looking from the boat, saw the *Sofala*, a black mass upon a black sea, lying still at an appalling cant. No sound came from her. Then, with a great bizarre shuffling noise, as if the boilers had broken through the bulkheads, and with a faint muffled detonation, where the ship had been there appeared for a moment something standing upright and narrow, like a rock out of the sea. Then that, too, disappeared.

When the *Sofala* failed to come back to Batu Beru at the proper time, Mr Van Wyk understood at once that he would never see her any more. But he did not know what had happened till some weeks afterwards, when, in a native craft lent him by his Sultan, he had made his way to the *Sofala*'s port of registry, where already her existence and the official inquiry into her loss were beginning to be forgotten.

It had not been a very remarkable or interesting case, except for the fact that the captain had gone down with his sinking ship. It was the only life lost; and Mr Van Wyk would not have been able to learn any details had it not been for Sterne, whom he met one day on the quay near the bridge over the creek, almost on the very spot where Captain Whalley, to preserve his daughter's five hundred pounds intact, had turned to get a sampan which would take him on board the *Sofala*.

From afar Mr Van Wyk saw Sterne blink straight at him and raise his hand to his hat. They drew into the shade of a building (it was a bank), and the mate related how the boats with the crew got into Pangu Bay about six hours after the accident, and how they had lived for a fortnight in a state of destitution before they found an opportunity to get away from that beastly place. The inquiry had exonerated everybody from all blame. The loss of the ship was put down to an unusual set of the current. Indeed, it could not have been anything else: there was no other way to account for the ship being set seven miles to the eastward of her position during the middle watch.

'A piece of bad luck for me, sir.'

Sterne passed his tongue on his lips and glanced aside. 'I lost the advantage of being employed by you, sir. I can never be sorry enough. But here it is: one man's poison, another man's meat. This could not have been handier for Mr Massy if he had arranged that shipwreck himself. The most timely total loss I've ever heard of.'

'What became of that Massy?' asked Mr Van Wyk.

'He, sir? Ha! Ha! He would keep on telling me that he meant to buy another ship; but as soon as he had the money in his pocket he cleared out for Manila by mail-boat early in the morning. I gave him chase right aboard, and he told me that he was going to make his fortune dead sure in Manila. I could go to the devil for all he cared. And yet he as good as promised to give me the command if I didn't talk too much.'

'You never said anything . . .' Mr Van Wyk began.

'Not I, sir. Why should I? I mean to get on, but the dead aren't in my way,' said Sterne. His eyelids were beating rapidly, then drooped for an instant. 'Besides, sir, it would have been an awkward business. You made me hold my tongue just a bit too long.'

'Do you know how it was that Captain Whalley remained on board? Did he really refuse to leave? Come now! Or was it perhaps an accidental . . ?'

'Nothing!' Sterne interrupted with energy. 'I tell you I yelled for him to leap overboard. He simply *must* have cast off the painter of the boat himself. We all yelled to him – that is, Jack and I. He wouldn't even answer us. The ship was as silent as a grave to the last. Then the boilers fetched away, and down she went. Accident! Not it! The game was up, sir, I tell you.'

This was all that Sterne had to say.

Mr Van Wyk had been of course made the guest of the club for a fortnight, and it was there that he met the lawyer in whose office had been signed the agreement between Massy and Captain Whalley.

'Extraordinary old man,' he said. 'He came into my office from nowhere in particular as you may say, with his five hundred pounds to invest, and that engineer fellow following him anxiously. And now he is gone out a little inexplicably, just as he came. I could never understand him quite. There was no mystery at all about that Massy, eh? I wonder whether Whalley refused to leave the ship. It would have been foolish. He was blameless, as the court found.'

Mr Van Wyk had known him well, he said, and he could not believe in suicide. Such an act would not have been in character with what he knew of the man.

'It is my opinion, too,' the lawyer agreed. The general theory was that the captain had remained too long on board trying to save something of importance. Perhaps the chart which would clear him, or else something of value in his cabin. The painter of the boat had come adrift of itself, it was supposed. However, strange to say, some little time before that voyage poor Whalley had called in his office and had left with him a sealed envelope addressed to his daughter, to be forwarded to her in case of his death. Still it was nothing very unusual, especially in a man of his age. Mr Van Wyk shook his head. Captain Whalley looked good for a hundred years.

'Perfectly true,' assented the lawyer. 'The old fellow looked as though he had come into the world full grown and with that long beard. I could never, somehow, imagine him either younger or older – don't you know. There was a sense of physical power about that man, too. And perhaps that was the secret of that something peculiar in his person which struck everybody who came in contact with him. He looked indestructible by any ordinary means that put an end to the rest of us. His deliberate, stately courtesy of manner was full of significance. It was as though he were certain of having plenty of time for everything.

Yes, there was something indestructible about him; and the way he talked sometimes you might have thought he believed it himself. When he called on me last with that letter he wanted me to take charge of, he was not depressed at all. Perhaps a shade more deliberate in his talk and manner. Not depressed in the least. Had he a presentiment, I wonder? Perhaps! Still it seems a miserable end for such a striking figure.'

'Oh, yes! It was a miserable end,' Mr Van Wyk said, with so much fervour that the lawyer looked up at him curiously; and afterwards, after parting with him, he remarked to an acquaintance –

'Queer person that Dutch tobacco-planter from Batu Beru. Know anything of him?'

'Heaps of money,' answered the bank manager. 'I hear he's going home by the next mail to form a company to take over his estates. Another tobacco district thrown open. He's wise, I think. These good times won't last for ever.'

*

In the southern hemisphere Captain Whalley's daughter had no presentiment of evil when she opened the envelope addressed to her in the lawyer's handwriting. She had received it in the afternoon; all the boarders had gone out, her boys were at school, her husband sat upstairs in his big arm-chair with a book, thin-faced, wrapped up in rugs to the waist. The house was still, and the greyness of a cloudy day lay against the panes of the windows.

In a shabby dining-room, where a faint cold smell of dishes lingered all the year round, sitting at the end of a long table surrounded by many chairs pushed in with their backs close against the edge of the perpetually laid table-cloth, she read the opening sentences: 'Most profound regret – painful duty – your father is no more – in accordance with his instructions – fatal casualty – consolation – no blame attached to his memory . . .'

Her face was thin, her temples a little sunk under the smooth bands of black hair, her lips remained resolutely compressed, while her dark eyes grew larger, till at last, with a low cry, she stood up, and instantly stooped to pick up another envelope which had slipped off her knees on to the floor.

She tore it open, snatched out the enclosure . . .

'My dearest child,' it said, 'I am writing this while I am able yet to write legibly. I am trying hard to save for you all the money that is left; I have only kept it to serve you better. It is yours. It shall not be lost; it shall not be touched. There's five hundred pounds. Of what I have earned I have kept nothing back till now. For the future, if I live, I must keep back some – a little – to bring me to you. I must come to you. I must see you once more.

'It is hard to believe that you will ever look on these lines. God seems to have forgotten me. I want to see you – and yet death would be a greater favour. If you ever read these words, I charge you to begin by thanking a God merciful at last, for I shall be dead then, and it will be well. My dear, I am at the end of my tether.'

The next paragraph began with the words: 'My sight is going . . .'

She read no more that day. The hand holding up the paper to her eyes fell slowly, and her slender figure in a plain black dress walked rigidly to the window. Her eyes were dry: no cry of sorrow or whisper of thanks went up to heaven from her lips. Life had been too hard, for all the efforts of his love. It had silenced her emotions. But for the first time in all these years its sting had departed, the carking care of poverty, the meanness of a hard struggle for bread. Even the image of her husband and of her children seemed to glide away from her into the grey twilight; it was her father's face alone that she saw, as though he had come to see her, always quiet and big, as she had seen him last, but with something more august and tender in his aspect.

She slipped his folded letter between the two buttons of her plain black bodice, and leaning her forehead against a window-pane remained there till dusk, perfectly motionless, giving him all the time she could spare. Gone! Was it possible? My God, was it possible? The blow had come softened by the spaces of the earth, by the years of absence. There had been whole days when she had not thought of him at all – had no time. But she had loved him, she felt she had loved him after all.

NOTES

THE GROWTH OF THE TEXT

The writing of the three stories in this volume spanned a period in Conrad's life (1898–1902) which saw the beginning and the end of Conrad's association with the publisher William Blackwood and *Blackwood's Magazine (Maga)*, in which Conrad's story 'Karain: A Memory' was published in November 1897.

'YOUTH'

In May 1898 Conrad put aside *The Rescue* in despair, wrote some pages of 'Jim: A Sketch', and left this to write 'Youth' which, according to G. Jean-Aubry, 'got itself written, almost straight off, in a few days' (*Joseph Conrad: Life and Letters*, I. 73). On 3 June 1898 Conrad was able to write to Mrs E. L. Sanderson, wife of his friend, Edward Sanderson: 'When your letter arrived I was finishing a short story ['Youth'] . . . Half an hour ago I've written the last word' (*L. and L.*, I. 238). It was accepted for *Maga* on 9 June and £35 paid for it. The story appeared four months later in the September 1898 issue of *Blackwood's Magazine*.

THE 'YOUTH' VOLUME

In June 1898 David S. Meldrum, literary adviser to William Blackwood, suggested that Blackwood, with McClure (in America), might publish a volume of short stories by Conrad which would include 'Youth'. Conrad wrote to Edward Garnett:

> I've sold (I think) the sea things [*sic*] to B[lackwood] for £35 (13,000 words). Meldrum thinks there's no doubt but still B must see it himself. McClure has been the pink of perfection 'We will be glad to get as much as we can for you in America' – and so on. He is anxious to have a book of short tales. I think *Jim* (20,000) Youth (13,000) A seaman (5,000) Dynamite (5,000) and another story of say 15,000 would make a volume for B here and for McC. there.
>
> (Letter of May 1898)

Of Conrad's suggested contents for the volume only 'Youth' was to be retained.

'HEART OF DARKNESS'
After completing 'Youth', Conrad went back to his struggle with *The Rescue*, which McClure hoped would be finished in July 1898, and at the same time he was expected to finish 'Jim' (still envisaged as a short story) for serialization to begin in September in *Blackwood's*. But *The Rescue* still flagged and again Conrad left it, this time to write 'Heart of Darkness'. That amazing story appears to have been written in just over one month, though Conrad had had it in mind for some time. According to Edward Garnett, Conrad had narrated it during a visit to Garnett's home, probably in September 1898.

On 31 December 1898 Conrad told Blackwood that he was at work on something for the thousandth number of *Maga*:

> I expect to be ready in a very few days. It is a narrative after the manner of *Youth* told by the same man dealing with his experience on a river in Central Africa. The *idea* in it is not as obvious as in *Youth* – or at least not so obviously presented . . . The title I am thinking of is '*The Heart of Darkness*' but the narrative is not gloomy. The criminality of inefficiency and pure selfishness when tackling the civilizing work in Africa is a justifiable idea. The subject is of our time distinctly – though not topically treated.

(*Conrad's Letters to Blackwood*, ed. W. Blackburn, pp. 36–7)

A letter from Conrad to Meldrum of 2 January 1899 suggests that he began writing the story about 23 December: 'I began the story for Maga 10 days ago . . . A mere shadow of love interest just in the last pages – but I hope it will have the effect I intend.' On 9 January he was able to send Meldrum pages 1–35 in typescript and pages 36–58 in manuscript. 'I am finishing in a frightful hurry a story for *B'wood* and it's an immense effort,' he wrote to the Hon. Mrs Bontine on 9th January (*L. and L.*, I. 265). 'Conrad's story is a very wonderful piece of writing, is it not? And such a "Show up" for the French!' Meldrum wrote jubilantly to Blackwood (14 January 1899, Blackburn, op. cit. p. 43).
On 6 February Conrad sent a telegram to Meldrum saying that he was sending the remainder of 'Heart of Darkness', presumably just finished. As so often happened with Conrad, the story had 'grown upon him', and instead of the two serial parts initially planned it covered three, appearing in the February, March and April issues of *Blackwood's Magazine* in 1899.

'THE END OF THE TETHER'
Conrad's name was then very much before the public as an *Academy*

prize-winner for *Tales of Unrest*, and Blackwood wished to take advantage of this by publishing the *Youth* volume at the end of April or in May 1899. Conrad, then writing 'Jim', suggested that this story with 'Youth' and 'Heart of Darkness' might complete the volume, but two circumstances delayed completion. 'Jim' grew into a full-length novel and was published separately by Blackwood (having first appeared as a serial in *Maga*), and Conrad was asked to write further stories for the *Youth* volume. But he also had to fulfil his obligations to other publishers and, after finishing *Lord Jim* in July 1900, he turned to these.

A year later, in 1901, Blackwood began to press for 30,000 to 40,000 words to complete the volume, and eventually, in March 1902, after finishing *Romance*, Conrad began writing the final story: 'I am in an hour or so going to begin my Blackwood stuff – "The End of the Song" – as Ford has suggested and advised' (letter to Elsie Hueffer, *Joseph Conrad: A Critical Biography*, Jocelyn Baines, 1960, p. 278). But the story did not come easily – it was 'all behind': 'I am tired – I am tired of sitting on the knees of the unpropitious Gods.' It was 20 May 1902 before he was able to write to Blackwood:

> This is 14,000 words. There are more written and you need not apprehend anything in the nature of Lord Jim's development. That sort of thing does not happen twice. There will be about 30,000 words . . . I have now blocked out in MS. about 6,000 words besides what you receive.

(Blackburn, pp. 147–8)

Although he had been generous in the past, Blackwood, later that month, refused Conrad a further loan: 'He was very kind but told me plainly that I was a loss to the Firm' (letter to Meldrum, 31 May 1902). Obviously very upset, Conrad wrote a long letter to Blackwood defending his convictions and method as a writer (31 May 1902), but his good relationship with Blackwood was coming to an end. The literary agent Pinker was now handling Conrad's affairs, and this contributed to the breaking of the personal link with Blackwood. There is a significant error in Blackwood's letter to Conrad of June 1902: 'I have had pleasure in desiring an early copy of the July *Maga* to be sent to you, and you will see that it opens with the first instalment of your story "The End of the Chapter" [*sic*]' (Blackburn, p. 158). As Conrad was reaching the end of the second instalment there was a disaster. He described to Hueffer what happened:

> Last night the lamp exploded here and before I could run back into the room the whole round table was in a blaze – Books, cigarettes, MS. alas! The whole second part of 'End of the Tether' ready to go to Edinburgh . . . This morning looking at the pile of charred paper MS. and typed copy – my head swam; it seemed to me the earth

was the turning backwards. I must buckle to, the MS. was due today in Edinburgh. I have wired Blackwoods.

(24 June 1902)

The story was probably finished on 15th July 1902 and it appeared in *Maga*, July–December 1902. The *Youth* volume was eventually published in November 1902, almost four and a half years after the original agreement was made. On 19 December 1902 Meldrum wrote to Blackwood:

> I knew Conrad was good – in fact 'Youth' I hold to be the most notable book we have published since George Eliot, and so do other judges. 'Lord Jim' and 'Youth' will go on selling for twenty years, I have no doubt.

(Blackburn, p. 172)

NOTES ON 'YOUTH'

Conrad was twenty-four when, on 19 September 1881, he signed on as second mate of the barque *Palestine*. The *Palestine*, 425 tons, was bound for Bangkok, and it is her journey on which the journey of the *Judea* is based. She was commanded by Captain Elijah Beard, owned by John Wilson of South Hackney, and built, of wood, at Sunderland in 1857. She was therefore twenty-four years old when Conrad sailed in her. Because of a gale it took her sixteen days to get from London to the Tyne where she was to take on a cargo of coal. According to the report of the inquiry into her loss held in Singapore on 2 April 1883, she left Newcastle on 29 November 1881 with a cargo of 557 tons of West Hartley coal and a crew of thirteen hands, but during heavy gales in the English Channel she lost sail and sprang a leak on 24 December. As in the story, the crew refused to proceed and the ship put back to Falmouth. The coal was discharged and stored and the ship repaired and she sailed again on 17 September 1882. Conrad mentions a stay at Falmouth of at least six months in the story and has the ship put to sea three times and return (p. 12).

The *Palestine* had a tedious passage because of persistent light winds. On 11 March there was a strong smell of paraffin oil (cf. p. 14), and next day smoke was seen coming from the cargo. Water was thrown on the coals and boats were lowered (cf. pp. 15 and 16). On the 13th some coals were thrown overboard. On the 14th the decks blew up fore and aft (cf. pp. 18–19), the boats were provisioned and the vessel headed for the Sumatra shore.

In 'Youth' the *Judea* is sighted by the steamer *Somerville*, but in the case of the *Palestine* it was the S.S. *Somerset* that took the *Palestine* in tow. Since the master of the *Somerset* refused to tow the barque on shore, the tow-rope was slipped at 11 p.m. on 14 March. The ship being on fire, the crew got into the boats – the mate and four seamen in one, the master in the long boat with three men, and the second mate (Conrad) in the third boat with three men. (Marlow has two men with him, cf. p. 26.)

Although Marlow steers many days before reaching land, Conrad landed at Muntock on the island of Banka, off Sumatra, after thirteen and a half hours, at 10 p.m. on 15 March 1883. The officers and crew of the *Palestine* were taken on to Singapore in the S.S. *Sissie*, where they arrived on 22 March 1883. The Court of Inquiry decided that the cause of the fire was spontaneous combustion, and that no blame was attached to the master, officers and crew. Conrad was discharged at Singapore on 3 April 1883 and paid 171.12 Straits dollars. (See Agreement and Account of Crew of the *Palestine*.)

Conrad spent six weeks in Singapore, probably staying at the Sailors' Home there as did Lord Jim. He left in May 1883, possibly on 1st May in the Spanish steamer *Leon XIII* for Liverpool.

NOTES ON 'THE HEART OF DARKNESS'

In 1889 Conrad was staying at Bessborough Gardens, London, writing *Almayer's Folly* and looking for another berth after his return from Australia. Through the influence of a relative, Marguerite Poradowska, he obtained a post as skipper of a steamer on the River Congo with the trading company Société Anonyme Belge pour le Commerce du Haut-Congo (SAB), which had its headquarters in Belgium. He was twice interviewed in Brussels by Captain Albert Thys, director of the SAB (November 1889 and April 1890) and was appointed master of the Congo river steamer *Florida*, a position left vacant by the assassination of Captain Johannes Freiesleben by natives at Tchumbiri on 29 January 1890. As in the story, the assassination resulted from a trivial argument, though Freiesleben was shot and not stabbed. Although Freiesleben lay unburied for some months, he *had been* buried by March 1890, before Conrad left Europe for the Congo, and Conrad could not, like Marlow, have seen his predecessor's bones (cf. p. 44). According to Conrad, however, he had been appointed 'to command of a steamboat, belonging to M. Delcommune's exploring party' (letter to Karol Zagorski, 22nd May 1890), and this is not part of Marlow's expectations.

Conrad sailed in the *Ville de Maceio* from Bordeaux on 10 May 1890, accompanied by another agent, Prosper Harou. The ship called at Tenerife, Dakar, Conakry, Freetown, Grand Bassam, Grand Popo, Libreville, Banana, and finally Boma, where Conrad disembarked on

12 June (cf. 'Heart of Darkness' pp. 48–50). During the journey his initial excitement seems to have waned. He began to worry about the possibility of dying of fever and dysentery: '60 per cent of our Company's employees return to Europe before they have completed even six months' service. . . . There are others who are sent home in a hurry at the end of a year, so that they shouldn't die in the Congo. . . . It would spoil the statistics' (letter of 22 May 1890).

From Boma there was a thirty-mile trip up-river to Matadi, Marlow's Company Station – 170 Europeans lived there, and there were four factories and the SAB station. The building of a railway had begun at Matadi and was to do away with the exhausting overland trek of 230 miles from Matadi to Kinchassa. Although there was to be great loss of life among native workers in the area two years later, it is unlikely that Conrad encountered Marlow's 'grove of death'.

The only two diaries of Conrad that have survived were kept at this time. 'The Congo Diary' (cf. *Last Essays*, pp. 161–71) shows that Conrad's strongest reaction at Matadi was dislike of the Europeans there: 'Prominent characteristic of the social life here; people speaking ill of each other.' He *did* approve of Gosse, chief of the station, and Underwood, Manager of the English Factory of Hatton & Cookson at Kalla Kalla, and of Roger Casement, who was taking part in the exploration of the Congo, and joined General Sanford's exploration in 1886: 'Thinks, speaks well, most intelligent and very sympathetic.' For some reason Conrad stayed at Matadi fifteen days – 13–28 June 1890.

Conrad's journey from Matadi to Kinchassa (Marlow's Central Station) was most gruelling, as his 'Congo Diary' records. He travelled from 28 June to 2 August with a rest at Manyanga from 8 July to 25 July, accompanied by the agent Harou and a caravan of thirty-one men. Marlow's experiences here closely mirror Conrad's – the exhausting nature of the terrain, the dead bodies, the trouble with the carriers, the sickness of the 'white companion' Harou. The most significant difference between the actual and the fictional journey was the time taken to reach the destination – Marlow took fifteen days, Conrad took thirty-five, and had already delayed at Matadi. Normally the overland journey took no more than twenty days and could be accomplished in seventeen. Conrad's relationship with Camille Delcommune, manager of the Kinchassa station, was bedevilled by this delay from the beginning and this is reflected in the story in the manager's attitude to Marlow.

Marlow spends some time at the Central Station salvaging his steamer, but Conrad left Kinchassa within forty-eight hours of his arrival on the steamer *Roi des Belges*. It was on this voyage that he kept his second Congo notebook, the Up-River Book, a seaman's charting of the river.

Like Marlow, Conrad was accompanied on the voyage to Stanley Falls by the manager (Delcommune) and by the agents (Kayaerts, Rollin and

Vander Heyden), and an engineer (Gossens). But Conrad was not in command of the *Roi des Belges*, whose master was Captain Koch. As his Up-River Book suggests, Conrad was probably there to gain experience of the river before taking over a river-steamer. The steamer covered the 100 miles in a little less than a month, a speed which merited a notice in the *Mouvement Géographique*, and the voyage would appear to have been a routine business trip to visit stations on the river and to go to the assistance of a troop carrier, *Ville de Bruxelles*, which had broken down. Moreover there was a considerable amount of shipping on the river, and a number of well-established settlements. It was not the uncharted world of Marlow's experience. It is unlikely that the kind of attack by natives that Marlow described took place, since no mention of any such attack appears in the records of the time. Marlow's Inner Station is a decaying ruin in the jungle, but when Conrad visited Stanley Falls it was a well-established station with a number of resident state officials and representatives of commercial houses. But the *Roi des Belges* certainly did take off a sick SAB agent, Georges Antoine Klein, who had arrived at Boma on 15 February 1899, and had become agent at the Falls station probably only a month or so before Conrad reached the Congo. Conrad himself appears to have been ill during his five or six days' stay at Stanley Falls, as was Captain Koch. Conrad was in command of the *Roi des Belges* when she left with Klein on board, about 6 September. A letter still in existence, from Camille Delcommune to 'Monsieur Conrad Korzeniowski' asks Conrad to take command, 'until the recovery of Captain Koch' (6 September 1890, cf. G. Jean-Aubry, *Joseph Conrad in the Congo*, 1926, p. 67). Captain Koch probably took command again by 17 September, and the steamer reached Kinchassa on 24 September. But Klein died on board and was buried in the European graveyard, 150 yards from the river, at Tchumbiri. His grave can still be seen there.

Conrad had been unhappy and ill during his stay in the Congo, and he had certainly made an enemy of Camille Delcommune. He wrote to Marguerite Poradowska from Kinchassa:

> Everything is repellent to me here. Men and things, but especially men. And I am repellent to them, too. From the manager in Africa – who has taken the trouble of telling a good many people that I displease him intensely – down to the lowest mechanic, all have a gift for getting on my nerves.

> (Letter of 26 September 1890)

And years later he was to recall to Jean-Aubry 'the hostile and disagreeable figure of Camille Delcommune'. The Katanga exploring expedition led by Delcommune's brother, Alexandre, arrived at Kinchassa between 20 September and 5 October, and is satirized by Conrad as the Eldorado Exploring Expedition (p. 68). Conrad's hopes of joining this were dashed when the expedition left without him on 17

October, and on 19 October he wrote to his uncle to say that he was returning to Europe. He was a very sick man and never fully recovered from his Congo experience.

NOTES ON 'THE END OF THE TETHER'

THE SOURCES

'The End of the Tether' presents an extremely accurate picture, historically and geographically, of Singapore which Conrad visited for three short periods in 1883, 1885 and 1887 as a seaman. The walk which Captain Whalley takes at the beginning of the story allows Conrad to describe that small part of the city of Singapore he would know as a seaman, the area near the sea front where the Post Office, Harbour Office, Officers' Sailors' Home, St Andrew's Cathedral, and the padang were grouped round the mouth of the Singapore river and Cavenagh Bridge. Conrad must have often seen the procession of carriages on the Esplanade from five o'clock till dusk (cf. pp. 145–7), the fashionable time for taking the air, and he was interviewed at the Harbour Office when he was given his first command, the barque *Otago*. *The Shadow-Line* makes use of the same material.

The historical detail which is used to build up Captain Whalley's life in the East must have derived from gossip Conrad heard in the port and from his reading about it. For example, the Consolidated Docks Company (p. 138) was the New Harbour Dock Company established in the 1850s (cf. Conrad's use of this name on p. 58). In the 1830s and 1840s Government House, built by Raffles, the founder of Singapore, was a bungalow on a hill, though in Conrad's time it was a 'many-windowed, arcaded palace', and the two Governors contrasted by Whalley (pp. 147–8) are based upon Samuel George Bonham (1837–43) and Sir Frederick Weld (1880–7).

Books such as Keppel's *A Sailor's Life under Four Sovereigns* (London, 1899), Sherard Osborn's *My Journal in Malayan Waters* (London, 1860) and Mrs Florence Caddy's *To Siam and Malaya* (London, 1889) may well have been used by Conrad for historical detail.

Conrad appears to have made a good deal in this story of one person he met once for a short interview, but of whom he must have heard much in the gossip of the port. This was Captain Henry Ellis, Master-Attendant at Singapore, who gave Conrad the command of the *Otago*. He retired in 1888. He appears also in *The Shadow-Line* and *Lord Jim*, and in this story he is Captain Eliott. Eliott's loud voice, sudden tempers, bluntness and essential goodness derive from Henry Ellis, and his power in the port reflects accurately Henry Ellis's authority in Singapore.

Ellis had a long-standing friendship with a seaman, Irish like himself, who was in the merchant service, trading in Far Eastern waters, who left the port eventually very poorly off, and this may be the origin of Captain Whalley, but Whalley's appearance, religious nature and dignity may well be based upon Ellis also, who had two distinct sides to his nature.

NOTES ON THE TEXT

'YOUTH'

p. 3, l. 8. *a director of companies* Cf. *Heart of Darkness*, pp. 37. In both instances Conrad is recalling his association with his friend, G. F. W. Hope, particularly just before and just after Conrad's Congo experience (1890–1). Hope was a director of many companies in his time.

ll. 8–9. *an accountant: a lawyer* On Hope's yawl, the *Nellie*, Keen and Mears joined the company. Mears had sailed in the *Duke of Sutherland*, as had Hope and Conrad at different times.

l. 9. *a Conway boy* The *Conway* and the *Worcester* were the two training-ships in existence at that time. Conrad's son, Borys, was trained on the *Worcester*. (Cf. also 'The Secret Sharer', p. 101.)

p. 4, l. 5. *sixty* The master of the *Palestine*, Captain Elijah Beard, was born on 2 May 1824, according to his application for Master's Certificate of 1868, and so was fifty-seven at the start of the voyage.

l. 30. *Mahon* The mate of the *Palestine*, Mahon, was born in Dublin and was fifty at the beginning of her last voyage. (Cf. Agreement and Account of Crew.)

p. 5 l. 6. *a palace* Conrad had previously sailed in the clipper *Loch Etive*.

l. 12. *love the old thing* But cf. Thaddeus Bobrowski's letter to Conrad, 11–23 September 1881: 'It seems to me that you are not satisfied with your post: is it because being on a "barque" touches on your honour? Then, of course, £4 a month is disrespectful to your pocket, and, finally, the captain seems to you to be merely a "creature.". . .'

l. 16. *Melbourne and Sydney* Conrad sailed to Australia in the *Duke of Sutherland* (1878–9) and the *Loch Etive* (1880–1).

p. 6 l. 5. *One of the ship's boys* John Brady and John Parish, both seventeen, both of London, were ship's boys on the *Palestine* from London to the Tyne. They were paid 7s 6d per month. They left the ship at North Shields.

l. 11. *tier* pier?

l. 13. *Colchester* Captain Beard was born at Colchester, according to the Agreement and Account of Crew.

l. 15. *a mulatto* Probably the *Palestine*'s steward and cook, Harry Stockbridge, from 'P. R. Island' (Puerto Rico?), who deserted at North Shields on 21 November 1881.

l. 25. *Sartor Resartus* (1833) by Thomas Carlyle, Victorian philosopher (1795–1881).

l. 25. *Burnaby's 'Ride to Khiva'* Colonel Frederick Gustavus Burnaby (1842–85), British soldier and traveller, wrote *Ride to Khiva* (1876) describing his winter ride across the Russian steppes.

l. 32. *shipped a crew* The *Palestine* appears to have signed on seven crew members at North Shields, including two boys.

p. 8, l. 20. *three months* Actually just over two.

p. 11, l. 22. *put back* The *Palestine* returned to Falmouth late December 1881.

ll. 36–7. *a new crew* In February 1882 the *Palestine* signed on ten new crew members at Falmouth (Agreement and Account of Crew). This would suggest the ship did leave Falmouth at this point and returned again, although this is not mentioned in the report of the Singapore Court of Inquiry.

p. 12, l. 7. *a Geordie skipper* Beard was not a Geordie, though he asked for his Master's Certificate to be sent to him at South Shields.

l. 16. *a fresh crew – the third* In September 1882 the *Palestine* signed on more crew at Falmouth, though they do not appear to be from Liverpool (pp. 13–14). Since the ship sailed on 17 September, this is the last crew and Conrad is embroidering fact for the sake of the story.

p. 16, l. 13. *she crawled on* Cf. *Lord Jim*, p. 17.

p. 17, l. 34. *About ten* Cf. this paragraph with *Lord Jim*, p. 30.

p. 19, l. 18. *lazarette* Space between decks used as a store room.

p. 22, l. 17 *two pounds ten a month* Able seamen on the *Palestine* were paid three pounds a month (cf. Agreement of Crew).

p. 24, l. 3. *kedge-anchor* Small anchor used in mooring or warping.

p. 25, l. 4. *cat-heads* Tackle used to raise or suspend the anchor.

p. 27, l. 20. *the oars were got out* 'The boats remained by the vessel until 8.30 p.m. on the 15th. She was still above water, but inside appeared a mass of fire.' (Report of the Court of Inquiry.)

l. 37. *jury-rig* A temporary rig.

p. 28, l. 32. *a high outline of mountains* Conrad landed at Muntock on the island of Banka, off the coast of Sumatra. Cf. Conrad's romantic description with his comment in a letter to Richard Curle, 24 April 1922: 'Muntok is a damned hole without any beach and without any glamour . . . the par[agraph], when pinned to a particular spot, must appear diminished – a fake. And yet it is true.' (*Conrad to a Friend*, ed. Richard Curle, New York, 1928, pp. 143–4.)

'HEART OF DARKNESS'

p. 38, l. 2. *mizzen-mast* The aftermost mast of a three-masted ship.

l. 17. *And at last* Cf. the similar description of sunset over London in *The Mirror of the Sea*, p. 103.

l. 35. *Sir Francis Drake* (c. 1540–96) His adventurous voyages were motivated partly by the urge to make discoveries, partly for plunder.

l. 35. *Sir John Franklin* Rear-Admiral, F.R.S. (1789–1847), famous Arctic explorer. The *Erebus* and the *Terror* were the ships taking part in his last expedition, searching for the North-West Passage, from which he did not return. Cf. also 'Geography and Some Explorers', in *Last Essays*, pp. 10–11.

p. 39, *l.* 5. *'interlopers'* Ships trespassing on the rights of trade monopolies such as the East India Company.

l. 17. *monstrous town* Cf. *The Secret Agent*, Author's Note, p. xii.

l. 21. *dark places* For Marlow's comparison of the Thames and the Congo cf. Henry Morton Stanley's reference to Pitt's speech of April 1792 on the subject, *The Times*, 4 October 1892. Cf. also *The Mirror of the Sea*, pp. 101–2.

p. 40, *l.* 33. *Ravenna* Chief Roman base in northern Italy.

p. 41, *l.* 15. *squeeze* Cf. Marlow's discussion here and on the attraction of Africa ('p. 42) with 'Geography and Some Explorers' in *Last Essays*, pp. 12–13.

p. 43, *l.* 3. *Company* The Société Anonyme pour le Commerce du Haut-Congo. It was Henry Morton Stanley who established trading posts on the Congo for King Leopold of the Congo, and he was much in the news in 1889 because of his search for Emin Pasha.

l. 9. *relatives* Alexandre Poradowski, a cousin of Conrad, and his wife Marguerite, lived in Brussels. Alexandre died in February 1890, but Conrad had for many years a close relationship with Marguerite, whom he called 'aunt'.

p. 44, *l.* 16. *deserted* Tchumbiri, where Johannes Freiesleben was assassinated on 29 January 1890, was visited by a punitory expedition and was burnt.

p. 47, *l.* 9. *Ave!* 'Hail!... Those who are about to die salute you.'

l. 31. *measure my head* In August 1881 Conrad's uncle had requested him to collect native skulls for a Mr Kopernicki, a craniologist engaged in the comparative study of human skulls.

p. 47, *l.* 7. *alienist* One who treats mental illness.

p. 51, *l.* 17. *a railway* The first rails and sleepers for a railway at Matadi were brought out on the vessel Conrad sailed in, the *Ville de Maceio* (*Mouvement Géographique*, 4 May 1890).

p. 54, *l.* 12. *chief accountant* Two accountants left to work for the railway according to the *Mouvement Géographique*, 26 January 1890.

p. 52, *l.* 11.   *Kurtz*   In MS. Klein, then cancelled.

p. 56, *ll.* 23–4.   *a carrier dead*   Cf. 'The Congo Diary': 'Saw another dead body lying by the path in an attitude of meditative repose' (p. 165).

l. 34.   *a middle-aged negro*   Cf. 'The Congo Diary' p. 163: 'Met an off^(er) of the state inspecting. A few minutes afterwards ... the dead body of a Backongo. Shot?'

p. 57, *l.* 4.   *got a fever*   Cf. 'The Congo Diary' p. 169: '[Harou] vomiting bile in enormous quantities ... put him in hammock'.

l. 7.   *quite a mutiny*   Conrad had trouble with the carriers and 'made a speech which they did not understand' ('Congo Diary', pp. 169–70).

p. 58, *l.* 22.   *a common trader*   'The manager is a common ivory-dealer with sordid instincts ... a kind of African shop-keeper.' (Letter of 26 September 1890, *Letters to Marguerite Poradowska*, p. 16).

p. 60, *l.* 23.   *a blaze*   There was a fire at Kinchassa, quite an extensive one, before Conrad arrived (cf. *Mouvement Géographique*, 1 November 1891).

p. 61, *l.* 19.   *assegais*   slender throwing spears.

l. 20.   *making of bricks*   There was a brick-maker named Deligne at Kinchassa, and a lot of bricks were made (cf. *Mouvement Géographique*, 22 November 1890).

p. 62, *l.* 31.   *chief of the Inner Station*   Arthur Constant Hodister was an important agent 'in the interior', 'the true ivory-country', with seven agents under his orders, including the one at the Falls station. He was associated with the antislavery movement and was against savage customs. He was an explorer, on terms of friendship with the natives, a great ivory collector; he charted the shipping at Bangala and made meteorological observations as well as publishing impassioned articles – a kind of 'universal genius'. Conrad must have heard of him in the Congo, and he may well be the original of Kurtz. In July 1892, while on an expedition, he and his companions were killed and eaten.

p. 63, *l.* 6.   *the new gang*   Hodister was supported by Thys (Director of the SAB) and Wauters (editor of *Mouvement Géographique*) who had supported Conrad.

p. 67, *ll.* 4/5.　*Huntley & Palmer biscuit-tin*　Cf. also 'The *Titanic* Inquiry', *Notes on Life and Letters*, pp. 233–4.

　p. 73, *l.* 2.　*guessing at the channel*　'Great quantity of dangerous snags along the star^d. shore. Follow the slight bend of the shore with caution. The Middle of the Channel is a S—B— [sand bank] always covered.' (Conrad's Up-River Book, *Last Essays*, p. 159.)

　　　l. 14.　*tight-ropes*　Cf. *The Secret Agent*, p. 116.

　　　l. 31.　*cannibals*　Crews of steamers on the Upper Congo were mostly Bangalas, who were cannibals. (Cf. W. Holman Bentley, *Pioneering on the Congo*, 1900, I. 210, 213.)

p. 74, *l.* 26/7.　*wood-cutters slept*　the *Roi des Belges* was a wood-burning vessel, and every evening wood had to be cut for the following day. (Cf. J. Rose Troup, *With Stanley's Rear Column*, 1890, p. 124.)

　p. 77, *l.* 11.　*Tower, Towson*　John Thomas Towson of the Sailors' Home, Liverpool, in the 1850s wrote on such subjects as 'Great Circle Sailing', 'Practical Information on the Deviation of a Compass'.

　p. 78, *l.* 7.　*boat*　1921 Heinemann edition gives 'float'.

　p. 81, *l.* 1.　*brass wire*　The mitako, or brass rod, was the currency among the natives of the Upper Congo (cf. Troup, pp. 103–4).

　　　l. 13.　*some stuff*　Manioc root made into a stiff dough and wrapped in banana leaves. (Cf. H. H. Johnstone, *George Grenfell*, II, 605.)

　p. 91, *l.* 39.　*Exterminate*　Cf. *The Secret Agent*, p. 303: 'Exterminate Exterminate! That is the only way of progress.'

　p. 113, *l.* 12.　*secular*　Centuries old.

'THE END OF THE TETHER'

　p. 127, *l.* 8.　*Serang*　Malay boatswain.

　p. 128, *l.* 20.　*monotonous huckster's round*　Conrad probably has in mind the voyages of the *Vidar* in which he sailed between 22 August 1887 and 4 January 1888 as mate. The S.S. *Vidar* traded among the islands of the S. E. Asian archipelago from Singapore to Berau in

Borneo, a journey of 27–35 days. (Cf. my *Conrad's Eastern World*, pp. 29–31.)

p. 129, l. 34.   *Isthmus of Suez*   The Suez Canal was opened in 1869, and cut 4,000 miles off the journey from Europe to India.

p. 130, l. 10.   *Travancore and Deccan Banking Corporation*   In 1884 the Oriental Bank in Singapore failed. (Cf. *Almayer's Folly* and *The Rescue* for the failure of the bank used by William Lingard, based on the Oriental failure.)

p. 134, l. 18.   *lee*   Side away from the wind.

p. 135, ll. 15/6.   *yellow funnels*   In January 1884 the *Straits Times* commented that the day of the sailing ships was almost gone. The advent of an Arab trader in a steamer into the river in *Almayer's Folly* reflects this situation, and William Lingard, original of Tom Lingard in that novel and *An Outcast of the Islands* and *The Rescue*, was similarly affected by the coming of steam into the Far East. (Cf. my *Conrad's Eastern World*, pp. 108–10.)

p. 138, l. 7.   *recently . . . thoroughfare*   In 1884 a new road was planned in Singapore from Fullerton Battery to Pasir Panjang.

l. 17.   *tigers*   In the 1850s and 1860s many Chinese were carried off by tigers within a few miles of the town.

l. 18.   *New Waterworks*   Probably reservoir on Mount Emily, Singapore, built about 1878.

p. 140, l. 3.   *'Song of the Shirt'*   Poem by Thomas Hood (1799–1845).

p.144, l. 17.   *small bridge*   Cavenagh Bridge which spans the Singapore River. (Cf. also *The Rescue*, p. 99.)

p. 147, l. 35.   *Evans*   It was William Cloughton who built the first dry dock in Singapore in 1854. Captain Whalley must have come to the island first in the 1840s when Samuel George Bonham was Governor.

p. 148, l. 19.   *caught fire*   There was a fire at Cloughton's yard at Sandy Point, Singapore.

p. 149, ll. 36/7.   *end . . . time*   Sir Frederick Weld, Governor of Singapore, retired in 1887.

p. 150, l. 16. *Cathedral* St Andrew's Cathedral built in 1861. (Cf. *Almayer's Folly*, p. 43.)

      l. 39. *a duke* The Duke of Sutherland visited Singapore in February 1888, and a steam launch was sent out to his yacht to bring him ashore.

p. 151, ll. 17/18. *Glasgow ship* Conrad is making use here of his appointment as master of the *Otago*. (Cf. 'The Shadow-Line', 'Falk' and *Lord Jim*.)

p. 152, l. 34. *Three girls* Henry Ellis, on whom Eliott is based, had one daughter.

  p. 153 l. 7. *in Surrey* He in fact retired to County Donegal, his birthplace.

      l. 25. *syce* A groom.

p. 155, l. 16. *Manilla lottery* The Manila lottery was very popular in the east in the 1380s. In 1887 the second prize was $15,000 (Straits dollars).

p. 194, l. 14. *King* Probably 'Kling' (Malay?), immigrant from Coromandel coast.

  p. 202, l. 2. *Denham Street* This would be Bonham Street in Singapore, named after Governor Bonham. Bonham is crossed out in the MS. and replaced by Denham.

     l. 8. *grog-shop* Cf. Mariani's grog-shop, *Lord Jim*, p. 49.

p. 240, l. 13. *fiddle* rail or frame to hold objects in place.

p. 249, l. 18. *pieces . . . pockets* Cf. Decoud's suicide in *Nostromo* and Cesar Cervoni's death in *The Mirror of the Sea*.